Praise for The Inn at the Amethyst Lantern

"The Inn at the Amethyst Lantern is a delight! A subtle and intriguing blend of fantasy and science fiction that thoroughly enchants!"

— Jonathan Maberry, NY Times bestselling author of Rot & Ruin

"Alive with magic, mystery, and mayhem, THE INN AT THE AMETHYST LANTERN, is a heart-pounding adventure you won't want to miss. With vivid, bright prose, Dotson weaves a story brimming with fantastical details and memorable characters who are given the daunting task of saving the world. Highly recommended!"

— Danika Stone, author of SWITCHBACK, ALL THE FEELS, and INTERNET FAMOUS

"J. Dianne Dotson has crafted a magical world young readers can get lost in until dawn. THE INN AT THE AMETHYST LANTERN is a glittering, luminescent mystery adventure that reminds us no matter how dark it gets, we are never truly alone."

— Kristy Gardner, author of THE STARS IN THEIR EYES

The Inn at the Amethyst Lantern

J. Dianne Dotson

ANDROID PRESS

For my children, who are my moons and stars.
For my beloved Gareth, who lights the way.

Contents

Acknowledgements

As a child in the 1980s in East Tennessee, I spent a good deal of my days and some of my nights in the rural countryside, exploring. Ever fond of the moon and the stars, and sometimes dreading the heat of Southern summer days, I felt a kinship with the night. The owls, fireflies, katydids, nighthawks, and other creatures of the dark kept me company when I would walk home from visiting friends. I wanted to recreate that safe, cozy night feeling in this book, despite its different setting.

The families and friends of Gen also channel some of my friends and family. And I hope to honor the memories of my mother Janice and my father Fred, now sadly gone, with that strong current of love written throughout this book. And thank you to my siblings Todd, Greg, and Brenda; we make quite the team.

My husband and fellow writer Gareth L. Powell cheered me along as I wrote this book, fueled by starlight and amethyst and love. I framed the entire story while on a return flight from England to visit him. Gareth is a constant supporter and source of joy and love. I love you, babe.

When I wrote the Solarpunk Magazine short story "Midnight Serenade" starring Mira Celestus, Gen's cousin, I knew there were more stories to tell in that universe. I would like to thank editor and publisher Justine Norton-Kertson for believing in the world I created, and helping this book take wing. Thank you also to editor J.D. Harlock. Thank you to Kim Herbst for creating the perfect cover art for this book.

Thank you to my supporters, Carrie Ancell, Michael Mulhern, Bradley Nordell, Robert Young, Richard Czernik, Carter Allen, Nathan Camp, Louise Murphy, Angela Blackwell, David Perlmutter, Melissa Davis, Gloria Thomas, and Catherine Watts.

Thank you to my friend, biologist Tim Wiltshire, Ph.D., for species advice.

Thank you to fellow writer friends Mya Duong, Bonnie Burton, Adrian Tchaikovsky, Dani Colman, Brian Schirmer, Dr. Janina Scarlet, Dennis K. Crosby, Karama Horne, Jonathan Maberry, Joanne Harris, Diane Duane, Jody Houser, Rachael Smith, Ryka Aoki, Paul Cornell, Lizbeth Myles, Sophia McDougall, Mike Chen, Lou Anders, Flo McGrath, Noah Kinsey, Tade Thompson, Lee Harris, Geoff Ryman, Melissa F. Olson, Tone Milazzo, Melissa Milazzo, Eddie Robson, Sarah Miles, Tori Eldridge, Greg Van Eekhout, Lisa Will, Henry L. Herz, Austin Farmer, Erika Ensign, Jackson Lanzing, Carolyn Hinds, C.E. Murphy, Ren Hutchings, James Moran, Antony Johnston, C. Robert Cargill, Aliette de Bodard, Jess Capelle, Premee Mohamed, Cory Doctorow, Alex Segura, Jonathan L. Howard, John Scalzi, and Chuck Wendig.

Thank you to extraordinary friends Pam and Hector Magnus and Jessica Springer.

Prologue

Midnight Serenade

Mira Celestus grew perplexed. She tapped her left arm bracelet, and it glowed a soothing, ethereal purple. Her harvester bots had not reported back from the root gardens, and her dinner prep would be delayed.

"Mira!" called her mother, Tam, eyeing her daughter's glazed eyes and half-raised hand, which held a vegetable peeler above the compost bot. The bot hooted expectantly for its quarry.

That startled Mira, and she continued peeling carrots.

"Sorry, Mom!" she called, grinning absently. She heard her mother sigh.

Mira was distracted by the previous evening's events as well as by the harvester bots having gone missing. The final invitations for the Glowworm Ball had been delivered dutifully in the night by opossums wearing the radiant, fuchsia-tubed helmets of the Gallant Twilight Society. The opossums had passed her house by and ventured on to the next along the lambent, ghostly glow-roads of her neighborhood. There, she knew, Amber Glistenad must have received hers, and she would, of course, attend the city's most illustrious event. But Mira could not because she was not yet fifteen.

The worst part of it was that Mira had, in her younger days, never paid much mind to the Glowworm Ball. That was where *other* people went when they reached fifteen, to promenade and preen and cavort, and who knows what all. That was not her business...or so she thought, but deep down, she viewed her coming of age with trepidation. She used to think such frippery meant nothing to her. But upon her fourteenth birthday, something changed. She found herself reading *The Biolumen Pen*, which was delivered to subscribers, including her mother, as a folded bud that bloomed after sunset into a newspaper. Upon completion, the *Biolumen* collapsed into itself and formed a seed, and these would be placed in baskets outside the door for collection by press workers, starting the whole process anew.

The *Biolumen* was all the rage, and whoever made it into its columns had, indeed, *made it*, so far as the town of Glimmerbight was concerned. Even across the bay, where the promontory with the lighthouse jutted above all else, the *Biolumen*'s news breached the more remote and placid village there. So Mira knew that her cousins must have word of it as well, though she suspected they collectively had far less interest in the Glowworm Ball than she.

Mira seethed with the unpleasant prickling of envy that traveled from the base of her neck down her spine, and she shivered. But it was not simply because she was left out, and her city friends were all attending the Ball. It was also because she and her family were moving in two months, well ahead of her fifteenth birthday, and she might *never* have the opportunity to attend the Glowworm Ball. She would be "out" in the far lands of the Northwest, in the bowl-like valley town of Umbradene. She knew that Umbradene offered deep canyons filled with lush, night-blooming flowers and that natural caves pocked the earth beneath it, and that appealed to her nature-loving side. But she knew she was changing.

She had grown interested more in the vibrant beat of a city, pulsing each night after the sun's rays dipped, a celebration of people and animals under starlight and moonshine and radiant neon: a revelry of civilization at night, not of the wilder lands of the Northwest, where the population was sparse. The Ball was a culmination of harvest, resplendent with song and dance, of moon exaltations and flowing potables that glowed softly. She wanted to go to that Ball, and she wavered between feeling irritated and depressed that she could not.

She finished peeling the purple carrots, and the compost bot, Blep, clucked indignantly and said as it waddled off, "Well, that took long enough! The earthwork team won't be pleased at my being late, no they won't!" Blep trundled out into the dark yard and down its little trap door into the cave gardens below, where the home's fungus farm grew.

Mira set her peeler down. "Mother, do you think I could work as an assistant at the Ball later?"

Her mother blinked in surprise and turned to look at Mira with her soft hazel eyes. "Sweetness," she said warmly, "you know you're not old enough. Anyway, I've got work starting in a bit, so I need your help."

"Yes, I know," Mira interrupted. "I know there's such a lot to do, but I don't...we won't...it's just that I won't be here for the next one. And Umbradene is so...it's so very dark. Wild-dark. I know you and Dad love that, but I just...I love being out in the city at night. It's different from being in the country. And the Northwest gets so much colder at night since it's not near the sea."

Tam lowered her chin and looked into her daughter's eyes, dark brown like her father's.

"Glimmerbight has been a good home for us," her mother said, "but you'll have your own space to make night music and create the sculptures we don't have room for here. It'll be good for your art. Plus, the School of Astronomy offers so much more than the local schools here for deep-sky viewing. It's so essential for your future science studies!"

Mira sighed. "What if I don't want to study science?" Tam widened her eyes. "What if I want to be an artist, but not in sculpture? What if...what if I want to work at the sea? And anyway, Umbradene doesn't have anything like the Glowworm Ball. There's no real society out there. Even the *Biolumen* doesn't reach out that far!"

Her mother smirked. "Well, of course, being a pioneer town at night has a very different flavor than a bay city. But you'll make new friends, and you can have your cousins visit any time."

Mira washed her hands and sighed again, and watched her father adjust the lights to pale purple inside the house. She knew that, outside, her home looked like a small dome with little circles for windows that glowed purple from dusk to dawn, when everything shuttered against the savage sun that they all found unsettling. Glimmerbight thrived at night.

Would Umbradene have anything remotely sociable or fun at night? She doubted it.

Mira walked outside into the soft darkness, which was lit only by wavering cables of egg-sized cobalt blue lanterns strung over the front walk of the house. These lights emitted a special hum to biting insects that did not harm them but essentially told them through sound that this home had nothing good to offer; so those insects would move on. Her mother stepped outside to join her. She followed Mira's upward gaze at the waxing gibbous moon above.

Her mother took three empty husks from her apron pocket. "I have an errand for you." She took from her apron pocket three empty husks.

Mira squinted at them. "What are those?"

"Old *Biolumen* seed husks. I saved them for Doc Bozzard on the quay. He needs them for a special gibbous moon incantation. I was going to deliver them myself, but I have a work deadline. Can you take them to him?"

"To his home or to his lab?" Mira asked, taking the small basket of husks in her hands.

"To his lab," answered her mother, the corner of her mouth twitching. "Now, hurry on, he was expecting me, but I will send a phial of else-liqueur with these to make up for not being able to chat. He can be long-winded, so you might not want to stay too long."

She winked at her daughter and tucked a dark amethyst-hued little bottle into the basket next to the pod husks. Mira noticed a little note was folded carefully and tied around the neck of the bottle, but she did not unravel it.

Mira sighed, nodded, and said, "Very well. I know I'll feel a little miserable walking past the Glistenad house because Amber is getting ready for the ball..."

Her mother kissed Mira's forehead and said, "Have a lovely walk, Mira."

Mira hoisted the basket and walked along the path, which lit as she stepped, one foot in front of the other, in a soft, pale pink circle. From above, the circles looked like a string of glowing pink polka dots that would eventually fade, but for now, they set the trail alight, and little glow-drones bobbed about in the air above the trail past the Glistenad home. It indeed buzzed with activity, echoing with laughter and fussing and squeals, and out of the home burst Amber, dressed in all her finery for the Glowworm Ball.

"Mira!" she cried, breathless and fanning herself with her hand. "Oh, I wish you could go, Mira! We're about to set off to the Ball."

Mira smiled at her friend, wincing a bit inwardly, knowing Amber would never intentionally snub her. Amber looked completely transformed, from the conventionally pretty cheerleader type of teenager to a suddenly regal and sophisticated socialite, her hair magnificently coiffed in glowing orange bows, her gown sparkling with real amber gems radiating from lights embedded beneath them. Her skirt rotated and shimmered in shades of fire and gold. Her arms bore radiant bangles of copper and bright orange. Indeed, Amber lived up to her name and seemed remote from the girl Mira had known most of her life. Until her face creased in a smile, and she laughed.

"I look ridiculous, don't I?" she snickered, and Mira would have said something, but a carriage hovered up, coated in dark violet lights and paler blue neon. "Ah, here I go! Bye, Mira!" and she was whisked away to the Ball.

Mira walked on, under wavering magenta lanterns along the trail to town, until she eventually made it to the quay, where the wind lifted its twinkling turquoise fairy lights and set them dancing. Along the quay, excitement bustled, with emerald-lit boats arriving every second, and bedazzled and bedecked Ball attendees stepped carefully onto stable ground to then walk toward something most extraordinary: the Glowworm Pavilion, the site of the Glowworm Ball. Mira tried not to get distracted, promising herself she would deliver Doc Bozzard's materials before taking a better look at the glowing dome in the distance.

The apothecary kept a laboratory-pharmacy at the corner of Fourthlight and Lux in the Twilit District, and there he sold potions, wrote incantations, and made crystal communicators. He was a busy gentleman in his ninth decade, with tufts of white hair poking out of his ears and a wild white shock of hair. Bright green spectacles made him look like a barn owl. Mira wove in and out of the crowds heading for the shop. In the distance, the buoys of the outer bight chimed the arrival of the evening fog, and everyone picked up their pace to try to make it to the ball before the fog would shutter out the gibbous moon. Doc Buzzard stood at the doorway of his shop, with its iridescent window panes softly emitting light and endorphins that attracted beneficial insects to the window gardens for night pollination. He waved.

"Best be quick, young Mira!" he called to her. "Let's see what you've got there."

"Hi, Doc!" she said, cheered by the sight of him. He used to give her Glo-Tarts when she was a little girl. He kept them next to his cash register, wrapped in iridescent cellophane made from leaves. Every child would receive one if they behaved well inside his shop.

Doc Bozzard waved Mira inside, and little teal lights sparkled on, illuminating the many shelves, making the rows upon rows of small bottles gleam like a bioluminescent algal bloom in an ocean wave.

"Did Mother tell you I was coming?" asked Mira, handing him the basket.

He plucked out the husks and said in his craggy voice, "Ah! Yes, just what I needed," and pushed his spectacles up his nose. "Not as such, dear. Your mother said she'd send the husks, but I expected her to deliver them. Ah, but I see there's a little bit extra in here!"

The old gentleman's eyes lit up as he withdrew the little phial. He curled the paper around the neck, took off the stopper, and sniffed. His bushy, white eyebrows shot up like two small, startled doves.

"Well, that ought to clear the mind!" he exclaimed. "Now, what have we here?"

He thumbed through the little scroll of paper, and then looked over his glasses at Mira. His face rose into an accordion of wrinkles, all of which formed a smile.

"Right!" he said. He pulled out a pocket watch that looked like a violet button mushroom and opened it. "We've little time. The Ball starts at midnight, and it is eleven thirty-six now."

"I had better get back," Mira said.

"Not if you're going to the Ball," said Doc Buzzard, opening drawers throughout his little lab shop, and leaving them ajar.

Mira laughed, "No, I can't go to the ball, you know that! I'm not old enough."

Doc glanced up. "Well, for tonight, you will be. Just this once. I know you're leaving. Your mother asked me to help."

Mira gasped. "What! She did? When? In that note?"

Doc grinned and brought forth bolts of what looked like cobwebs.

"She did indeed. I owe her a bit of a favor, as she's helped me over the years. Oh, how I will miss your dear family! Consider this a parting gift."

He held out the diaphanous, soft grey cobwebs to Mira, who wore only a simple skirt and top, and clunky boots. "That ought to do," he murmured.

He pulled out the mushroom watch again and held it over the cobwebby cloth. It lit up in bright purple, activating the fabric's tiny nanowires, and then the cloth began to march and warp and fold. Finally, the engineered gown stood rigidly on its own in the middle of the shop.

"When you put the gown on," explained Doc, "it will warp time around you very briefly, and offset the age detectors at the ball."

He opened the back of the dress as if it were a door, and said, "Step in while I call a carriage for you." Doc walked over by the door and pulled a cord with a sapphire at its end, and a little "toot-toot" rang through the shop.

Mira stepped in, fully clothed, and the gown stretched and twisted and covered her outfit completely, only showing the radiant purple. Part of the gown then snapped off and made its way to her hair, combing and tucking, until it was bound up in ribbons of the same fabric, and she could see it softly irradiating among her dark curls, reflected in the shop's mirrors.

The carriage pulled up, pilotless, ready and waiting to whisk Mira to the ball.

"Oh, Doc!" she cried, and she hugged him.

"No need, no need," he said gruffly, smiling, and he slipped her a Glo-Tart. "Eat a bit of something along the way, child. Have fun!"

And so it was that Mira was carried just above the ground in a bobbing, bejeweled carriage, toward an immense, pale green-yellow sphere with offshoots like octopus legs. The dome had been charging all day, every day, in the harsh sunlight no one could bear, and the reward was this wondrous sight, toward which hundreds streamed. Dazzled, Mira made her way to the entrance, where a little arbor of night-blooming, garnet-black roses hung, which were embedded with age detection technology. They shimmered like dark little eyes when she stepped under them, but they tinkled an acceptance, and she walked through.

"What will the *Biolumen* have to say about this?" she whispered to herself, her face beaming in glee.

All throughout the glowing, vast realm, people promenaded toward the Infinite Ballroom, filled with purple light-bubbles. The roof of the great, glowing dome opened to reveal the waxing moon at midnight. Voices began singing as Mira gazed up, full of longing and gratitude and grace, and the lights dimmed, and the moon shone high, filtering out the stars around it. Mira smiled up, knowing she would never see this place again, and she realized she was more excited about her future move, where the moon would glow more brightly in the night, among the innumerable stars.

"You have to know the past to understand the present."
—— **Carl Sagan**

Moth Borne

G en Lightworth never sat still for long, though she did love her books and her art. She was far more interested in exploring, which usually took her down to the waterfront to weave among market stalls and watch the harvest boats coming in just before sunup. It was a race against time and the brutality of the sun, yet they all managed it, and often it was quite a parade of glittering glow-masts and lights flickering among the sails, or gurgles of engines sputtering at the very end. Then the dash to get the harvest in before dawn's harsh rays. The thrill of adrenaline pumped through Gen, and she could hear the sailor's vibrant voices shouting to hurry.

While she loved the tumult and bluster of the bayfront boats, she adored far more exploring the villages between the bay and the Point. This took her through little tunneling thoroughfares both underground and over it, or beneath densely tangled vines grown as another barrier to sunlight. She never ventured forth during the solar day if she could help it, as it required shielding. The few times she had, she felt on edge and in danger.

Nighttime was different, and so she would slink along lit paths like everyone else. Jas didn't like the lit pathways, as he was more sensitive to light. He usually ventured farther inland to darker trails and haunts with his friends, getting up to who knew what business. Gen and Jas both seemed a bit out of sync with their parents.

Thinking along these lines, Gen muttered, "I'm going for a walk," and her father took his spent *Biolumen Pen* leaves and put them in a basket.

"Would you mind taking these out, Gentian?" He smiled.

Gen grinned back and nodded.

"Need a shawl, dear?" her mother asked.

"Nah, I'm good." Gen kissed her parents on their cheeks and nearly tripped over the cats as she headed out. She closed the front door behind her and set the basket down for collection. It wouldn't be long until the possums who worked for the *Biolumen* would stop by to take up the husks and replace them with the next issue's seed pod.

Gen never expected that two giant Luna moths would invite her to the end of the world.

They wafted their pale wings in the deepest portion of twilight, just as the moon rose to the east and the last of the sun's rays gleamed only as a smear of deep magenta on the horizon to the west. They carried between them a letter made of iridescent paper, which flickered in hues of cerulean, lavender, and deep, ethereal pink.

By and by, the moths found their destination: a little thatch-roofed adobe home painted periwinkle, which seemed to glow from afar in the darkness. It did not, but the cheerful lights within it radiated out like two bright eyes on either side of the front door. Gen sat with elbows propped on one of those windows, gazing dreamily with brown eyes into the darkness, a peacock quill tucked behind her left ear under her chin-length indigo hair, and she sighed.

For everyone in this land at this time, the concept of daytime had flipped with night, to cope with the savage sun. Once the sun went down, the violet light of the lighthouse called the Amethyst Lantern shone for all to see, lighting the way for everyone at sea and for their night-day to begin.

Gen never expected anything to change; it was all she'd ever known. But the giant moths carried a different fate for her than anything she could ever have imagined. They brought her all the adventure she ever wanted in her life, but the price might be an apocalypse.

It was the day after the great Glowworm Ball down by the bay, and everyone in the town of Glimmerbight who was of age and out in society had attended. Gen didn't see the attraction. She was far more interested in being outdoors and exploring. She had some vague idea that the old Inn on the promontory had once been just as bustling as the bayfront, but she wasn't sure. The Inn sat behind the Amethyst Lantern, the lighthouse still in operation.

The Inn once hosted splendid galas, and guests might arrive in extraordinary ways, such as air gondolas from above and balloons from boats below. The arrivals were as much a part of the spectacle as the festivities within the grounds of the Inn. At one point, this was where the society of Glimmerbight came to see and be seen.

That changed over the years, of course. The Ball, once the pinnacle of the gala season at the Lantern, long since moved down along the bayfront.

"Do you know why?" Gen asked her parents, but neither did. Her older brother Jas was completely disinterested in this sort of thing, too busy studying moon jellies for exams. Gen herself cared little for old society traditions except for their novelty. The past was a very different time, and her curious nature was drawn to imagining the bygone era.

"Ask Mira," her mother, Reggie, suggested, "Or ask your Aunt Tam. They'll know."

Gen nodded. "So, at some point," she mused aloud, craning to see the top of the lighthouse, "whoever lives there must have seen that change. They must be really old."

Her father looked up dreamily. "Oh, nobody who lives there now would have been alive back then. That was ages ago. I think that was in the Golden Hour era, wasn't it, Reggie?"

Gen's mother raised her eyebrows. "Had to have been. Maybe it was deemed too risky for night activities, or at the very least for accessibility, so during the Dawn of Dusk, the Ball was moved. Come to think of it, maybe the librarian is a good person to ask. I want to say she was related to the last Keeper of the Lantern."

"That was forever ago as well," Gen's father said, gazing over the curling pages of the latest *Biolumen Pen*, daydreaming.

"Yes." Her mother halted her work to gaze in the same general direction.

And so, the two adults sat lost in thought, in their wing-backed chairs, books close by and the *Biolumen*'s leafy pages floating away after being read. Sylvia, the lilac-pointed

Siamese cat, slinked around the legs of their chairs while Smudge, the mottled calico with a mask-like swath of tabby pattern over her nose and mouth, preened under the coffee table.

A distant, low moan echoed across the Bay.

"Fog's coming in," her mother sighed.

"I'll get tea," her father offered.

This was the way of things with her parents, a calm and quiet existence with cozy chairs, many books, glinting vases with herbs tucked hither and yon, and well-worn quilts or throws on every available surface, each threaded with luminescent strands that glowed when the lights went off.

It was a quiet middle of the night, after everyone had already eaten lunch, and doubly quiet because everyone was exhausted from the Ball the night before. So, the trails throughout the wooded neighborhood were empty at the moment. Gen stepped along the glow-turf paths and looked back at her shimmering footprints, which faded slowly. She had begun focusing on her exploration when her bracelet chimed. It was her cousin, Mira.

She answered, and the bracelet projected Mira in soft purple beside her.

"Oh, you're walking?" Mira asked, her eyes sunken, her hair mussed, but with a grin on her face.

"Yep, I was bored," Gen said. "You alright? You look a little... wild."

Gen smirked, and Mira's smile expanded. "Guess where I was last night!"

"Studying?" Gen ventured. Mira was quite studious, making her seem more closely related to Gen's parents than Gen herself. So, she was quite amazed by her cousin's answer.

"I went to the Ball!" Mira almost squealed.

Gen stopped in her tracks, and the hologram of Mira halted as well.

"Wait, what? *The* Ball?" Gen's eyes grew huge.

Mira lifted herself up and down on her toes, a purple-edged holographic sight at which a   passing fox sniffed in disdain.

"But... you're not old enough!" Gen said.

"I was, briefly," Mira said, clearly exhausted. "I'll have to tell you all about it. Oh... you were going somewhere. I'll let you get back to it."

"No, it's ok, I'll walk and talk. Besides, you said you were *briefly* old enough. I'm surprised you went. I know there's a story there."

"But where are *you* headed?" Mira asked, her image locked beside Gen as she meandered along the trail. Gen dodged a low-hanging berry-light, a natural lantern that hung like a great, head-sized golden raspberry, radiating its captured solar energy softly into the night.

"Well, I was going to go check on some root tea over in Ketcher Holler, but—well, it's just funny you mentioned the Ball. And that you went!" Gen shook her indigo hair. "Because I was talking to Mom and Dad a bit ago about the old Inn. Did you know the Ball used to be there?"

Mira tilted her head. "Yeah, I've heard that story. Maybe from my Mom? But I'd forgotten. Wonder why it changed? And when?"

Gen stopped mid-gait and huffed. "I think there's something to it. You know what? I want to find out. Want to join me?"

Mira tried unsuccessfully to stifle a yawn. "Yes. But I'm a little tired. Tell me what you find out. I'm going to take a little nap."

The cousins ended the call. Gen's bracelet went dark. She took a small globe off her necklace and put it in her mouth. The globe dissolved and released juice. She drank it down in a flash and kept moving, her boots falling in the darkness with satisfying thumps.

She turned at a fork in the path, where one trail grew narrower and steeper, and advanced up to a ridge overlooking her village. That wasn't the direction of her root tea in Ketcher Holler. If she didn't get the tea tonight, it would ferment just a bit too long and become something... not less pleasant, but far more potent. Not that it was a bad thing, but it wasn't exactly *allowed* at her age either.

The ridge-bound path beckoned, and her fingers and neck tingled in anticipation. Of what, she was unsure, but the air felt *expectant,* as though everything waited for her to make that decision, take that step under a cathedral of vines and up that rocky trail. She turned and chose the path.

Soon she sweated, pushing her flopped-over hair away from her eyes, and she popped another beverage globe into her mouth. The trail climbed among dark vines strung along darker conifers that had long since recovered from ancient fires in days before her village existed. Gen skidded a bit among the pine needles that had made it to the forest floor. This was not the sort of footpath one just sauntered onto. She'd previously thought this was a familiar old trail. But now that she was on it, she realized she'd never been there before.

She finally had to turn on her headlamp and adjust it so it wouldn't disturb the quiet wildlife she knew watched her from the treetops and their littered roots. She stopped briefly and looked back down the path, a wedge of soft blue-green light from her forehead casting shadows on the path below. Then she realized how steep it was, and for a second, a wave of vertigo overcame her. She shivered, turned back to look up, and pressed forward. The wind caught the treetops of the firs; they creaked and sighed. Vines thinned as she neared the ridgetop.

It opened suddenly before her, and she felt the full strength of the briny wind. The ridgetop flattened before sloping again. She caught her breath for only a moment when a brilliant purple light poured down her body. The light lingered, then slowly faded.

There stood the Amethyst Lantern, the lofty lighthouse of old, striped with great, dark purple bands. They appeared almost black in the darkness. Gen could barely make out the old Inn, but only when the swing of the light briefly illuminated it. The Inn itself was never open during the day and was never lit at night, so while growing up, the children of the area assumed it was haunted.

Gen thought it must be quite terrifying during the harshness of daylight. At night, it seemed merely sad and empty compared to the gaiety of the bayfront. Looking at the scene before her, dark then briefly purple from the Lantern, then dark again, Gen wondered why the Inn stood abandoned.

She shivered, regarding it from afar. With the blankness of its exterior, it seemed a great shell without its creature inside. Devoid of a soul, its eyes shuttered against both day and night, a derelict from another time.

Gen couldn't explain why she felt drawn to walk up to this spot and look out on that Inn, but now that she saw it again, her thoughts stirred. The wind lifted her hair, and she trembled as cold fog tumbled over the Point. The way back down grew even more slippery than the fir needles had left it, for now a fine drizzle made its way down to the rocks. She braced herself against a fall and realized her headlamp only scattered the light in the mist.

So, she switched it off. She made it clumsily to the bottom. Brushing herself off, she looked around and found herself back at the junction of trails she found before.

Gen couldn't explain it, but she felt different. That sort of prickly sensation still marched up and down her neck. She looked over her shoulder, and she felt absurd doing that. There'd be no one there but the trees and the animals. This wasn't the sort of place and time in which darkness should ever make anyone feel uneasy; those days were long ago, and now the opposite held true, for the sun meant doom and unpleasantness while the night was when life felt fresh and renewed.

The Invitation

Gen walked swiftly back toward her house and found its glowing little windows comforting. And just as she walked up to the door, two immense Luna moths descended from above and bobbed in front of her face. The shimmering envelope they held between them plainly read "Gentian Lightworth." The moths let it fall. Gen caught it with her hands, and the moths flew away. She watched them go, stunned, and then she opened the envelope.

She walked into her home in a distracted daze, dodging a hanging plant and taking note of the scent of berry muffins, and watched the purple seal on the envelope fall away after she folded the invitation back. Anticipation crackled in the room, like she was about to reveal an award winner. Her parents watched her.

"Well?" Reggie queried, with a nervous energy that surprised her. She glanced at Harris, who sat in the dining room, but he raised an eyebrow and returned to reading the *Biolumen.*

Gen examined the words on the invitation. They were embossed in a deep, shimmery violet, in a script that confused her. For a moment she wasn't sure she could recognize the language. Her own handwriting horrified her teachers. But she did, at least, write simply. This wasn't just writing, it was art; the words looped and spiraled with elegance unmatched. She touched their plum-colored curves and blinked.

"It's... hard to read," Gen stammered, unsure why she suddenly trembled. The invitation twitched in her hands.

"Try your best," her mother encouraged her, the corner of her mouth working to fight back an expression. Whether it was a frown or a smile, Gen was unsure.

Gen tried to read the invitation, but blushed because despite its artistic scrollwork, the person's scrawl was every bit as illegible as her own.

"Maybe I *should* write better," she muttered, and her mother laughed so hard that her father walked quickly into the living room to see what was happening.

"What's that?" His soft, dark eyes were kind and inquisitive.

"An invitation. Maybe," Gen still squinted at the letters. "I can't read it."

"Oh, did *you* write it?" Harris asked, tilting his violet-rimmed glasses, which were embedded with phosphorescent stones around the lenses.

"Very funny, *Harris*," Gen grumbled. Her father grinned and Reggie snickered. Both Gen and Jas could be quite merciless in the banter between them, and also with their parents. When they called their parents by their first names, it was meant as a cheeky barb. But if their parents rattled off their first, middle, or Luna be praised, their complete names, Gen and Jas knew they were in trouble.

Harris approached his irritated daughter to take a closer look at the invitation. "Hang on. I know that writing!"

Reggie glanced up at him from where she sat by the door. Gen didn't see her face, but her mother wore a knowing grin.

"Who's it from, then?" Gen asked him.

Her father rubbed his bushy salt-and-pepper beard.

"Well, come to think of it," he said slowly, eyes glazed a bit, "we never knew *whose* writing it was... just suspected. Wait, was there a seal on it?"

"Yeah." Gen shifted her feet, looking at the floor. "It... seems to have disappeared."

"Purple?" her father's eyes brightened.

"Yeah..." Gen drew out the answer into multiple syllables.

Harris looked quickly to Reggie, who inclined her head a fraction.

"Delivered by giant moths?" Harris pressed, rubbing his hands together, eyes glimmering. "They used to be called 'letter-flies,' long ago..."

"Yes?" Gen grew exasperated.

"It's from the Inn!"

"The *what*?" Gen's skin prickled on the back of her neck. *Surely not* the *Inn*, she thought. *The same one I'd seen earlier?*

"Inn! The Inn! The one at the lighthouse," her father said. He looked most excited, and Gen was bemused. She had never seen Harris act like this. The years seemed to melt off his face. "Mind if I take a look?"

"May as well." Gen shrugged. "I'm getting nowhere with this."

Harris took the invitation into his fingers. He held the paper with reverence like some ancient text that might crumble from age. His dark eyes darted over the jumbled, curling letters.

"By Luna!"

Reggie stood and stepped next to her husband. "Well, you two weren't kidding about the writing."

Harris stared at her, while Gen rolled her eyes. "I can't believe it!" he said. "In all my life, I never thought it was *him*. And... and now this?"

"Harris," Reggie lowered her voice and looked up at him with a teasing expression, "are you alright? Do I need to call Doc Bozzard?"

"Oh my God," Gen hissed, stamping her foot. "What does it *say*?"

"Gen!" Her father looked at her, beaming, "it says you've been invited to the Inn of the Amethyst Lantern by the innkeeper himself, Bendin! He wants to offer you a job!"

Reggie gasped and took the letter for one moment before Gen lunged forward and seized it back herself.

"Who's Bendin?" Gen wondered aloud. "And what job?"

"I'm not entirely sure," her father said, "because it seems unlikely to be the same innkeeper from..." his voice softened and fell away. He walked to the window and looked outside. The light of the Lantern cut a long, lavender wedge into the indigo sky.

"Can I ring up Mira?" Gen asked

"Sure," Reggie said. She looked over Gen's shoulder at the invitation. "The words are fading!"

"What!" Gen's eyes flashed over the page.

Her father quickly stepped back, his face split into a smile. "Just like the notes of old!" he said, rapping the table with his knuckles. "This must be the same person. How? I don't know. But Gen, did you catch the time of your meeting?"

She let out a squawk. "It's gone! Besides, I couldn't even read it in the first place."

Not only had the words vanished, but the paper also began to fold in on itself, smaller and smaller, until finally, it became a tiny kernel. It fell from Gen's hand onto the floor and rolled out of sight.

"Good thing *I* caught the time," her father said.

Gen exhaled a massive sigh. "When? And why didn't you just say that in the first place instead of asking me?"

"Sunup tomorrow." He didn't answer the second question.

"Sunup?" Gen's heart pounded. "This had better be worth it."

Mira held the retrieved kernel in her fingers. "Well, I'm not impressed," she said. She took off her jaunty hat, set it on the desk, and smoothed her shoulder-length brown hair.

Gen snorted. "No kidding."

"Tell me again." Mira paced the room. Her asymmetrical yellow outfit clashed with Gen's homey living room. Mira was slim, angular, and far more stylish than Gen liked to admit. Mira drew a pen out from somewhere, along with a small, dark magenta notebook.

"What, you're a reporter now?" Gen raised her brows high. She adjusted her shabby patchwork tunic.

Mira turned to her and shrugged. "Maybe. Now, go on!"

Gen rehashed what her father had read from the now-vanished invitation. "It said it was from the innkeeper at the Lantern, and that I—"

Mira's head tilted. Her eyebrows wrinkled and one corner of her lip turned upward.

"Don't look at me like that! It's what it said! I'm invited to meet with him at sunup about a position he wants to offer me."

Mira shuddered. "No name?"

"Oh, I forgot. It's Bendin."

"You're sure?" Mira pressed, scribbling in her book.

"I mean, that's what Dad said. I couldn't read it."

"You'd think *you* would be able to." Mira grinned.

Gen rolled her eyes. "Oh, stop! Let me see *your* handwriting." She snatched Mira's notebook.

"Hey!" Mira tried to grab it back.

Gen took one glance inside and laughed. "It's just as bad as mine! Guess we really are cousins."

Mira's face turned crimson. "Anyway," she went on, dismissively tossing her hair, "we're going."

Gen crinkled her nose. "What do you mean, *we*?"

Mira smiled. "I'm going with you."

"It's at sunup though. We'll fry!"

Both girls shivered.

"I'll shield myself well," Mira promised.

Gen sighed. "It'll be so disorienting, going in the morning. Maybe we could have a look now." Her eyes brightened at the prospect of an exploratory outing.

Mira searched Gen's eyes. "Do you mean, spy on The Inn before the meeting?" She grabbed her notebook from Gen's fidgeting hands.

"Yes," Gen said firmly. "I was just up that way earlier. It's stopped raining. Let's go!"

The two girls slipped out while Gen's parents busied themselves with their board game, Firefly Flick, their flashing beetle-shaped game pieces floating in the air as they tried to score points. Out the hall they went, through the door and past the snoozing housebots, which were locked into the ground for the night to heat the cave crops beneath the home. One opened a slow, radiant green eye, blinked at the girls, and tutted in disapproval before shutting it again.

Gen took Mira to the fork in the paths she'd reached earlier in the evening. Something rustled to their left and both girls jumped.

Why are we so nervous? Gen wondered. *I didn't feel like this when I was here earlier.*

The wind whistled, setting the tree branches creaking over the path. The woods took on a shadowy, almost sinister aspect, which was not something Gen had ever associated with her nighttime explorations. Goosebumps coursed their way up her arms and she shivered.

Suddenly the dark branches of the wooded path opened, revealing Jas loping through, yawning, and rubbing his face. "What're you two doing out here? It's late. Only a couple hours to dawn." He let the bag on his shoulder slip to the ground, then bent to inspect its contents.

"Well..." Gen wasn't sure where to begin.

"Gen got an invitation to the Inn!" Mira inserted breathlessly.

"The Inn?" Jas raised his eyebrows

"Yes. The Inn," Gen said, pointing at the purple light in the distance.

"Um, what?" Jas stared off at the lighthouse. "Why?"

"About a job," Gen shrugged. She felt embarrassed, and silly, and wondered if it was all some sort of prank. Telling her older brother—her accomplished and brilliant brother—about such a thing made it seem ridiculous, and she suspected he thought so too.

"At sunup," Mira chimed in again.

Jas shook his head and raised his hands, shaking the glowing instruments on his wrists. "Hold on." His brow pinched. He ran a hand through his rumpled, dark hair, and brought both hands together under his chin. "You got an invitation to the Inn about a job at sunup?"

"Well, to be fair, the job's not at sunup." Gen's eyes widened. "Oh, God! At least I hope it's not. The interview is."

"So... okay." Jas cut in. "That's... weird? Congratulations, or something. Do you have more data? Who's it with? What's the job?"

Gen's uneasiness increased. *This is a bad idea.* "I couldn't read the name, so Dad read it. It's with the innkeeper, Bendin."

"There *is* no innkeeper," Jas said matter-of-factly. "Hasn't been for decades. Eons. Who knows?"

"You seem to know a lot about the subject." Gen snarled at his skepticism. "Well apparently there is *now*. We're going to suss things out."

Jas looked from his sister to his cousin and back again and raised his hands, palms out. "This sounds insane."

Gen and Mira stared at him, puzzled.

"Why?" Mira asked.

Jas shot her a surprised look. "You're suggesting trespassing in the hours before dawn. Two bad ideas."

"But you just said no one's kept the Inn for, like, a million years," Gen pointed out.

"Okay, not *that* long," sniffed Jas, grimacing.

"But if no one's there, then it's not trespassing," Mira added.

"Anyway, we're going. Bye," Gen walked past her brother. She and Mira laughed and turned to hike up through the wooded path.

Jas groaned.

"Wait," he said. "This is a bad idea, and I'm older than you. So, I better come along."

Gen and Mira snickered ruthlessly. Gen dashed up the dark path, leading the way. But the stars were growing faint, and soon the savage sun would rise.

They advanced on the trail, panting as they climbed, bit by bit. With worry in his eyes, Jas glanced over his shoulder at the horizon.

"Gen," he said quietly, "the animals have retreated. Not long now."

He was right. The darkness had taken on a muted tone as the sky changed to a sort of tired, deep blue and green. Dawn indeed approached.

Gen shivered. "I had it in my head that sunup was hours away," she admitted. "But it's summer, nearly; shorter nights. If we go back and I return alone, I'll be late for the interview."

"Oh no," said Mira. "I'm sorry."

"Well," Jas remarked, "since you're already here, why not knock?"

They reached the hill overlooking the Inn. Light swung through the deep purple twilight, and Gen could see the horizon out at sea. She shuddered with dread. Her ancestors greeted the dawn with great relief, but not so Gen and her family. The Inn loomed in the changing light, shifting from royal to a soft, baby blue with purple shadows from the approaching sun.

"We're not shielded," Mira gasped, tugging at her hat as if it would pull down into a hood.

Jas twitched open his backpack and brought forth two wide-rimmed fieldwork hats and a spare sunshield jacket. He handed them out. "I should've known you'd forget."

Gen moaned. "We're going to roast."

"Gen!" Mira cried suddenly, just as the sun edged the horizon in a thin line of fire.

The three glanced down at the Inn. Gen's hair plastered to her forehead. Jas's face dripped with sweat. Mira panted. Her keen eyes found something that filled them with both trepidation and relief.

"The door!" whispered Gen.

"It's open." Jas said, urgency in his voice.

"Run for it!" Gen shouted, and the three hurtled down the steep hillside. The sun gave chase, heat nipping at their heels. Gen looked back over her shoulder as they stumbled through the Inn's dark, open door, which slammed shut behind them just as the sun's rays engulfed it.

Bendin

The trio found themselves engulfed in a profound darkness. There was no evidence of the sun's power here other than the temperature of the door. But then, suddenly, the door disappeared. So they no longer even felt *that*.

"We're moving," Gen breathed as the three lurched in the pitch dark and reached out to find each other by touch.

"I can't see a single thing," Mira complained.

"It's like being in one of the undeveloped caves up north," Jas whispered.

"Okay, it's dark," Gen snapped, then winced at how loud she sounded. "But we're definitely moving."

"Downward," Jas agreed.

"This... doesn't seem like an interview," Mira said in a low voice.

"Whatever it is," Gen said, "we don't seem to have a way out. And maybe this is better than facing the sun."

"My detection instruments don't work here," Jas said suddenly. "You'd think we'd have some working light. Anything. Gen, I don't like this."

Gen swallowed, her mouth suddenly dry and salty. She looked beneath her feet. "Uh... I think... I'm not sure—I could be hallucinating—but I *think* I see a light below us. Anyone else see it?" She looked just under her feet, realizing at that moment that they stood on a crystal clear surface. She felt disoriented and clung to her family.

"I see it," Mira answered softly. "It's—it's purple. Very faint."

"Or we're very far from it," Jas mused, squeezing his sister's and cousin's hands. "What *is* this place?"

"Not an inn," Gen replied in a flat tone.

She trembled. *I should never have asked them to come.* Her newfound sense of dread in the darkness unnerved her. Always the dark had been a safe place. And here she was, feeling a lancet of fear: unfamiliar, novel, and disturbing.

"It's getting brighter," Mira said.

"Or we're getting closer to it?" Gen was starting to sound like Jas.

"Gen," he said suddenly, "I've got your back. I have some tools that could be weapons."

"Jas!" Gen hissed, her judgmental instinct pushing down her irrational fear. "Where is this coming from? We don't even know where we are. You want to fight like in the old times? Just because something's unfamiliar?"

She felt Jas tug at her hand, and she squeezed his in return, trying to relax. She noticed a faint lavender glow on his chin. She looked at Mira and beheld the same on her cousin's cheeks. She looked at her own hands and saw their dark silhouettes outlined in deep purple. The light grew much brighter, then finally stopped. The radiance glowed beneath them. And Gen could swear that the light... pulsed. Very,

very slowly, over and over, like the great heartbeat of something ancient and enormous.

"You've made it!" a voice suddenly piped up to her right, and the trio jumped and cried out. Someone stood in the shadow, partially illuminated by lavender light from below.

"Who are you?" Gen demanded.

"Where are we?" Jas asked.

"What's that light?" Mira piped up.

The person chuckled, a sound like dried bamboo chimes knocking together in a breeze.

"I'm the keeper of the Inn. My name is Bendin. The light? It's the Source. Welcome, Gen Lightworth. But I only invited you!"

Illicit Magic

The figure joined them, and the light around them expanded. But the floor lost some of its clarity and became opaquer. Gen could just make out the scale of the room—if that was what it was—for it stretched above them into what might be a rotunda, but the light below them dazzled her too much to see it clearly. Gen shivered and her nose tickled from the ashes of old incense, made from forgotten blooms of a faraway place. The trio released each other's hands.

The always keen Mira pressed this shadowy Bendin.

"What was that light?" she demanded. "And are you *really* the keeper of the Inn?"

Bendin's face fully emerged into the light, and they found him indescribably old, his skin pocked and stained and damaged from radiation: the sun's. He smiled, and when he did, he revealed pale purple teeth and innumerable wrinkles. Gen wondered what adventures had played across the valleys of that face and forehead.

"And you must be Mira Celestus," Bendin said softly. He glanced at Gen, and she puzzled over his expression. Looking back to Mira, he said, "You might be in for a bit of trouble from the incident at the Ball."

Mira's already pointy eyebrows raised.

"What incident is that?" she asked, her face otherwise composed. "And how the hell do you know my name?" She stood straight and still. Gen admired her posture and lifted her own shoulders back and down. She felt uneasy.

Bendin snorted. "The little age distortion trick, of course." He ignored the second question.

Jas gasped and turned to stare accusingly at his cousin. "What did you *do*?"

Gen clenched her teeth. "Come off it, Jas."

Mira cleared her throat. "Well, technically, *I* didn't do anything but show up at the Ball, and be let in. And anyway, what would you know of that?"

Bendin looked down at the light radiating below their feet. "I have a pretty good view from the Lantern."

Gen scrunched up her face. "The Lantern? What did you do, spy on Mira from the lighthouse?"

Bendin shook his head, and that seemed to take some effort.

"No, and I didn't have to. The Lantern *showed me*. And I know who's responsible, Mira, aside from your mother, Tam."

Mira lost her composure. "My mother? How dare you! We don't have to listen to your insults. Come on, let's go." She looked over at Gen and Jas.

Gen turned to cousin. "And just how are we going to get out of here? The door disappeared. Remember?"

Mira flashed, "I don't know, I don't care, but we are going. Jas?"

Jas shrugged. "I'd like to leave, yes. But not before hearing more about this. Besides, if we leave right now, we'll fry in the sun." He turned to Bendin. "What happened?"

Bendin looked expectantly at Mira, whose face looked as hot as the sunlight outside was by then. "Go ahead, Miss Celestus."

"Why?" Gen protested. "Why should Mira say anything? You just said she and Jas weren't invited. I was. Maybe I don't need to be here either. Come on you two, let's go."

The light beneath their feet flickered and pulsed like a captured aurora. Bendin looked down, and Gen saw a troubling downward twist in his mouth.

"Because Mira triggered this," he said, gesturing downward.

Mira looked down, the flickering violet light making her pointy eyebrows look even sharper, and she snorted. "I did no such thing."

"Mira Celestus!" Bendin said, his voice chopping the air between them. "Do you deny that you passed the age detector at the Ball?"

Mira's eyes darted up to Bendin's, and then she glanced at Gen. Both girls turned their eyes to Bendin. Jas stood with his mouth agape, "What!"

"No, I did," Mira admitted. Gen and Jas gasped.

"Okay, first of all, *how?*" Jas asked, "And second, *why?* Why would you do that?"

Gen reached out to halt her brother, but he shook his head, dark eyes burrowing through the distance between himself and his cousin.

Mira bit her lip and twitched her hat on her head, agitated.

"You know why," she said to Gen, refusing to answer Jas.

Gen took a deep breath and let out a heavy sigh. Like her brother, she shook her head.

"I do," she said. "You're moving. You've talked about the stupid Ball forever, and you were going to miss your chance. But, you what... you *lied*? That's not possible. The age detectors are flawless. Nobody gets in under age fifteen."

"But I did," Mira squirmed.

"How?" Gen pressed her.

Mira sucked in her lips and her eyes grew wide. "I don't want anyone to get into trouble."

Gen opened her mouth to say something, stopped, rolled her eyes back, and then opened it again to say, "Are you kidding me? Someone helped you and you're going to take the fall for it? Whoever did this is responsible too."

Bendin spoke then, "You're already in trouble, Miss Celestus. Now we all are."

Gen put her hands on her hips as Mira wobbled a bit. Gen could see her cousin was shaken.

Jas huffed. "Ridiculous. Mira went to the Ball. It's not like she *killed* someone and we're her accomplices!"

"You know what? I've heard enough," Gen said. "There is no reason for us to be here, and if you're going to snitch on Mira, that doesn't even make sense. The Ball's over. I'm sure other people saw her there and didn't make a fuss, though maybe they didn't know she wasn't fifteen. But really, who cares?"

"I do," Bendin said vehemently, "and you *need* to. That was illicit magic."

The teens snorted and groaned and laughed.

"Magic!" scoffed Mira. "It's just a trick that—"

"Stop!" Bendin cried. "Mention no names. I already know. And I don't want anything to hear." He cast his eyes all around them, and down at the light again, mesmerizing and swirling and throbbing like a living thing. "You broke a law, Mira, and the person who helped you did too," Bendin continued. "These are things that happened, and on their own merit punishment."

"That's ridic—" began Mira, but the old man stared at her, his eyes locked onto hers until she blinked and shuddered. She looked exposed and even ashamed. She clutched her arms around herself, and looked nervously at Gen.

"What you did goes much farther than this, though," Bendin said, "and that's why you're here, Gen. Your cousin awakened something that should never have been disturbed. Now we're all going to suffer for it."

No three people could have protested more vocally than the cousins did just then, arguing among themselves and shouting at Bendin who for his part stood placidly, hands folded behind his back, head down and eyes up. He watched Gen.

She gritted her teeth and breathed quickly. "Get us out of here, you complete weirdo," she hissed at Bendin.

He nodded, to her surprise.

"I understand," he said. "It's a lot to take in. It doesn't make sense to you. You've each lived a gentle way of life, as your parents did, and their parents, and so on, going back generations. But it wasn't always so. Allow me to show you something. If, after doing so, you still wish to leave and hear nothing more about what I have to say, then so be it. But first, allow me this. You didn't learn any of this in your histories, in your peaceful night-filled young lives... nor did your parents. Although I suspect Harris, when he was a young boy, came close to learning more. Now watch this and follow me. I'll show you the Inn and the Lantern as they were *before*."

"Before what?" Gen asked, dithering, for she didn't like this circular discussion. A strange unease such as she had never felt before in all her fourteen years marched through her.

"Before Night Living," Bendin answered in a soft, low, almost musical voice. "Before the Golden Hour, even... Come, walk with me, and I'll show you what happened all those years ago."

The Inn and the Lantern

Jas began to protest but shut his mouth quickly as the purple light beneath them brightened all around them. Bendin marched forward and gestured for them to follow. He stepped onto a swirling, spiraling path, and it wasn't clear to Gen whether it was going in an actual circle, or if they descended or rose. Music echoed throughout whatever space this was, and Gen put her feet forward on the path behind Bendin. Mira followed her, and Jas brought up the rear. Each marveled as the purple swirling light changed into a kaleidoscope of colorful images.

Gen watched the images flow past and above her. Below, the pulsating purple light remained but grew faint. She felt sure they must be spiraling slowly upwards, but she was so disoriented by what she saw that she couldn't make any sense of direction at all. The images were diaphanous, and if she turned to look straight at them, they held the uncanny quality of stars gazed upon. But if she looked just aside, they appeared clearer. What she saw confused her, but she marveled just the same.

The music looped oddly too, and she couldn't make out what kind of music she heard. Part brassy, part vocal, deep and melodic. It was a bit like the peppy music sometimes played at Glimmerbight pops concerts held out on the Spindle Pier on summer nights. But there was sadness in this new music, a longing among the beauty. As if even when it was first played, it knew something was ending.

She shook herself out of her reverie and continued walking until she bumped into Bendin. He stood, waiting for her brother and cousin, and extended his arms.

The images coiled up above him, then down, flickering and warping—again so very like auroras—just as the light below their feet had. But they showed places, people, things Gen didn't recognize... great birds, fire, strange contraptions shoveling mounds of earth into immense holes. Everything whirled past her, and although none of it went by very fast, she couldn't comprehend any of it. She wanted to slow it down so she could understand what she saw.

Bendin stepped closer to her and addressed the three teens, "This is what once was."

Mira's eyes darted hither and yon, absorbing as much as she could. She knelt occasionally to place her little notebook on her knee and tried to scribble notes in the strange light.

"When?" she looked up for a second.

Bendin grinned. "Long ago. Longer than I can say."

Jas swept a sharp gaze to the older man, "Than you *can* say? Or than you *will* say?"

Bendin dipped his head. "You're becoming a true skeptic, Jas Lightworth."

Jas flared his nose a bit and folded his arms, but he nodded almost imperceptibly.

"What are we seeing?" Gen asked. "It looked like destruction. Big holes being filled."

She swept her gaze in all directions, her brown eyes rendered dark violet by the light beneath her. In one flowing scene, much like a living watercolor painting spreading across a blank page, she saw rolling hills and distant mountains beyond them.

"Are those… the mountains out West?"

Bendin raised his left hand, and the flowing image halted. Gen, Mira, and Jas all stared at what they saw. There, indeed, a mountain range emerged from a verdant landscape; atop the mountains, deep glaciers shone in brilliant sunlight.

It was almost too bright for them to behold, yet Gen braved it, absorbing everything she could from this moment. "If that's the mountain chain, then there should be a city… where's Umbradene?"

At that, Mira stepped closer to the image. It responded to her, rippling and moving farther away.

"There's nothing there," she murmured.

"Can we see the rest of this land?" Jas wondered aloud.

Bendin clapped his hands and twisted them together. "Indeed."

The images shifted, rotating as if they all stood in the middle of a field. Then they felt as though they rose above it and looked down on the landscape as their vantage points swerved first north and then east… and finally south. No one said anything. The music grew fainter.

Gen could then hear a soft ringing in her ears. "Wait," she murmured, pointing at those images, which now stood stationary on all sides of them. She and Jas and Mira stared due south. "Where's the ocean?"

"To the south," Bendin said.

"I don't see it." Jas squinted. "Nothing but hills and valleys to the south. Show us west."

The images rotated. Gen saw a blue arc on the horizon. "There it is." She felt satisfied.

"Something's not right," Mira added. "If this is accurate, Glimmerbight is out there to the west, and the Lantern and its headland face south."

"It's all land," Jas agreed.

"Hold, please." Bendin waved his hands. They appeared to rise high above the scene, or it retreated far below them. A strange smear in the landscape just below where they were, far below, indicated human activity, but it was subtle, bent grasses in rectangle shapes. That wasn't what intrigued Gen the most, however. From this height, she spied the ocean to the South.

"How is the sea so far away?" she puzzled. "This doesn't make sense! Is this that far inland? I'm confused."

Bendin nodded. The images swirled back into a coil again and moved on to other locations. "Keep following."

Mystified and intrigued, no one objected.

Bendin then looked over his shoulder at Gen, "Yes, it's far inland. Or it *was*." He gestured his fingers a bit, and the swirling pictures all around them shifted into focus. It looked as though they were standing in headlands, and off to their right, to the west...

"The Lantern!" Gen gasped. "And the Inn!"

"What?" Mira cried. "It looks completely different. How?"

Jas cleared his throat. "Erosion."

"Correct," came Bendin's simple reply.

Jas began shaking his head again. "But this would have been—this would have taken—*when* was this?"

"As I said," Bendin chuckled, "long ago."

"A *very* long time ago." Brow pinched, Jas continued, "Glaciers on the mountains. All this land. No cities. I can't even think how long ago this must have been."

"In some ways, not long enough," Bendin said.

Gen noticed a twinge of bitterness in the man's voice. He sighed. Then he clicked his tongue. "Enough of that for now. Keep going, there's more to see."

The images shifted toward the Inn and descended quickly so it looked like they approached it. Only then did Gen clap her hand over her mouth.

"All this time you've been showing us *daylight*." Her voice was hushed. "And we can't even bear it normally. But I didn't even *flinch*."

"Ugh, God!" Mira's face turned a light shade of red. "Neither did I."

Jim blinked, his forehead pinched together, lost in thought.

Bendin's eyes glistened. "Your brains remember. Somewhere deep, vestigial, private, and quiet... they remember what it was like. *Before*."

The three teens huddled together, shivering. It felt so unnatural. But Gen stepped away to take a better look at the Inn.

"Look at it!" she breathed. "We could never see it like this during the day. But this..." she gestured toward the scene, "this is another time. Look at all the people!"

The Inn was vibrant and alive and surrounded by orchards and vineyards. The great lighthouse stood on the curve of a cliff that stretched for many miles off to the east. The cape, where Glimmerbight lay now, looked more or less the same, although only a small seaside village rested there.

All around the Inn, however, was an entirely different village. In fact, it was a bustling town. Gen watched in wonder as people streamed toward the Inn, and musicians dotted verdant lawns or played instruments in little alcoves covered in strange flowers. Laughter bubbled and music swelled among many voices stretched ever so slightly, just a tiny bit muffled. She felt the hairs on her neck rise. She had never imagined anyone enjoying daylight, which meant pain and suffering in her era.

Ancient times, she thought. Yet still, to this day the Inn stood, as did the Lantern.

They stood, but they stood alone.

Gen felt a stab of some deep ache. *What happened?* she wondered.

As if in answer to her silent question, Bendin said, "This was the time of the Golden Hour, and let me tell you, people lived it up. Just hang back and watch the spectacle."

Mira scribbled furiously with her pen, certain nothing she wrote would be beautiful to behold, but it would be greatly important, she felt. *I'll submit it to the* Biolumen Pen*! s*he fancied. *Maybe I'll even win awards! Nobody's seen this, I'm sure.*

As for Jas, he stared intently at the trees, the flowers, the birds, and every growing thing surrounding the Inn back in this forgotten time. He knew almost none of the species he saw.

Bendin watched him and lowered his head almost imperceptibly. "Things have changed," he said, as much to himself as to anyone. "Yet the Inn and the Lantern hold fast. For now."

Gen had wanted to know the history of the Inn her entire life, and here it was swirling about her, a painting she could live in. She was like a voyeur spying on the jubilant people streaming in. She watched one couple waltzing on a terrace that no longer existed. Children played in a garden long since wilted and weathered into powder. She could hear all the music. She didn't realize as her face grew wet from gently spilling tears.

Mira, meanwhile, couldn't help it. "This looks like *so* much fun!" Her eyes shone. "Oh, what I would have given to have been there. Even"—she shuddered— "in broad daylight."

Bendin clasped his hands together in front of him and watched the three youths. "Your innocence is beautifully endearing. But I have come to see it's hideously lacking in pragmatism. And it won't save you or any of the rest of us."

Gen shook herself out of her mesmerized state and stared at him, eyes narrowed.

"Okay, what the *hell* does that mean?"

Bendin smirked. "That's the spirit. That's what I was looking for. I brought you here for a reason, Gentian Lightworth. And it is clear to me now that I need all three of you to help in the fight ahead."

"Fight?" the three echoed.

"One thing at a time, though," Bendin cautioned. "Gen, you're invited to take over the Inn and the Lantern."

Gen gasped loudly. "What! You *cannot* be serious. Me? Why me? I'm just a... well, not really a kid, but kind of a kid?"

Bendin hooted with laughter. "That's right!" He rubbed his withered forehead. "That's one reason why I want you to take over. Because I can't do much these days, and I—we—need the energy you kids bring."

"For running an *Inn*?"

"Yes, but not just that..."

The images all disappeared, and they stood above the pulsating purple light again, surrounded by darkness.

"We need all of you to help," Bendin continued.

"Help *what*?" Gen asked.

"Save the world."

Cause for Alarm

Gen burst out laughing, and Mira joined her. Jas made a sound with the back of his throat. Bendin didn't look amused.

"Do you hear yourself?" Gen asked him, halting her laughter and wiping her brow. "This sounds absolutely absurd."

"Ridiculous," Jas agreed.

Mira looked unimpressed. She kept her notebook shut. She adjusted her couture hat. "Even if I get into trouble for getting into the Ball, it's not going to end the world or anything."

Bendin shook his head. "You're going to learn soon enough what's at stake." The three teens shifted on their feet as he continued. "I'm trying to prepare you before it's too late. You're going to need more help. Find friends you trust. Gather them here; I'll arrange for the Inn to be open. One week, perhaps?"

He held his hands out, beseeching. Mira and Jas turned away and Gen stood facing him. She shrugged.

"I don't see any cause for alarm," she told him.

Bendin nodded and tapped his chin with his finger. "I see," he said slowly. "I must step back and take your view of things. It seems like a bit much, I'm guessing, to lay all of this before you. Your father, though, Gen, and your mother and your aunt... they might know enough town lore to tell you of the past."

Gen sighed. "I've asked about the Inn, and I know as much as you've told me, aside from the society bit, and I'm *never* interested in that."

"I am," interjected Mira, "and Mom's told me a fair bit about how the *Biolumen Pen* has been around as long as Glimmerbight, if not longer."

Gen thought she heard Bendin sniff in... what, disgust? She wasn't sure. She pulled on her tunic and stood very straight, as tall as she could considering she was barely taller than the hunched-over Bendin.

The man watched her ball her fists and place them on her hips. "We need to get going. How long have we been down here?" She knew she was making excuses, but she didn't know what else to say; she only wanted to get out of there and forget the whole thing.

"Ah," said Bendin. "In that case, give Harris and Reggie and Tam my best," he told them. "It's been many a year since I sent them their puzzles in their youth."

Gen felt a pang of guilt. The man seemed sincere enough, and he looked very tired just then, wizened beyond imagining, and quite ancient. She wondered just how old he was. He glanced up at her then and gave her a little smile.

"Look," she said, holding her hands palm up, "I appreciate the offer. I do. But there's just... I mean, it's empty here. What use would we be sitting around an empty old relic?

And as cool as all those images you showed us were, I don't see how any of them applies to us. The old days are long gone. We have good enough lives now. I know you skipped the really bad stuff, the stuff from history, and I don't understand why, but that doesn't really matter."

"I did, yes," Bendin nodded, "but only because I wanted you to see what was... sacrificed, *before* the great twilight of society. There is much to tell you about the years even before that, and what followed... what led to the Inn's closure. And we need to talk about the Lantern."

Gen sighed again, and Bendin stopped. He held out his hand to shake hers, and she took it.

"Think about it, Gen Lightworth," he advised her. "Think about taking on the Inn. I can't do it for much longer, for... well, obvious reasons." He gestured to his bent form. "I'd rather it went to families I like. It's got a rich legacy. A lot of good things happened here. And that etches into a place." He lifted his hand and ran it along the wall, looking lost in memories. "But mainly," he continued, "it's a base of sorts. It holds more than you realize, and it will be the only place of refuge one day, I fear. Within these halls lies power beyond description, and in the wrong hands, we'd all be living in the ancient ways again. But I fear it will be worse than that. Something isn't right out in the world. I feel it's pretty close to us now. We have to be ready."

Despite herself, Gen shivered. She noticed Mira gripping her notebook to her chest like a tiny shield. Jas looked unimpressed. He swung his head to look at his sister and raised his eyebrows.

"Right," Gen said. "We'll be off. And yes, okay, fine. I'll *think* about it," she grumbled. "You didn't tell me about the pay or anything, by the way. And trust me when I say, getting the title of *World Saver* is not an actual income. You got it?"

Bendin closed his eyes halfway. "Got it. Follow me, and I'll guide you out. But be warned, it's sunset above and you'll need to mind your eyes."

Heeding the warning, they followed Bendin in whatever direction they had come from. Gen couldn't discern any-more which way was up, and she was too tired and disori-ented to care. The images of the Inn's past had imprinted in her thoughts, but no longer flashed by them. The purple light below their feet, however, waxed and waned like a slow, steady pulse. Gen wondered what the source of that light was, but she didn't have time to ask because Bendin led them into the original, high-vaulted room and stopped.

"Here is where I'll say goodbye," Bendin said to the three of them, "but only for now. Each of you, please think of oth-ers you trust, people whom you would want to protect, but also who you think could fight. They must have considerable skills and of course, choose a team you get along with."

"Hmm." Gen shrugged. "I can't think of too many people I don't like."

"That's one reason I offered the job to *you*." Bendin point-ed at her. "You seem to get along with everyone. Now, go on, and come back when the time is right." He paused and Gen opened her mouth to speak, but he answered her question before she got it out.

"—You'll know when. Believe me." He inhaled deeply, exhaled slowly, and nodded at each of them, shaking their hands. "Mind your eyes," he reminded them, and opened the door.

The three of them held their hands up over their eyes and hissed at the amber light of the golden hour, so bright after having been in the dark inn for the entire day. The door shut behind them, and, squinting as she looked back, Gen found it looked as if there'd never even been a door; only a smooth surface of quite ancient stucco remained. Jas pressed something into her hand. She stared down at a pair of sunglasses.

"Do you have *everything* in your pack?" she asked him, amazed, for he had already passed a pair to Mira and wore one himself.

"Never know when you'll need these," he admitted, "because fieldwork has strange hours sometimes."

Her eyes didn't hurt as much as she thought they would, and that surprised her. Still, she avoided looking to the west, as the sun seemed to melt from a curiously clear sky into the sea. If she had watched its final descent, she would've seen a green flash. But she didn't dare. And as soon as that sun dipped, a marvelous purple wedge of light enclosed the trio: the Amethyst Lantern lit up for the evening, shining. Gen's shoulders relaxed. They could head home.

Stumbling over roots and skidding among leaves, they made their way back to the Lightworth home, saying little in their exhaustion. Each pondered what they'd seen and heard, and they were almost home when Mira broke the silence, "I don't like this."

Gen gazed at her cousin, whose brow furrowed, not unlike that of Jas.

"Look, I don't think you're gonna get in trouble," Gen said.

"Really?" Jas asked. "I think she will."

"Oh please," Mira scoffed. Gen raised her eyebrows, surprised by the bitter edge in Mira's voice. The three of them had only ever argued in fun before. Something felt different here.

"Maybe if you don't say anything, she won't," Gen snapped at Jas. "What's got into you?"

Jas stopped and looked back, but they had long since passed into the small valley beyond the forest separating their little village from the Inn. The lighthouse stood in placid stillness, a calming sight, a purple and welcoming light rotating for anyone who needed it.

It had always been there.

"I wonder," he said, watching it, "how old do you think that thing is? If it was around back then, like what we saw, in those... well, whatever they were, it must be ages old. A thousand years? I don't even know. Does anyone?"

"Bendin, obviously." Gen felt uncertain as soon as she said it. He was the keeper of the lighthouse, but not its maker. Or was he? *Did* he know? Did it matter? Gen couldn't decide. But it was rightfully a marvel, one of the lone monuments left to that distant past, when everyone lived during the day and slept at night.

For once in her life, Gen felt tempted to do just that: sleep at night. The last time she took a nap she was... a little kid. But the fact remained that the three of them were staggering with exhaustion. It felt like they'd been in that Inn far longer than they actually were. Gen shuddered.

"There's something off," Gen said at last.

Mira nodded. "Exactly."

"Was it already... off?" Gen wondered aloud.

Jas bit his lip. "Well, no..." he said slowly.

"Why, what do you mean?" Gen asked. She and their cousin stared at Jas.

He looked down at his pack and opened it. "You know I collect samples of fungi and test them sometimes?"

The girls nodded.

He took some paper sachets out of the backpack and held them up.

"Something's happened to one of the hardier strains. Some sort of rot." He opened one for them to see. Something black and twisting curled at the bottom of the stem in four out of his six samples. "I've never seen anything like it. I didn't think anything about it until—well, until we saw some of those images back there."

"Okay." Gen shrugged. "So, what did you see?" But a tinge of something unsettling crawled through her skin.

"There was one," Jas began slowly, "from above. Inland. Far from the coast. Do you remember that?"

Mira said, "I do. Why?"

"There was something down there," Jas said. "Something in the land, it looked... marked or something. Burned. I'm not sure."

"I saw it too," Gen agreed.

"Well," Jas went on, "when I found these mushrooms, there was a patch of earth like that. It looked... singed or... or rotten. Maybe it's nothing, but it sure looked a lot like what we saw."

"I don't like this," Mira cringed.

They walked in silence for a while and almost reached the path home when a shiver ran under their feet. Gen wobbled for a second, disoriented.

"What was that?" Mira gasped.

It happened again, but much stronger. The trees shook.

"That," Jas said, "was an earthquake!"

"An *earthquake*?" Gen gaped at him, disbelieving. "Why? How? We never—"

And the ground shook again.

The three of them looked at each other wide-eyed, and instinctively, they all turned to look at the Lantern. It still shone, but something seemed off. It seemed... dimmer.

"Um," Gen reached up and grabbed a clump of her own hair, "maybe we do have cause for alarm after all."

A Most Unusual Selection

T he earth stopped shaking, and Gen and Mira, and Jas hurried their pace back to the little periwinkle house. Gen found her parents pacing along the front path, and her mother gasped and ran at them.

"I'm so glad you're okay," Reggie said, hugging Gen and Jas together, and then hugging Mira. "Tam called, wondering where you were, Mira, and I thought you had told her you were staying with us. Then you were all gone for so long, and then the earthquake!"

Harris looked more frightened than Gen had ever seen him, and this in turn frightened her.

"It's fine," he said, his voice shaking as if trying to convince himself, "It's alright. You're safe. We're safe. But maybe we should check on the neighbors."

"Was it a bad quake, Dad?" Jas asked.

Harris shook his head. "I don't know. We've not ever had to worry about such a thing before!"

Mira touched Gen's elbow. "I'll help check in on people with you, but then I'm headed home. Can... can we talk for a second, privately?" Her voice fell to a whisper. She and Gen stepped off to the side, and Jas joined them.

"We can't tell them what we saw," Mira said.

"Are you kidding me?" Gen hissed. "Why wouldn't we tell them?"

"I just—I just think the fewer people who know, the better." Mira looked flustered, twitching her thin shoulders and adjusting her hat.

Jas sighed. "You're right."

Gen looked at him, incredulous. "But why? If we can't trust Mom and Dad, who can we trust?"

"You know what, Gen?" Jas asked, his voice harder than she'd ever heard it before. "I don't really know. But if he's right and there's something bad coming, then we better take him up on the idea of building a team. An army."

"An army?" Gen almost shouted, and she glanced sheepishly at her parents, who watched them with confused faces.

"Everything alright?" Reggie called out.

"Yes, fine, we'll be along soon," Gen said, "but we need water and a snack. We'll tell you all about it on our walk."

Reggie and Harris entered the house just as the housebots waddled out, glowing from the day's cooking duties. They shuffled into position along the home's walkway and plugged their heated legs down into the soil to reach the airspace of the cave beneath. Gen watched them and wondered what Jas said about the mushrooms he'd found. In their fungus garden beneath the home, they grew their own domesticated variety for food, as many people did in the town. But what Jas had told her gave her pause for the first time.

Mira met her eyes and nodded. "Makes you wonder about everything else, doesn't it?" Her voice lowered as Reggie and Harris emerged again, bearing snacks and water, and the teens looked at each other.

"We'll have to talk about this later," Gen said.

"Later needs to be tomorrow," Mira agreed, "since I need to get home."

Gen walked toward her parents and fell upon the snacks. Jas and Mira followed suit, and they felt somewhat refreshed, maybe even able to get through the night without a nap.

So the procession began, calling on various homes, checking to see if everyone was safe after the quake. Gen felt jumpy, expecting at any moment to be shaken more. But the shaking had indeed stopped, and there seemed to be no aftershocks. No matter what else might happen, Gen was glad that was over.

Will it come back? she found herself wondering, and she did not like thinking this way at all. It felt wholly unfamiliar, and she realized it also felt obscene. She pondered that, rolling the word "obscene" over and over in her mind, for she had never quite understood what that meant. At least not until now.

Gen awoke the next evening feeling leaden. She'd slept for so long her skin was creased and sticky. She stumbled into her shower pod and hissed in protest at the temperature of the scalding water that heated in the above-ground tank. She let the tap flow over her and was mindful of how long she took. The fresh night-blooming moon flowers her mother had placed in the base of the shower smelled like honey, and that woke her up a bit. She stumbled out, toweled off, and placed the towel in a slot in her wall to be recycled into another household item for later use. Then it would morph back into a towel and start the process over.

Gen put on her robe and slippers and scuffed her way into the kitchen. Her father was out already, off to town, and her mother painted a new set of scrollwork for the front door's archway. She did this a few times a week. It would all be swept away by the house when she grew bored of it, and then she would start anew.

"There you are," Reggie said, smiling, her dark brown hair bobbing from a new sculpt. She walked over to kiss Gen on the forehead, stroke her deep blue hair, and retrieve a mug for tea. "Sit tight, I'll help you out. You must have had quite the day! Even Jas isn't up yet."

The "even" irked Gen more than it might have another time.

"Yes, even the lofty Jas, the oh-so-responsible Jas," she muttered under her breath. Reggie had already entered the living room again, so she didn't hear. She brought back a familiar-looking envelope.

Gen's blood went cold. *So, it wasn't all just some strange dream that made me think I'd eaten sour mushrooms.*

"This came for you," her mother said, "but there were no Luna moths this time. It was just propped against the front door. Your father found it on his way out earlier."

Gen took the iridescent envelope in her hands and sighed.

Reggie noticed. "Do you want to talk about the interview?" she asked her daughter.

"Not really." Gen blew on her tea, holding the steaming mug gingerly in her hands. She wondered why they must drink hot drinks in the summer. Still, the thought of lukewarm tea disgusted her. "I don't think I'm qualified for the job."

Reggie turned her head to one side to look at Gen. "Why is that?"

Gen shrugged. "I don't know. It doesn't suit me, being cooped up somewhere, you know?"

One of the ovenbots marched over to her and delivered fresh toast from its bulbous midsection. She let the pieces dance in her hands, swiftly nicking bites, and then let the toast fall onto a plate.

"Hmm," Reggie said. "Well, let's see what your new letter says, hey?"

Gen picked the thing up and dropped it again. She rolled her eyes. She picked it up again and turned it over, and then she squinted. The handwriting was just as gorgeously chaotic as before, but this time there was very little of it.

"Gen," it read; it left off her last name, and the script was stretched as if it had been dashed off quickly.

She turned it over and found the seal, and it fell away instantly. She fumbled the contents out and stared at them. It was a letter, and it was terse and profoundly messy. Just the same, somehow Gen could finally decipher what it said:

"Come to the Inn. Something has happened."

"Well, yeah," Gen whispered under her breath. "An earthquake, Mister Brilliant. It can wait until after my breakfast."

Reggie watched her expression as if trying to decipher it. Gen's brows marched together, and she chewed the inside of her cheek. She turned the letter over and over but found nothing else interesting about it.

At that moment, Jas walked in. He looked as tired as she felt; his olive skin bore dark circles under his eyes, and he rubbed his curly head and threw himself on the couch without saying anything to Gen or his mother.

Gen blinked at him. "Um," she said, "I think you might want to see this." She held the letter out to him. He lay with his arms behind his head, and he smelled sweaty. He groaned.

"Can it wait? I've had a day of it," he drawled.

"I know, but it's kind of urgent."

Jas heaved a great sigh and sat up. Taking the letter from Gen, he skimmed over its contents.

"I can't read a word of it. Did *you*—?" He grinned at her and yawned.

"Oh, for Luna's sake," Gen snapped. "I didn't write it. Yes, it looks terrible. Yes, so does my writing, but you know what? I finally see a use for that. I can read someone else's bad writing. It took some doing. Shall I translate it for you, O wise elder of mine?"

Jas yawned and nodded, so Gen read the scrawl to him aloud in a low voice. And just at the end of it, the letter began to fold in on itself.

"Not again!" Gen cried. Reggie looked up from the table where she'd been sitting, ostensibly busy with something, but she'd been listening to their conversation the whole time.

The letter collapsed into a kernel and became so slippery Gen couldn't grasp no matter how hard she tried, and it fell out of her hands. Off it rolled, away and out of sight, just like the first one; the seal vanished in a puff of smoke.

"Why does this have to be so difficult!" she wondered, glancing at her mother. Reggie feigned innocence, but the lines at the corners of her mouth betrayed her.

"How much did you hear?" Gen demanded, her hands on her hips.

"Enough to know I better pack some food for you both. But try to get more rest, first," she cautioned. "Whatever it is can probably wait."

Gen wanted that to be true, but her heart raced in her chest. She faced this unfamiliar experience with intense anxiety. She didn't enjoy it at all. She wondered, then, how many emotions a person could feel in a short period of time. For so many flooded through her that she couldn't name them all.

"Mom," she looked down into her mother's open, caring, positive eyes. Gen felt bad for resisting her, and not only because she was nervous. "I think we'd better go now. I don't like this. Something's wrong. And... well, Bendin did ask *me* to take over the inn. I figure the least I can do is check to see if he's alright."

Jas sat up and stretched. He shook his head. "I don't like it any more than you do, and I'm *exhausted*. But as your big brother, I can't sit back and let you do this alone. Especially not if something's gone really wrong."

Gen nodded, meeting his eyes in silent agreement. "Calling Mira now," she said, and he gave her one short nod.

Mira answered and projected into the room. She wore an athletic outfit, as if ready to exercise or hike. It was only slightly less fashionable than her normal gear. Her shoulder-length hair was pulled tautly in a ponytail, but her angled bangs sprang free.

"I'm ready when you are," she said before Gen could open her mouth.

Tam peeked into the same hologram and said, "Reggie, I'm sending some snacks over."

Gen gawked. "Wait, how'd you know?"

"I didn't know anything, but I thought if you called, and you had that crease thing going on in the middle of your forehead, you'd need me," Mira said shortly. "I'll be over in a few. I have a couple more things I have to do first."

Hands sweaty with nerves, Gen fidgeted and dropped things, even the water pouch her mother gave her. "Shit." She blushed.

Meanwhile, Jas methodically went through his gear, as he always did for his outings. Gen by turns raged inwardly and felt impressed by his cold demeanor. *Why, why did you pick* me, *Bendin? I can't even pack my bag under pressure!*

She went to her room three times and shook from head to toe while she searched for anything that might help. She felt absurd packing a rope, but thought, *Never know when you'll need a rope, like Dad always said.*

She stopped and walked into the living room.

"Where's Dad?" she asked. "Shouldn't he be home by now?"

Reggie shrugged. "I'm sure he'll be back before long. Just focus on getting ready for your adventure."

"Adventure?" Gen exclaimed. "I didn't sign up for this. Isn't an adventure something a person *wants* to do? I don't want to do this. But I feel like I need to."

Reggie stood facing her daughter, and for the first time she looked tired and even a little aged to Gen. She said to her daughter, "All of life is an adventure, Gen, and that can be good or bad, depending on the circumstance and your approach to it. You've got a new job and a new path, and maybe we all do now." She nodded very slowly at Gen's frightened look.

"I know something's changed," Reggie admitted. "I can feel it. It's not just earthquakes, or moths inviting you to an inn. It's everything happening in such a short time. So, listen to me, both of you: look out for each other, and your cousin, and don't forget that you *do* need each other."

Gen felt her shoulders relax, and she mulled over her mother's words. She took some deep breaths and began focusing more on preparing... for what, she couldn't say.

After a few more minutes, the door chimed and Bloop, the bot just outside, opened it to reveal Mira and several other people behind her. Mira stood surrounded by Amber, Lyn, Nyota, and to Gen's surprise, Phan and Anisette.

Behind them stood a tall girl with very long, wavy black hair and brown skin. Her eyes were quite dark and surrounded by long, dark lashes. In contrast to everyone else, she wore a dress in a rich, mint green color with a gold sash across her chest. Gen had never seen her before.

"Right," said Mira, "we've got ourselves a team."

Flabbergasted, Gen asked, "Where did you find everyone so fast?"

Mira rolled her eyes and twisted her mouth. "Where there's food, there's"—she gestured dramatically at the group— "all these people. But no, seriously, I thought they'd be willing to help out. And maybe the new girl too, Dhatura."

The young woman waved at Gen shyly. Gen tilted her head and said, "Nice to meet you."

"So," Lyn asked, "what's the plan? Mira said you needed us."

Gen looked up into Lyn's aqua eyes and stopped for a moment.

What was my plan again?

Jas cleared his throat, and she snapped out of it.

"Plan! Yes. Um..." She blushed. "We need to go to the Inn, before sunup obviously, and see if Bendin—that's the keeper—is okay. Something's happened. He needs me. He needs us!"

Reggie said from behind Gen, "Be safe. And good luck. May the moon shine on you all tonight."

The door shut behind Gen and Jas, and they faced the other teens awkwardly.

"Are we really sure there's an innkeeper, though?" Anisette pressed, her eyebrows wriggling.

Gen bit her lip. "Yes. And... well, there's a lot to catch you all up on."

Amber looked at everyone else and giggled, her pale gold hair shining in the dark like silken moonlight. "Quite the group you've got, Gen," she said, smiling. "It feels like we need a name before we go off and rescue anyone."

Looking at them, Gen felt a surge of pride. Nervousness too, but pride overrode that for the time being. "Alright then. Let's go, Fireflies!"

The Fireflies

Amber looked the tidiest of them all, with very basic pale blue and white clothing, perfectly tailored. Lyn was disheveled, as though he had just awakened from a nap, and his bright ginger hair stuck up more on one side than another. Nyota looked elegant and imposing, her hair woven with opalescent lights, a vibrant purple and fuchsia cowl over her outfit, and a tall staff by her side. *She looks ready to take on an army*, thought Gen. Phan and Anisette, who were fraternal twins, both wore blacks and grays. Anisette's short, dark brown, straight hair was tipped teal, and her brother Phan's was tipped gold.

The newly minted Fireflies stared at each other awkwardly. Gen self-consciously looked over her shoulder, caught Reggie's eye watching through the window of the periwinkle house, and gave her mother a pained look. She mouthed, "Love you!" and Reggie opened the window.

"I'll tell your father you're off on an adventure." Gen groaned at the word and covered her face for a second. "Hopefully we'll see you before sunrise."

"Thanks, Mom." Gen looked at Jas, and the siblings took big sighs as they turned back to face the assemblage of teens.

Gen cringed. *What did I get myself into? What was I thinking?* She looped these thoughts over and over in her mind as she approached them.

Mira watched her cousin's eyes grow larger with each step. Gen reached her and swallowed, taking each person in. They looked at her; no, they looked *to* her, for... *For what?* She couldn't answer this. She felt sick to her stomach, and wanted to turn tail, walk into the house, shut the door, lock it, eat the key—or smash it into bits, maybe—and go try to cuddle the aloof Sylvia and the anxious cat, Smudge. *Just forget it. Can I just forget it?*

It felt like an out-of-body experience to Gen, looking at her fellow Fireflies, and in some ways far stranger than being surrounded by purple light and visions of the ancient past. Somehow, she could almost get her head around those things. But leading a group? Not so much.

Mira reached forward and squeezed her shoulder briefly.

"Um," she said, so loudly that she blushed again, "well. So, we all felt the earthquakes, right?"

Even just saying that out loud made Gen want a trapdoor to appear beneath her feet so that she might slide all the way to the sea, swan-dive into the ocean, commandeer a ship, and sail away forever, laughing maniacally, maybe. *So much for taking charge.*

Even worse? Someone laughed.

But that did the trick because it angered her. *The gall!*

Flushed, she took off her well-worn beret and pushed her jagged, indigo hair out of her eyes (conscious, the whole time, of Amber's lustrous, model-perfect hair and outfit, and her willowy, tall frame, and her general Amber-ness, which annoyed Gen, and yet Amber actually was kind… and that annoyed Gen even more).

Gen cleared her throat and said, "Yes, ha-ha, okay. The earthquakes were *not* normal," and even Lyn bit his lip at such a statement. Gen felt ill from the way things were going.

"So," Mira prompted her cousin, "we were asked by Bendin, the Keeper of the old inn at the lighthouse…" and then she turned, eyes silently pleading with Jas to pick up the thought.

Jas took a moment before saying, "Oh!" He rubbed a hand through his hair and said, "Bendin is the Keeper of the Inn, yes, and he asked us to build some kind of team to help prepare for… what's ahead."

Phan raised a hand. Gen, bouncing on her heels, pointed to him like a teacher, blushed again, and asked, "Yes?"

"A team?" the tall young man asked. The moon shone on his short, highlighted hair to make him look like he bore a crown of stars on his head. "So, what *is* ahead? And who is this Bendin person?"

Gen took a deep breath. She said, "Bendin, the innkeeper, showed Mira, Jas, and me a record of the past. The far, distant past, before Night Living. It was incredible. Everything was different; there was land stretching out into what's now the sea. There were glaciers in the mountains. The Inn was alive, and people were…" She remembered the wondrous sights and sounds, and the sadness that pierced her while watching them. She caught her breath. "People were happy and sad at the same time. Like they knew their way was ending, but something better was coming. This."

And she spread her arms around them all, pointed to her own glowing necklace, to the housebots, to the swaying berry-lights under the trees, and to the pair of armadillos that wandered past, their coats sparkling with glow-pearls in the twilight. Her home, her beautiful home. At that moment, a shaft of purple light caught her and seemed to hold her suspended before the others, making her indigo hair look ultraviolet.

It was the light of the Amethyst Lantern, of course, wheeling slowly, just beyond the very inn she spoke about. The effect was something she didn't see, but the others did. Gen wasn't glamorous. She wasn't considered beautiful. She was clever, but never sought the highest marks in school like her brother, and she wasn't competitive like her cousin.

Before the light passed beyond her, and she was held in its sway, she continued. "Bendin said things were changing. That—that some of us," and she carefully avoided Mira's alarmed gaze, "that some of us might be changing things ourselves. But something triggered a chain reaction, I think… rotting things in the fields, earthquakes, and… and something else. We're changing, and something bad is happening." The light then passed her by. She told them, from her darker perch, "I felt… I felt afraid in the dark for the first time in my life the other night."

Anisette gaped at Gen, as did her brother Phan. Nyota lifted her staff, which glowed in the moonlight. She stepped forward, using it as a walking stick. She stood in front of the others and looked down at Gen. Gen realized she was almost the shortest person there, except for Anisette, who was just a couple of inches shorter. Nyota looked imperious and regal, as ever, and more so tonight. Her high, dark cheekbones shone in the moonlight, and her elaborate hair swirled atop her head, woven with the same colors of threads as the ones in her vibrant shawl.

Now she *looks like a leader*, thought Gen.

Nyota said, "I, too, have felt something shift. I checked my cards," and she patted a little pouch hooked onto the belt at her waist, "and they foretold danger, instability, and betrayal."

Lyn asked, "What does the sky tell you?"

Nyota looked up. "In terms of science, we have a waxing gibbous moon, nearly full, that can give us ample light to do whatever we need to do. In terms of astrology, we're in trouble. So, whatever you want us to do, Gen, I suggest we do it while we still have time and light."

Amber then stepped next to Nyota and could not have seemed more different: a chilly, stiffer presence versus a warm, more dynamic one. Yet Amber held her own unique qualities, and her position in society didn't hurt, either.

"How can we help?" she asked Gen, folding together her immaculately manicured fingernails, each shifting in color and light at their tips. It was the only adventurous aspect of her whole appearance. "Do we need boats? Do we need air bikes? My family has equipment. All you need to do is ask."

Being rich must be great, Gen pondered, *but having a rich friend is somehow... better?*

Gen nodded. "Thank you, Amber. I... I have no idea what we need just yet."

Lyn took the chance to speak, meeting Gen's gaze under the moonlight. She flinched and looked at his pale neck.

"I'm happy to help, Gen, but should we maybe go see what we need to do? Nyota's right. It's the best possible night to head to the Inn."

Gen shot her head up and said, "Yes. To the Inn."

She began marching forward, and everyone followed her. This made her uneasy, so she stopped, grabbed Mira and Jas by their arms, and made them walk ahead of her.

"Remember the path I took," she murmured to them.

Mira took the lead, then Jas, then Gen, and then everyone else. Gen glanced back at them all when she began climbing up, and again her eyes fell on the new girl, Dhatura, who walked in front of the twins, lifting her elaborate skirts. Dhatura looked up then, locked eyes with Gen, and she smiled with brilliant teeth even at night. Her long, night-dark, wavy hair swung down her shoulders. Gen blinked, half-grinned, and turned back around.

Who is *Dhatura?* she wondered, but she needed to focus on the pathway and its slippery detritus. They would soon reach the Inn, and Gen hoped it contained answers... and some sign of Bendin.

She began to dread what might lie beneath The Inn. She hated this new feeling of anxiety. It felt like a virus spreading beyond control. She wondered if it could be stopped.

Luminous

Under the filtered moonlight of high summer clouds, the troupe climbed the steep pathway to the forest ridge looking out at the Inn. There was much protesting and occasional swearing; Anisette slipped, hitting her brother Phan, who stumbled backward and knocked heads with Jas, who brought up the rear. Gen heard snatches of barbed talk and a few choice epithets, and she wanted to turn and tell them all to stop. But if she turned, she might strike Mira, who pushed just behind her, or Lyn... and then start a domino effect down the narrow path. So, she ground her teeth and moved onward.

She reached the top and looked out. Moonlight edged the billowing little altocumulus clouds with silver, contrasting their pewter centers. The diffused glow cast strange, muted shadows from tall trees. Gen felt the familiar sea breeze in her hair spiking around her face, and she took off her cap to let it wash over her, carrying in moisture and nutrients from far out at sea; it was this wind and the moisture within it that helped the trees grow so tall, particularly on the hills and in the forests to the east, despite the punishing sun of daylight. This was the source of the evening's dew all along the promontory from which the Amethyst Lantern shot upward, a lone sentinel in the dark up where only bats, owls, and moths travailed the starlit skies. The stars were muted by the watercolor wash of creamy moonlight overtaking the night. Gen could have gazed forever at the scene of the Lantern's slow-wheeling light, the softly dappled, dark sea on the horizon, and the pale Inn below.

Something nudged her elbow. She turned and found Lyn and Nyota next to her, and she felt a startled jolt back into the present. She chewed on her lower lip.

"Just beyond those trees," Gen led the group on the path around the trees above the Inn. Their boughs creaked in the evening wind, and far off, she could hear a buoy clanging; but other than that, this side of the shore was abandoned. Completely unlike the ancient days that Bendin showed her.

They followed her, and she stopped just above the Inn. It lay in silence, but for crickets in the shadows. The filtered moonlight made its angles look softer, more weathered, and—somehow, to Gen—forlorn. She turned to face the team.

"Hi," Gen said so loudly that an owl catapulted from a nearby tree and brushed the top of her head in its indignant flight. Her cap twirled off into the dew-rich grass. She knelt to pick it up, grunted at the effort, and then blushed; for again she forgot one most unusual thing.

Everyone was staring at her. *Everyone.*

She tried unsuccessfully to look anywhere else: to the sky, to the roving hedgehog couple that she spied trundling along next to them all, to the watch on her wrist. Still, she couldn't look away from them now. Some deep instinct guided Gen, and she felt it best to see how that went. Still, she didn't like speaking in front of a crowd. Mira could tell, and stood with her cousin, giving her a little nudge.

"I—" Gen began. She blew air out of her mouth, and it fluffed her choppy, dark blue bangs upward. "I know this sounds crazy," she went on, "but I think something's happened to Bendin, the innkeeper. But I don't really know what to expect. The Inn was full of purple light from some source beneath it, and I don't know what else is in there, or where he might be. All I know is he said something happened, and he wanted me—us—here. But the inn isn't small, and I don't know where to start. I think we could each look for different things in small groups. You've all got lights?"

Murmurs and nods of agreement met her ears.

"Then let's go find Bendin," Gen said.

She privately hoped a hole would open beneath her and pop her right out of the cliffside, where one of the ancient balloons from the Inn's party days might show up and lift her away. She felt nauseous and sweaty, and she absently took one of her beverage globes off her necklace and put it in her mouth to dissolve.

At this rate I'm going to need to pee soon, Gen thought, and she wondered what the toilets were like in the Inn. Then she wondered if there even were any toilets, after all this time. That stopped her for a second, and while she led the group down to the Inn's backdoor where she entered the first time, her thoughts wheeled over Bendin. How had he been able to function there? She had never seen him out and about, and suspected, based on the mystery surrounding him and the inn, that he probably never did get out, and had things like food delivered. Her father, Harris, had spoken about the letters that the old gentleman had sent forth decades prior. Was that something Bendin always did? For how long? And how old *was* he, anyway?

Gen found herself staring at the door, having fallen so deep in thought that she completely forgot anyone stood behind her. Jas cleared his throat. Gen swallowed and turned to see him and the others.

"Okay," she said, "Jas, Mira, each of you take a couple of folks. We can split up inside."

Mira chose Phan and Amber, Jas chose Anisette and Dhatura, and Gen faced Lyn and Nyota, both of whom had joined her before anyone else could. Gen's face tingled. She would have been happy with any of them, but she was especially pleased with these two. She faced the spot where the door had been, and dark purple handles appeared. She reached out, slowly resting a hand on those handles. She paused briefly and took a deep breath. She pulled them.

The strangely blank darkness within the Inn disturbed Gen much as it had the first time, but she lit her headlamp. Lyn followed suit, and Nyota held her staff out; its tip shone forth, the light slicing through dust motes. The others entered behind her. Gen looked back and saw that the door stood ajar.

"Can someone shut that?" she called out. Her voice echoed faintly in the dark space of the hotel, and she shivered.

"Why?" Phan asked.

"Because," Gen said, and then she stopped. *I don't know,* she thought. *It seems proper? But what if we need to run out?* She hesitated. "Well, I don't want anyone sneaking in behind us," she finally said. "If Bendin *is* in trouble, maybe we'd better think like that. In fact, maybe we should lock it."

"Nope," Jas said, emphatic. "I vote we keep it unlocked. In case we have to run out of here, I don't want anything in my way. This place is old. The lock could break or something. I don't know."

Murmurs of assent met Gen's ears and she blushed, not that anyone could really see that she did among their bobbing headlamps, staff, or in Amber's case, a wrist lantern. *Maybe Jas should be in charge. Maybe anyone else.*

She felt frustrated. "Okay, we leave it unlocked. As for light, I—I know there's a big purple light in here, somewhere, but I'm not sure where. The center of the floor? Maybe it... shows up? But until then, let's see if we can find another light source. I don't know what, if any, kind of power there is here. It's not like any other place I've ever seen."

"You can say that again," Anisette murmured dryly as she drew her hands across a long-shuttered windowsill, revealing thick dust. She wiped her hands together to get the dust off, and it scattered in the light of her headlamp. Dhatura sneezed.

Even her sneeze is pretty, Gen thought, mildly irritated.

"Split up," she told the Fireflies. "Look for Bendin, and let's meet back here in... let's say an hour?"

And so, they went off in their groups, and Lyn and Nyota joined Gen on either side of her. Nyota's staff glowed upon the walls as she walked along. Their footfalls echoed throughout the Inn, and Gen would have given much to have been able to see it fully lit, for its ceilings were high, and truly it must have been splendid so long ago.

Nyota halted her steps then. "Look at this." The tall girl raised her staff. The bangles on her forearms and wrists clinked together as she did so. She shone the light on a painting, as high as she could lift her staff, and it was an enormous piece of art stretching perhaps twenty feet up, Gen guessed.

The art looked at first like an oil painting, but something in the surface, upon contact with light, set it flowing and reflecting Nyota's light. Gen aimed her own light up at the work, and it moved more quickly, shifting scenes.

"It's responding to light," Lyn said, sweeping his own lamplight across it.

"And it's changing the scene as it does," Nyota's dark eyes darted across the piece. "Is this the Inn?"

"Yes," Gen said, recognizing some of the exterior, the gardens, the many tumbling vines and flowers and fountains. The colors swam about, the scene shifted, and it was in some ways a slower, silent version of the images Bendin showed her, Mira, and Jas.

"It was gorgeous!" Nyota breathed. "Wow! And now look at it."

Lyn said, softly, "Nothing lasts," as Gen turned to him and squinted.

The inn was quiet but for the scooting shoes and chatting Fireflies. And some of that chatting held a nervous undercurrent that Gen recognized in her own voice. She couldn't shake the sense that they were intruders. It didn't help that she already felt so much impostor syndrome by trying to lead this group.

Suddenly, she heard a gasp. She turned swiftly, and, finally, she could see a faint purple light in the floor.

It grew and pulsed slowly, as it did before. Gen walked swiftly to it, and her fellow Fireflies joined her, encircling it as it expanded. It ceased at about four feet wide and seemed to come from underneath them, and yet felt suspended as well. Gen couldn't quite understand what she was looking at; it had no discernible shape, it simply *was*.

But it had a beat, a slow heartbeat, like a living thing. And that beat pulsed, sending out enough light that she could look up and see the room growing brighter. She gasped and pointed.

"Look!" Her overenthusiastic voice echoed powerfully through the great space. And now everyone could see exactly what lay within that space: doors, several of them, perhaps as many as twenty. Gen had trouble counting them due to the pulsation of the light, for in its dimming phase, she couldn't discern fine details as well.

Mira said what everyone was thinking: "I wonder what's in those?"

"I don't know," Jas spoke up, "but you might want to look at this."

Gen walked over to her brother and clapped her hand over her mouth.

Across the floor, before what looked like an old front desk for the Inn, papers fanned out in disarray and a bottle of ink lay spilled on its side. Gen could see that it was no ordinary ink. It was iridescent and glowing, and the paper quite distinct. It was the same type of paper Bendin used both for her invitation... and for her warning.

Chambers

Gen held her hands out as if to say, "Back off," as she knelt to consider the papers. Lyn sat on his heels next to her.

"Don't touch them," she cautioned the group, her voice trembling. "They might disintegrate like Bendin's other letters."

Nyota sighed and swept her staff around, looking at the front desk. It was ornate, carved from an entire piece of wood, something that must have made an enormous tree in its day. She ran her fingers across its dust coating and revealed a gleaming, rich, varnished surface, deep reddish orange. The top of the desk was a fine pearl-hued stone that, when wiped free of dust, sparkled in purple and copper veins among the white.

Mira joined her in looking at the desk. The light on Mira's hat bobbed, and she could see a wall of key hooks beyond the desk. Some keys even glittered on the hooks like gemstones. She found the entrance to the desk, a well-disguised door blended in both paint and wallpaper to match the walls around it. She opened the door and stepped into the little chamber so that she looked out on the other Fireflies in various stages of examination.

Nyota tilted her staff. "Do you need better light?" Her rich, melodious voice would have been soothing in any other situation.

Mira bent down, squinted, and sneezed. "Yeah, thanks," she replied, and Nyota held her staff higher. Mira's own headlamp found a set of cubbies, like a little mailroom, beneath the desk surface. "There's all kinds of stuff in here," she said.

Meanwhile, Gen finally decided to pick up one of the papers. It was blank, save for one small blob of ink stretched across one of the corners. She turned the sheet over in her hands and waited.

Nothing happened.

"Okay," she said, "Lyn, can you look at each one? Let me know if you see any with writing."

Lyn reached out and scooped some of the papers in his hands, avoiding the ink spill.

Gen examined that for a moment and wondered. She set the bottle upright; the outside was sticky, but not wet. She touched the spill and drew her fingers back to look at them under her headlamp.

"It's a little wet," she said. She looked up at Lyn, who balked at her headlamp, so she dimmed it, saying, "Sorry."

"So," Lyn tilted the blank sheets of paper in his hand, "it wasn't spilled too long ago. But there aren't any words written on these pages."

"Are we sure?" Jas chimed in.

"Maybe there are some invisible letters?" Dhatura wondered. She leaned over, her dark hair swaying in front of her face.

Gen shook her head. "I don't think so. Bendin didn't go to any lengths to hide his handwriting in the other things he's written. He just made it really bad. Like mine," she added ruefully. "And after I looked at the letters, they crumbled into nothing, basically. Which makes me wonder—"

"Gen! Jas!" Mira called. "We found something."

Gen stood and brushed off considerable amounts of dust from her pants. Dhatura sneezed. The two girls, Jas, and Lyn approached the desk, while Anisette, Phan, and Amber lingered in the background, examining something on the far side of the great hall. Mira and Nyota's expressions were those of curious uncertainty, if Gen was reading them correctly.

"Come around, Gen and Jas," Mira suggested, and so the siblings entered the doorway to the front desk area. Mira pointed at the cubbies and looked from where she knelt up to her cousins. Various old envelopes could be seen in different slots, in different stages of fading and decay, along with bottles of the distinctive shimmery ink, just like that spilled upon The Inn's floor. Three envelopes, however, didn't bear the patina of time upon them, and they were tucked enough to the side and down that a casual viewer might not find them. But Mira was no casual viewer; she thought herself a reporter, and she had made a find.

"Don't touch them yet," she cautioned. "Can you see?"

Gen and Jas looked. In swooping, wild scrawl, letters shone in iridescent ink, and it was jagged and smudged as if someone had written them in a hurry and accidentally smeared the ink. She knew that handwriting; it was clearly Bendin's. She said loudly, "They're addressed to us three!"

Jas reached for his envelope and Gen blocked his arm.

"Wait!" she warned. "Once we touch the things, the countdown is on. They'll be destroyed. We've got to be careful. Let's do one at a time. You ok with that?" She glanced between Mira and Jas.

Jas sighed. "Fine."

"I'll go first, Gen." Mira's bright eyes shone with excitement. She smirked, but her hands shook a little as she reached into the cubby and retrieved the letter addressed to her. She held it under Nyota's staff light for everyone assembled to see the words "Mira Celestus" sparkled and shifted on the paper. Mira nodded to herself and opened the envelope.

She drew out a letter, and something else fell out as well and hit the floor below with a faint tinkling sound. But she had the letter in hand and fretted over how much time she might have to read it, so she focused on that. She glanced over the words and raised her pointy eyebrows. She glanced at the floor, then back to the letter.

She looked up at Gen, and said, "I'm not supposed to share what's in the letter, Gen," and her cousin shrugged. Mira sighed. "I don't feel good about this." She reached down to find the object that had fallen on the floor and cringed as her fingers searched the old cobwebs and dust of the dark corners until they came upon the object. Mira drew the little, oblong metallic object into her fist and cried out in dismay as the letter began its telltale disintegration, down into a kernel too slippery to grasp, and it tumbled off and away, gone.

"Again with this!" she hissed.

Jas then reached for his envelope and opened it. He poked his fingers down inside the envelope and found a hard, small item, like a large coin. He held onto the envelope and fished out the letter within. His brows twisted together, and he frowned as he read the letter. Gen knew that look; she saw it whenever Jas had to do something unpleasant that he'd rather not. He took a big breath and let out a long exhalation.

"I'm also not supposed to share what's in this." He tapped the envelope and its hidden object fell into his hands; he pocketed it before anyone could see it, but Gen caught a flash of silver reflected in it. She grew hot from irritation. There was one final envelope, with her name on it. She extended her hands into the cubby and pulled it out, shaking.

She pressed the thing before opening it, and hers indeed contained an object. She felt the eyes of her companions on her, and chills ran up the back of her neck.

"I—" she began, but she couldn't explain her sudden unease. "I'd like some privacy if you don't mind."

Mira and Jas stared at her. She glanced up to Nyota, who tilted her head and stepped away. Everyone left the little office except for Gen.

She adjusted her headlamp.

Please be okay, Bendin.

She traced her nearly illegible name, Gentian Lightworth, with her fingers, and looked at her fingertips. The ink didn't rub off. But she could tell that the writer's hands had shaken badly; it was similar to her own. Whenever she wrote in a hurry, it looked akin to this, dashed and drawn out and even more unrecognizable to other readers. She swallowed and found her throat dry and irritated from all the dust in the ancient inn.

Her hands trembled, much to her irritation. She tugged at the back of the envelope and could see paper inside it. Chewing on her lip, she paused for a moment. Then she withdrew the letter.

In shimmering letters, written by a swift hand, the letter said:

"Gen, I apologize for not warning you sooner. Things are happening very fast, and I must leave. I've decided it's the only way to keep all of you safe and try to stop, or at least hold off, what's coming. I made some mistakes a very long time ago, and I thought I had fixed them, but it appears I haven't. And now you're all in trouble. I hope you've gathered a group you can trust, because you're going to need every single person to stop what's coming. And to rebuild after.

"I need you to go to a place on the other side of Moonbow Valley. There is a person there who can help you. I'm beyond all of you now, but I'll put up a good fight. I've left you something that only you can use. I hope you use it well. I may not see you again, but if I do, it might be a worse situation. So don't look for me: look for the truth. It's all here in this inn. Try not to dig up roots that are dead. And Gen, keep the light going. The one in the Inn, and the one inside you. Now go write the future you want for yourself and the people you love. Write a good one, one that lasts this time. Ad astra per lunam, Bendin."

Gen's eyes stung and blurred, and her heart raced. She felt something inside the envelope and brought it out. It was a fountain pen, made of purple crystal, like amethyst. She held it to her chest for a moment, and then put it carefully into a deep pocket in her tunic. She looked up through her tearing eyes and felt the paper in her hands slip away and begin to fold in on itself. She watched it deteriorate and fall away into its final little kernel.

Will I ever see another one? She wondered. But she didn't have much time to grieve.

"Gen!" called Amber, her voice urgent. "Come over here!"

Gen left the little front office and walked across the great hall, lit softly but not completely by the purple light in the floor, which continued its strange pulsation. The ceiling, otherwise pitch-dark, held a chandelier that caught the purple light and sent soft violet and lavender and magenta glints in all directions. The other Fireflies followed Gen, and then halted when she did to take in what Amber, Phan, and Anisette had found. They all stared down at a dark streak on the floor that disappeared behind a doorway. Gen shuddered.

Anisette said, "We don't know what happened."

Phan continued, "But it looks like maybe a struggle."

Amber reached out toward Gen and held one hand against her pale neck. "Gen, I think—I think Bendin might be hurt. That—that looks like blood."

Lyn and Jas bent down to examine the streak. Gen shivered uncontrollably, staring away from the smear, about two feet long and five inches wide, that led from the floor to a door.

"Ugh," she murmured. Mira pushed in next to her and looked down at her cousin's wide-eyed expression. She put her arm around Gen. "I guess... we'd better open the door."

Lyn stepped quickly toward the door, towering over her. "No, wait, Gen, let me, Jas, and Phan do this."

"Are you kidding me?" called Anisette. "My twin gets to do this, and I don't. Why? Because I'm a girl? Is that it?"

Every girl there turned to stare at Lyn, whose aqua eyes bulged wide. He held his hands up.

"That's not what I—I didn't—"

"Step aside." The edge in Nyota's tone made them all whip around to see her. She stood in an attack stance with her staff aimed at the door like a spear.

"Um, wow!" Gen said, admiring Nyota's regal posture. She looked from Lyn to Nyota and back, and she shrugged. "You heard her," she said, giving Lyn a lopsided grin.

Lyn nodded in respect. "You're the one with the staff! Makes sense to me."

So, he stepped aside. Gen then noticed something flash at Jas's side. She glared at him. He looked back into her eyes and shook his head very slightly.

Disturbed by what the shiny object might be, Gen stepped aside with him. But she did not back away entirely.

"I'm going to open the door," she told them. "And Nyota, you're more ready than we are, but please be safe.

Nyota, Jas, and Phan stood ready... for what, Gen couldn't guess. But it was time to find out what happened to Bendin, whether she liked it or not.

She turned the knob and pulled hard, prepared to yank the door open, and... it didn't budge. It was locked.

"Oh." She awkwardly rubbed her forehead.

Mira cleared her throat and stepped forward. "Well, I have something that might help. Bendin gave me this."

"Wait!" Gen held up her hands. "We aren't supposed to share—"

Mira shrugged, rolled her eyes, and pulled from her pocket a purple key. She held it up for everyone to see.

Gen's fingers felt the fountain pen in her own pocket, and she felt her breath quicken. She exhaled loudly and said, "Then we try the key. Get ready."

Mira inserted the key, hesitated a moment, looked back into Gen's brown eyes, and she turned the key with a stiff click. Mira pinched her lips together and looked sternly at Nyota, Phan, and Jas. She stepped back, letting her cousin do what she had said she would, and Gen turned the knob and yanked open the door.

A gust of wind whistled out and smelled briny, but not unpleasant. What lay beyond was pure darkness, and Gen worried about pressing forward, for fear Bendin might be on the other side on the floor.

Nyota's staff glowed brighter, and she thrust it into the dark rectangle of a door. Jas was at her side, and he brought forth what Gen feared he would: a small dagger, gleaming from Nyota's light. Phan stood in a fighting pose with his fists at the ready, and they advanced into the darkness. Nyota went first. She stumbled and fell but braced herself with her staff before tumbling further.

"By Luna," she hissed, "it's stairs!"

Jas teetered at the top and nearly fell himself but caught hold of the door frame. He turned his headlamp up and looked down at Nyota, who sat up stiffly.

"You okay?" he asked.

Nyota grunted, then gave a short laugh. "My pride's a bit hurt, but I'll be alright. I slipped in something," and she brought her hands up from where she'd landed hard. Something was smeared all over her hand, and she held her light to it and recoiled.

"It *is* blood," she said, and Jas and Phan shone their lights on the stairs to get a better look.

Gen pushed forward and squeezed between them. "Let me see," she urged, though she really wished she didn't have to see.

The top of the stairs grew crowded with everyone jockeying to look in a fit of macabre fascination. Nyota stood and made a disgusted sound, casting her staff light down the stairs to see how far they went, and how far the blood went. Gen stepped down carefully and could see dark red drops heading off into the darkness.

"How far do the stairs go down?" she asked.

"Not sure," Nyota answered.

By now Phan had helped her up, and Jas pushed forward, dagger at the ready. His own headlamp did the work Nyota couldn't, and he continued down the stairs to a landing.

"It's one floor down," he announced. Gen joined him then, as did Lyn and Mira.

"What do you see?" Amber called out, her voice unusually high. Gen saw Amber trying not to look at the blood, as dizziness flashed across her face.

Gen and Jas glanced this way and that, with their headlamps swinging.

"Um, the blood disappears." Gen tried to figure out what she was looking at. It was a long hallway, extending quite far into the darkness, yet it sloped downward. All along it were doors on either side.

"What is this?" Jas wondered aloud. "Hotel rooms?"

"I'm not so sure," Gen said. "They aren't on the main or upper floors, and they aren't aligned like rooms. They're some kind of chambers. They... they keep going down."

"Chambers?" Nyota echoed. "What sort of chambers? I'm not sure I like the sound of that."

"No idea," Gen replied, "but the blood disappears at around the fourth one on the right. I guess we'd better see what's inside."

The Scroll

G en held her breath, and Mira tried the key. It opened. They looked at each other, and Gen closed her eyes for a moment, adjusted her headlamp, and walked in. Despite growing fatigue from hours of exploration, she jolted to alertness at what she beheld.

An oval room met her, and the second she set foot inside, four sconces began glowing along the curved walls. They were a deeper blue-violet than the Lantern's light, tinged toward the unnamable hues of deep twilight at the blue hour, with just a touch of purple in their flames. Except, on closer inspection, they weren't flames at all: they were crystals, each pulsating in their notches. Gen wondered if this was the same sort of thing powering the Lantern, but Mira nudged her out of her reverie.

"Look," said Mira, pointing at the floor.

Gen stared down. A few spots of blood could be seen, but nothing more than that. There weren't any footprints. The floor was a deep blue and strangely unmarked, whereas the walls looked much older, ancient stucco covering stone that peeked out in small chunks here and there. A long crack spread from floor to ceiling, forked like a bolt of lightning, and it looked like a fresher wound upon the walls.

"The earthquakes," said Gen, and her own loud voice startled her.

"Subtle much?" hissed Mira.

The other Fireflies crowded in the doorway to see the room.

"What is that?" Amber called, pointing at one of the sconces. Something was tucked around its base, in shadow. She entered the room, and the sound of her boot heels seemed off to Gen. The tall blonde towered over her friends and tossed back a wave of flaxen hair as she advanced to what she had found. She retrieved the item, which was tied in dark violet ribbon to the sconce. She held it out: it was a scroll.

For a moment, Gen beheld Amber in quite literally a new light: the blue-purple crystal lights shone on her pale hair, making it pale blue, and her blue eyes looked violet. Holding out the scroll to Gen, Amber looked like some ancient goddess of the moon. Then Amber grinned; the one thing asymmetrical about her face was her smile, and the effect was broken. Still, Gen felt stirred, especially when Amber bequeathed the scroll to her.

Gen said, "If this is from Bendin, maybe it'll vanish as soon as we read it, so I want to make sure everyone hears what it has to say, okay?"

"Let's hear it," said Lyn, nodding to her with encouragement. She glanced up at him, and his red hair shone magenta in the light.

She nodded and unrolled the scroll and found the familiar iridescent ink and challenging handwriting. She was growing better at reading it.

"Gen, Mira, and Jas," she read aloud, "by now you have discovered the gifts I left for you, or at least, I hope that you have and that no one else is reading this. Either way, expect it to melt away, and so take it to heart and mind.

Lyn's eyebrows shot up, and Amber bit her lower lip. Gen breathed in deeply and exhaled before continuing.

"I am going away, as something has happened, and I fear that it is something I have tried to prevent for far longer than any of you has lived. I must be sure, so I am leaving, but I have paid a price to do this, and I do not know whether I will succeed. If I am too late, then we might all be as well.

"I want you to take the team you've hopefully made by now and seek the wisdom of the priestess Andraste, at the outer edge of Moonbow Valley. You may have heard of her; some of the tales are true, and some are... embellished. But either way, know that you can trust her. She is wise, if eccentric, and she will advise you and give you what you need for what I hope is not coming next, but likely is. I wish I did not have to be so cryptic, but in case this was opened by anyone but you three, that is all I dare to write. Do not come looking for me. And although you may want to more than anything, do not go looking for anyone else who might be missing. It's too dangerous, and they're lost for a reason. I'll do what I can. In Luna's light, Bendin."

Gen watched as the scroll burned up into a tiny cinder, leaving only a tiny spark in the air before it vanished. There were no kernels remaining. Like Bendin, it was simply gone.

"But where is he?" Jas wondered aloud. "This door was locked, and there's no evidence he was here except for the scroll."

"And the blood," Anisette pointed out.

"There's nothing left of Bendin at all, it would seem," said Nyota, leaning on her staff.

A sneeze startled them all, and they turned to face Dhatura, who covered her face in shocked embarrassment. Gen looked at the girl with half-lidded eyes and wondered. *Just who is this girl? I swear I don't know her from anywhere...*

"Excuse me," the girl said, and there was a moment of awkward silence. A flicker of confusion passed over several faces as if they, like Gen, wondered just who she was.

Mira piped up, "Andraste... I've heard Mom talk about her, but not anytime recently. I didn't know she was still around, to be honest."

Nyota sniffed and crinkled her brow. "Of course, she's still around!" she exclaimed. "I know her."

"You do?" Gen asked, marveling. *What doesn't Nyota know, though, really, if I'm being honest?* she thought.

"She's..." and Nyota looked down for a second, whether in hesitation, embarrassment, or something else Gen couldn't quite decipher. "She's a character. But she's also been a mentor to me. She taught me astrology lessons; not the ones like in school, but ancient guidelines. There's a lot we don't know anymore, but she... seems to? I don't know how else to describe her. But it sounds like you're going to find out for yourself!"

Phan yawned loudly, and said, "It's getting late. The sun will be up in an hour."

"What?" cried Gen in shock.

"We've barely explored the Inn!" protested Mira.

Phan shoved a power bar into his mouth.

"I'd like to explore the Inn's kitchens, to be frank," he said, smirking. Mira scowled. "But I don't want my precious skin bubbling up in the sun, ya know?"

"Might be an improvement," his twin Anisette said in a low voice. Lyn snorted.

Gen shook her head. "Yeah, I know, I'm hungry too, now that I think about it. And I really want to see what else is here, what's in those chambers, and all that."

"The rooms, too," Amber pointed out. "What's in all the rooms upstairs?"

"I'm more interested in what's in these chambers downstairs, and why this inn is built like it is," said Lyn.

"The sun, though," Jas said, hands on hips.

Gen sighed. "We've got to get going. I think we had better do what Bendin wants us to do. Maybe we can explore more tomorrow night." She yawned, Lyn yawned too, and then they all grumbled and shuffled out of the room. The sconces went dark instantly, as if the Inn were aware of their every word and movement. Gen shut the door.

Mira held out her key toward Gen.

"Should we lock it?" she asked.

Gen shrugged and blinked in exhaustion. "Sure. I don't know. Yeah. I guess"

So, Mira locked the door and pocketed her key.

They made their way back to the main floor where Gen noticed her wristband buzzing.

"The signal in here is terrible," she said, "let's get outside. Someone's been trying to reach me."

They found their way to the Inn's main door, and the deep light embedded in the floor dimmed somewhat as they passed by. Too tired to think much about that strange pulsation, Gen waited for everyone to leave, looked around the darkened interior, and closed the door behind her.

"Mira," she shouted as her cousin began marching up the hill toward the woods.

"What?" Mira replied.

"Can you lock it?" Gen asked. "I just... it just feels like the right thing to do."

"If you say so, innkeeper," Mira called out as she came back down the hill. "Or should I call you *Genkeeper*?" and the two girls laughed. Mira locked the door, and they walked up the hill together, as different pairings of Fireflies ascended and chatted. Gen noticed Dhatura speaking quietly with Jas, and she wondered what the strange girl might be saying to her brother.

Gen's watch then crackled, and a hologram of her mother Reggie burst forth, startling Gen and Mira.

"Mom! Um, hi. We're on our way back."

Reggie exhaled with a small hiccup. "Oh, thank Luna." She clutched her throat. "Your father. He's still not back. Gen, come home soon. I'm worried."

Gen felt like a spike of ice had been thrust into her chest, and she stopped dead in her tracks. "Oh!" she said in a loud voice. Reggie's image vanished.

The others ahead of Gen overheard her and looked down the hill at her. Mira put her arm around her cousin.

"It's probably nothing," Mira tried to reassure her.

"It's—it's not nothing," Gen stammered through chattering teeth. "Bendin said... Bendin warned us about losing someone. If Dad—"

Jas stepped away from Dhatura and walked down to Gen, taking her arm in his.

"Gen," he said to his younger sister, his face calm, "try not to worry. Let's just get home. Dad'll probably beat us there."

Gen hastened with him and the other Fireflies up the hill, and she looked back down at the Inn, solitary and silent. The circuit of the Lantern's light wasn't as strong as it had been, for dawn approached. So, she and her friends hurried through the woods and back to their little village, back to their homes, to escape the sun.

Headlines

Gen, Mira, and Jas each let out a collective sigh of relief at the sight of the Lightworth house quickly turning a paler blue in the coming dawn. The night-blooming jasmine that entwined the little home steeped the air in sweetness, the little starlike flowers glowing in the fading darkness. The housebots murmured hellos to them and then set about docking to charge for the coming day. On the front step, a *Biolumen Pen* bloom sat like a great flower bud about to open. Yawning, Jas scooped it up and turned the doorknob.

It was locked.

Stunned, he tried it again. He glanced over his shoulder at Gen and Mira, who reflected confused looks.

"What?" he asked, and then he checked his wrist. He called into his watch, "Mom? Are you home?" and they all heard the *click* of the door unlocking.

The doors barely opened with a creak, and Reggie peeked out and waved them all in.

"Hi Aunt Reggie," said Mira, "can I stay overday?" Her aunt nodded but said nothing.

Reggie herded them all inside, shut the door, and to Gen's surprise, locked it again. Once she did that, Reggie set about making plates for each of the teens and set her mouth in a thin, downturned line. Mira held out her hands to Jas, who still held the *Biolumen* like a ball in the crook of his arm. He, meanwhile, was ignoring her, watching his mother with his intense, dark eyes, his brow stern. Gen kept blinking from exhaustion, but she felt anxious and was almost afraid to ask the question she and her brother wanted to know.

Jas tossed the *Biolumen Pen* to Mira, who caught it and sat on the couch, messaging her mother Tam before opening it. Reggie still said nothing, but operated in a rather machinelike manner, like she was on autopilot as she portioned out their food onto little trays and heated them with what remained of the prior night's charged oven. Usually, this was a housebot task, but for some reason they were all still outside.

Gen said, "Mom, what happened?" just as Mira gasped. Gen turned to look at Mira and saw that Reggie had jerked her head upright and stopped what she was doing.

Tam's hologram vanished, and Mira opened up the *Biolumen*.

"Mira," said Reggie, "what is it?" Her voice, low and urgent, reflected the mood of the house.

Mira answered, "Mom says Doc Bozzard's gone!"

Reggie dropped the spatula she'd been holding and marched into the living room.

"What?" Her eyes widened.

"She said to look in the *Biolumen*," Mira said, cradling the curled-up paper bud. "She'd gone to get a treatment and the Doc's apothecary was closed. She tried calling him for days. The *Biolumen* says he's missing!"

"Let me see," Reggie said tersely, in a tone Gen had never heard from her before, not even when she'd been in trouble.

Mira stroked the bud just so, and it unfurled its leaf-pages. The first leaf peeled back and released, and Reggie actually snatched it before anyone else could. She held it up, and bold letters blazed across the leaf: "DOC BOZZARD MISSING." Her hands began to shake. Gen put her arm around her mother, and read the article aloud with an intense, high-decibel voice.

"In an exclusive scoop, the *Biolumen* learned tonight that Glimmerbight's treasured Doc Bozzard has been missing for two days," Gen shot Jas and Mira a stunned look before continuing, "after having been on a routine expedition to the north foraging for his renowned treatments and tisanes. All attempts to reach the doctor have been unsuccessful, and his shop remains shuttered at this printing. Residents are advised to seek the services of the following apothecaries on the outskirts of the Bay."

Gen stopped there and skimmed the remaining article leaf. At the bottom, the footer read, "Strange Sightings and Missing Persons in the Northeast Reported..." and Gen let the first leaf fall while she seized the second page from the remaining bud, which Mira still held.

Then Gen read aloud, her pulse thundering in her ears, "Luneton District officials say that strange animals were seen at the end of the night chasing goats and shepherd dogs..." She skimmed ahead again: "Nighthawk Square resident Valerie Lux tells the *Biolumen* 'I saw two large creatures, like people, but much taller, and strange... twisted up, coming out of the fields at the edge of my property—scared me half to death. The peacocks screamed and I nearly jumped out of my skin. I heard some commotion out in the barn, so I locked my doors. I've never locked my doors in all the time I've lived here!'"

Reggie sat down suddenly on the arm of the couch beside Mira. Gen squeezed her shoulder.

Jas said, "Mom, how long has Dad been gone now? Two days?"

His mother nodded, her eyes looking straight ahead. Sylvia, who sat on her cat perch across the living room, tried meeting Reggie's eyes, and meowed. Smudge slinked in and rubbed against Reggie's ankles, sending up concerned purrs.

"Mom?" Gen said, nudging her.

Reggie shook herself out of the reverie and reached down to scratch Smudge's orange and black ears.

"Two days," Reggie said, her voice dull.

Mira rose then, and carefully set the *Biolumen* on the knotty pine coffee table in front of the quilt-covered teal couch. She hastily called out, "Shades!" and her command set the windows closing off all light, for the first hint of dawn had begun to break, and nobody else had remembered. Then she went into the kitchen and finished the food preparation her aunt had begun.

Jas and Gen helped Reggie sit fully on the couch rather than its arm and sat on either side of her. The only sound was the purring of Smudge at their legs, an occasional meow from Sylvia, and Mira slicing something in the kitchen.

Jas then said, "Mom, Dad's probably fine," and his calm, almost clinical tone of voice reminded Gen more of her mother than she had ever noticed before. Gen then realized that she was more like her father, and she'd been avoiding the awful thought that something might have happened to him.

"He's never done this before," Reggie murmured, so quietly that Gen could hardly hear her. Somehow that made it worse.

She glanced behind her mother at Jas. She knew her brother must be thinking the same thing: Harris and Doc Bozzard had also been missing for two days, and something strange was seen up in Luneton at about the same time. *It couldn't be them, could it?* Gen wondered. Then she shivered.

What if it wasn't them. What if... what if whatever it was took them.

She drew in a sharp breath and Jas gave her a stern look, very subtly shaking his head for her to say nothing. He knew her well enough to know she could let her thoughts run rampant, but he was more disciplined.

"Right!" Mira chirped with feigned cheerfulness as she considered the three of them facing the door and windows, expectantly, nervously. She swept into the living room bearing the finished trays of food, wobbling a bit and nearly dropping them, but managing to put them on the coffee table. "We should probably eat."

They sat in a strange, sad silence, and jumped when one of the housebots alerted them to a delivery. It would have to wait, for now, the sun was up, and Gen frowned in irritation.

"Who's leaving something at this hour?" she complained. "We should all be in bed. Tomorrow we've got to get going to Moon—"

And Mira cleared her throat to try to stop Gen from continuing.

Reggie, who had been methodically eating, snapped out of her near-fugue state to say, "You're not going anywhere tomorrow."

Jas and Gen tilted their heads as if they hadn't heard their mother correctly.

"Sorry, what?" Jas asked.

"I said," Reggie wiped the corners of her small mouth tidily with her napkin and rising, took all their finished trays, "you're not going anywhere. Not until your dad comes home."

Gen shot up. "We can't! We're supposed to be some—"

"Where?" her mother demanded, ice cold. Gen shrank back, stunned by her mother's tone. "Where are you supposed to be? Your father is missing!"

Gen chewed on her lip and twisted her fingers together. "I—we—we promised—"

Mira spoke up airily, tossing her head back, "They're escorting me home, Aunt Reggie," she declared. "Seems like the right thing given all the missing people, doesn't it?"

Reggie's shoulders relaxed. "Ah, yes, that's fine. I'd rather you three went together." Gen exhaled in relief, but then Reggie continued. "Maybe I'll come too."

Gen almost shouted, but Jas caught her look and said, "Actually, you should probably stay here, you know, in case Dad comes back."

"He hasn't messaged, he's not back, I—I don't know what to do," Reggie finally admitted. Her eyes welled up with tears that didn't quite spill out, and her lower lip trembled. She looked exhausted, and Gen realized it was late in the day for them all to be up.

"Let's go to bed," she said, yawning so widely that her jaw popped. She rubbed it and motioned to Mira.

Reggie finally relented. Jas set the trays in the sink and they soniced themselves clean, and then he and Gen hugged their mother as she readied for bed. She glanced back at the front door, but Jas goaded her on.

Mira and Gen quietly cleaned their faces and teeth, and Gen pulled out the spare trundle bed for her cousin. They whispered for a few moments, but neither could manage to stay awake for long. Gen felt herself drift away, thinking of her dad's excitement at seeing her invitation to the Inn. She could envision his kind, delighted face, and that carried with her into her dreams.

The Parcel

The slow, methodical chime of Gen's mushroom-shaped lamp clock rang in her mind, pulling her out of the shadowy echoes of her dreams, and she fought those chimes, for in some ways she wasn't eager to wake up and face the unpleasant facts tugging at her mind like thorns caught on pant cuffs. Groggy and a bit numb to the events of the past twenty-four hours, she stumbled into the kitchen and found Bloop there preparing toast for her.

"You left something at the front door," the bot chided her.

"Well," she said, yawning, "I wasn't about to step into the sun to get it, was I?"

Disgruntled clicks emitted from the bot as it placed the toast on a plate for her.

"Thank you, Bloop."

It made some sort of irritated pops and gestured toward the living room. "I left it by the door. The cats climbed all over it, so there's no accounting for taste."

Gen munched on her toast and considered the object from where she leaned against the kitchen bar.

"Purr-owl!" said Smudge, trotting toward her to wind around her legs, nearly tripping her.

"Not for you, kitty," Gen said between chews. "Not the toast, and not... that. Whatever that is."

Jas shuffled into the kitchen behind her, yawning, and took a hot cup of his usual tea from Bloop. He paused on his way out and stared ahead at the package.

"Oh," he said. "What's that?"

"No idea," Gen said, "but Bloop brought it in for the evening. It sat outside all day."

"Well," Mira said, emerging from Gen's room, her hair in a disheveled top knot, "I hope it isn't food."

Reggie walked through the hallway to stand behind her children and Mira.

"Is it from your father?" she asked.

Gen turned to look at her and felt a stab of worry at her mother's face, which looked sunken, as though she hadn't slept in days. *Maybe she hasn't*, Gen considered.

"We don't know what it is, or who it's from," she told Reggie.

The woman approached the package and studied it. It was cube-shaped and knee-high. Papered in dark blue-gray, it was bound by a deep, iridescent blue and black cord, and where it was tied, a glossy black feather stuck out. Attached to the feather was a small, silver tag. Reggie knelt, took the feather out, and opened the tag.

"Lightworth," she read aloud. She looked over her shoulder at her children and her niece. "I'm opening it," she said firmly.

There was no denying the light in her eyes, and Gen glanced at Mira, who looked back at her with sympathy.

"She thinks it's from your dad," Mira whispered in Gen's ear.

"I know," Gen whispered back.

Jas walked over to the box, and Gen and Mira followed.

The wrapping paper fell away, and the box did as well, collapsing outward, and a soft lump of something sat in the center. Reggie picked it up and found it nearly weightless.

"It's a sack," she said, her brows flickering in puzzlement. Another dark, iridescent tie bound this sack. She loosened it, and it too fell open.

Gen, Jas, and Mira approached the contents and weren't sure what they were looking at. Small pieces of fabric glistened in the soft light of the living room, and they were not of any one color that Gen's eyes could register. They seemed in flux. Mira reached down to pick one up, and it unspooled in her hands to reveal a much larger fabric, as long as her own body. It flowed outward into a sort of gown with long sleeves and an open front.

"It's a cloak!" she exclaimed.

"They all are," Reggie said, and she began to drape them all on the back of the couch. Sylvia and Smudge instantly sprang onto them and tried to knead them with their claws, as cats do.

Everyone shouted at them to stop, and the cats let forth outraged yowls and leapt down from the couch. Smudge growled and darted off in offense.

Gen examined the gowns with a flushed face and shot Sylvia a look. Sylvia made the feline equivalent of a shrug and sat sphinxlike on the coffee table, staring at the gowns.

Mira wasted no time putting one of the gowns on. It billowed for a moment as if to decide something, and then began to shrink to fit her form. They all watched in amazement as the gown fused with her own clothing, which could barely be seen at all now but for its odd, glittery texture transposed on top of Mira's fabric.

"I want to try," said Gen, and she shoved her arms into the sleeves of another gown, and again it shifted and warped and shrank. Jas did the same, and so did Reggie. That left seven other gowns, all identical to their four.

Reggie took a deep breath and said, "I suppose your father *could* have sent these. But probably not. He'd have just... said they were from him." She sighed, and they all heard it. They looked at each other in silent worry.

"The feather," Jas said. "Let me see it."

Reggie picked it up from the collapsed package and handed it to her son.

He held it in his long, dexterous fingers and studied it with his naturalist's eyes.

"It's a raven feather," he declared.

"A raven!" said Mira. "I've not seen a raven in... well, come to think of it, I'm not sure I ever have."

"There used to be a lot out north of Umbradene." Reggie's expression softened, lingering on some memory she didn't share with the teens. "I've not seen any in years. But I do know of someone who might have a raven, if anyone did."

"Who's that?" Gen asked.

"Someone on the other side of Moonbow Valley. And I've not seen her in many years, either." She took the feather back from Jas and examined it herself.

Gen and Mira and Jas all glanced at each other.

"Who?" Gen asked again.

"A woman called Andraste," Reggie said.

Mira gasped, and then covered her mouth... too late.

Reggie turned and looked at her quizzically. "Do you know her, then?" she asked her niece, whose face went scarlet up to her pointy eyebrows. The girl pressed her thin hands onto her burning cheeks.

"I mean, no, not really," Mira stammered. "Mom... knew of her, so I guess that's how you know, too?"

Reggie smiled and watched the three of them carefully. Gen could see her mother's face ease into the more comfortable mother position and wondered for a second if she were about to call each of them out by every one of their names.

We're in big trouble, maybe, or not, I can't tell, Gen thought nervously.

"I don't know everything Tam has ever done, and I've not personally met Andraste, but I've heard of her, like you Mira. She's a bit of a local legend in the area where we grew up. But I'm wondering. If this package is from Andraste, why would she send it? And why would there be so many of these cloaks, or whatever they are?"

Gen blinked and Jas scooted his feet back and forth on the floor.

Reggie asked her children, "Is there something you'd like to tell me?"

Gen's skin crawled because she didn't want to tell her mother what had happened in the inn. At the same time, she hated to lie about it.

"We—we—" she began.

"We're going to see her, actually," Mira piped in, jittering.

Reggie raised her eyebrows at the two girls and then turned to Jas, who visibly flinched.

"Um," he said, completely unmoored. "Yes. I'm escorting them... us. We. We are going to see Andraste."

Reggie glanced at all of the gowns on the couch. She nodded slowly.

"Okay," she said to them, "obviously this has something to do with your club, or whatever. So, I won't pry much. Just... I'm worried. I don't want anything to happen to you, that's all."

"Mom," Jas said, "what would happen to us?"

Gen realized Jas was addressing her as well, that it wasn't only a rhetorical question, but also a pointed one. She wished she could answer.

Reggie gave a soft, sad little laugh, "Well, I never thought your father would just... not come home one day. And that Doc Bozzard would go missing. I'm being a mother, that's all. I don't want you getting hurt. But I know when I have to relent, too. We can't stay cooped up in here waiting for news. And maybe you'll... maybe you'll see your dad when you go."

Gen blurted out, "So we can go?"

"Yes," Reggie agreed with a sigh. "Wait! Before you do, know that what I've heard about Andraste doesn't mean I necessarily approve of her. She's very strange, and she never goes out and about. I'm not even quite sure where she lives; nobody is. But I have a feeling those cloaks have something to do with that. I don't know what this fabric does, but she wouldn't have sent these if there wasn't some reason for them, I'll bet."

"She sent more than we needed," Mira pointed out.

Reggie tilted her head at her niece. "Did you think I would give mine up? And I'll be giving one to your mother as well."

"You're not going with us, are you?" Gen nearly shouted.

Reggie laughed at her red face. "I'm not going to be so 'uncool' as all that," she said. "Maybe we'll never need them, but just in case, I'll take the spare one to Tam. Looks like you have deliveries to make, meanwhile. And get going; it'll take a while to get to Moonbow Valley."

"Any way to get around that?" Jas asked.

"Take the Owl Bus," Reggie suggested, grabbing her purse. "And be home before sunup!"

The Owl Bus arrived twenty minutes after they hailed it. Everyone left the house, and Reggie locked the door behind them. She stopped and leaned down to Bloop, who had already embedded itself into the ground along the outside walkway leading up to the house. She whispered something to the bot, and the red lights around its midsection winked on for a second. Then those lights turned blue, and then they switched off entirely, leaving the bot dark. Reggie kissed them all and walked out into the night on the northwest trail, which would take her through the tree-covered path down to her sister Tam's home closer to town.

Gen had messaged everyone except Dhatura, since she didn't have the girl's information. She also wasn't sure how well Dhatura might fit into the group, going forward, but she kept an open mind. She heard back from Nyota first.

"I know how to get to Moonbow Valley my own way," Nyota told her, "So I'll find you when you get there."

Mira got off a call with Tam and looked up to see the Owl Bus twitching, waiting for her, Gen, and Jas to enter.

"Oh, sorry," she said, and she entered the bus, followed by Jas and finally Gen, who took another look at her little periwinkle-hued home and sighed.

Gen secured the lightweight sack of cloaks over her shoulder.

"I hope you're back soon, Dad," she whispered.

"Get on, will you?" squawked the bus, and she entered.

The Owl Bus was so named because its headlights were round and immense, like those of an owl, and also because it levitated, having no wheels. The headlight-eyes were phosphorescent yellow. The sentient drone bus was as cantankerous as any housebot, and disliked waiting. It traveled a course over the village roads, as it wasn't made to fly high into the sky, per the city's flight ordinance rules. Luckily for them, the bus only stopped once for another passenger before cruising near to Anisette and Phan's home a few turns to the north. That passenger wore a greatcoat and a brimmed hat, both a deep taupe in hue, and Gen couldn't tell who it was that sat hunched over on the ride.

Phan and Anisette climbed aboard and passed small packets of noodles to Gen, Jas, and Mira, who took them gratefully, tore them open, and promptly slurped them down.

"Hey!" the Owl Bus called, "be considerate of other passengers, will you? You're not supposed to eat here. Also, that's putting off quite a reek."

"You've got no taste," Anisette called, "in multiple ways."

"Mind yourself!" the Bus barked, "or I'll let you off ahead of your destination and warn the other buses!"

Anisette rolled her eyes and turned back to her friends.

They stopped next at the Glistenad house to pick up Amber, and then Lyn, and just as the young man was about to enter the bus, a shorter figure ran up behind him, breathless. It was Dhatura, and she smiled at him. Gen watched this transpire. Dhatura wore her hair mostly down, but the sides were tied back in copper cords among her thick, long hair. Today her sash shone a similar copper against a deep magenta dress with an empire waist. The smile Dhatura gave to Lyn unsettled Gen, but she didn't know why.

Lyn, however, merely nodded politely to Dhatura, and let her enter the bus first. She walked down the aisle and smiled at everyone. Jas nodded to her. Mira stared at Gen until she looked back. Then Mira jumped across the aisle to sit next to Gen before Dhatura could... or Lyn, for that matter. He chose to sit next to Phan, Anisette changed seats to sit next to Amber, and so that left an empty spot next to Jas. Dhatura then took that place. Anisette leaned over her seat in front of Gen and Mira and glanced over at the new girl.

"What do you think of that?" Anisette whispered. Amber turned to look at her seatmate and scowled a little.

"Oh, be nice," she whispered, "she's new."

"We don't even know who she *is*," Gen whispered back.

Amber looked indignant, tossing her perfectly coiffed, golden hair. "Because she's new! I think she's nice."

Anisette crossed her arms and shrugged.

"Okay," she grumbled. "Meanwhile, the news."

"Oh!" Amber said excitedly. "I saw the news about Doc Bozzard missing!"

Dhatura, who had been making small talk with Jas, stopped her speech, "What?"

Everyone turned to the girl then, and her eyes opened wide. She straightened, however, and looked somewhat regal. Gen noticed then how carefully poised Dhatura was.

"Doc Bozzard," Amber repeated, "was reported missing. In the *Biolumen Pen* today. Don't you get the *Pen*?"

Dhatura opened her mouth and closed it. She adjusted her copper sash.

"I don't," she answered simply. Her right cheek twitched.

"Oh, we know she's a weirdo for sure then," Anisette whispered to Gen and Mira; Amber heard and sniffed angrily.

Amber said aloud, ramrod straight and imperious, "The *Biolumen Pen* is the local news, and I'm sure your family will subscribe at some point; everyone eventually does. The town keeps up with it because all of the goss—I mean breaking news—is in the *Biolumen Pen.*"

"Yes," Dhatura said carefully, "I am sure my family will." She cleared her throat. "I—I'm surprised, that's all. I'd gone to—to Doc Bozzard shortly after arriving. So, it comes as a bit of a shock to me that he's gone. Does this... happen a lot in Glimmerbight?"

"Never," Lyn told her. "But don't worry. I'm sure he's just on one of his foraging missions or something."

"He'd have told us, Lyn," Jas interjected. "I didn't get any word. Did you?"

"Well, no," Lyn admitted.

Phan whistled and said quietly, "Someone's sure keen on staying on board with us," and he pointed to the unknown person in the coat near the front of the bus. Just as he did so, that figure pulled the cord and the Owl Bus slowed. The stranger bolted out of the bus and into the night, out of sight.

The bus wheezed and sighed and rambled, hovering over the countryside, lit by the gibbous moon, with few clouds disrupting the deep indigo sky. The land to the north was hillier, and so the bus began descending as it twisted through thick forest, trees gnarled and tough and resistant to the intense and dangerous sunlight, but shielding the lands beneath their boughs effectively. Finally, the bus stopped.

"Moonbow Valley," it announced with no fanfare.

Only the Fireflies remained on the Owl Bus at that point. They each began disembarking, but Jas stopped and bent down to pick something up. It was a torn piece of paper, and something was written on it in smudged, black ink.

"Keep a watch out for Doc Bozzard," it said.

Jas considered telling the others about it, but instead pocketed it, at least for the moment, because what he beheld outside the bus pulled his attention away from everything else.

Moonbow Valley

The early evening, still warm from the day's heat, unfolded in a vibrant parade of melodies across Moonbow Valley, which spread like a dark vein of life across the countryside to the northeast of the bay. Gen couldn't see the ocean from where she stood but knew by the thin line of marine layer drifting in from the west that, just over the next set of hills, it was there. The heat of the northeast siphoned it in, and the cleft of a river cutting through the land made its way to what once must have been a rich delta to the north of the bay, which had long since dried up and given way to fertile farmland, which in turn was baked by the sun and then ultimately settled over time by small communities. Those communities gradually diminished as well, and finally the desalination projects moved in to help sustain the population until the climate, shifting back and forth, settled ultimately on something new and unpredictable. One unique thing began to occur, however, as prevailing winds shifted along the western and southern coasts, and that was the intake of marine moisture by the land itself. The lay of the land to the east allowed that moisture to collect, and formed its own microclimate, creating Moonbow Valley.

In that valley, trees had adapted to the harsher climate, and over the centuries the tougher species with thicker leaves and hardier trunks grew to a great age, sheltering a vibrant ecosystem beneath and among their canopies. The temperature differential between the canopy and the layers beneath it varied dramatically. In this way, Moonbow Valley could house permanent standing water in long sets of pools and small lakes, deep beneath tree cover.

There were springs also that bubbled up from deep below the valley, where a network of karst caves extended in all directions like its own arterial network. Those whose homes sat above natural caves benefited from a place of cooling refuge, but artificial caves—like the one beneath the Lightworth home—were much more common. Moonbow Valley's caverns were all natural, and they were labyrinthine, their waters pristine. Not many homes were built in the valley itself, though, due to the large number of caves beneath, and the risk of cave-ins. Some sinkholes had formed over time, and while some were explored, others remained mysterious. Some were rumored to be hidden from the outside world, undiscovered by anyone.

When the Fireflies stood awkwardly staring at the dark blue sky, with the vivid yellow moon above the deep green-black valley, they seemed for a moment quite small to Gen. They were part of this greater whole, sure. But teenagers rarely have time to think about such things, so busy are the many turbulent and wondrous thoughts tumbling about in their growing minds as they figure out their places in the universe.

The valley, to Gen, seemed timeless somehow. Some part of her believed it had always been there, though she knew that valleys only formed over time and didn't simply appear fully formed. Listening to the crickets and katydids singing and scraping their calls into the pulsating night, Gen felt both part of the greater whole and yet insignificant at the same time. She didn't understand what it was she felt. She thought of her father, Harris. *Where are you, Dad? Are you okay? Why haven't you come back?*

Jas watched his sister stand at the edge of the valley, on a little rocky outcropping overlooking it.

"Gen," he approached her. He waved Dhatura away, and she seemed a tad miffed, but Jas just wasn't the sort of seventeen-year-old who dwelt long on the concerns of others. He was always analyzing problems and making discoveries, and here he was watching a mystery unfold right before him for the first time: his younger sister.

She looked back at him with her large, dark eyes, messy indigo hair sprouting out at odd angles under a cap, and her mouth tightly drawn.

"What are you doing?" he asked her.

Gen looked out at the valley again, and then back at Jas. A few glider bikes sped around and down to where the group stood by the roadside, waiting.

"I don't know." Her eyes hurt from holding back tears. "I don't know what I'm doing, Jas."

Jas folded his arms. "Yeah, I think we all get that from you right now."

"What do I do?" Gen asked him desperately.

"What did Bendin tell you—tell us—to do?"

"Find Andraste."

"Then let's go find her." Jas's tone was matter-of-fact.

Gen snickered in spite of her wallowing doubt.

"It's that easy for you, isn't it?" she marveled at him, standing there so confidently.

Why didn't you pick him, *Bendin?* she thought for the thousandth time.

Jas sighed. "I don't know if it's easy, but it's what he told us to do. Specifically, you. We're here, we're waiting."

"But I don't know where Andraste is. She could be any-where down there!" Gen said, turning back to the valley. She could just see little glints of lights of all colors winking on and off under the thick valley forest. She wondered if they were from houses, giant insects, robots, or something else entirely. Curiosity began to stir inside of her.

"Nyota can help us once we're in. She's supposed to meet us here. Let's just get everyone down there, together," Mira said from behind her cousins, giving Gen a reassuring pat on the shoulder. The rest of the group approached them. "Give everyone the cloaks, Gen."

"Oh," Gen said, slipping the sack off her shoulder, "I almost forgot."

She distributed the strange cloaks and watched in wonder as everyone donned theirs. She had kept hers on, and it had formed a sort of semi-transparent skin over her other clothes. Now the others wore theirs as well and looked down at themselves. Phan and Anisette pointed at each other and guffawed. Amber's face scrunched up as she touched the fabric.

In the darkening night, Gen could see they twinkled a bit, reflecting the moonlight above. Just then, an eerie call rang out over the valley, and Gen shivered.

"What the hell was that?" Lyn cried.

"I don't know," Gen replied.

"Probably a night heron or something," Jas said with a shrug.

"Well, you'd know, right?" Mira asked him.

"Yeah, Nature Man," Phan said, "shouldn't you know?"

"I don't like it," Amber chimed in.

"No shit," Anisette scoffed.

Feeling annoyed at the Anisette-Amber antagonism, Gen heaved a massive sigh at them.

"Look," she said firmly, walking around the group and slightly down the hill, "honestly, I don't know if it's a bird or a creature from the news stories, but either way, let's get off the road, shall we? Come on."

So, irritable and frustrated, but not immune to the beauty and eeriness of the night, she led the Fireflies into the valley below.

As they walked, Gen noticed the sparkling of her cloak-skin began to increase. She wondered what might be causing it when they reached a great archway of trees, the main entrance to the valley. A narrow road twisted ahead of them and several trails forked off in all directions.

The entrance itself was spectacular. Someone had made a magnificent stone entrance, and the words "Moonbow Valley" were hewn from ancient river rocks that made an arch over the road. The valley's foliage was dense and tall, and had long since grown high above the arch, effectively forming its own curving entryway. Among the tall trees, globes of many colors drifted or hung affixed, lighting the way for visitors and residents of the valley. The pathways coursed along lit by walkers, glowing pale blue green, much as they did in the village, but instead of being artificially paved, they were naturally carpeted by phosphorescent groundcover. The trunks of some of the trees were encircled by soft illumination, and

Gen couldn't discern which sources of lighting were natural and which artificial. It was a glowing wonderland, and she could soon see that moisture had led to mushrooms of tremendous size, taller than her head. Foxfire twisted around their bases and trailed through the undergrowth.

Out of that undergrowth, from the left, a rustling met Gen's ears, and she could see a shape walking through a tunnel of softly glowing vines; it carried a long rod or something, which glowed at the end.

"Nyota!" Gen cried, rushing toward her friend.

Nyota smiled broadly at the group and accepted the cloak Gen gave her.

"Ah," Nyota said, nodding confidently, "Andraste's work, for sure." She put it on without questions.

"I'm so glad you're here," Gen burst out, loudly enough that Nyota put a finger to her lips.

"The valley doesn't like a lot of noise, not from drivers, nor from visitors," Nyota told everyone. She smirked, and held out her staff a bit. Then she bowed. "Welcome to Moonbow Valley."

She led them off the main road and into the labyrinthine paths snaking through the undergrowth of the waxy trees with their bobbing globes and berry-lights swaying in the evening breeze: pale blue, green, lavender, and fuchsia lights that could follow them along or stay suspended, as they chose.

The farther in they walked, Gen could feel the air grow heavier with moisture from condensation. As she and the Fireflies descended deeper into the valley, the temperature decreased. She paused under a tunnel of vines with flowers that glowed ultraviolet and watched the dance of moths dipping in and out of the tangle of blossoms to reach the nectar within them, and in turn pollinate the flowers. The calls of nocturnal birds could be heard in the distance. It was still early enough in the evening for actual fireflies to begin rising from the underbrush, and sheltered as they were in this vast, cool, shaded expanse, they made use of whatever edge environments they could away from the densest portions of forest, and rose up slowly as they winked on and off. Gen knew that as the night went on the fireflies would fly into the upper reaches of the canopy, their lights spinning and signaling.

"Look at them," she said suddenly, halting. The murmurs and laughter of her friends behind her quieted, and she pointed at the fireflies rising slowly. "They're just like us, making their way in the world."

"You picked a good name for us," Nyota said. "Now, off the main trail, you lot. It gets a little trickier from here."

Nyota steered them through narrow crevices choked with thick vines, all sheltered from the sky. No lights bobbed in this part of the valley, so it was quite dark. Her staff and their headlamps, however, shone softly and from a distance—as their own lights flickered among the foliage—they really did look like fireflies.

The trail meandered, dipped, rose, and then skirted what sounded like running water. Nyota halted on a rocky outcropping and gestured for Gen to step beside her. Here there was a view of the valley, and to her surprise, a waterfall. Nyota looked up and laughed softly. The moon, quite plump and gibbous, cast its light down into the valley. That light caught the spume of the waterfall and formed a moonbow. Everyone crowded around the two girls to see, and for that moment, they all felt a sense of bliss and camaraderie.

"I hate to be that person," Phan piped up, stretching his arms above his head in a half-hearted moon salute, "but are we there yet?"

"Is your brain there yet?" his sister Anisette drawled. They bickered and hissed at each other.

Nyota shook her head. "On down we go. Not much longer. You *will* know when we get there."

Gen wondered what she might mean, as, one by one, her friends all filed out behind Nyota. But Gen cast her gaze into the lovely deep blues and blackish greens of the valley, and the delicate, diaphanous moonbow in the secret oasis. She walked behind the other Fireflies for a while, and since no one seemed to notice she wasn't leading, she felt intense relief.

She thought about her father.

Did you ever come this way, Dad? she wondered. She sighed and stepped forward upon soft, decaying leaves that stuck to the bottom of her scuffed boots. They lingered back a bit for Dhatura, who was next in the line, was chatting with Jas again. Gen felt momentarily lonely, and thought briefly that it might be nice to just stay in that cool valley rather than deal with whatever was happening at the Inn. Yet when she thought that, she felt suddenly that she missed the comfort of the Amethyst Lantern, for it didn't quite reach this far out into the valley. Down she walked, down past the rushing water, around precarious, ancient limestone boulders where she shot out of her reverie.

"It's raining!" she said, and her booming voice startled everyone ahead of her.

Amber wheeled around, saw her, and laughed. "You scared me, Gen!" She waved for her friend to join her. "What are you doing back there, oh fearless leader?"

Gen twisted her mouth back and forth. "I can't say I'm fearless," she confided to Amber. *I can't say I'm much of a leader, either.* Amber, in turn, stepped back to join Gen at the end of the line. Lyn noticed, and he fell in with the two girls.

"Did you have any idea how big this place was?" Gen asked him.

He avoided her eyes and said, "No, not quite." Gen looked at him quizzically, but he continued, "At least, not this part."

"How is it," Gen asked, "that it's raining down here?"

Lyn wiped his damp, misty brow. "It's the condensation. All the water below is being trapped by the trees above. The valley basically has its own weather system!"

Gen grinned. "I love it," she said, and she glanced at Lyn.

He smiled down at her. "I do too," he said, and she felt her insides grow warm.

Amber smirked at the two of them and sauntered just ahead. The line suddenly halted, however, and she stepped aside for Gen to walk past her. Nyota was waiting at the front of the line. She stood in front of a nondescript thicket of vines where the trail swerved off in one direction, but one part seemed to end at her feet.

"We've reached the boundary," she said quietly. "Now we'll see if Andraste will let the rest of you in."

"But she'll let you in, right?" Gen asked, straining to whisper.

"I hope so!" exclaimed Nyota. "I left my homework there last time." She laughed, smoothed her purple-tinged hair, adjusted her jewelry and her earrings and her poise, and glanced over her shoulder at the others. "You should know," she said to them, "there's a guard here. And it's not like any other guard you've ever seen in your life."

"That sounds a bit ominous," Mira remarked, glancing nervously at the others. She saw Gen and waved for her to stand next to her. Gen noticed Mira had her notepad in one hand, curved against her thigh, hidden from the others.

Nyota held her staff against the interwoven tangle of thorns and vines before them. Gen watched, amazed as they untangled and curled back as if drawn like curtains by unseen hands. The vines strained and shivered.

"Hurry," said Nyota, "because they won't hold long for anyone. Not even for her."

The Fireflies bolted through, Gen leading them forward, with Nyota waiting and holding back the collapsing doorway of plants as best she could. The vines became unruly, and Gen could swear they hissed. Just as they closed behind Nyota, some of the vines shot forth, snatched their ankles, or in Dhatura's case, her waist, and tripped them up. They fell into a pile of disarray and swearing.

Unscathed, Nyota marched up among the mass and shook her head, looking down at them. From her position where she had fallen on her rear, Gen could see that Nyota's lips trembled from a desire to laugh, but she swiftly tidied her expression.

Masterful! Gen thought. *I could just never hide how I feel. Not even once.*

Nyota glanced down at her, held out her hand, and pulled her up. Gen's hat slid off, and Nyota raised an eyebrow at the thing.

"Oh." Gen picked it up and stuffed it into her pocket, out of sight. She ran her hands through her hat-pressed spiky hair, and Nyota looked serene but still a bit pained.

They faced a small opening in the sky, and the moon shone overhead, a comforting sight. The vines' presence corresponded to the light and they slinked back to their gateway, having had their fill of harassment. Before the group, a patch of woods stood tall and dense, its depths impenetrably dark. Yet it was free of vines.

Just as Nyota drew herself into her most regal pose to say something, a great wind gust howled from out of nowhere, sending dust and dried leaves eddying upward in spirals. They all coughed and wiped their eyes in the maelstrom. Then someone yelled. Gen looked up and her breath caught.

An immense shape burst out of the canopy, blotting out the moon, edged in sparkling blues and violets and greens. It swept down towards them. It took Gen a few seconds to realize it was a *bird*. A bird with a wingspan the size of a bus!

It descended, and as it did so, it cast off more whirlwinds among the Fireflies so they couldn't fully see what it was. Gen looked at Nyota, whose eyes were huge and her mouth set. Then the creature landed, its wings still outstretched. Gen's mouth fell open and stayed that way for a long time.

Andraste

I t was an owl. A simply enormous owl. Its head looked very like a great horned owl, and its eyes were monstrously large, glowing pale gold with bottomless black pupils. But in the place of feathers across its chest were countless, glistening, tinkling cylinders of several colors: violet, magenta, azure, emerald, all shimmering in the moonlight, like the gorgets of a hummingbird yet huge. And still this wasn't the most remarkable feature of the gigantic owl.

Below the chest gorgets, its body was a mix of copper and silver tubing and facets with flickering lights. Gen's eyes darted back to the wings, and she found that parts of the wings were made of bone and flesh and feathers, and the rest were mechanical, jointed copper. Its legs were flesh, but it wore two copper bangles on each ankle, and these blinked with red lights. This winged behemoth bent its great head down and stared at them with its lamp-like eyes and then it opened its mouth.

What came out of that fearsome, sharp-tipped beak the size of two human heads sounded mechanical and robotic, like hearing something travel from a bellows in a cave through a synthesizer. Creaks and rattles and clangs and wheezes and layered, deep notes echoed around in its gullet. Then it cried again: "Who-oo-oo!"

"Well, owl be damned," Anisette said.

Phan guffawed and the others turned away or openly snickered, but then the great owl stretched its neck toward Anisette and faced her with its ghastly eyes. She squirmed and stepped back onto Dhatura's foot; that girl yelped, and then the two of them seized each other in horror as the owl tilted its tufted head at an impossible angle while stretching closer to them.

Another hoot sounded, but not from this creature; it was higher in pitch and definitive at the end, a "Who-hoo-oot!"

The immense owl paused, then shifted its head back into a more palatable position and ruffled its feathers, shivering its tinkling gorget armor. Its breath seemed to bounce within its chest as though encased in rusty metal. Then the owl turned to stare at Gen and Gen alone.

Swallowing, she looked up at the impressive bird-thing, and said, "Oh. Hi!"

Nyota shot her a look of warning, and so Gen hesitated.

Not knowing what else to do, Gen bowed awkwardly.

Someone tried to stifle laughter in the group, but she ignored them.

"Anyway. Hi, great owl," she began, and at this even Jas laugh-coughed into his fist. Gen's blood flooded into her face, but she went on, "we seek the mighty Andraste—"Nyota cleared her throat and rubbed her temples. "—to seek help for a missing person."

Amber looked at Gen with performative pity, and Gen felt her prim and proper society girl gaze. Then she felt guilty that she would interpret Amber that way, and once again Gen wondered why suddenly there seemed to be new shadows to everything around Amber in a world that already lived by night.

The owl shook its feathers, again sending whirls of dust and debris flying, and then turned around, tucked its wings in, and walked back into the forest as if it were made of hanging beads. Gen turned to Nyota, who shrugged.

"So, now we go in," she said simply, and she stepped forward into the dark foliage curtain. They could no longer see her or the owl, but they could hear... something: a quivering of leaves and a crackling of boughs.

Gen turned to face the remaining Fireflies. "You don't have to go in if this is... um... well, if it's too weird."

"What else would we do, though?" Jas asked. "We came all this way."

"Yeah," Anisette added, "I'm gonna need to see more of GigantOwl."

Mira patted the pocket where Gen knew she had stored her notepad. "I'm not missing *anything*," she said, and she winked at her cousin.

So, Gen took a deep breath and announced, "Ok. Headed in."

It was the strangest sensation Gen had ever felt. She could see the skin of the cloak she wore light into thousands of sparkles, and the air seemed to fizz and sting a little bit on her exposed skin as the forest enveloped her on all sides. And then, quite suddenly, she was inside, standing next to Nyota.

"Holy shit!" Gen cried out.

For within the strange boundary, the dark trees stretched taller than any Gen had ever seen, and she knew there must be no way for them to have reached such a height without some... unique aspect of the place. Maybe it was the micro-climate, or something... less scientific. Her eyes darted this way and that, taking in floating lights like small balloons, little whirring machines flying above piloted by mice, garlands of crystalline ropes draped over shrubs, and alcoves full of mushrooms of enormous size. Those mushrooms flickered with myriad facets of electricity coursing visibly through them, and the other great fungi seemed to respond.

Wingbeats drew Gen's eyes to the ceiling of this secret forest, and she followed what looked like a copper-colored peacock's flight as it dipped down and touched a glowing bayou that extended in the shadows of ancient trees. The cascades of fountains embedded in petrified logs tumbled into that slow-moving, brilliant blue water, through which ducks and river otters plied, the latter fussing at the former at every chance. The sounds of bamboo and glass wind chimes knocked and tinkled everywhere, swaying from a breeze under the long, intertwined boughs of the trees above them.

On the far end of the bayou, a low cottage sat, encrusted with trembling vines and softly glowing night-blooming flowers. Rimu trees, with their shaggy boughs draping the ground, stood on either side of the cottage. An empty gondola floated along the bayou toward the Fireflies, while their namesake insects danced above their heads. The immense owl was nowhere to be seen.

Nyota stood confidently and looked satisfied at everyone's expressions. Even Anisette was struck silent by this place. Nyota stepped forward, caught the tip of the gondola, and pulled it gently up onto a ramp of moss and bracken.

"Our ride's here," she said, "and it's a pretty good one. Normally I have to try to make my way to class by tiptoeing on the shore without falling in, but sometimes she doesn't like that because she wants me to stay off her plants. And I *know* she doesn't want you all trampling her stuff."

"I'm sorry?" Dhatura spoke up, her face reflecting the wonder and near stupefaction of everyone besides Nyota. "Did you say to *class*? Is Andraste your teacher?"

Nyota grinned and closed her eyes for a second, savoring the question; her eyelids sparkled with turquoise and purple glitter. She opened her eyes and said, as casually as she could, "Yep!"

"You've been holding out on us, Ny!" Amber said, impressed. Nyota's shoulders shook from suppressed laughter as she covered her face in her hands.

"To be fair," she gasped, "do you blame me? I didn't want everyone knowing about this place."

Then her face turned serious, and she said to them all, "Look, Andraste is not... she's not like anyone else you've ever met or known or anything. She's... special. Powerfully special, emphasis on the power part. Just... don't piss her off, okay?. Don't wreck her plants. Try not to get caught in her vines. None of you would've made it through that barrier without the cloaks, either. So she clearly thinks you should all—" she looked pointedly at Dhatura's questioning face "—should be here."

Nyota used her staff to pull the gondola a bit closer to the shore and hold it in place. "All aboard," she said, and one by one they stepped in: Mira, Amber, Dhatura, Anisette (scuffling with Phan of course, who followed), Lyn, Jas, and Gen. The boat bobbed and swayed with each entry. Finally, Nyota stepped onto the boat and remained standing. She took her staff and pushed the boat off, and Gen noticed the water's flow change the other direction so that the boat now coasted down the slow current. Where Nyota's staff swept through the surface of the water, it broke apart in dazzling, vivid azure, and so their wake was luminous. Birds swooped overhead, and bats skittered down along the water's surface before launching skyward again. The forest was full of calls: hoots, clicks, the music of katydids, crickets, buzzes, rustles, yips, distant howls. Such a vibration of nocturnal life Gen had never heard or seen before. And none of it was human.

The gondola glided smoothly forward, thanks to Nyota's agility, and pushed up into a small cove with a set of stone steps above it. A night heron flew up from a nearby thicket of cattails and soared upward into the verdant dark canopy and out of sight. Two knee-high kākāpō parrots waddled from the top of the stairs to the bottom, greeting Nyota where she stood.

Each flightless, sturdy green parrot wore sparkling vests of similar material to the cloaks everyone wore. The one on the left had a jaunty turquoise bandana around its neck.

"Hello, Rangi," Nyota said to the leftmost kākāpō.

"Greetings, Nyota!" Rangi the kākāpō said back.

The right hand kākāpō wore a little purple cap studded with tiny white lights all around its rim.

"Hello, Papura," Nyota greeted the bird with a grin.

"Hullo there, Nyota!"

Gen jumped out of the gondola and watched the exchange. The parrots saw her, and both bowed low. She grinned down at the sturdy green birds with their flashes of color.

"The Lunadatrix Andraste welcomes you," they said in unison.

"So formal!" Nyota remarked. "You never greeted me that way," she teased them, reaching down to scratch them both

at the napes of their necks, which they very much appreciated.

Papura reached a foot up to scratch behind its ear and
said, "Well, you're a student. Gentian Lightworth is a
leader."

Gen cringed as she looked between Nyota, Papura, and
Rangi. Nyota gave Gen a sidelong look, and Gen quaked
from impostor syndrome. Someone as self-assured and dynamic as Nyota surely deserved a better title than student,
and Gen felt again that Nyota obviously made a better leader
than she did.

Rangi tugged at its bright blue bandana to tidy it, and
then stood quite straight. Papura straightened too. The
teens arrayed themselves in a semicircle on the landing at the
base of the stairs and stared at the two birds. The kākāpō
then turned and hopped up the stairs, and Gen and Nyota
followed, with everyone else trailing behind the two girls.

At the top of the stairs, a path of stone embedded in
starry-flowered groundcover curved toward the low cottage,
which upon closer inspection was quite large, although
from a distance it had looked more intimate. It was made
of stone, glass, thatching, and found materials of all sorts
glinting in many colors, especially deep reds and greens. The
vines traversing its exterior shifted restlessly across the home.
A deeply recessed veranda stretched along its front and sides,
with ancient wooden stairs climbing up to its floor.

Gen climbed those stairs and with each step they groaned
and popped from great age; their surfaces were smooth and
deep, reddish orange. Black and red jewels flickered, embedded in the wood of the ornate stairs and their accompany-
ing handrails. On the veranda, many inviting cushions of
vibrant, deep jewel tones were piled everywhere. The chimes

she had heard from afar now knocked together close to her ears.

She faced the door, which was also of considerable age, carved from multiple kinds of wood, both the reddish wood of the veranda, a black wood, and a pale, blonde wood, fused together. The black wood was carved into an intricate raven with curved, archaic symbols and elements, but Gen did not know what those were. The door knocker was a roughly carved garnet the size of Gen's fist. It was made to look like an amulet hanging from the raven's neck, and it glimmered with some inner light. She looked back at her friends and Nyota, and down at the two kākāpō on either side of her. It was as if the world hung expectantly: a dewdrop on the tip of a leaf, just about to release, but stubbornly hanging on. She took hold of the garnet knocker and clapped it onto the door three times.

The wind whistled down from the dark basket of woven treetops above and whirled through the veranda, setting the chimes dancing; the bamboo ones knocking in their hollow voices, the glass ones jingling brightly against each other.

And then everything went silent and still.

The door opened with a long, scraping creak.

Inside the structure—for at this point Gen was reluctant to refer to it as a house anymore due to its strangeness and size—she found a room with several levels. The uppermost level extended in a U-shape from where she stood, all around the windows of the home. It tricked her eyes, because at some moments the shape looked angular, and in others it appeared curved. Under the windows, soft cushions and blankets lay in piles; some held cats, others foxes, and still others looked like oversized hen nests. Low, red candles flickered in those windows. Some were mushroom-shaped, others shaped like crystals, and Gen felt the urge to look at the latter, for they reminded her of the crystal sconces in the Inn. On the far side of the U-shape was a grove of slender, pale-trunked trees with waxy leaves that formed a wall for all of the levels.

Dark wood stairs extended from this level to the second, and here along the U-shape there was a vast library set below the earth. Shelves full of books, bottles of gemstone colors and shapes, vines, and hovering berry-lights clustered the entire perimeter. Several creatures—cats, possums, and ground squirrels among them—sat curled up or explored or chatted.

Gen stepped down to the library and to her right, Mira scribbled surreptitiously on her notepad, recording everything. Jas murmured, "Look at those ancient books!" in an excited but reverent tone. Lyn reached down to scratch the ears of a tabby with fur similar in color to his fiery hair. Amber walked over to admire something on one of the shelves when a raven called out, startling her and everyone else. It sounded as though the raven must be below them.

On the lowermost level, incense hovered in the air, obscuring the many candles and floating lights and any other details of what the bottom floor might hold. So Gen descended, her hands holding the smooth, wooden railing of an ancient, pleasantly gnarled tree trunk, and the thick haze of incense parted. There sat a figure, up against the groove on a great, chartreuse and teal wing-backed chair, and on the back of the chair sat three sleek ravens. The figure also held a raven on each arm. Gen stopped several feet in front of this person to gawk openly.

It was a woman of an age Gen couldn't discern, but clearly not young, with wild, frizzled, large hair, much of it gray.

Underneath, some of it was gold and auburn, and her skin was golden, what little of it was exposed; for she wore a dark, patchwork velvet kaftan that shone with silver threads, and her arms were covered in bangles and bracelets. Around her neck an extraordinary necklace of silver, curved into an intricate crescent moon, extended from her chest and wrapped around her neck. On her feral hair, a tiara of similar shape and hue rested. Long raven feathers hung from her ears, interspersed with garnet beads. Her eyes were deep-set and a strange hazel color, nearly gold but flecked with greens and browns. Wrinkles gathered on her brow and at the corners of her eyes, but her high cheekbones lifted the deep grooves at the corners of her mouth into a smile.

Nyota stepped forward and knelt, but the woman waved her hand and rolled her eyes, not unkindly.

"That will do, Nyota, thank you," she told the girl. Her voice was low, husky, and lilting with an unrecognizable brogue.

"Gen," Nyota said, and Gen noticed the pulse jumping in her friend's neck, "this is the Lunadatrix Andraste."

"At last, Gentian Lightworth," the woman said. The three ravens croaked in unison, "*Gentian*." The girl shivered.

"C-call me Gen," she said.

"Call me Andraste, dear," the lady said. She turned her head to the right, and one of the ravens bent its beak toward her; she whispered something, and off the raven flew through the grove of trees forming the wall behind her. "Come," she said, "you and Mira and your brother, and sit by me."

She gestured to a couch and a chair, each piled with colorful cushions, some with metallic threads, others with beads, some with mirrored glass diamonds. Gen could see, then, that there were many more cushions and couches in this lowest room, which was dark and soft and velvety, yet shimmering with candlelight and smokey incense curling from hanging, multi-faceted lanterns of teal and gold. Her friends found nooks and crannies immediately, with Anisette roaming the alcoves and shelves, Phan pulling a hookah pipe from a corner and holding it up while Lyn laughed. Dhatura walked around the room and gazed at everything, fascinated, with her copper sash gleaming in the dim light.

Amber, meanwhile, looked the most out of place, and she tried to settle herself on a round chair made of a tapestry showing, of all things, the sun. Her outfit was nearly colorless, and she felt about to sneeze at any second. Still, she was tired, and she sat chiefly in support of her friends, to listen to what their plan might be next. Then one of the two ravens behind Andraste shot forward, flapping its large wings, and aimed straight for her.

"Oh!" she cried, ducking, but the great bird landed on her shoulder. She froze and gasped, some of her blond hair caught across her face. She clawed it away and sat very still, with the great bird perched serenely next to her face. It was a striking thing to see, the pale, tall girl in white and the blue-black raven perched with her. Anisette and Phan fell into spasms of laughter at her between hookah shares, but Gen was struck by something strange. Amber looked, somehow, for the first time, *correct*. She was slightly disheveled, her pale cheeks flushed from the terror of the bird, her cobalt eyes staring out toward Andraste in shock.

"What—what do I do?" she asked in a shaky voice.

Andraste smiled, curling her hands over the arms of her chair. The remaining raven leaned down and clicked in her left ear.

"Yes, I think so, Sapphire," she murmured back to the bird. More loudly, she said to Amber, "Let Onyx settle. He's getting to know you, child. What is your name?"

"Am-Amber," the girl answered. "Amber Glistenad."

"I thought so," Andraste said, and she unfurled a small scroll that she pulled from her voluminous sleeve. She held this scroll upon her lap and gazed back to Gen, whose mouth had fallen open at the sight of it. She made eye contact with the girl and nodded slowly.

It's Bendin's! Gen thought, and a thousand questions percolated up in her throat, but Andraste spoke before she could.

"I know why you are here," Andraste told the group.

Gen took a deep breath and looked at Mira, whose writing hand twitched, but she didn't dare take notes just then. Jas watched her with unblinking, dark eyes, his brow furrowed in concentration. The incense and the atmosphere made him sleepy, but he fought it.

Andraste continued, "Bendin alerted me that you would come." Gen sat bolt upright, pulse quickening. She noticed Dhatura had rushed up and now stared at Andraste with her hands clasped under her chin.

"Where is he?" Gen asked quickly. "Is he alright?"

Andraste closed her eyes and took a deep breath. The remaining raven, Sapphire, lifted her wings and glided off through the pale woods wall. "I think not," she said, her voice low and mellifluous, "or he would be here himself. It has been a long time since he ventured this way, and he was going to meet me here on his way north. He told me that you, Gentian, would need to bring a group to see me, to help prepare you for your task."

"My task?" Gen looked uncomfortably from Andraste to the Fireflies and back again and asked. "What task?"

Andraste stared into Gen's brown eyes. "You are the new keeper of the Inn at the Amethyst Lantern. Or Lembrar, as it was called long before this time."

Gen's eyes flew open wide, and her mouth formed an "o."

"Seriously? I'm really the new keeper?"

"Lembrar?" Lyn tilted his head.

"The grand Hotel Lembrar," Andraste told them. "An old word, from another time and place, meaning 'to remember.' It will be your task to keep it sound, and to keep the Lantern going; you will need help with that. It's your inn now, Gentian Lightworth, and your task is to protect what the Inn protects."

Gen mulled over those words in her mind and was about to ask more questions, chief among them: what it is that the Inn, and now it seemed she too, was supposed to protect? But just then, Dhatura marched straight up to Andraste and said, "No. It's my Inn. I'm the only remaining heir of Bendin."

Heir Apparent

The room fell silent. Everyone stared at Dhatura where she stood, squeezing her hands together and clenching her jaw. Gen couldn't believe what she just heard. Nyota, meanwhile, leaned forward a bit, holding onto her staff, and glared at Dhatura.

"This is what you've been hanging around us for?" Nyota demanded. "You thought you'd spring this on us, on the Lunadatrix *herself*? The disrespect!" Nyota then stood straight and tall and glanced over her shoulder at Andraste, whose face was unreadable, her lips drawn thin, and her golden-hazel eyes half-lidded as she sat watching Dhatura.

Gen blurted out loudly, "I didn't know Bendin had any relatives at all!"

Mira chimed in, "It does seem awfully convenient," and her sharp eyebrows sank downward as she squinted at Dhatura.

Jas held up his hands and said, "Maybe let her speak?"

Andraste locked eyes with Dhatura, and for a long moment she simply looked at the girl. Dhatura twitched her thick, dark, wavy hair over her shoulders, and pulled at her long, magenta skirt.

Then Andraste said in her rich, low, musical voice, "Tell us, Dhatura, how you came to think Bendin of the Inn might be your relative?"

Dhatura exhaled, swallowed, and stood straight and regal. She glanced briefly at Gen, who watched intently.

"I moved to Glimmerbight a few months ago," Dhatura said slowly. "I live with my aunt. My parents died when I was little, and my aunt wanted me to be here when I came of age, because she told me I was to inherit a great inn."

Phan made a disbelieving snort, and Dhatura trembled. But while Gen felt confused about everything, she did feel badly for Dhatura just then: the girl was thrust into a situation just now that she hadn't asked for. Much as Gen had been when she received the invitation from Bendin.

"Go on," she encouraged Dhatura. The girl looked at Gen with an amazed expression, but it softened into gratitude and she relaxed.

Dhatura went on, "I followed my aunt's advice and went to Doc Bozzard recently. We'd heard that he was an expert on the history of Glimmerbight, the Lantern, and all that. So, we met with Doc—"

"When?" Mira interrupted. "Was it before or after the Glowworm Ball?" For she had also gone to the Doc for very different reasons, as her mother Tam had helped make possible her trip to the Ball, and all the domino effects of what happened after that. Not that Mira wanted to dwell on that part.

Dhatura blinked and thought for a second before saying, "Before the Ball. And, well, he sent me to the Inn."

"He did *what*?" Gen exclaimed, incredulous now. "You went to the Inn? Before any of us?"

Dhatura sighed and paced back and forth before Andraste, Gen, Mira, and Jas where they sat. Nyota watched her with a savage gleam, her jaw working, teeth grinding in anger.

"I went to the Inn," Dhatura admitted. "But I couldn't get inside. I tried. I knocked, I shouted... no one ever answered. I even said my name at the door and... nothing. So, I never got to meet my ancestor."

"*If* Bendin *is* your ancestor," Nyota said tartly.

Andraste held her hand up and dipped her head at Nyota.

"Dhatura," the older lady said, "thank you for sharing this with us. Your honesty is appreciated. Please, do sit, child. Let us take a moment to ponder everything, but I do not want to address this situation before we've broken the fast. I know you're all tired, having traveled a long way. And you have a long way back."

Andraste clapped her hands together, and her bangles chimed against each other. Sapphire flew back in, presently, weighed down a bit by a deep burgundy velvet bag with a golden cord that she carried with her feet. The other raven flew in from the pale woods just then as well, carrying a basket. Two foxes trotted in behind them also with baskets in their mouths.

The animals set everything on a low table in the center of the room, and Phan shouted, "Food! Thank Luna!" So, he rushed forward, joined by Lyn. Anisette sidled up next to the spread of breads, fruits, flapjacks, and moon cheeses, while glancing back toward the woods, searching for something.

Amber attempted to stand with the raven Onyx on her shoulder.

"Nice, nice Onyx," she said, voice shaking. "Do you... uh... want to eat?"

Onyx clicked his beak and said, "Yes!" and Amber gasped. The bird then flew off her shoulder, and she rubbed where he had perched. She watched him fly to the back of Andraste's chair again, and for a moment she felt sad that he had done so.

Andraste watched her keenly as one of the foxes brought her a plate. She reached a hand out to Nyota to help her from her chair. Nyota offered the woman her staff, but Andraste drew a carved walking stick from beside her chair and walked forward to the table. She looked back at the Lightworth siblings and Mira, and gestured for them to join in.

The three cousins, however, held back. Mira and Jas whispered at once to Gen.

"Something's not right with Dhatura's story," Mira hissed.

Jas said in a low voice, "She talked to me, said she was new, but she never said anything about Bendin, just that she wanted to help. I thought she seemed alright, but now? I don't know."

Gen sighed and rubbed her face. "I don't know what to think. I think she was brave. I just—I'm tired. I'm worried about Dad. And I'm hungry. Let's eat and talk more about this later."

Lyn approached her with a bowl of some food.

"Here," he said softly, looking down at her with candles glinting in his aqua eyes, and his ginger hair glowing softly. "You look super tired. Eat something."

At first, they stood awkwardly eating, but Jas and Mira left their seats, smirking at each other and giggling as Lyn sat down and Gen joined him.

"Thanks, Lyn," she said. She glanced around at everything and then shoved an entire seeded roll into her mouth and chewed.

He smirked. Then he looked around the U-shaped room and said, "This place is amazing, isn't it?"

"Guess so," Gen said, growing more fatigued by the second. She realized she had felt tense the entire time they had been there, at least until Lyn came to her with food.

Dhatura came up to Gen then, and standing before her, said, "I'm sorry. I really didn't mean to hide anything. It's just that I was new, and then everything happened so quickly, and…" her voice trailed off and she shifted back and forth from one foot to the other. "No hard feelings?"

"No hard feelings," Gen agreed between chews. She swallowed, took a cup that Lyn handed her, and drank its contents all in one go. Whatever it was, it tingled on the way down, and left a fruity and flowery taste behind in her mouth. "So," Gen said slowly, "you're Bendin's relative. He never mentioned he had any relatives. I know he contacted my dad when he was younger. Did he ever send anything to you or your family?"

Dhatura tilted her head. "Not that I know of. But maybe he did, and I just didn't know about it."

"Oh," Gen said, thinking of the two immense, green Luna moths wending their way toward her home to the south, "you would know."

The two girls looked at each other and Gen felt uneasy. Dhatura's eyes fell away from hers, and she wandered off to eat. Andraste settled back in her chair and observed. Amber touched her shoulder absently and looked back at Andraste. The older woman smiled.

"Sapphire," she said to the raven, "bring me the bag."

The raven hoisted the burgundy velvet bag and eased it onto Andraste's lap.

"Gather round," the woman said, "for it is time to give you what you need to help you in the fight ahead."

Gen turned her head quickly and said, "Fight? But what fight? Who are we fighting?"

Andraste glanced sidelong at her and then patted the sack in her lap.

"I wish I could tell you 'no one.' But Bendin warned me for many years that, one day, we would have to defend this land of ours from invaders. If the stories I'm reading about in the *Biolumen Pen* are true, it's already begun. But I've always known they would make their move; they've been biding their time, and now that time has come."

True North

Gen watched as Andraste began to open the velvet sack in her lap.

"Who are these things we're supposed to fight?" Gen asked. "Are they the reason people are disappearing? We've heard about animal sightings... or something. Is that really all it is?"

Andraste set the sack down and looked at Gen with an unreadable expression in her golden eyes. "Some things needed to stay buried," she said, and Gen felt a chill course through her spine. *What? Is she being serious?*

The lady then said, "Gen, Jas, and Mira, I want you to show me the gifts that Bendin gave you from the Inn."

The three rummaged in their pockets and brought forth the pen, the key, and the pocket watch.

"Do you know what these can do?"

"Yes," Gen and Mira answered in unison.

"It... just seems to be a watch," Jas said, opening the silver item.

Andraste laughed richly. "Oh, dear boy, *that* is no mere watch. First of all, lift the face."

Jas stared at the lady for a moment and then examined the opened watch. There was indeed a tiny groove below the six o'clock position. He stuck his fingernail in and pulled, and it opened to reveal a vibrant green face with a needle spinning wildly.

"A compass!" Jas explained. "Well, that's neat."

"Neat? This isn't just any compass, child," the woman said. "It is also a dosimeter, and as such, a de facto detector."

"A dosimeter!" Jas exclaimed. "We don't really need those if we wear the right clothing, though, do we? And don't venture out into daylight?"

Andraste folded her hands under her chin. "It is not for solar radiation," she told him. "And indeed, it is not for any conventional radiation."

By now, the other Fireflies gathered around Jas to look at the item.

"Then... what *is* it for?" Jas asked. "What's it going to detect?"

"It is to help you know how much of something you've been exposed to."

"Such as?" Jas pressed. He was growing impatient; and Gen knew it took some doing to get her brother to that point.

Andraste took the bag in her lap and stood. Nyota moved closer to help her, but the older lady waved her away.

"Now it is time to distribute these," she announced, and Jas cocked his head to one side and furrowed his brows, still waiting for an answer. She glanced at him and nodded. "It is also time to warn you of what I know and what I think. Anisette Sao Duong, come."

Anisette jerked out of the reverie she had been in and, looking startled, walked forward, her typical bravado growing a bit frayed. Andraste, it so happened, was taller than she, and she felt suddenly intimidated by the woman: her age, her wisdom, and some sort of enigmatic power she wielded even just in her gaze.

Andraste pulled an object out of her bag and held it out for Anisette: a small conch shell-shaped, deep red gemstone on a long, black cord. Anisette took it and smoothed it in her hands. It flashed and winked at her.

"When you have need, make the call," Andraste told her. Then she dipped her head, and Anisette placed the amulet over her head and held it against her chest, staring at it in wonder.

"Amber Månstråle Glistenad" Andraste said next. "Onyx has made the choice to remain with you, but he is not my gift."

The blonde stood, with the raven Onyx on her shoulder. The bird flew off to the back of Andraste's chair to sit next to the other two ravens. Amber approached the Lunadatrix.

"I feel I shouldn't take anything else from you," she said to Andraste, "since I have Onyx."

Andraste laughed indulgently. "Child, Onyx was never mine to give, and he is no one's to own, any more than you are. You found each other: that is all. Now, this, however, is my gift," and she brought forth an iridescent black necklace with three raven feathers hanging from it. But these were no ordinary raven feathers, they were metallic like the necklace, and something shone within the iridescence. Amber thought they looked a bit like circuits. "You will never be lost," Andraste said.

"I think these are... are just lovely," Amber said, trying to gather herself into her normal persona of a confident, popular rich girl, rather than being underground in a forest surrounded by strangeness. "I just don't... I'm not sure they're really my sort of thing. I mean no disrespect," and she glanced at Nyota, who made eye contact with her and gave her a short nod. "But this just doesn't feel quite right."

"Tell me, Amber," Andraste said, "how did it feel when Onyx left your shoulder?"

Amber considered. "I... I hadn't realized how heavy he was, until he flew away. I guess I had got used to him being there."

Andraste nodded. "I thought so," she said, looking pleased.

Amber looked flabbergasted. "I don't think he'd be happy with me," she said, not knowing what else to say. "I live... I live in a house with a lot of glass and lights and... oh, and there's our dog, Milton. I don't know if Milton would approve at all. Let alone Mom and Dad! What would they think of a raven in the house?"

"You're of age," Andraste said, "and you are also, clearly, of mage."

Amber laughed again, bewildered, and said, "What on earth do you mean?"

"Perhaps a better question might be, what on the moon do I mean," Andraste said cryptically, adjusting her silver crescent moon necklace. Amber noticed and her smile faded.

"You're quite serious, then, about Onyx?" she asked.

Andraste shrugged and began to walk away from Amber. "Ask him."

Amber looked from Andraste to the raven and back again. Gen watched her friend.

"Nothing really makes sense right now, if that helps," Gen said to Amber. "So why not take the raven?"

Amber's expression changed to one that Gen read as fear.

"I don't know the first thing about ravens!" the tall girl exclaimed, staring over at Onyx, who preened his feathers with his great beak. He raised his head, then, caught her eye, and croaked at her.

She blinked several times and gulped.

Gen smiled. "I've never seen you like this," she said to Amber. "Usually, you know exactly what's going on, all the time, and how everything fits together."

"I don't think I can do this," Amber moaned, and then quite suddenly Onyx stretched his wings out and set flight, heading for Amber.

This time, she was ready, and she flicked her hair over to the side. Onyx alighted upon her right shoulder, and she stood very still while the bird adjusted. She turned her face to look at him, and he touched his beak delicately to her nose.

"Hi," she said to Onyx. "I guess... I guess we're friends now?"

Onyx preened Amber's long hair in his beak.

"Hi," he said.

Amber grinned at Gen, who nodded approvingly, beaming. Anisette walked over and stared at the blonde girl with her black bird.

"I never thought I'd see the day!" Anisette said, shaking her head. "Amber's gone full goth!"

"Lyn Afon Hooper," Andraste called as the girls giggled. But as Lyn approached her, the teen's expression changed.

Gen noticed it and thought, *She looks... proud?*

Andraste held forth a strange, round object, and Lyn took it. "This only amplifies what you already hold within you, child," she told him cryptically.

Lyn joined Amber and Anisette, so Gen was craning her neck to see whatever it was.

"Phan Hồ Duong," Andraste announced.

Phan, running his hands through his gold-tipped dark hair, smiled and loped forward, holding his hands in a prayer pose as he bowed.

Andraste laughed at him. "That's more than enough of that, lad." She brought forth something wrapped and gave it to him. "Only as necessary," she said, and the look she gave him wiped the smile off his face. He stepped backward, turned, and then joined his sister and friends.

"Mira Jessamine Celestus," Andraste called as if Mira was on the other side of the room rather than practically at her elbow already.

Mira stood, adjusted her asymmetrical skirt and top, and walked to face Andraste.

The Lunadatrix brought forth a pale green, small object that glowed. Mira took it and held it up. It was shaped like a large jasmine blossom.

"It is clear," Andraste said, "that this could only have been made for someone with your name. You don't need to go off seeking the advice of apothecaries anymore, if you get my meaning," she said with a wink. "You may not need it now, tomorrow, next week, or even next year... but if you fancy yourself a reporter and you need to bend the age rules, this will get you where you need to go." Mira's mouth twisted in a wry grin, she curtsied and joined the others.

"Jas Larimar Lightworth," Andraste announced next, "I know you have a useful device already; you three cousins are unique in that regard. But consider this gift a counter-balance to the compass." And she handed Jas a long, pale crystal on a silver chain. "It looks like tourmaline, but I assure you, it is not."

Jas hung the crystal around his neck and gazed at it as he walked slowly to join the other Fireflies.

"Nyota Ariki Marama," Andraste said then, and she smiled fondly at her student as Nyota stood proudly before her. "It is time you graduated, dear. Hand me your staff."

Nyota did so, and on its tip, Andraste fused a deep red crystal that sent shards of crimson light scattering in all directions of the U-shaped room before it extinguished. "Sometimes," Andraste told Nyota, "we need to cast a light in the darkness."

"Dhatura Lal," Andraste said next, and the girl jumped. Looking uneasy, she stepped forward. Andraste brought forth an exquisite copper brooch that looked like one of the valley's copper peacocks in miniature. Its tail bore tiny emeralds. "We inherit many things in life, and sometimes not from our own blood. There is knowledge here that may prove useful. Failing that, it's a blunt object. Sometimes, you need both."

"Gentian Opal Lightworth," Andraste said finally.

Gen's palms sweated. She stood before the Lunadatrix and time seemed to stop. The room went silent. She could hear a voice, but Andraste's lips didn't move. Gen almost said something, but a tiny shake of Andraste's head stopped her.

Child, a voice inside her said, *look for friendship in unlikely places. Search the Inn with all the tools and help you have before you; there are stories upon stories, and each one is important for what's coming. Understand the past. The Lantern holds more than light, but should you need more than that, you have your own light now.*

And then Andraste gave Gen a brooch as well, of a gold and black firefly half the size of her hand. Its tail shimmered within for a moment and then went dark. "You are the firefly," Andraste told her, "and the firefly knows when to signal, and when not."

Andraste then clapped her hands, and the three ravens and the foxes gathered close to her.

"It is time for you to leave," she told the Fireflies. "I would advise you not to take a northern detour, but I know you shall anyway. You might get an early test for your gifts, if you do. Mind the time; it is three hours until dawn."

She turned to Nyota and said, "Take them through the woods; the passage north is easier that way."

The Lunadatrix Andraste then stood and bowed to the assembled Fireflies. Onyx croaked to his sibling ravens, and then launched from Amber's shoulder into the pale woods forming the back wall of the great house. Nyota leaned to touch Andraste forehead to forehead, and then she bowed and entered the woods with her red-tipped staff shining.

Gen said to the other Fireflies, "You go on ahead. I'll bring up the rear."

And so, the others thanked Andraste one by one and entered the woods. Each one seemed to vanish as they did so, Gen noticed, but she could still hear their voices, and the calls of Onyx croaking.

Andraste saw her hesitate and said, "It is not that you were made for this, Gentian Lightworth. I know you do not want to lead. It is that you dwell in the present. Go forth. Listen to what seems wrong and make it right. That is a better compass for you than that which Bendin gave your brother."

Gen nodded, not sure what else to say. She felt turbulent, wanting to stay and yet needing to go. Yet forward she stepped, between the ghostly trunks of the next forest, and when she looked behind her, she could only see dark trees and their tall canopy, as if there had never been a house there at all. She touched her firefly brooch and then hurried to catch up with the others.

Dark and Tangled

"No, no, no!" Mira moaned as Gen caught up with her.

"You okay?" Gen asked.

Even in the shafts of moonlight between the slender trunks of the pale forest, Gen could see Mira was flushed and agitated. She swore, and Gen threw her hands up in the air. Finally, Mira shoved her little notebook at Gen.

"Look at it!" Mira cried, practically spitting with rage. "Just look at it!"

"Wow, jeez, hold on," Gen said, "calm down!"

She saw Lyn slow down ahead of them and then shuffle back through the dried leaves and fallen, dried moss toward the two cousins. Then she took the notebook that Mira waved in her face.

"Open it!" Mira insisted.

Gen opened it. "Oh. Oh shit, Mira."

It was blank. There was no writing, no sketching, nothing, not even the imprint of Mira's pen from her scribbling.

The two girls stared at each other, trying to make sense of it. Lyn, cringing slightly, rubbing the back of his neck with one hand and holding the other out to them palm-up, said, "I guess Andraste didn't want any of her secrets to get out."

Mira turned to Lyn in a fury, "I worked on this! This would have been my biggest story ever! I could have overtaken the *Biolumen* and—"

"Whoa, whoa," Lyn said, backing up. "Don't blame me for it! And honestly, can you blame her?"

Mira gave Lyn a look that could have melted lead and stomped ahead of him and Gen to catch up with the others, her voice rising and falling from a string of swear words, many of which she invented on the fly, gifted writer that she was.

"Sorry!" Gen called after her cousin. She turned to look up at Lyn and sighed. "Say, what exactly did Andraste give you?"

"Oh! Right," Lyn said. He drew forth the gift from his shirt vest and held it in his palm as he and Gen walked slowly behind the other Fireflies, their feet making swishing sounds among the leafy litter.

Gen reached out to touch the object. It was a smooth, milky stone, round and slightly flattened, with four longitudinal bands, two on each side, in a dark pewter metal.

"What is it, do you think?" she asked Lyn. He shrugged.

"It might be a charmstone?" he answered. It fit perfectly in the palm of his hand, but it didn't glow. "I've heard of them, but never seen one before."

"What do they do?" Gen asked.

Lyn rubbed his chin with his free hand and said, "I'm not really sure, but I think something to do with healing?"

Gen looked shyly into the boy's serious face. "She seemed really pleased to give it to you, you know."

"Did she?" Lyn said, surprised.

"Yeah, I saw it in her face. She didn't look like that with anyone else. Not even Nyota, not quite."

"Weird. I mean, not her. I mean... Okay, she *is* a little weird. But... good-weird. You know what I mean?"

Gen laughed. "Well, look at all of us. We're all good-weird, at least I hope so."

Lyn smirked. He said quietly, "I love that you're our leader."

Gen blushed and felt a bit rebellious at the title. "Yeah? Well, your leader is literally at the back of the line. Race you!"

And she bolted off into the woods, hoping to burn off the wild sensations she felt while talking to Lyn. He followed close behind, laughing, and Gen had never felt such a rush from being alive before. She caught up with Phan, Anisette, and Dhatura.

"Can you believe it, though?" Anisette whispered. "Amber, of all people!"

"Hey, gang," Gen said, and the three others jumped from her loud voice. "What's up? Is Amber alright?" for she didn't see the girl ahead of them, nor Mira, Jas, not even Nyota.

Anisette looked up at Gen and scrunched her mouth outward. "She's gone full Bird Woman. Maybe she's the next Andraste!"

With that, all of them burst out laughing at the absurdity of such an idea. Then a cry broke through the woods, and Gen held up her hand to hush everyone. She heard running, and then from the darkness, Mira emerged, and then Amber. Onyx croaked and wheeled among the trees over their heads, only perching on Amber when she stopped running.

"Gen," Amber gasped. "Something's happened."

"What!" Gen cried.

Mira bent over, wheezing and pointing.

"They—they reached the boundary," she coughed, "Jas and Nyota. Nyota went through first, and something grabbed her as soon as she was out. Jas went through to help her, and I—he didn't come back."

Gen's heart hammered. "Go!" she shouted, and she began running forward. The others followed her. Phan patted his pocket where the object Andraste had given him rested. He glanced sideways at his sister. Anisette clutched the shell-shaped gem at her throat.

Amber raced forward on her long legs, and then met the boundary. It was a strange, amorphous sort of wall that stretched up and along the ground and appeared to extend underground as well. It looked rather like a soap bubble, swirling and multicolored, yet beyond they could see the moors to the north of Moonbow Valley, the hillsides lit softly by moonlight.

"Gen," Amber whispered, "I don't see them. They were just here."

Gen pressed her hands to her temples.

"Okay. Look, if something grabbed them, it could grab us too. Amber, I hate to ask this, but can you send Onyx through the boundary to fly up and check things out?"

Amber gasped, and held Onyx to her, stroking his sleek dark feathers and touching his beak.

The bird tapped her cheek and said, "Yes," and Amber looked at him with a troubled expression.

"Alright," she said, hesitant. Gen admired her willpower. "Come back soon, Onyx."

Onyx clicked his tongue and flew up and out of the boundary. Amber watched intently as he soared ahead, and then she cried out, "Oh God! What is that?"

Something hurtled in the sky toward the bird, dark and twisting and long, whipping around. But Onyx flew too high for it. He circled above the thing several times, swooped down, dodged another coil from it, and then burst back through the boundary to land on Amber's shoulder.

"What was that?" Amber asked, astonished and a little freaked out.

"Dark," Onyx said simply.

Gen asked urgently, "Onyx, did you see Jas and Nyota?"

"Tan-gled," the bird said.

"What is that thing?" Gen pressed.

"Dark," insisted the bird, dipping his head and flicking his wings out. "Dark tangled."

"What the hell does that mean?" Anisette said. "Gen, I think we'd better take a look."

"I'll do it," Phan said, patting his pocket.

"The hell you will," Anisette growled at him. He rolled his eyes at her.

"I'm going," Phan said, and before anyone could stop him, he ran through the boundary.

Gen watched, frightened beyond rational thought as something dark and tangled indeed leaped forward in the air toward Phan. But he dodged and thrust something at it, backed up, dodged and even jumped over the thing again, and plunged forward. Then he ran back to the boundary and re-entered.

"I killed it, I think," he panted. Gen saw that he held a short blade of solid green metal. On its tip, something dark shone. He did not touch it.

"Phan," Gen said to him, "What was it? And where are Jas and Nyota?"

Phan dropped the knife on the ground and bent over, gasping for breath.

"No clue," he gasped. "No idea what the thing was. Like—like a dark vine, but not made of plants? It was about the size of a dog—not a dog though. But there were things coming out of it, like tentacles, and I thought—I thought for a second it was gonna get me."

Anisette gave him a quick but fierce hug.

Gen's breath caught in her throat, and she felt cold all over.

"It has to be what the news has been talking about," she said in a shaky voice. "And now it's got Jas and Nyota!"

"Not that one," Phan said firmly. "I killed it. Whatever grabbed the others, I don't know what it was, or where it went."

Mira put her arm around Gen.

"Let's get Andraste to help us," she suggested.

Gen shook her head. "What's Andraste going to do? She's way back there, and the longer we wait, the farther away whatever this is has gone with Jas and Nyota."

Dhatura said, "We'll do whatever you think we should do, Gen."

Gen gave her a grateful look.

"Okay," she said to them all, "let's do this—let's go out there, take a look, and if we see anything threatening at all, or you feel unsafe, it's back to this boundary. *Immediately*. Okay? I need to get a handle on this, I need to see for myself."

"You're not going out there alone," Lyn said emphatically.

"We'll all go," Amber agreed, and with that, Onyx flew up and out again.

He soon flew back and croaked, "Gone."

So, Gen nodded and walked through the boundary to try and find her brother and Nyota.

Ominous

Passing through the boundary out of Andraste's land almost hurt; it felt to Gen like thousands of pinpricks of static electricity. She turned to look back at it, expecting to see a dome, but she could only see trees, thick and dark stretching all the way back into Moonbow Valley, and seemingly impenetrable. Ahead of her, the moorlands of the northern country rose and swooped back down, their daytime golden brown a muted gray at night under moonlight. Onyx soared aloft, circling, doing figure eights, and then swooping back down to Amber, who no longer flinched when he landed. On the ground, yards before her, Gen saw a warped, black shape. She approached it warily.

Phan walked with her and reached down to wipe his flinty blade upon the ground, but kept it at his side, just in case. They approached the shape on the ground, surrounded it in a semicircle, and stared at its steaming remains.

"What in the blue moon hell is this?" Anisette breathed. She then glanced up at her brother. "You killed it, eh? Rad."

Phan grimaced at it and shuddered.

"Ugh, God," Mira said. "By Luna, it stinks."

She was right. Whatever it was that lay sprawled on the earth before them, the reek it sent up set them gagging and covering their noses.

Gen thought, I've never *smelled anything more dead than this, whatever this is.* It made her shudder.

Pulling up the collar on her shirt to cover her nose, she said, "Do we think this is what's been in the *Biolumen*?"

Mira stepped gingerly toward it and peered down. It spasmed, and she screamed and jumped back. They all crammed together. Onyx flew over to it, circled it twice, landed near it, and Amber cried, "No!"

The bird tilted its head from side to side to look at the thing better. Then he made knocking sounds and flew back to Amber. He croaked, "Dead."

"What do we do now?" Lyn asked. "Are you okay with going forward, Gen?"

She hesitated. She hated this now, officially. Phan had put himself at great risk, and her brother and Nyota were missing. She felt like her innards were collapsing and taking all her moxie with them. She put her hand to her throat. And there she felt the firefly brooch.

She opened her eyes and said, "We need to see what we came to see. I have to believe this is all connected. Right? Doesn't it make sense? And we have to find them. I think we can do both."

"We can," Mira said firmly.

Dhatura said, "I will help you look."

"You sure about this?" Gen asked her. "This is a bit more than you signed up for, isn't it?"

"It is," Dhatura agreed, "but I'm not backing down."

Gen nodded, and started marching up the nearest hill. The Fireflies followed.

From time to time, Onyx flew high above them and back again. There were no more of the strange creatures, or whatever they were, and on they trudged.

"We're running out of time," Lyn said uneasily. "It'll be daybreak in two hours. We need to get back home, Gen."

"No," she said stubbornly. "Not yet."

She crossed another hill, and then she motioned to Mira.

"Is this it?" she asked her cousin.

"Is this what?" Mira replied.

"From what Bendin showed us. Does it look familiar?"

The two girls looked out at the rolling lands before them.

"Yes, I think so," Mira said.

"Then down in that valley, there should be those rectangles we saw."

"Gen," Mira said quietly, "I'm worried we won't get back in time. We aren't prepared. Besides, didn't Bendin say not to go looking for missing people?"

"Please, we have to, Mira," Gen begged her. "I can't go back and tell Mom that Jas is missing too."

Mira threw her head back and sighed. "You're right. Okay, let's go down and take a look."

The group followed Gen and Mira down, and then from a distance, Gen could see something odd. She glanced back at Amber, and Amber nudged Onyx. Onyx shot upward and pulsed his wings ahead. He quickly curved and steered himself back at great haste and flew right above Gen.

"Hurry!" he said.

Gen wasted no time and bolted forward.

Then they all heard a cry.

"Nyota!" Phan shouted, and he and Lyn bounded ahead with everyone else close on their heels.

Gen beheld something then that seared her mind.

They found the rectangles: they were massive, several feet in length and width. There were two, and they were blackened as if burned, but also, they were *moving*, writhing with shapes that shot out of grates below them. Some of the writhing forms held Nyota and Jas in their grasp. The two fought them, but were being dragged back into the grates, and Gen could see that one was ajar, and pitch black below it.

She screamed and ran forward, and Phan jumped in the fray, stabbing and slashing. Gen found Nyota's staff and was about to wield it, but Anisette grabbed it from her and screamed, "Get back!"

Anisette joined her brother attacking the mass of wriggling black shapes that snaked in the air and whipped and lashed in all directions, including toward Gen and the others. Lyn dashed in to stomp on the smaller tendrils.

Each snaking tentacle joined another and then two immense masses pulsated near the grates, pulling Nyota and Jas, squeezing their ribs. The two yelled and gasped as one tendril whipped around and squeezed Jas's arm. His cries horrified Gen. She ran forward to try and grab hold of the thing that had him, but it shot forth another tendril and tripped her, and she fell hard on her back and lost her breath for a moment, stunned. She felt arms around her, picking her up and running to set her down: Lyn's arms. She sat gasping, and Mira and Dhatura tried calming her.

Amber ran just as another tendril hurtled forth and grabbed her ankle. Onyx screeched and shot down at the thing, stabbing with his beak until it released her. Phan and Anisette were relentless, dodging and parrying.

"All the parkour finally paid off!" shouted Anisette.

"Eat this, shitstain!" Phan yelled, plunging his blade deep into the gullet of one of the creatures. Pus-colored liquid shot out and onto his arm, and he howled and fell back. But his mark was true, and the creature fell still, releasing Nyota.

Gasping, the girl seized her staff from Anisette and ran straight at the other beast that squeezed Jas and then snaked around his neck until he began to choke. Nyota stabbed with the jeweled tip of her staff, and it glowed like radiant blood. The creature made an inhuman bay and recoiled, and then fell still. Phan, for good measure, used his uninjured left arm to stab it again.

The things hissed and steamed and twitched, and finally seemed dead.

Gen ran to her brother and helped him, gagging and limping, and Lyn and Amber walked Nyota away from the area.

But the great rectangles were still partly open in the ground.

Dhatura said quietly, "Those are ventilation shafts."

Gen half-heard her enough to say, "For what?"

"Don't know," Jas gasped, coughing and rubbing his throat, "but they're super deep. If you hadn't got to us in time—"

Gen shuddered and her eyes stung.

"How are we going to get out of here in time?" Mira wailed. She could just see the horizon become slightly muddy.

Everyone else looked too, and a pall settled on them.

Nyota leaned over and vomited.

Gen felt like doing the same; for as bad as the first creature had smelled, these larger ones were far worse. *And if we don't get out of here and away from the sun, we're done for.* She knew they were all thinking it.

"We can make it back to the boundary," Lyn suggested.

"I don't think we can before sunup," Gen said sadly. "We've got three injured. And once that sun comes up, the rest of us are injured too."

"Leave us, then," Jas coughed.

"Hell no!" Gen cried. "I'm not leaving you."

Anisette paced, threw her hands up in the air and swore, and then looked at her chest. The deep red conch shell jewel shone there.

"Okay. Whatever," she said, and she put her mouth over the hole and blew.

Silence.

She made a disgusted noise and went back to shaking her head.

"Look!" cried Dhatura.

Onyx squawked and bolted skyward. An immense shape soared over the hills toward them from the south, with bright lights shining forward like headlights.

"Oh my God!" Anisette cried. "It's GigantOwl!"

And there it was, the huge cyborg owl, soaring forward and then circling the area. It landed and they could all hear clanging and wheezing. It bent down, its bright, huge eyes illuminating the dark moors.

Onyx cawed out, "Climb!" and they didn't need to be told twice. They clambered onto the back of the creature, with Gen holding onto Jas, Lyn securing Gen, Amber and Dhatura supporting Nyota, and Mira and Anisette helping Phan. The superb owl then huffed and clanged and beat its huge wings, and it pushed up into the air, swooping south-ward.

By and by, Gen could see something to the south, and finally she let out a whoop: it was the great lighthouse, the Lantern casting a swath of purple light, and it crossed the flight path of the enormous owl. Gen exhaled: they were almost home.

Residuum

The great bird coasted above the village just as the sky began to pinken along the horizon. It alighted on the front lawn of the Lightworth home and set off every alarm imaginable, much to the chagrin of the housebots. Sylvia and Smudge bolted in terror through the cat door and into the house, which in the growing light took on a purple cast. The door flew open and Reggie and Tam both spilled out, gawked for a second at the immense bird, and ran forward as the teens slid off it onto the yard.

"Thanks, GigantOwl!" Anisette said, stroking the huge creature's beak.

"Thank you!" Gen gasped, and she and Mira helped Jas to stand; Reggie ran forward and took over for Mira. A great gust of wind blasted them all as the bird lifted up from the earth. Gen looked over her shoulder at it, and it sailed into the sky. "Get inside!" she hissed to her friends, and they tumbled inside the house, shutting the door just as the sun rose.

Inside, chaos unfolded, and Lyn bolted over to clear the coffee table. Tam hurried into the kitchen and gathered cloths. Phan sagged in a chair at the dining room table, Nyota sank wincing into a living room chair. Jas lay on the couch.

"Antiseptic and bandages," Lyn said to Tam urgently.

Reggie took scissors and cut away Jas's shirt, revealing pocked weals from where the creatures' tentacles had soaked through to his skin. She tried cleaning them with wet cloths, and Jas roared in pain and began to heave. Gen rushed forward with a bucket as he vomited. His pocket watch fell onto the floor, bouncing open. Gen saw it and froze.

"The dosimeter," she said, as quietly as possible, but Jas heard her. He glanced down, spasmed from pain, and then lay back. His throat was starting to bruise, and the abrasions oozed a bit as well.

The dosimeter had changed from bright green to a darker hue, a deep teal.

Troubled, she glanced at Nyota. Tam was cleaning her wounds, and Nyota briefly made eye contact with Gen.

"Maybe we should have stayed with Andraste," she said miserably, but Nyota shook her head.

"It was going to be last night or another time," Nyota told her. "Sooner or later. Now we just have to figure out how to stop it again."

"What can we do for them?" Gen asked her mother.

Reggie shook her head. "I've never seen anything like these wounds. Tell me everything."

Gen recounted the ordeal with a burning-red face, and Tam and Reggie's mouths fell open in astonishment. The sisters looked at each other and then pursed their lips.

Dhatura knelt next to Jas, her face full of anguish. Gen could see she had grown fond of him. "I guess Doc Bozzard..." Dhatura began, but then she trailed off and her face sank.

"Still missing," Tam said briskly. "Can you and Mira get these three some water?"

Dhatura and Mira obliged, and Mira checked on Phan. She noticed Anisette favoring her left leg.

"Not you too!" Mira wailed.

"It didn't get to my skin," Anisette said. "Don't worry about me."

Tam came over to inspect Phan's wounds. The tall boy hissed when she cleaned them. His skin looked cauterized in streaks.

"Acid burns," she said grimly. Mira gawked in horror.

"Ow!" Lyn cried suddenly, and everyone turned to look at him. He snatched something out of his pocket and bounced it in his hand. It was his charm, and it was glowing.

"Where did you get that?" Tam asked him quickly.

"Andraste," the redhead answered.

"Do you know what that is?" she asked.

"Um... no," Lyn said.

"It's a healing stone," Tam said. "Bring it over here."

Lyn obliged and knelt by Phan.

Tam looked at Lyn with an intense expression, her brows furrowed, her hair wild, and she said, "You know field dressings well, but this heals in a different way. You need to hold it close to a wound."

"It hurts!" Lyn cried, nearly dropping it. "It's burning!"

"Because it works," Tam said. "Now, give it to me."

"Gladly," he gasped, handing it to her. It went dark instantly.

"It feels cool to the touch for me," she told him, "because it's not made for me. It's made for you. It will only respond to you and your touch; only you can make it work. So, take it back, and hold it over Phan."

Lyn took it back gingerly and he broke into a sweat. His pale fingers turned red, but he gritted his teeth and breathed slowly as he held the white stone over Phan's burns.

"Closer," Tam encouraged, "don't touch the skin, but get it really close. Even closer," she guided, and then Phan gasped. "There," Tam continued, "now swipe it over him. Anywhere he's been hurt."

Phan cried out and then it was his turn to vomit, which Anisette deftly ducked. Amber rose to get something to clean the mess, and Onyx croaked and jumped from her shoulder to the top of another dining chair. Sylvia howled from her perch in disapproval and Smudge ran back to Reggie's room to hide.

"Dude!" Phan gasped to Lyn. "Stop!"

"Okay! Okay!" Lyn said, and he threw the stone on the table to recover for a second. His hands looked pink but were otherwise unharmed. Phan's wounds appeared shiny and cleaner, but not completely healed. The important thing was, they looked better than they had before.

Phan touched those areas delicately and nodded, giving Lyn a thumbs up. Tam brought a tube over to him and squeezed out a thick, dark blue-green paste, and applied it to his skin. Then she nodded to Amber, who gave her cloth bandages. Once bandaged, Phan threw his head back in the chair and exhaled.

Anisette said, "Guess you're sticking around a bit longer, then. Good. Maybe Gramps won't ground me now. 'Cuz if you'd died, I'd never see the outside of the house again."

"Priorities," Phan groaned.

"Absolutely," Anisette agreed. She held her hands to hide their trembling, but Gen saw.

Lyn looked warily at the stone on the table. Gen approached him.

"I hate to ask you to do this," she began, and she cringed. *I'm going to have to ask everyone to do things I hate to ask them to do*, she realized.

Lyn glanced down at her, took a deep breath, and said, "It's alright. I can handle it. Nyota, you ready?"

Nyota looked exhausted. She opened her eyes and said, "No. Jas first. He's worse off."

"I'll get to you soon, I promise," Lyn assured her.

Jas was at that point delirious from pain. His mother brought him a juice globe laced with analgesic and put it in his mouth. It burst so that he could swallow it, and within seconds he relaxed. Lyn then set to work moving his charmstone over Jas's injuries. Jas winced and ground his teeth, even with the analgesic taking the edge off his pain.

"It's working," Gen said, and she felt her shoulders ease from tension. She gave Lyn a grateful squeeze, but noticed again that he winced from holding his stone. Reggie held Jas's hand while Tam applied the dark green salve to his wounds and bandaged him. Gen stepped across the room to Nyota, who Lyn approached next.

Nyota sat stoically while Lyn moved the stone over her, and after he was finished, she managed a half-smile.

"Thanks," she said. "You know, you need something to hold that thing with. Like... a wand or something. Then again, it would look like a scepter. You'd be a healing king." She chuckled, and Lyn joined her.

"Hmm," he said, "the stone's gone cold now." He flipped the pale thing in his hands and then pocketed it.

"Like it knew you were finished," Nyota noted.

"How would it know that?" Gen wondered.

Nyota smirked. "How does it even work to begin with, right?"

"Well, yeah," Gen agreed.

"I think there's more to Lyn Hooper than we thought," mused Nyota, and she shrugged. Tam came to her and gave her the special ointment. Nyota adjusted her clothing over her bandages and reached for her staff, using it to help her stand.

"Easy," Tam warned the girl. Then she announced to everyone, "I'm calling your parents and guardians now. Nobody's able to leave until night, so I'll get things set up so you can sleep here overday."

"In that case," Nyota said, "I think I'll sit back down."

"No," Gen said, "you and Amber and Anisette can take my or Jas's room. Go rest."

"What about you?" Amber asked, yawning. Onyx already had his head tucked back, snoozing on her shoulder.

"Mira and I will share Mom and... Dad's room," Gen said, with the spasm of worry for her father jolting her again.

Nyota, Anisette, and Amber walked back to the bedrooms to sleep.

Tam and Reggie brought bedding out for Lyn and Phan, who immediately threw himself down and fell asleep. Lyn remained in a dining room chair, head in hand, and watched Gen's troubled face. The house fell silent.

Gen looked around the room at everyone's exhausted eyes. Her mother approached and hugged her.

"Still nothing from Dad?" she asked Reggie in the softest voice she could manage.

Her mother rubbed her furrowed brow. Gen had never seen her look so tired.

"Not yet," she said. "I was so worried about all of you. And... well it looks like I was right to be!"

She glanced down at Jas, who had finally fallen asleep on the couch, one of his arms across his abdomen, the other hanging from the couch's side. His dark, curly hair was damp on his sweaty brow.

"We don't have a whole lot of medicine here," Reggie said to Gen quietly. "And with Doc Bozzard gone? I mean, there are other doctors. But he had—maybe I should say has—the best apothecary in the area."

Tam walked over to her sister and put her arm around her.

Mira then said, "Why don't we go there and see what we can find?"

Gen stared at her. "He's not there, though."

Mira grinned. "Well, I've already used illicit magic. Maybe I should lean into that life."

Tam jerked her head around and said, "No you don't, young lady."

Mira put her hands on her hips. "If he's not there, he won't care," she said, with a mischievous gleam in her eyes. "We need medicine. For this and..." she looked to Gen "...for other reasons."

Gen paced. "We could go now."

"Not a chance," Reggie said firmly.

"We'll take the tunnels," Lyn said suddenly. "I'll go with them."

"I don't want anyone else getting hurt," Reggie said with an edge to her voice Gen had never heard before. She wondered if their full names would be deployed soon.

"Mom," Gen said, "we can do this. We'll be fine. I promise. By Luna."

Reggie looked at Tam. "Only if your aunt says yes as well."

Tam sighed and shook her head at Mira. "Fine," she said. "But if you see or hear anything strange, you high tail it back, alright?"

Mira gave Tam a breezy kiss on the cheek. She nodded to Gen, who looked back at Lyn. They walked to the back door, which had steps leading both into the back garden and down into the basement. Down there, a small den and library sat in darkness, and on the northern side a door stood closed. Gen opened the door, and a series of soft, ghostly blue lights came on beyond it in a tunnel. She stepped through the doorway.

In The Shadows

Some lights blinked on from above, and others underfoot. Just off to Gen's left, a tunnel branch winked on that led to the cave garden. Her nose tingled from the earthy reek of fungi within it and the tang of aging root milk cheese as well. Ahead, the tunnel stretched west and then north, sloping gently down. It eventually forked off to other tunnels, and as it dropped, its ceiling stretched high above. While Gen's family hadn't decorated their spur of the tunnel, other families sometimes made paintings or tiled their portions, and changed their light colors.

In this way, it was easy to know where you were based upon the differences in home tunnels. Almost all of them formed a subterranean network that led to the main districts of Glimmerbight, emerging aboveground before the earth changed over to silt from the sea. From there, transit could be made throughout the city either on foot, by bicycle, air bike, various buses, and mag lifts, or by water taxis on the crescent-shaped bay itself. Tonight, traffic was light, although several animals scurried at brisk paces carrying *Biolumen Pen* pods from town to their destinations.

When they reached a tunnel branch leading to other neighborhoods to the north, Gen, Mira, and Lyn came across one dark tunnel spur. This tunnel was unusual, as all others held some form of lighting. However, this was not the only strange feature of this tunnel, nor was a doorway placed within it that was partly open. It smelled off.

At this point, the power of the sea upon the land aboveground was apparent elsewhere; a particular tang in the air traveled up through the tunnel systems, so it was a good indicator of how close the bay was. For this dark spur, something seeped out of it into the main tunnel. The three teens looked at each other.

"Gross," whispered Mira, scrunching her nose.

"I don't like it," agreed Lyn.

Gen's pulse quickened. She covered her nose. "I know that smell."

Lyn looked sideways at her under the dim light behind them in the main tunnel. "*We* know that smell."

"Don't think we could ever forget it," Mira said.

Gen cleared her throat. "My point is, why are we smelling it *here*?"

They all looked at each other, and Gen shuddered.

"Maybe let's... let's keep going," Mira suggested.

So they did, but Gen glanced over her shoulder occasionally as they descended from the hillside and into the busier tunnels ahead. The stench, however, stayed in her nostrils making her uneasy. The thought of those things out on the moors, their black tendrils snapping and whipping, lashing at her brother and her friends... she replayed it in her head. And she was utterly exhausted by now. It was not until they could smell the sea that she finally relaxed enough to focus on what they were doing.

They emerged from the tunnel system and its eventual networks of underground shops and out into the thriving night markets of Glimmerbight, the streets covered in archways of lights, the trees hung with lanterns. The sea air at night was most welcome, and Gen could see the boats coming and going at the marina a few blocks ahead. The moon shone above but would set soon, and by the looks of things, the marine layer would absorb it before it had much chance to sparkle upon the sea itself. That was something she enjoyed seeing when she was a little girl when her father would take her and Jas for night walks along the bay, giving her mother time to work or rest. Gen would cry out at the sight of a full moon upon the waves, with the scattering of reflections dancing like glowing fish upon the surface.

"More moons!" she used to say, and Harris would laugh, but Jas would correct her and tell her it was just the moon on the water.

Gen stopped in her tracks, gazing up at the moon, and her throat ached.

"Hey," Lyn said, standing beside her and looking up. "Are you okay?"

"Just... just remembering," she replied. "And wondering where Dad is."

Mira stood next to her and laid her head on Gen's shoulder.

"Well," said Lyn, "we know he's not up there, anyway."

That made Gen laugh.

Mira said, her eyes lifted to the sky, "Do you remember there used to be stories that people actually went there a long time ago?"

"Yeah," Lyn said, chuckling. "Not sure I believe them, though."

"Why is that?" Gen asked him. "We did, didn't we? Befo re... before the Golden Hour."

Lyn shrugged and sighed. "I don't know. It seems... not right, though. Sort of... blasphemous."

Mira laughed mercilessly at him. "I don't know if it's blasphemous, but we sure didn't *need* to go."

Gen turned away from the sea, walked along a farmers' market, and asked a lady in a glowing umbrella hat for three moon cakes.

"Didn't we?" asked Gen then. "We don't even really know what happened... out there," she casually pointed out to the sea.

"The world ended," said Mira bluntly. "That's all we need to know. And we started it up again, from the darkness."

"Well, *we* didn't," said Gen, feeling irritable. "Our ancestors did. I just... I wonder. What if we had kept going? What if we had... not given up?"

She gave them each a moon cake.

"Gen," said Lyn, his eyes glowing an odd hue of green under the light of overhead magenta lanterns and his red hair nearly purple, "I don't think our elders had a choice."

Mira nudged her cousin with her elbow.

"Come on, Gen, don't be morose," she said.

Gen shook her head, walking forward through the markets, listening to the clinking of masts at the harbor and the bustle along the quay, and she could see the great dome of the Glowworm Pavilion to the north. She slowed and watched Mira's face as her cousin stared at it.

"It wasn't that long ago," Mira murmured. "I danced t here... I felt... I felt part of something grand." She brought forth the blossom Andraste had given her and looked at it thoughtfully.

"Risky, though," Lyn remarked, and Mira rolled her eyes.

"Not you too, Lyn," she said with a big sigh. "You sound like Jas." Then she sighed again and rubbed her temples.

Gen said, "We're in the Twilit District. It's at Fourthlight and Lux, right?"

"Yeah," said Mira. Gen could see her face had fallen.

It wasn't that long ago, Gen agreed with her in her thoughts. *But it sure feels like it now.*

They found Doc Bozzard's shop, where he kept his laboratory and a storefront selling his creations. While its windows glowed in iridescent hues, and the endorphins he had pumped out for pollinators set the place abuzz with moths, the place looked deserted. A looping turquoise neon sign read "CLOSED" in the door's window. Gen walked up to that door, took hold of its pewter handle, and tried it anyway. It was locked.

"Alley?" Lyn suggested.

"Okay," said Gen, and the three of them walked around to the narrow alley behind the shops on the block. Wind funneled into the dark slot, sending leaves and dried bits of *Biolumen Pen* husks rattling on the cobblestone. Gen could see her firefly brooch start to glow and pulse.

They found the back door to Doc's shop, and Mira pointed without saying anything. Her eyes were round. The door hung slightly ajar.

"I'll go first," Lyn whispered.

Gen nodded.

Lyn opened the door, and it screeched on its hinges. The three of them recoiled, looking this way and that in the alley, but Lyn proceeded anyway. Once inside, teal fairy lights began to wink on, and the floor responded to his footfalls by glowing with each step. He walked into the shop's main floor, and found it empty except for its wares.

"No one's here," he called back in a low voice.

The girls walked in then, and Mira stepped forward to stand in the center of the room and look all about her, hugging her arms, wistful. Gen watched the lights fade in and out, pulsating slowly like the lights of jellyfish and setting the many bottles and vials on the shelves of the apothecary aglow. There were buckets of treats all along the counter near the register, and Gen reached in one to pull out a Glo-Tart, its iridescent leaf wrapper shining in the dimly lit shop.

"I remember these," she said. "Doc used to give them out, I think, when we were little."

"If you were good," Mira agreed.

"I miss that," Lyn said, and the girls nodded.

Gen said then, "Look, we won't steal anything. We'll leave money behind the counter for anything we take. I just... I'm not really sure what we should get?"

Lyn rolled up his sleeves. "I'm on it," he said.

He began to pull items down from shelves, or open jars, weigh powders and wrap them in paper, and the girls helped package everything in bags. Gen slapped what she hoped were enough coins on the counter and scrawled, "Thank you!" on a note.

Then they heard a crash from the back door.

Mira yelped, Gen slapped her hand over her mouth, and Lyn froze. They stood in silence, not moving, looking at each other. Lyn looked all around and found a walking stick in a corner behind the counter. He brandished it like a club and motioned for Gen and Mira to stay where they were.

But the cousins were not about to sit and wait for anything to happen. Gen grabbed a pair of scissors on the counter, and Mira grabbed a candlestick, and the three listened.

Something shuffled, and then a sound of something rolling met their ears. They looked down and saw something fizzing on the floor. A stinging gas rose from the object and began to fill the room.

"Oh *shit*!" Lyn yelled.

"Run!" Gen shouted, and the three of them headed for the front door, fumbled at the lock and tumbled out of the store, slamming the door shut behind them. Pedestrians across the street stopped and stared at them, and then quickened their paces and walked on.

"God!" hissed Mira. "Someone tried to gas us!"

"Come with me," Lyn told them, and the three of them with their various improvised weapons headed around the side of the store to look down the alley. The light was still dim, but they could see someone... or something.

It looked man-shaped, and it was bent over, creeping down the alley away from the shop, and away from where they stood. The three teens backed up to peek around the corner, and whoever it was paused and looked back. A lamp at the end of the alley flickered, and they could see two shining eyes staring out. Gen thought they looked green, but they vanished before she could double-check.

Gen pulled Mira and Lyn back away from the alley and said, "Let's go!" and the trio ran hard down the street, east, until their legs burned. Gen collapsed onto her knees outside a bodega, startling the tuxedo cat hanging out at the front, who hissed at them.

The bodega owner came out with a towel over his shoulders, a scarlet-cheeked, middle-aged man with a white cap, and he glared at them with disapproval.

"Get on out of here, would you!" he bellowed at them. "We've had enough commotion tonight."

That made Gen angry. "Well, so have we!" she shouted. "Maybe cut us some slack. We've had a very bad couple of nights. We've not slept. We were attacked last night. And we just got gassed by someone up the street tonight!"

The man sniffed, looked left and right up and down the street, then said, "Fine. Come inside. I don't like how tonight's going myself. Someone's been spooking my customers."

"Someone?" Mira asked, and her hands twitched. She brought forth her magenta notebook—which, to her fury, remained devoid of the many notes she had taken at Andraste's cottage—and began to write.

"What, are you a reporter or something?" the man asked her, frowning.

"One day," said Mira confidently. "Maybe I'll work for the *Biolumen Pen*."

"That birdcage liner!" the man grumbled. "Though at least they're keeping up to date on what's happening around town. I reckon tonight's latest will be in the *Biolumen* within the hour. Look what they put out early: more missing persons!"

He lifted the leaf-pages from the latest *Pen* and showed them. The heading read "MORE MISSING."

Gen cried out.

Under the heading, her father's picture stared out at her.

Shaken

"Gen, slow down!" panted Mira. Gen bolted out of the bodega and walked as fast as she could toward the tunnel network, and then she broke into a slow jog. Lyn and Mira bounded after her.

"Gen!" called Lyn. "Wait!"

She was shaking and running, her lungs burning, tears streaming. Her only driving thought was *I've got to get home to Mom and Jas. I've got to.*

"Stop! Gen!" cried Lyn and Mira. The two looked at each other as they ran, and the seriousness they saw in each other's faces catapulted them forward.

Gen ran faster, and she began to wheeze. She started to gag on her tears, faltering just in front of the tunnels. Pedestrians stared at her.

"Are you alright, dear?" a silver-haired lady wearing a lighted, long pink dress asked gently.

Gen nodded, gasping for air, bent over, as Lyn and Mira finally caught up with her.

"Hey, Gen, sweetie," Mira said in a soothing voice, putting her arm around her cousin. "We're here. Let us go back home together. I don't want you alone right now."

Lyn said, "Gen, you dropped your medicine bag, and I picked it up. You okay?"

Gen's entire body was filled with adrenaline, yet she felt more exhausted than ever. She watched as a fox pulling a wagon full of pods of the *Biolumen Pen* trundled up into the tunnels, and then she started crying again.

"We have to beat those home," she said, pointing. "I don't want Mom to see it!"

"Gen, we'll get there in plenty of time," Lyn assured her. "Breathe, Gen. Deep breaths. Breathe. We're here. We'll get you home."

Gen gagged, and then she stood up, held her back, and lifted her head to look up at the moon, partially engulfed by the incoming fog. "I can't let her see. I can't let Jas see. It's too much. It's too *real*."

Mira shivered. "I know," she said. "If it were my dad, I would have freaked out. He's still out at Umbradene getting the house ready, and he may not know yet."

She did not say what else she thought, but Gen knew her cousin enough to know that her worries were similar to Gen's, and nothing seemed safe or normal.

Gen, meanwhile, gazing upward, caught the telltale smear of purple light sweeping from the Amethyst Lantern onto the low clouds. She straightened herself then and took a deep breath. She could barely see the lighthouse above the city. It comforted her, somehow. Then she made up her mind.

"I want to go back to the Inn," she said. "I want to see if there's anything we can use. If there are any clues.

"What, now?" Lyn asked. "I thought you wanted to get home."

Gen nodded and sighed. "I do. Yes. We'll go home first, and then I'm going to the Inn. I can't stand this. I don't want to wait around. Something's happening, and I just... I need to know."

"Fine, we'll go with you," said Mira, taking hold of Gen's left hand. "Now, let's get home before Mom and Aunt Reggie completely lose it."

Gen held her other hand out to Lyn, and not thinking, he placed her medicine bag into it. She looked up at him and tilted her head.

"That's not what I—" she began. Then she shook her head. "Never mind."

She began walking with Mira into the tunnels. Lyn looked confused. Then it dawned on him. He mouthed, "Oh," but Gen shook her head again and kept walking.

It was getting late, and the foot traffic inside the tunnels had slowed considerably, with some folks headed uphill to the villages and far fewer headed to the bayfront. They reached the one junction with the tunnel spur that reeked. The three of them stood there and stared into the black maw of the tunnel. Its smell was so foul that Mira stepped away from her and Lyn and began to dry heave. Gen wanted to throw up also, but she faced the thing. She even began walking toward it, staring into that blackness, the stench of it stinging her nostrils.

"What are you?" she murmured into it.

And then the earth shook.

The three stared at each other.

It shook again, harder, and pebbles knocked loose from some of the sides of the tunnel. The ceilings looked intact. But Gen felt the blood drain from her face.

"It's happening again," Lyn said, his voice grim.

"Let's get out of here," Gen said. She took one more glance at the dark passageway and then turned quickly.

An alert message startled the three of them badly as it began looping: "There has been a seismic event. Please exit the tunnel system. There has been a seismic event. Please exit—"

The three of them rushed up through the tunnels.

"Let's get overland, quick," said Mira, and she pointed to a tunnel spur.

It was exceptionally well decorated, with ornate tiles and pale, golden lights, and the floors were tiled beautifully as well. They followed it up, and another tremor shook the tunnels. Some calls of alarm echoed from below. They continued anyway and found themselves climbing up a set of tiled steps into a garden.

"Hey!" Mira cried. "I know where we are. This is the Glistenad garden!"

"Amber's home?" Lyn asked.

"Sure is," said Gen, and she felt a wave of relief crash over her.

The Glistenad home was splendid, built partially into a steep cliff with large picture windows facing the sea. The garden extended on either side of the house, even over its roof. It was an ornate structure, elegant and sleek with clean lines but with touches of artistry. At night it beckoned with golden lights both strung all through its shrubbery and even from the housebots themselves, which were glowing golden spherical robots plugged into the yard for their underground gardens. Those gardens surrounded a subterranean swimming pool. All of it screamed wealth and couture.

One of the robots spied the three and called out, "Hello, Gen, Mira, and Lyn. Amber is not home just now. Would you like for me to alert Dani or Göran?"

"No, thank you, Vass," Gen replied. "We're headed home. We... uh... took a shortcut."

"Travel safely," the robot replied.

"Thanks, Vass!" called Gen, and the three teens waved to the housebots and slipped up the embankment and out onto the lane headed toward the Lightworth home.

Gen was so tired and so full of upset and grief and worry that she could think of nothing more than getting home. So she barely looked at the mix of scattered cumulus clouds above the fog zone and how the nearly full moon edged those clouds with the elusive color between silver and gold. All she could think about was home, and she replayed over in her mind the last time she had seen her father.

Harris had been so overjoyed by Gen's invitation to the Inn, and he had mentioned his own letters from his childhood. She could not let that go, for why had Bendin sent those? And who else did he send them to?

Now Bendin was gone, possibly injured somewhere in the bowels of the Inn. The Hotel Lembrar, Andraste had called it. That meant "to remember," and at the moment, Gen wished she could remember all that her father had said about the Inn. And, for that matter, everything Bendin had told her. Her fatigue wrecked her memory, and her running and stress wore her down. She absently took a beverage globe off her necklace and popped it into her mouth. It gave her just enough stamina to stagger to her home. The round home beckoned with its blinking housebots, and Gen could make out the silhouettes of Sylvie and Smudge from a distance. Gen stopped.

"What is it?" Lyn asked her warmly.

She blinked in complete weariness, and she sighed. "I don't know. I—I know I need to go home, but I want to go to the Inn. I feel like... if I go home, I have to face everything again. I don't want to. I'm sorry. It just... facing it makes it so I can't back down from it."

Mira gave her a hug. "You're not going into this alone. Not any of this craziness. We're not going anywhere."

Gen glanced at her and managed a small smile. She then noticed that Mira and Lyn's eyes were sunken from fatigue. None of them had slept in a few days, and it showed. Gen felt guilty.

"I'm sorry. You two need to get some sleep. Let's go in. I may not want to, but I see you need to. I'm not leaving you alone, either."

So, they entered the house, yawning. Reggie and Tam were waiting for them, and in Reggie's hands hung the front leaf-page of the *Biolumen Pen*, with her father's face on it. She set it aside, seeing her daughter's stricken face.

"You saw it already?" her mother asked her.

Gen couldn't answer, so Reggie rose and folded the girl into her arms. Gen sagged into that loving embrace and let the tears flow. Finally, she could let it out. Everything else could wait, she decided; they needed to rest and recover for now. So, she climbed onto her mother's bed, fully clothed, turned on her side, and fell asleep within seconds.

Reflection

T he *Biolumen Pen* held other unsavory bits of news, showing blurred images of "animals," burn marks, crop damage, and other strange phenomena. Gen's one comfort from that awful issue came from its absolute lack of her and the Fireflies' attack by the creatures in the north.

"Good," said Nyota over a breakfast of porridge and toast, "because I don't want people poking around Andraste's home."

"Neither do I," agreed Amber, stroking the shimmering dark feathers of Onyx on her shoulder. The raven, between bites of toast she offered him, kept looking at the leaf-pages of the *Biolumen*.

"Shafts!" he croaked suddenly, startling everyone in the room.

"What do you mean?" Amber asked him.

He hopped down, took one of the leaf pages, and held it in his beak: the one with the obscure pictures of some dark creature. Gen felt chills dash up and down her spine.

"That wasn't taken near the shafts, though," Mira noted. She took out her notebook and scribbled something. "My guess is whoever or whatever got these pictures did so from far away."

"Shafts! Shafts!" exclaimed Onyx, flapping his wings. "Inn! Shafts!"

Then everyone halted what they were doing.

"Oh. Oh God," said Gen. "What if he's right? What if these are connected to the Inn?

Jas, sitting up and grimacing but with more color in his face today after taking some of the medicine his sister had brought, said, "We can't know if they're connected."

"How could they *not* be?" Anisette asked him. "Bendin had those weird chambers and some freaky elevator thing going underground. Then we see those things trying to get back to those ventilation shafts out there."

"That's not super close to the Inn, though," Lyn pointed out.

"Do we know that?" Gen asked. "What if"—and she visibly shuddered in front of them all—"what if there are tunnels down there. Leading to the shafts, leading to the Inn? We... we saw something yesterday."

"You mean we *smelled* something," Mira said, pinching her nose again at the memory and making gagging motions with her forefinger and open mouth.

"What?" asked Reggie. "What did you see?"

Gen bit her lip and thought back to the strange, dark spur of the underground tunnel network and the reek emanating from it. "It was an abandoned tunnel spur. It *stunk*, just like those... things we saw on the moors."

"It was a different smell from the gas bomb," Mira said absently.

Tam stood up. "I'm sorry, what? A gas bomb?"

Gen pushed her lips together in a tight line as Mira blushed deep red. Lyn turned his entire body away from Tam and Reggie.

"Um," Gen said, quaking, "there was... we... weren't entirely alone at Doc Bozzard's. Someone came in while we were in there, and they kind of... they threw in some sort of gas canister."

It pained her to say those words. She wished Mira had kept quiet, and she glared at her cousin, who avoided her gaze.

Reggie and Tam cried out, "What!" in unison.

Onyx, Sylvia, and Smudge fled the room collectively, and Amber followed the raven. The other Fireflies looked away from the two mothers.

"We're fine, Mom!" said Gen pleadingly. "Who knows what that was. Maybe it wasn't a gas canister. We don't know!"

"Lyn," said Reggie in a serious tone, "I know you're not going to cover up anything. Tell me exactly what happened."

Lyn turned so red that his ginger eyebrows glowed, and it was painful to look at him as he stammered out what happened at the apothecary and afterward.

"That's it," Tam said firmly. "We're going into lockdown. I'm calling all your parents again and updating them with this news. Nobody goes anywhere."

Great protests erupted in the room, with Gen and Mira shouting, Jas grumbling, and Reggie and Tam arguing with them all.

"We have to go to the Inn," urged Gen, "and look for more answers. Bendin showed us a lot of things, and I'm guessing there's more to learn. Maybe there's a connection between him and what's happening. It's my Inn now." Dhatura shot up out of her chair.

"He's my relative," she said, showing more steel in her posture than Gen had seen before. "I should go see."

"But you weren't there when he showed us," said Gen, "and if you *are* his last remaining relative, maybe you should stay out of it and stay safe!"

"I will not!" said Dhatura, dark eyes flashing, mouth set. "*We* will go together."

"You will not go anywhere," said Reggie. "We've lost three people now that we know personally. I don't want to lose you kids."

Gen shook her head.

"Mom," she said, "something awful is happening, and we've been given the tools to fight it by Bendin and by Andraste. I'm not sitting in this house waiting for things to get worse. Nobody else out there is as connected to this as us."

"You don't know that, Gentian," said her mother and the girl looked at her and blinked.

"Can I just say," Nyota said from her chair, "that Gen is right, we've been gifted some serious power?" The tip of her staff glowed deep red just as she said those words. "And these aren't mere trinkets. These are gifts from the Lunadatrix herself."

Tam sighed and said, "Look, I know you kids are going to do what you're going to do, whether we like it or not. But please, please be careful," and she emphasized that last part to Mira especially, taking her daughter's thin face in her weathered hands. "I don't want to get another paper like the one we got today with *your* pictures on it."

Gen looked down at her firefly brooch, and it responded to her touch by glowing. "Strength in numbers," she said.

"Fireflies, those of you who feel like going to the Inn, we'd better get moving. There's a lot to explore. Mom, Tam, I promise we won't stay longer than we absolutely have to. Besides, I want some of Aunt Tam's brownies!"

The sisters looked at each other, passing some old, familial recognition between them. Reggie then dipped her head.

"You can go," she said, "but if you see anyone… *anyone*, or anything that looks dangerous or doesn't belong, get back here quick. Got it?"

"Got it," Gen nodded.

Nyota brushed off any concerns and held her staff against her shoulder. Amber joined her. Phan decided he needed more rest, but Anisette felt ready. Her brother slyly handed over his dagger to her, and she tucked it into her belt out of sight. Dhatura stood next to her and adjusted her sash. Jas motioned for Gen to come to him.

He winced from residual pain, but the weals from the attack had healed well from Lyn's charmstone, leaving his skin tender and red. The medicinal potion he had drunk earlier helped him regain his strength. But he knew he could not go anywhere like this.

"Gen," he said quietly so that only she could hear, "are you sure you didn't see Doc last night?"

"What?" she hissed. "No!"

Jas grunted, readjusted himself, and said, "Lyn told me about what you three saw. Something about the eyes? You tell me."

"They… they were eyes, shining," said Gen, trying to remember and finding herself repeatedly disturbed.

"Could they have been more than just eyes?" he asked. "Could they have been glasses? Like Doc's?"

Gen leaned back and stared at him. She went cold. The eyes had been green, or she thought they had, but she wasn't sure. So were Doc Bozzard's spectacles. "What are you talking about? You don't think it was him, do you?"

"I asked Lyn, and he refused to admit it was even a possibility," said Jas, glancing over to Lyn, who was adding small packets of medicine to his vest in readiness. "But Gen, think about it. Whoever that was knew you were there, tried to attack you with freaking *gas*. And Doc would know what substance would have worked."

"I can't believe you!" Gen hissed.

Jas closed his eyes. "Fine. Just put a pin in it, will you? And meanwhile. I'm not going this time, but pretend you're me for a change." Gen snorted at that. "Be scientific. Be methodical. Dig for stuff that's not obvious. Maybe try different lighting too? I'll bet there's a lot of information in that Inn we've not seen yet. Bendin's, like, ancient and lived there a long time. There's no *way* he doesn't have things crammed into every nook and cranny of that place."

"Pretend I'm you," said Gen more loudly. "The moon would drop right out of the sky."

Jas rolled his eyes.

"Good luck, then," he said, and then she felt bad for teasing him. She leaned over and kissed him on the forehead.

"What was that for?" he complained.

"Don't make me regret it," Gen snapped.

"I love you, too," Jas said, and Gen smirked, kissed her mother goodbye, and opened the door into a new night, full of anxiety and purpose.

Buck Moon Blues

U p the forest trail and the stone steps, Gen and the Fireflies pushed themselves through lingering exhaustion mixed with a frenetic feeling that everything was happening at once. When Gen reached the overlook of the Inn and the Amethyst Lantern, she turned to look back at the friends who had joined her: Nyota, Mira, Anisette, Lyn, Amber, and Dhatura. Even though the newest addition to her group might contest the ownership of the Inn, Gen knew Dhatura was invested and determined to help. And Gen was not about to turn down any help.

The moon had grown robust and broke through any lingering clouds that night; there was no fog upon the southern shore where the light shone its purple beacon.

"We've got ourselves a full Buck Moon," Nyota told them.

"Hard to believe Hānuere is so far along already," Dhatura remarked. "Not long until school starts again, yes?"

"School?" Anisette hissed. "That's the last thing I'm thinking of. I'm in monster-fighting mode. That's all I care about."

Mira snickered quietly.

Amber said softly, "What's wrong, Onyx?" for the raven acted jumpy, flicking his feathers, bending forward, and swinging his head left and right. He said nothing, but his mood put Amber on edge, making Gen uneasy too.

It feels like we're being watched, she thought, and she felt exposed atop the hill looking at the still and dark old inn. She put her hand against her firefly brooch to calm her nerves; it felt smooth and warm. The wind was somewhat calm, making for a quiet evening. The only light nearby was the Amethyst Lantern, swinging its purple light around the promontory where it perched and out to sea.

"Let's go," she said, and she set off down the slope toward the Inn, with her friends next to or behind her. Nyota kept pace with her on the right, her upper arm bandaged, her staff glowing dull red at the end, and she used it as a walking stick. Lyn walked to Gen's left.

Onyx jumped up suddenly and flew high into the sky and circled them.

"What's he doing?" Gen asked Amber.

"I'm not sure," Amber replied, touching the feather necklace Andraste had given her. "He's been acting nervous."

"Is it because *you're* nervous?" Gen wondered.

"Maybe," said Amber, as she kept her eyes upon Onyx, now wheeling in slow spirals over the group and the inn.

As they reached the door, he flew back down, and Amber held her arm out. He landed on it and clicked quietly.

"See anything?" Gen asked the bird.

He fluffed his feathers and shook his head. "Dark," he responded.

Gen took that as a reassuring sign since Onyx had not added further details. She looked back at her cousin.

"You've got the key, right?" she asked Mira.

"Oh, hang on," said Mira, fumbling with a crossbody bag and pushing aside pens, paper, and other materials. She drew out the key and placed it in the lock. When she turned it, the click made the hair on the back of Gen's neck stand up, and she and Nyota looked all around them again, back to the hill and the woods.

"Get inside," she urged everyone, and they filed in, with her entering last and looking once more.

I don't know what I think I might see, she thought irritably, *but I kind of don't want to see whatever it is anyway.*

Once inside, she shut the door behind her. Then she turned to see an astounding sight.

The full moon shone through the uppermost part of the great hall, the zenith of its dome, down onto the pulsing purple light in the floor. The combination of the moon and the light lit the great hall beautifully, and Gen could finally see some vestiges of how the Inn must have looked in its heyday. Beneath the opening in the dome's zenith, the great chandelier shimmered. Although its bulbs no longer worked, it still caught the light of the moon and the Source beneath and sent sparkles dancing throughout the hall.

The two light sources illuminated artwork on the ceiling as well as the walls. Pictures hung everywhere, and metallic scrollwork glistened in the soft light. Off to the sides, tables had been moved, their chairs upended on top of them. Everything that had been mostly in darkness on the perimeter of the room now sat in soft light.

"It's exquisite," breathed Mira.

Amber walked off to a corridor they had never been down and said, "Oh, this has stairs going up! I see moonlight, I think, on another floor."

Everyone else joined her to look, and they found a staircase at the end of the hallway, with an upper-level balcony overlooking the hall below. Gen joined Amber and looked up.

"Is there a skylight up there or something?" she wondered aloud. "I don't remember seeing any windows that weren't boarded up."

"Let's go see," Dhatura suggested behind Gen, and the girl walked ahead of everyone else and began to climb the stairs.

Once at the top, however, they found that the light descended from yet another floor above them, and so they traversed that staircase.

Dhatura said softly, "Ahhhh!" and the others joined her.

There was a great picture window looking south as well as a skylight above them. Part of the window had been a door long ago, but the balcony it had led to must have fallen long ago. The opposite wall was completely boarded up, yet this one side was left open for some reason, and the glass was still intact. From this viewpoint, they could see the lighthouse and the sea. Gen could imagine that visitors to the Hotel Lembrar long ago must have enjoyed this view of the sea; they might have been able to see whales or distant boats.

There were broken pieces of furniture scattered on the floor, all of it quite aged, and the moonlight even revealed little alcoves with seats in them, covered with dust and deteriorated.

"Maybe they read books here or played games," Gen mused aloud.

"I would never have stopped looking at that view," Dhatura said.

"It *is* pretty spectacular," Anisette noted.

"Just think of it!" Gen said. "Coming here for holidays, shows, and just... just to see this! I wonder if the visitors appreciated the moon back then like we do."

"Well, remember what we saw, though," Mira said. "It was around the Golden Hour. So, I don't think the moon would have been the draw. Look on the western side. All the windows are boarded up. Back then, I'll bet they'd have watched the sunset in the west."

"So strange to think about," Amber murmured. "I can't imagine wanting to watch the sunset! Wouldn't that have destroyed their eyes?"

"Well, yes," Lyn answered, "but I don't think they'd have been stupid enough to look directly at the sun, even before it was like it is now. Would they?"

Anisette snorted. "I don't know," she said in a sarcastic voice. "They were stupid enough to let things get as out of hand as they apparently did, right?"

"Good point," said Lyn.

"Look at the Lantern," said Gen, pointing.

The barber-pole-striped purple and white lighthouse, capped with the vivid purple light, swept around and around slowly. Gen found it absorbing to watch, almost hypnotic. Something tickled the edge of her thoughts as she gazed out of what must have been a popular vantage point for the Inn's guests.

"Which came first?" she said under her breath, not realizing how loudly she'd said it.

"What do you mean?" asked Amber, shifting Onyx to her other shoulder.

"Oh," said Gen, embarrassed. She adjusted her cap and headlamp, and replied, "The Lantern or the Inn. Which do you think came first? Who built the Inn, and who built the Lantern? And what is it about this place? What's the light in the floor?"

"Maybe we should head down and start sleuthing it all out," Nyota said. "The moon will give us enough light to do so tonight; we could not have asked for better."

"It *is* good timing," Mira agreed. "Come on. I'll help go through any papers we might find."

"Onyx and I will check the upper floors," Amber said.

"I'll look for the kitchens," Anisette announced. When everyone else stared at her, she shrugged and said, "What? I'm not looking for fossilized food. But Bendin lived here, so I'm assuming he had *something*. And who knows, I might find a clue. Dang! Wish Phan had come with us. He'd have slain me with that joke." She sighed and headed for the stairway.

They clambered down the stairs, and Gen felt self-conscious that her steps might be too noisy or that someone still could be watching them. This time, Lyn brought up the rear, and he spoke to her quietly.

"I kind of want to check that chamber again," he told her.

"Not the one with the blood?" she asked, stopping on the stairs to stare at him.

"Yes," he said.

"Well, don't do it alone," Gen advised him. "And remember, Mira has the key to that area."

"I'll be fine, Gen," Lyn reassured her. "What are you going to look for?"

Gen just shook her head. "I have no idea. Something that can help us figure out what's going on. Some clue for where

Bendin might be. Anything to help. If I don't, I'll think… too much of Dad," and she swallowed, for she kept pushing that worry down, and now in the soft light of the full moon, she could not hide the concern on her face.

"I can see why you'd want to stay busy," Lyn said, "and I'll leave you to it. Let me know if you need anything, okay?"

"Thanks, I will," said Gen, and a moment of tension arose between them. They almost hugged, but both backed away at the same time.

Gen reached the bottom of the stairs, walked into the great hall, and watched the moonlight strike the floor with its purple light beneath. That light seemed more vibrant than before, and the room was much brighter from it. She wondered about that. Nyota and Dhatura stood on the perimeter of the light. It was now so vivid that it had become harder to look at. Nyota glanced up at the moon in the sky.

"It's going to move out of range soon," she said, "but look at how charged it is!"

"What do you mean, the light in the floor?" Gen asked her.

Nyota nodded and held her staff up to a cool column of moonlight. The effect was eerie upon the dark red stone on her staff. The stone began to glow.

"The moon is charging this crystal," she said.

Gen looked quizzically at it. "I thought that was just a myth."

Nyota shot her a fierce look. "Not to some of us," she said simply, "and certainly not to Andraste. What happens if you hold your firefly in the moonlight?"

Gen removed the brooch and held it under the moonlight, but there was no change in its slow glowing. She shrugged and put it back on her tunic. "It doesn't seem to affect this," she said, "but obviously, it's doing something for you. And hey, I am sorry. I didn't mean to insult you or anything."

Nyota nodded and said, "We've each got a different relationship with the moon, and that's okay."

Gen realized she had always wanted to have this sort of conversation but had not done so, aside from those with her father, Harris. He was always open-minded and questioning, never judging what others believed. She didn't find that easy and wondered how he did. She wished she could be more like her father or even more like Jas, who at least could see clearly what situations were through a lens of science. She wondered if she might fall somewhere in between the two of them. And once again, she felt uneasy with the role of "leader" and wondered just how she could lead in such a strange situation being thrust on her.

She thought mutinously, *I kind of just want to go home, pet my cats, and forget this whole mess.* She remembered what Jas had said about checking the lighting of things in the Inn. She looked back at Nyota's glowing staff and considered its color.

"Nyota," she called, "can we use that crystal of yours like a torch?"

"What, to go into a dark place?" the girl asked.

"Well, yes," Gen answered, biting her lower lip. "In that chamber, where we found the blood. Lyn said he was going to check it out."

"There are already lights in there, though," Nyota reminded Gen.

"I know," said Gen, "but they weren't like yours. Maybe let's at least try it and see what happens."

Nyota tilted the staff with its crystal so that she could get a better look at it. "Well, why not?"

They found Mira returning from helping Lyn unlock the chamber, and she frowned.

"I don't know what's so interesting to all of you about that room," said Mira. "It's empty."

"Humor me," said Gen.

"I was going to look through more papers," said Mira, "but do you want me to go back with you?"

Gen looked at the notepad peeking out of Mira's bag, slung across her chest.

"Yes," she told her cousin.

Lyn met Gen and the cadre of the others following her as he exited the chamber.

"Find anything?" she asked him.

He looked disappointed. "No," he said, "and I know this sounds ridiculous... but I actually waved my charm-stone around, hoping it would do something." He laughed at himself.

Gen grinned at him and looked behind her at Nyota, who raised her eyebrows and looked amused.

"Still, let's look again," suggested Gen. "Nyota, can you try your staff stone on everything? Wave it around, put it near the walls, I don't know. But let's at least see."

Nyota obliged, and she waved the staff around. Since that did not result in anything interesting, she began drawing the stone along the curved walls. It was a fascinating sight to see Nyota at work, with the flickering stone sconces casting light upon her even as her stone reflected onto her face. She seemed transformed into something other than a fifteen-year-old girl. She looked powerful in a fundamental and ancient way. Gen finally found a word for how Nyota seemed just then: impressive.

And then, quite suddenly, there it was. Nyota gasped. In between two sconces, just below eye level, Nyota's crystal revealed lines on the wall, organized into rectangles and other geometric shapes.

"What could that be?" Gen wondered aloud.

"No idea," answered Nyota.

Mira suggested, "It looks like a screen, maybe?"

"What?" Gen scoffed. "No."

"Close," Anisette piped up, poking her head in the room and watching. "That looks like a control panel to me."

Lyn nodded enthusiastically. "It does!"

Amber said, "Try it and see what it does!"

Gen looked at Nyota. "What do you think?" she asked.

Nyota replied, "I don't see that we have anything to lose."

"I'll do it, then," said Gen, "whatever happens, it's on me. Nyota, if you'll keep the stone shining on it?"

Gen looked at each of the Fireflies, now all crowded into the room in complete curiosity, and she swallowed. She pressed the shapes.

At first, nothing happened. But then the shapes became clearer, and she could feel their edges better. Two of them were triangles stacked on top of each other. She pressed the one on the bottom. The room jerked, and the Fireflies cried out. The room began to move! And it lowered a few feet so that the open door stood above them.

Gen panicked and took her finger off the button.

"What *is* this room?" she cried. "Hold on, I'm going to try something."

She pressed the upper button, and the room jolted again, sending them up to their original position. The door, to her relief, was aligned with the floor again.

"It's an elevator!" Mira exclaimed.

"Oh, by Luna," breathed Gen. "If it's an elevator, then it's got to go down... *where*?"

"Well, we've got to find out!" Anisette insisted.

"I don't think we do," Nyota objected. "Not after what we saw in the moors. I don't want to go anywhere underground anytime soon."

Amber said, "I don't think everyone would need to; it makes more sense that some stay up here, just in case."

Gen asked her, "Do you want to see where this thing goes?"

Amber looked at Onyx on her shoulder.

"I don't know. Onyx, what do you think?"

"No!" the raven said emphatically.

"Then no, it is," said Amber.

"I'll do it," said Anisette fiercely. "I don't care what's down there. I'm not afraid of it."

Nyota shook her head. "You just had a battle like I did," she said.

Anisette replied, "I can handle anything."

Gen looked at Dhatura. "If this is partly or fully your inn, do you want to know what all is in it?"

Dhatura held her arms against her chest and raised herself on her toes a few times.

"I... I don't know, Gen. I want to know where it goes, but I am not sure I want to travel with it to find that out."

"Fair enough," said Gen. "Mira? Lyn?"

"I'll go where you point, boss," Lyn answered with a wry grin.

"Are we even related?" Mira drawled with a sarcastic roll of her eyes. "Of course, I want to know what's down there!"

"Then those of you who want to come along, let's—"

At that moment, a tremor shot through the room.

"You didn't press the buttons accidentally, did you?" Mira asked Gen.

Gen said, "No, it's not that, it's—"

And a great jolt shook them all.

"Oh God!" cried Gen. "Earthquake!"

They all sprinted out of the chamber.

"Get to those old tables in the great hall," insisted Gen, "and get under them." The shaking had stopped temporarily, but she took no chances.

They all sprinted to the great hall and found the tables against the walls. One by one, they scrambled to get under the tables. A series of loud pops and bangs rang through the Inn. Another earthquake shook the Inn violently. The chandelier hanging above the Source light jangled and swayed, and then it fell, landing like a bomb on the floor and sending glass bits in all directions. Then, silence.

Downward Spiral

The tremendous crash of the chandelier frightened Onyx, and he flew upward from Amber's grasp in a panic.

"Everyone okay?" Gen asked. At least the other Fireflies' unconvincing mutters didn't send her into her own panic. "Look, go home. We might get more quakes, and you should be safe. Also, it's getting late in the evening. We can keep looking tomorrow."

With a shaky yawn, she dusted herself off and regarded the ruined chandelier before her. "We can take turns sweeping up the mess tomorrow," she added.

She stumbled out of the room, exhausted, stressed, and jittery from the quake. As her fellow Fireflies filed out into the remainder of the night, Gen looked back at the glittering wreck of the once-great chandelier. It was a mass of sparkles above the light in the floor, and she could not help but feel sad over the damage.

"It feels like everything is breaking in the world," she said to no one in particular, "and nothing can stop it."

Mira stopped walking and waited for Gen and linked arms with her.

"The Fireflies aren't nothing," she said to Gen, to which Gen grinned up at her and nudged her gently with her elbow. Gen touched her firefly brooch and nodded.

Anisette had bolted ahead of them all, to rejoin Phan. Lyn walked with Amber, Nyota, and Dhatura back to their homes. Mira sauntered more slowly with Gen back to her home, and the two girls shuffled in, looking and feeling monumentally tired. For a moment, Gen thought, *I have so much to tell Dad!* And then she remembered all over again that he was missing. It made her feel more tired and anxious than ever.

"Where are Phan and Anisette?" Gen asked Jas, seeing him propped up on the couch examining something small in the palm of his hand.

"Phan felt well enough to leave, so Aunt Tam took them home," Jas replied, scratching at his bandages. "Mira, she said to tell you that she'll be back soon."

Mira frowned. "I don't like her being out alone," she said, blushing. "I'm sorry about your dad," she added. "I bet he'll just walk in the door one day like nothing happened."

"I would be *so* angry with him!" cried Gen.

"Same," said Jas. "But relieved."

"Yes," agreed Gen.

One of the housebots outside chimed a message into the house: "Tam has returned," to which Mira exhaled in relief, and then she felt guilty being so obvious about it, considering her Uncle Harris being missing. But she could see that her cousins were glad as well.

Reggie emerged from the back room, and given her droopy-looking eyes, Gen realized her mother had been napping. *She needed it!* Gen thought. She endured a ferocious hug from her mother, and Gen allowed her to make a fuss about her... a rare thing because Gen was not so much a cuddling type.

Tam entered, holding the latest pod of the *Biolumen Pen*. They all stared at it as if it were a bomb about to explode.

"Remember when we used to love getting the *Biolumen*?" Mira asked.

Gen and Jas looked at each other and said in unison, "No." And Gen added, "I think you were always born to be a reporter. But I... I just don't really want to see the news right now. I mean, I do, but I don't." Mira sighed sadly for her cousins.

Gen's pulse rang in her ears, and time seemed halted as she waited for Aunt Tam to open the leaf-pages of the paper. Her aunt looked up at her and Jas and shook her head.

"No updates about your dad or Doc Bozzard," she said, "but there are new sightings of strange things in the north."

Gen looked at Jas, whose expression was stern. "So, nothing's stopped. That means... there's more of those things out there."

"What are they? Where are they coming from?" Reggie asked the very question all Glimmerbight, including the Fireflies, wanted to know.

Jas said slowly, cupping the object in his hand, "Whatever they are, there's something in them that changes people."

Gen shivered. "What do you mean, changes people?"

"Well," Jas replied, "Bendin gave me a strange device, part clock, part compass, part dosimeter. And it... changed color after being in contact with one of those things."

Reggie's face went pale. "You're not feeling worse, are you?" she asked quickly. She was about to say she would call

Doc Bozzard and caught herself in time. She put her hands to her temples.

"No," said Jas, and he stood and put the device in his pocket. "I'm actually feeling really good. I'm healing faster. So, I'm ready to get back to the Inn and find Bendin. I want to see that elevator!"

"After the quake and everything?" Reggie cried. "Jas, I think you've been through enough."

"Mom," Jas said in a serious voice, "I'm well enough. And I'm of age. You can't stop me. I want to do this. I just think Bendin had to know something bad was happening, and he's missing because of it. And I don't want Gen to think I'm letting her down."

"What?" Gen exclaimed, throwing her hands out. "Look, you were *attacked*. Nobody expects you to do anything but rest, including me!"

"You need me down there," Jas insisted. "You know you do, Gen. I can be another set of eyes and analyze what's happening. I'll bring some goggles and try different lights on the place."

Gen sighed. "Fine, but not until we've had a full day's sleep."

And with that, she marched back to her bedroom, fell on her bed, fully dressed, and fell asleep immediately.

The next evening, Gen's wrist phone chimed during breakfast, and she brought up a hologram of Nyota.

"I'm ready to get back to the Inn," she said.

Gen bit her lip. "Are you *sure*?"

Nyota nodded and said, "Yes. I heard there are more sightings of those creatures out in the north of town, and if there are, that means we didn't kill them all. They're still coming...

and if they're from those shafts we saw? They are coming from underground."

"You and Jas are on the same page with this, then," Gen said. "Okay. I'll call the others and see who's up for it." She called the other Fireflies, and everyone was ready to join in whenever she gave the word.

Another call came in at the same time for Reggie, and Gen heard her voice rise and fall.

She came out of her bedroom with a flushed face and a wild expression.

"What is it?" Jas asked.

"That was the City Council. They have no updates on missing persons," Reggie said. "But their message... those... those things attacked a home in the north. The Council is recommending we all lock down our homes, including any tunnel access, immediately. Gen, Jas, please—"

"No," Gen said, "we've faced those things, and we made it out. We know what to do. We're going back to the Inn and getting answers. It has something to do with Dad. I just know it. I'm going to find out *what*."

Once she said it, Gen felt more determined than ever and surer.

Reggie and Tam looked at each other with fraught expressions. But Tam rallied.

"Okay," Tam said stoically. "Then we will be ready here for anything. First, we'll barricade the cave tunnel."

Reggie nodded. "Go now, just in case things start to get worse and the town gets stricter about who's out and about."

"Has this ever happened before?" Mira asked.

"Never," said Tam, and her eyes gleamed. "And I don't want it to happen again. I'm furious! We should never live in fear!"

Mira straightened her back proudly at those words. Gen, however, felt more worried than ever.

Phan and Anisette arrived on their air bike, followed by Amber with Onyx, Nyota, Dhatura, and Lyn.

Gen urged them all to check their water and snack supplies.

She said, "The town is locking down the tunnels, sounds like, so we need to find out what's going on quickly."

With brief, no-nonsense farewells to Reggie and Tam, who looked energized to action, Gen, Jas, and Mira joined the other Fireflies and headed toward the Inn. Over the hills in the night, with the moon now barely starting to wane and the light dimmed by fast-moving clouds, they hurried, with Jas and Nyota and Phan stopping more frequently than they used to, but with their faces set. Amber marched along as Onyx the raven flew above, keeping watch. She looked sober and more mature than she ever had, to Gen's eyes. There seemed to be an air of resigned inevitability to them that Gen did not like, as it troubled her that something residual still affected them from their attacks. Jas, especially, having noticed the dosimeter change, worried her greatly.

She breathed through it and pushed on, and her team rallied behind her. Mira unlocked the Inn's door, and they entered, locking it behind them. Then they turned to see the wreck of the chandelier, and several of them gasped.

The broken crystals, which had scattered everywhere the night before, had coalesced above the light source in the floor like crystalline stalagmites, reaching skyward. Also unusual, the Source itself had quickened its pulsing, giving the impression of an elevated heartbeat.

"What *is* that light?" Gen wondered aloud.

"Elevator time," Jas declared. They all nodded and headed toward the room with the chambers. But Gen stopped them all from entering.

"No," she said, "we shouldn't all go down there. Right? Some of you must keep watch, and anything you can find for clues would be good. I'm going. Jas?"

"Yep, I want to see what it is," her brother answered.

Gen took a breath. "Who's volunteering to look around?"

"I will," said Amber, and then with an affectionate pat on the raven's beak, she added, "And so can Onyx."

Nyota said, "I'll stay. I'll use my staff stone to look for anything new."

"Great!" Gen said, pleased.

"I'll do some sleuthing up here, too," Mira said. Gen nodded.

Phan and Anisette looked at each other. "We'll guard," Phan said. "If things get dicey, we'll join you."

Then it was down to Dhatura and Lyn.

"I'm going," they both said in unison and then they looked at each other. Dhatura smirked, and Lyn shrugged.

Gen sighed. "Okay. I'll let you both go, but if anythin g... *anything* goes wrong, get back up here."

Lyn and Dhatura nodded.

"Let's go, then," Gen said, and before she left to hunt for more clues, Mira turned the key to the secret room. The two girls nodded to each other, not speaking their respective concerns, and Mira left the room.

Gen pointed to where Nyota's crystal had shown the control panel. Jas put his goggles on and adjusted their vision for different wavelengths until he could see in infrared.

"I see it," he told her. "Are we ready to head down?"

"Yes," said Gen, "and let's hope there aren't more earthquakes!"

They all glanced at each other nervously then. Jas pressed the down button, and the elevator began to descend. It lowered a full floor before a strange scraping sound startled them all... and then the room moved in a different direction.

"Uhhhh," said Gen uneasily. "What's going on?"

Lyn said, "We're going down, for sure, but not straight down. Are we moving sideways?"

Dhatura looked ill at ease. "I'm feeling motion sick," she said. "We're going in a spiral."

"A long spiral," Jas agreed. "And a wide one. But why? Why would this not just go straight down? Why is it going around?"

"You mean, *what* is it going around," Dhatura corrected him.

Jas stared at her. Then he turned to his sister.

"Gen, where are we in relation to the Source?" he asked.

Gen's neck tingled in dawning comprehension.

"We're going around it!"

"Which means..." Jas began, considering as the elevator continued its downward path, and they could not decide among them how far they had gone, "When Bendin showed us those images, we were moving. But we weren't in here, were we?"

"I don't think so, but we were spiraling, I think," Gen answered.

"So," Jas continued, "we were probably circling the Source then, too."

Lyn, Dhatura, Jas, and Gen stared at each other across the small room.

"How big is that light?" Gen wondered.

"Really freaking big," Jas answered.

"This is so strange!" Dhatura said.

"But you didn't know about this, right?" Gen asked her, trying not to feel annoyed and failing.

"I—I," she stammered. "There's a lot I didn't actually know about what was in here."

That was not an answer! Gen thought furiously, and she fought a blatant scowl.

Lyn noticed, though, and said, "This inn is one mystery after another. Nothing about it makes any sense. I'm getting the vibe that it's not an inn anymore, and I have no idea what it could be."

"It *was* an inn, though," Gen said. "It changed over time."

"Bendin changed it," Dhatura said, startling Gen. "That's the only explanation, isn't it? And now he's gone."

They each pondered the strangeness of the Inn over several minutes, and Gen began to wonder how deep underground they were. It made her slightly nauseous to think about it because, at this point, if they had trouble, Phan and Anisette might be beyond contact range to help. They were on their own.

At long last, the elevator slowed and came to a halt. Gen's heart pounded, and her palms sweated. Looking at Jas, Lyn, and Dhatura, they all bore the exact expression she felt on her own face: anxiety. The door opened.

A rhythmic humming met their ears. They could just make out a lavender glow. They walked out of the elevator, and no one and nothing met them, except for a short tunnel toward the glowing light. Gen walked ahead of the others, drawn to that light, and it was the same luminous purple of the Amethyst Lantern as well as the light within the floor of the Inn. She walked out of the tunnel into an enormous cavern chamber, and in its center was a gigantic structure that she could not comprehend. It was unclear to her if it were natural or manufactured, and even its phase confused her. It was brilliant and white-purple; in some moments, it resembled an immense crystal. In others, it was an amorphous blob of light. It pulsed back and forth between these two phases: the heartbeat. It stretched up, and out of sight, so Gen knew that it extended just beneath the main floor of the inn.

"The Source," she said, and her loud voice echoed in the chamber, startling her friends.

Jas, Lyn, and Dhatura joined her in gazing upon this Source, and then Dhatura noticed something off to their left. She walked over to it and then cried, "Gen!" Her eyes were wide and startled.

"What is it?" Gen asked.

Dhatura simply pointed: dried blood streaked off down a hallway. Gen swallowed and stepped forward to look at it. Lights flashed off and on inside the hallway in random order. She looked back at the others, and they joined her. She walked slowly down the corridor, far enough away from the Source that she needed her headlamp. Her firefly brooch pulsed almost at the same rate as the Source. Her heart pounded much faster.

The trail of blood stopped at the end of the hallway, at a door with a wheel lock, like a vault. But the door was not closed. It stood wide open. And from that door, a shape emerged.

Unsealed

Smoke and haze poured from behind the vault toward the Source, and the effect was striking, the coiling, diffuse purple clouds billowing all through the great rotunda. Gen could see something among the clouds, edged in purple light from the Source. It was tall and lean and half-violet, and to her eyes, from across the great hall, it did not seem human. But it did not appear monstrous either. *Godlike.*

The word jumped into her mind and burrowed there as she tried to reconcile that she was looking at someone who had come out of the other entrance to the chamber, and it was someone she had never seen before. For the first time in her life, she felt the sensation that someone she did not know might very well be dangerous.

"Maybe we should get out of here," whispered Lyn, watching Gen. From his vantage, he had not seen the figure. Or it had not seen him.

But it stared at Gen.

She shivered, stood straight up, and stared back. Lyn then followed her eyes and jerked alert.

"Oh shit," he hissed. "Gen, let's go!"

Gen slowly shook her head. The figure stepped forward slowly.

It was lean, taut, and somehow feral yet streamlined, with an air of savage ferocity like that of a falcon. Yet this was no falcon: it was a person. A person unlike anyone she had ever seen before. Its outfit was close-fitting with tubing and black, yet reflective, for its surface scattered the Source's purple light along its edges. Then it pivoted to face the Source, and Gen could see its profile: sharp, aquiline, proud. The face turned back to Gen and then walked forward. It stopped a few feet from the Source and looked over at her.

It was a young man with sharply pointed, pale hair, tinged lavender in the light of the Source, but she was not sure what color it might have been otherwise. His eyes were pale as well, almost as white as the whites of his eyes, yet with dark rings around the irises. He held her gaze until she blinked. She felt heat rising in her cheeks.

"You don't look particularly monstrous," said the young man to Gen in a strange accent but well-enunciated. "I'm glad at least something hasn't changed."

Confused, Gen tilted her head and said, in her too-brash voice, "What's that supposed to mean?"

It was his turn to blink, and he did, and then he tilted his head back and laughed. He ceased, then smirked and looked briefly at Lyn, who stared coldly and suspiciously back at him.

"Tell me your name, girl," the stranger commanded, not asked.

Lyn then burst out, "Are people that rude? Where you're from, then?"

The stranger's lips twitched, but he refrained from laughing. "You seem defensive, boy."

"I'm not a boy, I'm a—" Lyn spluttered, his face turning quite red, but Gen placed her hand on his shoulder and looked at him in such a way that he stopped. She turned back to the newcomer.

"I'm Gen," she told him. "And this is Lyn."

The pale stranger laughed again. "Gen and Lyn! How precious and poetic the two of you are. And how... soft," he added, lowering his voice, regarding them both.

Gen did not like the sound of "soft."

"Well?" she asked loudly, "who are *you*?"

He walked up closer, stopped, looked behind him briefly, tilted his chin down, and leaned forward to say in a low, silken voice, "Styx."

Lyn made a snorting sound and shifted uncomfortably. Gen began to walk toward Styx.

"Gen, no!" protested Lyn, but she was determined.

The two faced each other on the floor, with the pulsing violet-white light of the Source sweeping over them, and the newcomer stood several inches taller than she. Up close, she could see that he was younger than the shadows had made him from a distance, with his angular features. *Maybe about twenty? Maybe younger?* she guessed.

His eyes were so pale that, to her, they seemed made of liquid. His outfit was elaborate, covered in a strange, faceted tubing, and his skin was partially creased around his neck as if he had slept for a long time pressed up against something. His eyes held her transfixed, and she felt messy next to him, wild and unkempt, so she pulled at her tunic. The tiniest crescent of a smile curved in on the left side of his mouth. He bore high cheekbones and long, nearly white eyelashes.

Looking at him, she felt something shift inside her, as if the world had slanted without warning, and she might start sliding off it.

She swallowed and said, "I know your name now, Styx. But who are you?"

Styx

B efore Styx answered, Jas moved forward from where he and Dhatura had watched beyond the Source on the other side of the great chamber. Styx darted his eerie, pale eyes to them and worked his face into an expression Gen was unfamiliar with: smugness tinged with disdain.

"Ah, so there are more of you, then!" he said in a smooth, low voice.

Gen felt confused because she rather liked the sound of that voice, but felt as though maybe she was being insulted and did not know it.

"This is my brother, Jas," Gen told Styx, and he bowed.

"A family of you!" he exclaimed. "Nice to meet you, Jas."

"Hello," said Jas brusquely, not approaching any closer. His dark eyes locked with Styx's pale ones, and Gen had never felt such a chill watching two people before.

Styx inhaled slowly, hands interlocked behind his back, and he walked up to Dhatura and stared down at her.

"And who might you be, pretty girl?" he said mellifluously.

Dhatura smiled radiantly, mesmerized by the young man, and shook back her long, dark, wavy hair. The copper peacock brooch pinned to her sash glimmered in the light of the Source.

"I am Dhatura," she answered, but when she glanced at Gen, Gen gave her the tiniest shake of the head behind Styx's back. Dhatura lifted her chin regally but in secret acknowledgment.

"Interesting," murmured Styx. "Four young people, int act... mostly," and he swept his gaze back to Jas, which made Gen feel queasy.

What do you mean by 'mostly'? she thought.

"You don't seem like you're from here," she said out loud.

Styx smirked at her. "You're a brash one," he laughed. "I like you already, Gen. And no, I suppose I am not *from here* originally; I suspect none of you is, either. But tell me more about yourselves! Where are you from? What do you do? And have you had any troubles lately?"

"Look," Lyn said hotly, "we have no idea who you are and where you came from. We *are* from here; this is our home. We've never seen you before."

"What do you mean by 'troubles'?" Jas asked Styx pointedly.

"There's blood," said Gen breathlessly. "Did you see a—" but Jas shook his head at her. It was as if they all danced around secrets, but the greatest secret right now was Styx: who he was and where he had come from.

"Blood!" exclaimed Styx. "What, back there?"

Gen watched his sharp face, and he raised his eyebrows while looking back.

"Is that what that was?" he said then. "That's a little gruesome, isn't it? Well, luckily, it wasn't mine. But thanks for the concern." He looked at them all through half-lidded, ghostly eyes. "As for troubles, Jas—it was Jas, yes? Interesting name... anyway. Well, not everything went to plan, did it? I mean, *I* am complete and healthy, so I'm a success. But something's happened to some of the others. I'll have to let the commander know."

"What does all that even mean?" demanded Gen. "You don't seem to have any idea about what's going on, or our troubles. You have no idea what we've been through." Her lips quivered, thinking of her dear, kind father.

Styx turned to look at Gen and took her cheeks in his hands while he looked deep into her brown eyes with his lightning-like gaze. The ends of her indigo hair curled between his fingers. She shivered, having never been touched in this way before. It sent a shock through her entire body. She found it alarmingly pleasant.

Styx hissed, "I've been through more in my life than you can even imagine."

"Get your hands off her!" bellowed Lyn, balling his fists.

Styx laughed and let Gen go, but his right hand caressed her brow before he did.

"You have a vintage look," he said. "Like a silent film star."

Gen crinkled up her face, and Styx laughed again. "Well," he said, "not when you do that."

She exhaled, not realizing how long she had held her breath.

"I... don't know what any of that means," she told him. "Did you just insult me?"

Styx leaned back and guffawed. He glanced at Lyn and grinned. "I do like Gen."

"Who *are* you? Or should I ask *what*?" Jas asked.

Styx regarded him with an approving look and a nod. "You're a solid one and keen," he noted. "I'm the herald."

Gen, Lyn, Jas, and Dhatura instinctively moved closer together. Gen could tell nobody else liked that word, either. Yet she felt that the four of them could not fend off this one person, so formidable an air he carried about him, like armor.

"The herald of what?" Gen asked. "Those monsters?"

Styx smirked at her and the others and then looked up at the Source. "I wouldn't know of any monsters, Gen. I was chosen to help begin operations for my commander." He studied the great biphasic Source. "Someone must have built this just for us and our plan. That's a relief. He'll be pleased we aren't starting from scratch for his return! Fascinating power source. What is it?"

So, he really doesn't know what it is, either, Gen thought. *But Bendin definitely did.*

"We don't know," said Gen.

"Huh!" remarked Styx, looking intently at her. "You're too innocent to lie well, so I believe you."

He walked all around the Source, illuminated by it in such a way that he seemed almost a manifestation of it. Gen could not take her eyes from him. When he turned to her again, she breathed more quickly.

"Whatever this is," he said to her, "it's not natural. It's new tech, but as for what kind, I have no idea. And you don't either, which... how did you come upon it, then? We're very far down here. What are you doing here?"

Gen felt defensive. "It's my inn," she said.

"And mine," Dhatura chimed in, stepping forward. Gen gritted her teeth.

Styx laughed at them both and said, "An *inn*? What kind of inn has this giant power light in it? And why would it be so far down in the earth? This is the strangest thing I've ever seen or heard of."

"*You* are the strangest thing I've ever seen or heard of," Gen spat hotly. "You're even stranger than Andra—"

"Tell us, Styx," Jas broke in, jaw tight, as he moved next to his sister and gently nudged her. "Who are you the herald for? And what do you mean by it?" He glanced at his dosimeter, and Styx noticed.

Styx steepled his hands at his lips and squinted.

"See," he said coldly, "you're a little too strange and a little too eager. I need to know more. Are you armed? What is that?"

He pointed to Jas's dosimeter.

"It's a watch," Jas said simply.

"Then what time is it?" Styx asked him.

Jas looked again at the watch and said, "It's 2:53 AM."

Styx crowed at that. "What are you kids doing down here in the middle of the night?"

"What are you doing here *at all*?" Lyn demanded.

Styx took the four of them in and paced back and forth in front of them.

"I need a little more information," he said quietly. "What year is this?"

The four Fireflies blinked at him.

"What?" Gen asked, unsure if she had heard him correctly.

"It's a simple enough question, Gen," Styx said, smirking. "What's the year?"

"How do you not kn—" Lyn began.

Styx said through gritted teeth. "The year! What's the year?"

"It's 534 DD," blurted Dhatura.

Styx twisted his face up. "What the hell does that mean? DD?"

"Dawn of Dusk," replied Gen.

Jas stepped forward, face to face, his dark eyes meeting Styx's pale ones, and he asked, "What year is it *to you*?"

Styx stepped backward, and for a second, as fleeting as a spark from a fire, he looked unmoored. "It's 2027," he answered. "AD," he added.

"A...D?" Gen repeated, her eyes large and curious.

"Look," Styx said, his hands shaking, although he tried to still them, "I don't know what's going on here, and you'd better not be playing a joke. What year is it here in AD?"

Jas looked quite sober, but his brow betrayed confusion. "If you're being serious about this, then the year in AD is, if I'm getting it right, 2563 AD."

Gen watched in amazement as Styx staggered backward and whirled around. His expression showed emotions she had never beheld on anyone before. His face flickered between disbelief, horror, revulsion, and wonder, and finally, he broke into wild, long laughter.

"I want," he said between raucous spasms, "I want you to be full of it, I want you to be lying, and I can see... I can see from *you*, Gen," and she blushed, "that you're telling me the truth. Oh, God. Oh, my God."

Gen marched up to him, reached her hands out despite Lyn's protests, and said, "Tell me, Styx, do you really think it's 2027?"

Reeling, he took her hands and looked down at her clear, bright face, and he said, "It... it was. Before... before we froze."

"You... froze?" she asked.

Styx nodded. "Cryofreeze. We preserved ourselves. We t hought... we thought we'd just ride it out, you know? And Cybolag would open us up. But. They obviously didn't."

He slid to the floor, sat with his arms around his knees, and stared at the Source.

"But something woke us," he said. The Fireflies gathered around him. "Something or someone. I—I'm alive. I'm alive. How am I alive after... *centuries*?"

"You're serious!" exclaimed Jas. "If so, then you're the oldest person alive."

Styx laughed softly. "I was seventeen."

The Library

S tyx stood and dusted himself off. Gen watched him harden his face. He looked at her briefly, then turned away from them all.

"I have to get back," he said.

"What! In *time*?" Gen asked. "You can't!"

He sighed. "I know that. I have to get back to see if anyone else survived. I took a wrong turn and got here. Well, maybe it was the right turn," and he shot her a look that gave her a pang similar to the one she had experienced while watching the images of the past Inn.

"Do—do you want our help?" Gen asked.

"Gen," said Jas in a hard tone, "we don't know who this guy is, where he came from. And we have to get back home. It'll be dawn soon."

"It's fine," said Styx. "You don't want to get grounded."

"We have to get back inside before the sun rises," Dhatura told him.

"What, are you vampires?" laughed Styx.

They all gasped.

Gen felt sick.

"Don't. Don't ever say that," she told him. He twisted his eyebrows. "It's a… a slur."

Styx made a strangled sound and turned it into a cough. His eyes watered, and he covered his mouth.

"Are you… are you *laughing*?" Gen demanded.

"No!" Styx replied. "No. But… well… good luck avoiding the sun or whatever it is you have to do. I mean, we only need it to live."

"To a point," said Jas.

"We don't need it like you did," Lyn joined in. "We live our lives at night now. Thanks to your era."

Styx made a scoffing sound and said, "I'm fresh out of a time capsule, and you're already blaming me for your own weird ways. Gen, nice meeting you. The rest of you can—"

The earth shook again, and tiny pebbles scattered across the floor.

"Bye," said Styx quickly, and he fled out the door he had entered.

Gen took a deep breath, turned to her friends and brother, and said, "We'd better get out of here."

"I don't like that guy," Lyn muttered.

"I can tell," Gen replied. "Now, let's go home!"

The four of them ran to the elevator, and Jas set it going up. They felt both the upward and circular motion of its ascent and Gen pondered the Source around which that elevator traveled.

"The place keeps getting stranger," she muttered.

Once the elevator opened, she found Mira pacing.

"By Luna, you took forever. I thought you'd never get back!" she exclaimed, seizing Gen by the hand. "Come and look at something we found."

"Hold on," Gen said. She turned to Phan and Anisette, who had been guarding the elevator. "I need you two to make sure this thing doesn't go anywhere." The twins looked inside the empty thing and at each other.

"What is it, a possessed elevator now?" Anisette asked dryly.

Gen hesitated before finally answering, "No, but... I'll tell you later. Be ready to leave as soon as I've seen whatever Mira wants me to see."

Her cousin lifted herself up and down on her toes. "Come on!" Mira urged.

Gen followed her as she walked up out of the chamber hall and onto the main floor. From there, Mira took her along one of the hallways of hotel rooms.

"Up there," said Mira, pointing up at a spiral staircase at the end of the hall. "Nyota and Amber are waiting."

"We're running out of time to get back," said Gen, "can it wait?"

"I know you'll want to see what it is," Mira insisted, fidgeting.

"Fine," Gen answered, irritable, thinking of the stranger far below them and wondering what he was doing or what he *would* do.

Mira led her to room 217. Gen stared at the number.

"Seventeen," she whispered to herself. She pushed the thoughts of Styx down so she could focus better. She wanted to talk about him but at the same time, felt uneasy about doing so, and she could not decide why. It was as if the moment she said something, it might make everything change, and enough had changed for her already. She chewed on her lips and kept the revelation private.

Mira held out a key from a keyring she had draped over her wrist, full of keys to the various rooms of the Inn. She had looped her own special key given by Andraste on a cord around her neck. She turned the key and opened the door, and they found Nyota and Amber there. Onyx was not with Amber, but the girl was sitting on the floor sorting through iridescent papers.

Gen looked up from her to see bookshelves from floor to ceiling. Nyota stood on a ladder sorting through the books, with her staff leaning against the shelves below her. In the center of this room, set just out from the window, a desk sat, stacked high with papers that shimmered, and large, ancient books with cracked spines and silver font. Candlesticks with pale green, melted candles sat both on the desk and on a boarded-up windowsill behind it. On the wall where Gen had entered, two framed pictures stood on either side of the door. One of them was a diagram of a lighthouse. The other was a fancy poster.

Gen stared first at the lighthouse and realized the art within the frame was quite old and stained, but its shape was unmistakable; it was the Amethyst Lantern, showing its interior architectural design. She did not understand some of the elements marked on it, but she was impressed by the number of stairs illustrated. The poster drew her attention more.

It was beautifully illustrated with an Art Nouveau style and font. It read, "Welcome to the Hotel Lembrar, for a time to remember!" The image was of the inn in a stylized version of what it had looked like in the past images Bendin had shown her, Jas, and Mira. Beyond it, up the hill a bit, stood the Amethyst Lantern, and beyond that, billowing clouds in the sky. This was not a nighttime image, so it seemed alien to Gen. It was gorgeously rendered in faded paints, golden and green, and framed by twining, violet flowers like small trumpets, and a little airship with a gondola approached it from the sea cliff with the Lantern.

Again, Gen felt that ache, which made her think of Styx. Had he seen this place back... *then*? And she thought perhaps he had not. Because how could anyone forget such a beautiful sight? *A time to remember, indeed.*

"What is this room?" Gen breathed.

Nyota climbed down from her ladder, holding a book in the crook of her arm, and she turned to Gen, pushing the stray, purple baby hairs away from her forehead. Her soft, dark eyes glowed in the light from one of the candles, and she looked wistful.

"We think this was... is Bendin's office," she said. "Look at this!"

She handed Gen a book, and Gen took it and wiped its cover free of dust to see its title. She promptly sneezed explosively, twice in a row.

The cover read: "An Account of the Golden Hour, Years One Through Twenty," and the author's name shone in silver font below it, "Benjamin D. N. Lal."

"Oh, my Luna!" exclaimed Gen. "Is that... is that Bendin's actual name?"

Amber looked up and said, "We think so. Note the surname," at that moment, Dhatura walked into the room.

Gen turned to her and handed her the book.

"I guess you are an heiress, after all," she said, and she fought the urge to sound reluctant, but she failed.

I didn't want it to be true, she thought. *I don't know why. I... wanted the Inn, after all, I guess. Silly me. A nobody.*

Dhatura took the book into her hands reverently.

"Oh, this is marvelous," she murmured, her face gone soft. "Thank you! Did he write *all* these books?"

"No," said Amber, "but he wrote all the ones related to the Golden Hour in that series. Now, if only I could figure out what he's written on these papers... I *think* he's saying something like 'read in this exact order,' and then on the other sheets, there are just... random words." She closed her bright blue eyes and rubbed them from fatigue.

"That isn't all," Nyota said. She picked up a book from Bendin's old desk, and its front cover was exquisitely rendered with a tapestry depicting owls, kākāpō, peacocks, otters, and other animals, as well as symbols such as the moon, stars, and astrological constellations all along its border. Nyota's eyes glistened as she held it lovingly and turned it over for Gen to see: "ANDRASTE" was written in all capitals on the back and filigreed with silver and copper.

"Wow!" Gen exclaimed.

Jas stuck his head in the door just then and said, "I found some writing on the walls downstairs with my goggles. Did you tell them, Gen?"

"Tell them what?" Gen asked, but she blushed.

Jas raised his eyebrows. "About our... visitor?"

The room went silent as everyone turned to look at Gen.

"I did not," she said, twisting her hands together behind her back nervously. "To be honest, I was not sure how or when to say it. But... someone... a guy... came out of a vault. Down... down in the elevator."

"What?" exclaimed Mira. "Why didn't you tell us? Was it an attacker?"

"Gen," said Nyota sternly, "what sort of vault?"

"Where is this person now?" Amber asked.

Phan and Anisette, craning their necks in from the hall after overhearing them, looked at each other and frowned.

"Nobody's come up the elevator," said Phan.

"Is that why you had us guard it after you came out?" asked Anisette.

Gen felt her spirits sink. It was too much to deal with just then, she felt, all those eyes on her. *I didn't ask for any of this!*

Aloud, she said, "Phan, Anisette, you're right. I was too focused on gathering up everyone and getting home, and I—I just wasn't... ready. I wasn't sure what I would say. It's a young man, and the vault? I don't know. But we found the bottom of the light under the floor out there. The elevator moves around the Source. It's huge. It stretches down several floors. And it's... I don't know *what* it is. Enormous. Brilliant."

"It seems to be a biphasic form of matter," Jas said. "If I had to guess, it constantly switches between plasma and crystal. I've never seen anything like it before."

Nyota turned toward the library, moved the rolling ladder over to her left, and climbed up. She pulled out a slender turquoise book, climbed back down, and handed it to Jas. "Something like this?"

Jas took the book from Nyota and read aloud from the cover, "Exotic Frustrated Systems Between Phases of Matter," with the author Benjamin D. N. Lal underneath.

"That's not..." Jas began.

"Yeah," Gen said. "It's Bendin!"

Jas stared at the book and turned away from everyone as if lost in his own world, thumbing through the pages with excitement. He walked into the hallway and met Dhatura there, and the two looked with interest at the book. Dhatura's face shone again with what Gen guessed must be pride.

"Gen," Mira said, her voice a bit higher than usual, "who was this person? Tell us more!"

Gen opened her mouth and closed it a couple of times.

Lyn, leaning through the doorway, said, "He's a bit of an ass from the past, that's who he is." His face was flushed.

"Lyn," Gen said in a low tone. "Really?" The others in the room looked at Gen in confusion.

She then said, "There is a person, a young man, named Styx, and he's just appeared out of nowhere down in the caverns underground. He says... he says he was frozen? For centuries, and now he's awake. It sounds like... he's not the only one who was frozen, either. And that he's the herald for someone else."

Everyone spoke at once, with Amber disbelieving her, saying, "Oh, Gen, someone is really pulling a bad prank on you!"

Gen swallowed and said, "I believe Styx."

Lyn made an irritated sound and left the room.

Nyota stared into Gen's eyes. "I believe *you*," she said. "But do you know whether this Styx is safe?"

"Thank you, Nyota," Gen said, relieved. "I don't know much about him. He seemed so... electric. So alive and awake and... and *different* from us. Casual, callous, maybe."

Mira watched Gen's face intently as she wrote, without looking, into her notepad.

"He sounds very interesting," said Mira, "and I wish I had met him! If he's telling the truth—which I doubt, but then again, we've seen a lot of insane things lately—then this would be the biggest story we've ever had. The *Biolumen Pen* would be all over this!"

Gen looked at the others in the room and was about to say something when Jas ducked and yelped in the hallway. Great black wings flapped in excitement, and Onyx burst into the room. Amber stood, and he alighted upon her shoulder and croaked, "Dawn soon!"

Instantly they put everything down, extinguished the lone candle burning, and bolted from the room. Mira hastily locked the door, and they all ran down the stairs, joining Lyn.

The twins sprinted up to meet them, and they all ran for the Inn's door, with Mira and Gen lingering behind.

"Mira," said Gen, "I'm not sure we should lock it."

Another tremor in the earth, and Mira stared at Gen.

"I'm locking it. What's got into you? We have to go! Look!" and she pointed to the dulling of the remnant of the night as twilight began to take hold of the sky. Then Mira said, "Wait. Is this about that... Styx person? Gen, honestly..."

Gen looked back at the dark interior of the Inn and the heartbeat pulse of the Source light in the floor. She sighed and nodded, and Mira shut the door and locked it.

They all rushed along the path back to the village, with Nyota, Amber, Phan, and Anisette going their separate ways over land since the tunnels were shut. Gen watched Onyx soar in the remaining night sky. She then slowed a bit to bring up the rear, continually looking over her shoulder.

What do I hope to see? she wondered. *We didn't find Dad. But we found someone.*

State of Readiness

What met them when they arrived at the Light-worth house in the pre-dawn hours was not what they expected. The housebots had arranged themselves in front of every entrance and window, and their eyes glowed red. Each bot scanned the teens.

"You are allowed entry," said Bloop.

"By Luna!" cried Dhatura.

"We'd better get home," Lyn told her. "I'll escort you." He looked back at Gen, who gave him a small wave. There seemed to be turbulence between them, which bothered Gen.

"See you soon," she said, and Lyn nodded and walked with Dhatura quickly down the lane.

Another earthquake rattled the Lightworth home when Gen reentered. She noticed Jas checking his dosimeter.

"Any changes?" she asked him in a low voice.

"Nothing new," he answered. "...what do we say to Mom and Aunt Tam?"

Mira piped up, "I think we'd better not tell them about Styx. It's a bit much right now, don't you think?"

"What's a bit much?" her mother, Tam, asked, coming out of the kitchen with a terrifying-looking object thrown over her shoulder.

"Mom," said Mira, pointing, "what's that?"

"It's a crossbow," said Tam casually.

The cousins all gasped.

Then Reggie entered, and she had a long stick slung over her shoulder.

"Uh... Mom?" Jas asked. "What are you carrying?"

Reggie lowered the object, and it had some heft to it. Gen cried out when she saw what it was.

"An axe! Mom! What are you doing? What are you and Aunt Tam doing?"

Reggie grinned at her sister, who shrugged.

"We're ready to defend this home," said Reggie.

"What about our home, Mom?" asked Mira.

"I locked it down," said Tam. "Your father isn't back from Umbradene, so I told him I would stay with all of you until he's back. I also told him he might want to hold off because nobody can use the tunnel network. It would take a while for the commute... plus with these new sightings in the north, I don't know if I want him coming back at all!"

"Mom!" cried Mira. "You can't mean that!"

Tam said, lowering her crossbow casually, "Just until we know what's going on and things quiet down. That's all."

"Now," said Reggie, "you've been gone all night, and it's bedtime. I don't want any excuses. The housebots are guarding the perimeter, the tunnel door is sealed off, and if another quake hits, get under a table. We've got you covered."

Gen marveled at her mother. "Mom, wow! I didn't know you had it in you."

"For you kids?" Reggie said with a spark in her brown eyes, "I'll do anything. Watch me."

"I hope we don't have to, Mom," Jas said, leaning down to hug his mother goodnight. Gen hugged her too, and she and Mira went to her room.

"What will we do tomorrow?" Mira asked as the two girls stared up at the ceiling in Gen's room. The sun shields had activated, and the room darkening closed every light source except for the little glowing stars Gen had projected upon all her walls and the ceiling. She remembered how much fun she had making star maps with her dad and felt conflicting emotions.

Because every other thought she had was of Styx. Of his pale eyes burrowing into her, of his poise, alertness, and his momentary weakness when he realized he lived out of his own time.

"We go back," Gen decided. "We learn more."

"Good," said Mira. "I want to take every story we can to the *Biolumen*."

"Why?" asked Gen. "They don't seem decent. Showing Dad's photo before we even got an official missing person report. I hate that paper now. You know what?" And she propped herself on her side to look at her cousin, whose hair finally was loosed from any fashionable hats and tied into a small knot on the top of her head. "You should start your own paper. Forget the *Biolumen* and anyone involved in it. Report the news yourself!"

Mira laughed in delight and turned over to think about this until she fell asleep. Gen waited for that moment then stared at the projected stars, thinking of Styx and missing her father. *I don't know what night will bring me this time*, she thought, *but I hope I'm ready for it.*

The overday delivery of a new *Biolumen Pen* coincided with messages from Phan and Anisette that nothing had remained calm while Gen and her family slept. After the last night's quake, daybreak brought a series of attacks along the northern perimeter of the down and once again encroached on Moonbow Valley. The Duong twins had the most astounding story of all: their housebot had been overtaken by one of the creatures right outside their home and had responded by creating a flaming ball to kill the thing.

As Gen and Jas chewed their cereal and watched the twins' hologram message with increasing horror, Mira sifted through the *Biolumen*, poring over every detail about the attacks.

"There's a pattern to them," she announced. "They're all within a larger perimeter of those shafts we found. She opened her notebook and drew a rudimentary map of Glimmerbight and its villages, including Moonbow Valley. She placed an "x" on each sighting or attack of the creatures, adding in the ones that had attacked the Fireflies. Gen and Jas looked at the map and at each other.

"So, they're still coming out of those shafts," Jas said in a grim tone.

Gen bit her lip. "If they're coming from underground, Styx is in danger."

"Would you let that weirdo go?" Jas hissed.

"No," said Gen emphatically. "We found someone from the *past*, Jas. I'm not letting him go."

Mira looked sidewise at Gen's flushed face and pressed her lips together forcefully to stop herself from making the comment she wanted to.

"Here's what I don't understand," Mira finally said. "Styx does seem to be totally fine. Especially to be as old as he said he was. So, the cryo-thing that he stayed in worked for an incredibly long time. How would it have? Wouldn't the chance of it lasting that long be really rare?"

"Insanely rare," agreed Jas. "I've thought about that too. And the only thing I can come up with is that he had to have been kept alive by a reliable power source for hundreds of years. How?"

Gen stood up from her seat. "The Source," she said.

"Wait, we don't know how long that thing has been there," Jas said.

"It doesn't matter when it was made. It matters why," Gen replied.

The three of them looked at each other.

"You're not implying that Bendin… made the Source to keep Styx alive, are you?" Mira asked her.

Gen paced back and forth in the living room.

"It might be the only thing that makes sense out of any of this," she said. "Because I think you're right, Jas. There's no way a power source could last hundreds of years and keep someone alive."

"But he's just a kid like us," Jas remarked, absently tapping his chin with his dosimeter. "What's so important about him that would make Bendin want to preserve him? Are they relatives, maybe?"

"Even if they were," Gen said slowly, "Styx didn't seem to know him or mention him. Maybe he did know him, but you'd think he'd have said something."

"What else did you say he told you, Gen?" Mira asked. "Something about being a 'herald' or whatever?"

"Yes," said Gen, "a herald."

"But a herald for what?" Jas wanted to know.

"Or who?" added Mira.

Gen put her hands to her cheeks and thought of Styx's touch with his hands. She brushed her jagged indigo bangs from her forehead.

"There are other people down there," she said slowly. "Somewhere in that vault."

"Other people?" Jas said, suddenly stern, "or other *creatures*?"

The room went silent but for Smudge yowling over a half-full food bowl, demanding more. Sylvia jumped down to inspect Smudge's bowl and received an unwelcome swat on the nose from Smudge.

"Don't mess with the leader," Gen chided Sylvia.

The three teens looked at each other.

"The leader," breathed Mira.

"I'm calling the others," said Gen. "We need to get back to the Inn."

Jas took hold of her arm, and she noticed he had better mobility from healing.

"Gen, are we ready for this? We don't know who or what might be down there." And he looked at her with brotherly concern. "I feel like you're too connected to all this."

"We can't be any readier than we are," Gen told him and Mira. "Andraste gave us things to help us, which must be why. We need to find out what's going on underground and see if it's related to Bendin's disappearance. He could be trapped somewhere by one of those monsters or by an earthquake. Either way, he needs us. And so does Dad."

Jas nodded. "Then we're ready."

Vaults Within Vaults

"All that was great in the past was ridiculed, condemned, combated, suppressed — only to emerge all the more powerfully, all the more triumphantly from the struggle."
—— **Nikola Tesla**

"Officially, I do not like the thought of any of you staying in that inn overday," said Tam after their breakfast.

Reggie sighed and checked the backpacks that Gen and Jas, and Mira stuffed with snacks, water, and various bits and bobs that each thought might be important. Jas, naturally, had his various research tools and the book Nyota had found by Bendin.

"What are you going to do? Throw it at a monster?" Gen asked dryly.

Jas looked down his nose at Gen. "I'll have you know that this book contains pertinent facts about building a biphasic power source. Like *the* Source. I'm the scientist. Let me figure all this out."

"You're the scientist like I'm the reporter," Mira scoffed, grinning.

"Like I'm the leader," Gen said, grimacing.

"One of these is true," Nyota said, entering the Lightworth home. "The others *will* be true one day. Gen, the housebots are vicious, I have to say…"

"We have the security up as high as it'll go," Tam told her. "But I'm sorry if it's a little *too* high."

Everyone heard a raven's distinct, indignant croaks just outside the door, and Tam said, "Oh. Well, that doesn't sound good."

Amber entered with a fluffed-up and angry Onyx, who she tried to soothe. The raven looked balefully at Tam and Reggie, flew straight to the kitchen bar, and tapped his beak on the counter. "Snacks!" he bellowed. Reggie and Tam looked at each other and winced.

"A little too high," Reggie agreed. "Sorry, master raven."

"Onyx," said the bird, and he tapped his beak again and strutted to and fro on the bar.

"On it, Master Onyx," said Reggie, the corners of her lips twitching. After placating the raven with a bowl of nuts and some scritches around his neck, Reggie welcomed Amber and gave her snacks for her bag as well.

The Duong twins and Dhatura arrived next, each with bags slung over their shoulders. Dhatura also brought a second bag full of treats and flowers for the two mothers. While Reggie and Tam exclaimed over that and praised Dhatura for her good taste, Gen answered the door to see Lyn standing there. Between them, a flicker of uneasiness passed, and it made Gen feel both irritated and sad at the same time.

How did we get here? she wondered.

Lyn double-checked his stores of medicinals and herbs, and Tam placed some ointment into his pack for anyone who might need it. She and Reggie looked at all the teens gathered in the room and then at each other. A look of resignation settled on their faces.

"Just don't end up on the cover of the *Biolumen Pen* tomorrow," Reggie told Gen and Jas. "For *any* reason."

Gen adjusted her cap and smirked. She quickly kissed Reggie on the cheek and headed for the door. She noticed her mother and her aunt's array of various weaponry, most of them household objects improvised for who knew what purpose. She did not pretend to understand why a broom would be a good weapon, but there was a lot she did not understand about adults, so that just seemed part and parcel of the bargain.

Gen turned at the door before exiting. She said, "We're going hundreds of feet down under an ancient inn with earthquakes and monsters on the loose all around us. I don't have anything inspiring to say. So don't look to me for that. You don't have to look to me for anything. Ever. But... I'm glad you'll be with me above and below, in the dark or, Luna forbid, in the day."

The Inn lay silent, still, and pale, again reminding Gen of a great shell housing a sleeping creature. She knew that at least one form of life dwelt within it, and she wondered what he might be doing or if he were still there. Had Styx ventured out? Her heart pounded. What else would they find in the bowels of the Inn? The only thing Gen felt sure of was the Lantern, with its reassuring purple light wending its way back to shine upon her and her fellow Fireflies as they stood on the hill above the Inn.

"We could use eyes above," Gen said. She looked at Amber, whose hair had gone a bit wilder than usual, and Onyx sat dutifully on her shoulder. Amber's feather necklace sparkled in the waning gibbous moonlight.

Amber stroked Onyx and asked, "Can you do a sweep and see if there is anyone—or anything—out of the ordinary?"

Onyx made a knocking sound and booped Amber's nose, then shot up into the night. She watched him go, smiling, and Gen reflected that Amber seemed to be changing before her eyes.

Amber is changing. Maybe we all are.

Onyx wafted back toward the party, and the Lantern's beam caught him and gave him an amethyst outline before he dropped more altitude. Gen felt a surge of gratitude for Andraste, who did not outright give Amber the raven but made it possible for them to meet. Seeing Amber's pride as she held her arm aloft to the bird put a much-needed smile on Gen and fueled her forward. She looked back at the group, each bearing gifts from Andraste, and took a big breath.

The raven said, "Clear," and Gen nodded and began walking down the hill to the Inn. Her friends and her cousin fanned out on either side of her, and from above, they would have looked like a small army approaching the decrepit inn. Before they entered the Inn's shadow, Gen felt a sense of unease. She glanced over at Onyx, who Amber was trying to soothe, and the bird looked agitated.

"Do you want to fly up again?" she asked the bird.

"No," he answered. "Inside. Quick!"

Something shivered in the trees where they had just been moments before. Gen saw something dark and shapeless oozing down the hill toward them.

"Run!" she shouted. "Mira, open the door!"

"It's one of them!" hissed Phan, and Jas and Nyota both jerked their heads up to look and winced.

"Hurry," said Nyota.

Mira fumbled with the key, opened it, and then dropped it in nervousness. She looked at the ground between the bottom of the hill and where she stood.

"It's coming fast. Go!" she cried.

Everyone filed in except for her and Gen, and she reached down to get the key when a long, black tendril shot forward from the creature and slapped around her wrist.

"Mira!" shouted Gen.

Phan, who bolted back out the door, drew his dagger, and swiped at the thing, and the rest of its amorphous shape was approaching fast, but Phan sliced it just the same. It fell away. He seized Mira and jumped inside, and Gen slammed the door. Mira locked it, wincing, and they could hear something pound against the door, and a deep, eerie moan erupted from it.

"How good a seal is on this door?" Lyn asked.

"It's good," Gen gasped. "Get over here and help Mira."

Lyn hastened over and looked at her wrist. It blistered with sucker shapes, but the skin was otherwise unblemished. Mira was in pain, however, so Lyn moved his charmstone over her wound. Her shoulders relaxed.

The thing outside thumped against the door again and then suddenly quieted.

"Oh, Luna," Nyota said suddenly. "The doors and windows upstairs!"

Gen looked at everyone. "I don't know if that thing will figure out how to climb up and get in, but let's assume we're not safe in here. Get in the elevator, and we'll go down to the Source."

They hastened along, and Gen noted the light of the Source shining up through the door. The quickened heartbeat pattern unnerved her.

"I hate this," she muttered under her breath. Lyn glanced at her.

"You okay?" he asked, and she looked up at him.

"I don't know," she answered truthfully. He nodded.

"I'll do whatever I can to help," he said to her, and she knew he meant it, and she felt relieved.

With all of them in the elevator, it was more crowded than it had been, but not so tightly that they did not have room to move. Phan and Anisette promptly sat down, backs against the wall. Amber joined them while Dhatura, Nyota, and Lyn stood. Mira, Jas, and Gen huddled together.

Jas took hold of Mira's hand and inspected it. Lyn's charmstone work had kept the wound from festering, but Mira pulled a brave face. Gen could tell she was in pain. Jas took some of the salve Tam had mixed from Doc Bozzard's stores and dabbed it on Mira's skin. She hissed but tolerated it. Then he bandaged her carefully.

"You don't want to get any more of those things on you," he said, his face grim.

"Agreed," said Mira, gasping a bit. She breathed deeply as the salve did its job.

The elevator circled downward, and Gen thought of the encounter with Styx and wondered what they would face when that elevator door opened. She felt nauseous and took off a beverage globe to drink. She knew she was not dehydrated, though; she was nervous, not just for the unknowns that awaited them. She was nervous about seeing *him* and angry at herself that she felt that way. She also felt guilty that she was excited to see him again because he was so unlike anything she had ever experienced.

The elevator wound to a halt with a deep *thoom* and slid open. Gen turned to the Fireflies.

"I'm going ahead first," she told them, "and I want you to promise me that you'll get out of here if whatever we find is too much. It won't make you a coward. It'll make you live. And honestly, I just want you all to be okay. Got it?"

"Got it," murmured Lyn, and everyone else nodded.

Gen chewed on her lower lip, glanced sideways at her brother and cousin, and stepped out of the elevator.

The brilliant pulse of the huge Source shimmered in the great chamber of the cavern, and she could hear gasps and "No way!" from the friends who had not yet seen the thing.

Nyota looked especially excited, and she approached the Source. It put out warmth, but not unbearable heat and her staff's crystal responded by pulsing at the same frequency. She held the staff out to get the stone closer but did not touch the great light.

"It's incredible!" she exclaimed, her dark eyes reflecting the light and the purple lights in her hair shimmering from the Source's own purple cast. "What is it?"

Jas stood next to her, stared up at the thing, and said, "I think I'm right about it being a biphasic... object or force, I'm not sure which. It's both light and crystal, fluctuating between plasma and lattice."

Slow applause rang through the great space, and Gen whirled around to see Styx walking slowly toward them all. Her entire body went cold for one second, then flushed the next.

He slinked along in his dark, faceted suit, and she finally realized that he must have worn this for centuries to help him survive and recycle his own bodily fluids.

"Very good, Jas," he said in a lilting voice. "Hello," he then said, dipping his head to the rest of the Fireflies. Lyn glared at Styx, which made him smirk. Dhatura nodded politely.

Gen approached him, flanked by Nyota, Amber, Phan, and Anisette. She introduced them to him and said, "This is Styx. He is... from the past."

As Styx greeted them, Onyx flapped his wings, and Amber winced from his talons.

"Old!" croaked the raven. Styx laughed out loud.

"Bit harsh, feathered friend," he said. Then he sighed. "But you're right." Then he turned to Gen and said, "Come, I've found some other interesting things back in my vault."

She looked back uncertainly at her group, and they gave her looks of encouragement or, in Lyn and Phan's cases, skepticism. Jas kept his own expression neutral, and he kept glancing back at the Source. Gen thought, *Now we find out more about this guy*, and she followed him out of the chamber through the vault he'd emerged from.

It was a dimly lit hallway, its walls roughly hewn from rock, and several fallen pebbles and larger fragments gave evidence that the quakes had tested its integrity. That troubled her, but she focused more on avoiding tripping on those rocks than what might happen in any more quakes. The hallway twisted down and was dank and smelled acrid, like preservatives.

Everyone's light sources were activated; Nyota's staff, Lyn's headlamp, and so forth, and then Gen halted while Styx continued. Mira bumped into her and yelped.

"Sorry," Gen said, "but listen for a moment."

They all listened, and two distinct sounds met their ears: a heartbeat pulse from the Source reverberating down these tunnels and music. It was not music like Gen had ever heard before: its rhythm was choppy, and its vocals, warped by the Doppler effect of the twisting hallway, were harsh and garbled.

"Gen," a voice called from ahead, and she turned back to look ahead and found Styx silhouetted by a distant light source, his hair spiked, his form slim and dark. "Come on ahead, all of you. Sorry about the music. I realize it's out of date. I made myself a lot of playlists before... before I went to sleep."

Gen caught up with him, and she could hear more of the strange tunes. There was something chaotic and erratic about that "music," and she thought it was rather fitting for Styx himself. She did not know what to think of him or his music.

The humidity of the tunnel had increased, and she found it stifling, and the reek of chemicals tickled her nose. The air had become so moist, in fact, that whatever the source of the light ahead, it was obscured by fog or steam.

"Just a bit farther," Styx encouraged, and he held his hand out for Gen to take.

She heard a whisper, "Gen, don't," from behind her, and she knew it was Lyn. They were crowded in the narrow tunnels, and she fancied she could hear everyone else's heartbeats, or at least her own, and in tandem with the beat of the

Source far behind them yet echoing around them. She felt disoriented and dizzy. She took Styx's hand.

He pulled her through an open, metal doorway, and she saw then that it also had a wheel lock and was part of an entirely different sort of chamber, one with flickering lights and steam. She drew in her breath at what she saw.

All along the walls stood vertical capsules, dozens of them, or perhaps more, yet she could not tell. They stretched farther into this strange, sleek room, out of sight. Each capsule held... something. And that something was obscured in each one by what looked like steam.

Styx looked at her with glittering pale eyes, a wild excitement kindling in their depths, and he led her farther along.

"I hoped you'd come back down here tonight," he said, holding her gaze, and she felt as if her spirit were being pulled away from her body simply by its power. "Because I'm about to do something extraordinary. I'm about to wake him up."

He approached one of the capsules, taller than the others, with many blinking lights all around its edges and its contents hidden by mist. With his left hand, Styx gently pulled Gen forward. With his right hand, he began to press buttons.

"Gen," blurted Mira, "there's something wrong. Some of the other pods are already open."

Gen turned her head quickly to squint into the distance, but Styx took her face in his hands and said, "Hey, don't worry about that. This is the one that matters the most. And you get to be here for it!"

Lyn, Phan, Anisette, and Dhatura stepped forward to look at the other chambers. Styx kept his eyes on Gen, grinning, and the lights around the capsule before them began winking. A beeping sound startled everyone, and they all turned to see the lights flash more quickly.

Jas watched closely and said, "You're reviving some-one. It looks like those are vital readings?" he pointed at various numbers and levels on a small panel. Mira, Gen noticed, had leaned up against one of the unopened capsules to write something in her notebook.

"That's right," Styx said, still holding Gen in his sway.

"What is happening now?" Jas asked, pointing. "What are those pulses?"

Styx shrugged and said, "Muscle revivers."

A crack and hiss made them all jump. Mira almost fell as she sprang back: the chamber she had written against began to light up and beep.

Styx glared at her. "That was a bad idea," he said harsh-ly. "We don't want that one opening first."

"There are already others opened," Lyn said through gritted teeth, "so who was in those, and where are they?"

Styx shrugged again. "No idea. They were like that when I was awakened."

"So, who awakened you?" Nyota asked.

"Again," Styx said testily, "No idea."

Onyx squawked at that. "Monsters!" he hollered.

Styx burst out laughing. "That bird is quite the chara cter... Amber, was it?"

Amber stroked Onyx's back and fingered the necklace she wore, and she looked deeply suspicious now. Styx shook his head and returned to Gen and the capsule be-fore him.

Lyn began walking back toward them while looking ahead. Phan drew his dagger.

"Something's moving up ahead," Anisette said.

Styx snorted, looked annoyed, and grinned at Gen. "Your friends sure are jittery."

The capsule next to Mira hissed again, and she skipped back toward Amber and Nyota. The capsule opened like a door, and out something fell and slapped on the floor, hissing and steaming.

"God!" yelled Mira. "What is it?"

It was a blob of shining red, gray, and deep blue, and it spread out onto the floor and spasmed.

Styx's grin faded, and he looked stern.

"Damn," he said. "Don't think that one's going to make it."

Gen gasped, "What is it?"

Styx shook his head. "It was someone," he said, "but it looks like they've decayed."

"It's alive," Jas said in an urgent tone. "Can we help it?"

"Gen," Nyota said, thrusting her staff forward to point at the thing, "We need to get out of here."

"Um, Fireflies," Anisette called, "something is coming our way. I think it's not something we want."

Gen said, "Okay, everyone out," but Styx held her fast.

"Not yet! Hang tight. He'll sort out everything. Here he comes—"

And the capsule next to them exploded.

Shards of its cover flew in all directions. One struck Dhatura in the thigh, and she fell over screaming. Another flew toward Amber and Onyx, and the bird launched himself and pushed out with his talons to deflect the shard from striking Amber.

Gen could then hear whipping, snapping, slithering, and deep moaning sounds from the far reaches of the room, and she yelled, "Run back to the elevator!"

The blob on the floor then rose, slid quickly toward the tunnel back to the Source, and blocked the exit.

"Kill it!" cried Nyota.

"What!" yelled Styx. "That's a person, and besides—"

Everyone then went silent because something stepped out of the exploded capsule. It was a tall being wrapped in an obsidian-hued suit, its face covered with facets that made it look like a person made of black crystal. It stepped onto the floor, the steam of its capsule spilling around its ankles and joining the reeking clouds of the room.

Lyn ran forward to pull Gen away from Styx and this being when it caught him by his collar and held him up into the air. Then it hurled him across the room, and he struck a wall and collapsed.

"Lyn!" screamed Gen, and she rushed to him and knelt.

The being walked on long legs toward her and said in a resonant, powerful voice, "Stand!"

She turned back and looked up.

The being peeled off his black, crystalline face mask, layer by layer, starting at the neck and going upward.

Gen let out a wail of disbelief and horror.

"Dad?"

Skaarden

"You may live to see man-made horrors beyond your comprehension."
—— **Nikola Tesla**

Gen reeled, staring up at this man with her father's face, his eyes as dark and cutting as flint, and she gagged. Behind her, Mira and Amber scrambled to wrap Dhatura's leg. Nyota faced the blob at the door, and it rose taller and quivered; she stood prepared to stab it with her staff like a spear. Jas, who had knelt to help Lyn, jerked his head up at the word, "Dad."

He stood and rushed to Gen's side, and the man simply put his gloved hand out and struck Jas in the chest, sending him on his bottom. Styx watched Gen in fascination, and a flicker of confusion crossed his face as he looked between the man and her.

"You're not him, you're not my dad."

Cold and deep laughter rang from the man, and he stared into her eyes.

"Assuredly not," he hissed. "I am Skaarden."

Gen could not stop shaking. It was too uncanny, too horrible, and far too strange that his person should appear just when her father disappeared. She did not want to accept what was happening, and her own thoughts gaslit her for a terrible moment.

Is it actually Dad? She found herself wondering. *Did he get transformed? And he doesn't recognize me?* She felt so sick that her legs began to buckle, but she fought the urge to collapse.

"Who are you?" the man asked her. She stared at him. He narrowed his eyes. "Did Styx hire you?"

"Styx?" she asked, still not quite processing everything that was happening. Skaarden sniffed.

"If you're not here to help, you can get out of the way," he said coldly. He jerked off electrodes on his wrists and on his neck and tossed them onto the floor.

"This place is a mess," he said next, ignoring Jas and Lyn, and Gen glanced down at the electrodes and felt a spike of anger toward the man. "Where's the soak chamber?"

"The what?" Gen asked.

Skaarden turned to glare at her and said, "Are you stupid, girl? The soak chamber. With the stimulant solution. It should be right here."

The man knelt to examine the floor. There was an oval mark upon it that Gen had not noticed before.

"It *was* here," he muttered. "But it's been removed." He stood quickly and faced her, his sharp nose above her forehead, his sour breath gusting in his choppy speech. "Who did this? Tell me, or I'll cut you."

"I don't know!" Gen cried. "I don't know anything. Styx brought me here."

Skaarden sneered. "What did you call me, Dad? Nothing I could ever make would be as weak as you."

Gen recoiled for a moment, and then, looking at her brother and Lyn and Dhatura, she turned to Skaarden with a face purple in rage and shouted, "You could never be as strong or good as Dad. You hurt my friends!"

Skaarden lunged forward, but Styx danced in between him and Gen and said quickly, "Don't mind her, she was helping us."

"With what?" spat Skaarden, walking around and scowling at everyone. "All I see is a mess. What happened to Crockett?" and he gestured toward the door, where Nyota faced off the blob-creature.

"I—I don't know," stammered Styx.

Skaarden marched over and shoved Nyota out of the way, and she yelled, "Hey!" but he ignored her. He stared at the blob, which lowered before him and quivered.

"Disgusting," he growled, and he spat on it, and then plunged his fist into the mass and pulled out something deep red and bloody. He threw it on the floor. Gen felt bile rise in her throat: it was a heart. Skaarden raised his boot and squashed it under his heel. Amber fainted, and Onyx flapped his wings over her and croaked in alarm.

The blob stilled and melted all around Skaarden and Nyota's feet. She sprang away.

"Guys!" yelled Phan, facing the other direction, "we need to get out of there! Those things are back!"

And out of the dim light sprang black, whipping, tendrilled masses, five, six, ten of them, on the ceiling, on the walls, attaching to the other unopened capsules.

Skaarden bellowed, "Move!" to Phan and Anisette, and he faced the creatures. One looked coiled to spring.

Skaarden held his hands aloft and said, "Stand down."

Gen gasped.

Each of the creatures dropped down before Skaarden and sat on the floor as a group, quivering.

Gen glanced at Jas, making eye contact, and nodded toward the door where the blob had been. Jas slowly hoisted Lyn, and Phan dashed back to help carry the unconscious boy. Nyota awakened Amber with a small vial from her pack, and Mira helped her stand. Dhatura clung to Nyota then, the bandage on her thigh stained with blood. They moved slowly and intentionally toward the door while Skaarden faced the creatures.

"I see," he said in a long, stretched hiss, his long, dark, lank, greasy hair tossed back over his shoulder, his fierce eyebrows furrowed. "Styx," he said, looking at the boy, "it appears there has been a problem with some of the chambers. Did you know?"

Styx shook his head confidently. But Gen saw something that gave her some small consolation in all this: the boy's jaw twitched, and she could almost feel fear coming off him.

"I've... not seen this before. I'm not sure what we're looking at."

"It's my team," said Skaarden coldly. "Something has disrupted their integrity. The nanovirus altered their DNA somehow. Maybe an introduction of a foreign agent? I'll need to run tests. Put them back in their capsules, will you?"

Styx balked at that, and Skaarden jerked his head toward the boy and gripped his arm until Styx broke into a sweat and breathed heavily. Gen watched, horrified, just as her friends slinked back toward the exit.

"I—I am not sure I can—"

"Why not?" demanded Skaarden, clenching him further.

"They—they only answer to you, right?" Styx gasped desperately.

Skaarden tossed Styx's arm away casually. He stepped toward the horde of creatures and brought his hands together almost as if in some maniacal prayer. As Skaarden did so, Styx looked back at Gen and noticed her friends slipping past the dead blob one by one, with Jas and Phan awkwardly supporting Lyn between them. Styx gave Gen a very slow wink.

She took a breath. And, seeing that everyone else had got out of the vault, she looked back.

Skaarden raised his hands and said, "Back to your pods, friends."

The creatures jumped at lighting speed back among the other capsules to the ones opened at the far end of the room and into their pods.

"Good," Skaarden said silkily. "I can work with this."

Quaking with horror and nausea, and reeling from the man's similarity to Harris, Gen then walked backward, carefully, out the door and pulled it slowly shut. She turned the wheel, knowing it was not a lock but that it might slow Skaarden down.

Then she ran.

She ran as she had never run before in her life, and all but Jas, Phan, and Lyn had sprinted ahead and out to the final door with the wheel lock. She eased past the boys, darting ahead, and made sure the girls had all run toward the elevator as best they could. Once the boys were out of the hall, Jas joined her in shutting the door to that tunnel and turning its wheel as hard as he could.

Gen stopped for a moment and stared at the Source. It was pulsing faster still, like her own heart.

Once everyone was within the elevator, Gen watched its door closing, shutting off that light, and she felt sick. Up they slowly traveled, and she looked down at Lyn, unconscious, and wondered what they had all unleashed in the belly of the inn.

<h1 style="text-align:center">Afoot</h1>

The journey back to the Lightworth house strained every single Firefly, with Gen checking on everyone while feeling completely exhausted mentally and physically. Dhatura winced and limped on her injured leg as they advanced slowly up the hill. Phan and Jas carried Lyn between them, still unconscious, while Onyx kept an eye on things from high above in the deep cobalt sky.

Gen and Mira fell in step beside Jas.

"What do we tell Mom?" Gen asked quietly.

"That was so not your dad," Mira answered vehemently, her brow stern.

"Obviously," muttered Jas. "But it's uncanny."

"You don't...you don't think..." Gen began, and she did not want to utter what she felt, but knew she had to get it out: "Could he be our ancestor?"

Mira made a gagging motion.

"Oh, *Luna wept*," she groaned. "I hope not."

"Well, he wouldn't be yours, at least," Gen reminded her.

"Yes, okay, technically not? But I feel tangentially awful for you if he is," Mira replied.

Anisette slipped back to them and said, "So what do you think Bad Hair Dude is going to do next? I'm guessing he'll be pretty pissed off that we locked him in."

Gen grimaced, as she had been wondering the same.

"I don't think it'll take long for them to get out," she answered, feeling miserable.

"Nothing that guy does will be good," Jas said firmly.

Nobody denied that.

Reggie met them all outside the house and put her hands over her mouth at the sight of Lyn. She quickly opened the door and once again the couch was used as a makeshift hospital bed. Her mouth pursed to a razor thin line and her face looked flushed. Tam came from the kitchen with the medicines procured from Doc Bozzard.

Opening Lyn's eyes, Tam announced, "He's concussed. If he doesn't wake soon, we'll have to get him to the hospital. Either way he needs to be seen." She then examined Mira's wound, but it had improved enough that she felt satisfied.

"What happened this time?" Reggie demanded, and both Gen and Jas cringed. "I thought you were just going to stay overday at the inn, and now this? You're risking too much, and it needs to stop."

"But Mom, he—" began Gen.

"I don't want to hear it, Gentian!" snapped Reggie. "Jas, you're still recovering. You shouldn't have been carrying him."

"What was I suppose—" Jas started.

"Not one word," said Reggie, her tone deadly calm. Then she caught sight of Dhatura. "By Luna, what's happened? Tam, she needs cleaning up and bandaging."

With a long, frustrated, worried sigh, Reggie then said, "Okay. All right. Nyota?"

"Yes, ma'am?" the girl asked, her eyes gone round with alarm. She gripped her staff from anxiety.

Reggie said, "I want you to tell me exactly what happened in that inn. Every single thing. And after that, I want you to go home so you don't worry your family half to death."

Nyota swallowed and stammered out a summary of everything except for one detail: Skaarden's looks. Gen, Jas, and Mira looked at each other nervously.

Finally, Mira stood up and said, "There's something else you should know."

Reggie, having experienced shock upon shock from Nyota's account, closed her eyes for a moment. "Go ahead, Mira."

"Skaarden looks exactly like Uncle Harris," Mira told her.

Reggie blinked a few times, and looked at Gen and Jas. They looked at each other and back at her, and they nodded.

"I mean, not exactly, he's too tall, but Mom, his face," Gen said, voice shaking. "It's—it's too close to Dad. I mean, it's not Dad. But he's missing and...and I—I—" and finally she broke into tears. She was just so tired and worried and haunted by it all and missed her father so much. All of this was too much for her. She bent over and sobbed.

Reggie melted then, and sat between her and Jas, hugging them both.

"I'm sorry," she said, and the guilt in her voice rang in the silence of the room as the Fireflies looked on, and Lyn lay still. "I shouldn't have fussed. You've been through trauma. Let's just...focus on getting Lyn some help. And you can all rest here before going home."

"But what do we do now?" Gen asked her. "Skaarden won't stay down there. I know it."

Tam agreed. "He has that helper boy, Styx, who sounds smart for his years."

"He's actually ancient," Jas pointed out.

Tam sniffed. "A seventeen-year-old is a seventeen-year-old no matter *what* century it is."

Gen managed to giggle and thought for a moment it would have pleased Styx. Then she shook her head to try and toss the thought from her mind.

Lyn stirred just then and grunted. Gen rushed over to him and held his hand. He smelled like the sea, and she realized she had never noticed that about him before, but now that she had, she felt a surge of affection for him. He blinked and groaned and put his hands to his temples.

"Ohhh, ow," he muttered. Tam came over and helped him to sit up.

Phan finally relaxed and leaned back with his hands behind his head. "The dead awakens," he said. "Welcome back. Can we go home now?"

Anisette pointed to the door and said, "You can leave *anytime*."

Phan snorted and rose and bowed to Tam and Reggie.

"Tell us our plans for the next catastrophe when you get the chance," he said to Gen. He and Anisette left then.

Amber and Onyx made their way to the door, but not before she whispered to Gen, "Call me. I know we've got a big situation. If my father can help, let me know." Gen squeezed her hand and Onyx allowed her to stroke his beak.

Dhatura felt better after being bandaged, so Nyota offered to walk her home. Dhatura looked determined despite her injury.

"Gen, I'm ready for whatever you need."

Gen nodded in appreciation and said, "Hope you feel better soon."

With the crowd dwindled, Gen turned her focus back to Lyn. He drank water that Tam gave him and smiled at her.

"Glad you didn't stay behind," he said.

Gen stared at him. "Um, why would I have?"

Lyn shrugged. "Styx," he said simply.

Gen rolled her eyes. "I wasn't leaving my team behind with those monsters."

"So, you're not Team Styx anymore?" Lyn asked her, avoiding her gaze.

"Lyn," she said, heated, "I don't really know him. But he was alone until now and I don't think he's in a good place. You know? That Skaarden is cruel. Who knows how he's treating Styx?"

"They knew each other," Lyn pointed out. "So, Styx must've been okay working for him. What if that's his father?"

Gen shook her head. "No, I don't think so," she said, though she had no logical reason to feel certain about it. "I think we need to get Styx away from him."

"You're not going back to that inn," Reggie said firmly, "not for any reason at all! Look what's happened tonight? One of you concussed, another cut, and these...these monsters you're talking about, which it sounds like are the same things people have been seeing up north, and that the tunnels have been shut over?"

"Mom," said Gen, steeling herself, "you can't stop us from going back there. And I am not sure we will be any safer here with those things out in the world."

A chime at the door interrupted them, and Bloop waddled in, carrying a *Biolumen Pen* seed pod. Mira grabbed it, said, "Thanks!" and brought it over to the coffee table by the couch. She unfurled it with twitchy hands, her pointy eyebrows dancing as she pulled back the leaf-pages. The front page read: "MONSTERS AFOOT." Skimming below the headline, Mira murmured, "Oh no."

"What is it?" Gen asked.

Mira read aloud, "Mayhem erupted in the waning hours of the night as reports of monsters attacking homes, latching onto power sources and sending Glimmerbight residents indoors. This as the tunnels were recently secured..."

She set the page down and looked at Gen.

Gen said, "They didn't waste any time finding a way out. I wonder if they found a way *in*, to the inn. To the Source."

The Unveiling

As they sat pondering the unsettling news, Gen began to doze, but something woke her: a light flashing. She looked down and found that her firefly brooch was glowing in patterns. She took the thing off and held it in her palm.

"What do you think this means?" she asked aloud.

Mira and Jas leaned in to watch the blinking. Lyn said from the couch, where he now sat up fully, "Andraste."

"What?" asked Gen.

"I think she's messaging you," Lyn answered.

"Um," said Gen, rubbing her indigo bangs away from her forehead and blinking from fatigue, "how do I... message her back?"

She did not have to wait long. Pressing in on the flashing bulbs of the brooch projected a hologram in their room, sparkling and golden, with the tall figure of Andraste in her many drapes standing before them all.

"Gentian," she said, "the creatures have advanced upon the town openly. They seem to have come forth from the shafts near my Valley. Do you know if they have breached the Inn?"

Gen, amazed, stood and faced the shimmering image of Andraste and said, "I don't think so. We locked the door."

Andraste, her face expressionless, said, "That is good. I will converse with the mayor about sealing the city off, but those creatures endanger all of us. How many were there?"

"I'm not sure," and Gen glanced back at Jas and Mira, who shrugged. "A lot, maybe, and there's... there's a man. There are two men. Well, one of them is a teenager; he's okay."

Lyn groaned.

Ignoring him, Gen continued, "The other is a tall man, and he's violent. Terrible. They... they're from the past. They were... cryo-frozen? For centuries. It looked like there were a lot of other people frozen, but some of them had... what's the word?"

"Mutated," Jas offered. "And not intentionally. Like something went wrong with their chambers. Skaarden mentioned the nanovirus?"

"Skaarden," repeated Andraste, and the way she said it sent shivers all through Gen. The older woman closed her eyes and put her fingers to her lips. She opened her eyes and looked stern in a way Gen had not seen before. "That man cannot be allowed to reach the light in the Inn. Do you understand?"

"The Source?" Gen asked.

Andraste nodded. "Yes."

"Why?" Jas asked next.

Andraste sighed. She told them all, "I hoped, I planned... we all did... that this would never happen. I wonder if the decisions we made were incorrect after all. Skaarden and his group are from a time that did not respect life the way we do now. They chose to freeze themselves rather than stay accountable for the actions of their time. And now they are loose. Something triggered the... Source, as you call it, to generate the power that finally awoke them. It was not something we wanted to happen in this way. If Skaarden gains access to the Source, he can access unlimited power."

Gen could have dropped where she stood from the shock of it all.

"Styx knows," she said quietly. "He's seen the Source."

"Styx?" asked Andraste, her voice stern.

"He's the one who woke Skaarden. Young, like us. But I thought he was okay. He seemed... nice," Gen said, and she felt wretched. She saw Lyn shake his head out of the corner of her eye as if to say he had told her so.

Andraste let forth a rueful sigh. "Then Skaarden likely knows about the Source. Which means we are in far greater danger than I feared. I'll alert the mayor. We will need to seal off the city above and below, and I will help with that."

"Dad and Bendin and Doc Bozzard are all missing," said Gen. "Please don't make it so they can't come back!"

Andraste shook her head. "We have to ensure the safety of our city first and try to stop Skaarden from getting out into the world again."

"How do you know so much about him?" Mira asked.

Andraste turned to her and said, "Child, I was married to him."

Gen let out something between a gasp and a wail.

"What! How? You—you're not that old! Are you?" she cried.

Andraste looked downcast. "I am, Gentian Lightworth, *that old*. Oh, the regrets I have... he is worse than you can imagine, yet somehow it sounds that time has not helped him even while he slept.”

Reggie and Tam had stood at the revelation and looked at each other in alarm.

“Does he know you’re still alive?” Reggie asked.

“Dear Reggie, I hope that he finds out in the worst possible way for him,” Andraste said with a wry grin. “For now, we will keep that secret to ourselves. I trust each of you can do that?”

Gen and Mira nodded generously.

“Count on us,” Gen told her.

“I am,” Andraste said firmly. “Now, haste. I’ll alert the mayor. And Reggie, dear, as for Harris and the others, hold the faith and watch the skies. And let these Fireflies fly as they see fit. They might be the only wings of hope we have left at this point.”

With that, Andraste vanished, leaving the Lightworth residents stunned and silent for some time. This was broken by a plaintive mew from Smudge, and seeing the judgmental blinking of Sylvia, Reggie walked over to the dining room and fed both cats. She also retrieved her weapon, and Tam revealed the crossbow again.

“What do we do now?” Mira asked Gen.

Reggie shook her head and looked at her sister. Tam said, “You go to bed. No objections. Lyn, your parents are on their way. Rest. It’s almost dawn. We’ll figure all this out.”

“Together,” said Reggie, her voice hard.

Gen marveled at her mother and her aunt. “Together,” she agreed.

The Engineer

Reeling from everything that had happened and that they had just heard, Gen found it hard to go to sleep at dawn, and she fidgeted with anxiety about what might happen next. But eventually, she did fall asleep, and her dreams shifted between fitful and deeply disturbing. In the worst one, she heard her father's voice calling to her, and when she ran to look for him, she found Skaarden instead, grinning malevolently, his fists holding hearts that dripped with blood. He told her, "It's all Mira's fault, you know. She woke me up. Here, let Daddy hug you."

In the dream, Gen ran from Skaarden, found Mira, and shouted, "You got us into this!"

"You've got to be kidding me, Gen!" cried Mira. "All I did was go to the Ball!"

Even in the dream, Gen didn't care how the hot outrage in her felt. She wanted to hammer it, polish it, make it sharper, a blade of pure rage that might somehow make her feel better about all of this.

"You *broke the law*, Mira!" Gen hissed. "And you triggered something terrible!"

"I didn't do *any* of this!" Mira shouted back, her usually clear and composed face blotchy with fury. "I wasn't the one who gave me the spell that changed my age! How was I supposed to know that would set off... some end-of-the-world scenario? That's stupid. And you know it!"

Gen roared back, "This isn't fair!" she cried. "Why invite me to do this? I can't do any of it. I don't *want* to do any of it! Why would I be asked to? Why would he pick me? Anyone would be better; anyone would be smarter, be willing to be inside an inn all the time and never leave, like Bendin. I don't want this!"

Mira panted and put her hands on her hips. "I know you don't! But he saw something in you that you couldn't see for yourself, I guess."

Gen jerked awake, sweating.

She looked at Mira, who slept soundly, her bandaged wrist flung up toward the headboard, her thin face bearing a slight scowl, which was in many ways her default expression. Gen felt a surge of anger at her cousin and then felt badly for it. *Illicit magic.*

She looked at her nightstand, where her firefly brooch sat dormant and dark. She was tempted to use it to speak to Andraste, for she had so many questions without answers and so many fears unnamable. She checked the time. It was not yet dusk but getting close; the house shields were easing on the cooling as the punishing sun had dipped. Then she heard a commotion.

A series of muffled beeps rang out from the hallway. She swung her legs over her bed, seized her robe from its hook on her wall, quietly left the room, and shut the door behind her. She padded down the hall and listened to scuffling.

"Enough!" a man growled, and Gen heard indignant beeps. The housebots!

"We will contact the authorities for this intrusion!" one of the bots droned, and she heard a distinct yelp of pain.

"Stop attacking us!" another male voice said. "Will you let me in, you garbage pail with eyes!"

A crackling sound could be heard, and a separate yowl of pain rang out in the second man's voice.

Reggie shuffled out into the hallway, and Tam slinked behind her with the crossbow.

"Gen," whispered her mother, "what's going on? I got a perimeter alert!"

"Someone is outside the house!" Gen hissed. She stared at her aunt's crossbow with round and quite alert eyes. "The bots seem to have it under control. But what if it's Skaarden?"

"I dare that demon to set foot near your house," growled Aunt Tam.

The sounds of struggles, zaps, and profanity rang out. It sounded like an all-out attack by the bots. Smudge ran for the door and batted the handle, turned to look back at Gen, and meowed over and over.

"Smudge!" cried Gen. "Get back!"

Something slammed up against the door, and Gen felt sick... what if it were one of the creatures?

"Gen!" a voice said through the door. "Gen, is that you? Let us in!"

Tam said urgently, "The cameras are showing shapes, not faces, so we have no idea who it is. Don't answer it!"

Reggie ran forward. "Who is it?" she called through the door.

"Reggie!" said the voice.

Gen and Reggie looked at each other, and before anyone could stop her, Gen flung the door open and winced in pain at the dying sunlight. In fell two forms, one of them caught snugly in the grip of a housebot. They were cloaked in something, and Gen gasped. These were special cloaks, like the ones the Fireflies had worn into Moonbow Valley. She pulled at the diaphanous material.

"Dad!" she shrieked, and then, "Bendin!"

Reggie hastily pulled Bloop off Bendin and chided the bot before rolling it back outside. She slammed the door, locked it, and joined Gen in flinging her arms around Harris, who looked haggard, disheveled, and gray but also relieved and grateful. His spectacles were gone, and for a fleeting moment, Gen felt a chill, thinking of Skaarden and her nightmare.

Bendin wheezed and shook, so Tam helped him to the couch. The old gentleman coughed and looked nearly cadavcrous.

Jas and Mira spilled into the hallway, looking aggrieved at their rude awakening, but Jas quickly jolted himself awake at the sight of his father. It was a reunion of tears, shock, and more questions than Harris could answer. Mira brought him and Bendin water, and then dusk settled over the land. The curtains and shades of the home opened, and the breeze outside set the berry-lights bobbing pleasantly.

"Oh, I'm so glad to see you," Harris said in a shaky voice, tears flowing from his eyes. This comforted Gen even as it saddened her, for she could not imagine someone like Skaarden in tears like her beloved father. "I'm sorry, I'm so sorry. I know you must have been so worried."

"Harris, where *were* you?" Reggie asked him, her left hand entwined with his right hand as he held onto both Gen and Jas with his left arm. Reggie's voice quaked, full of anguish and fear she'd felt, and she let her own tears spill down her cheeks.

Harris released his children long enough to accept water from Mira, and he drank it greedily and leaned back for a moment, his cheeks wet and hollow. Gen felt a stab of worry for him. He did not look well.

"You might want Bendin to answer that for you when he feels up to it," her father said.

Bendin, meanwhile, huddled under a throw blanket he had pulled from the back of the couch. He looked lost in thought but focused on Harris at the sound of his name.

"Dear friend," he said in a rasping voice, which had lost some of the dynamism Gen had first heard, "that is a long telling. But Reggie, Gen, and Jas, I do apologize. We did not mean to be away so long or for such chaotic reasons."

Tam said sharply, "You've been injured!" She gently pulled his arms away from his chest. His shirt was soaked with dried blood, and Gen then noticed his sleeves were too. She thought back to the blood she and the Fireflies had seen at the Inn.

"It's okay, dear Tam, I'm fine," said Bendin, and then he coughed deeply for a few minutes.

"I'm getting you some tea," Tam insisted, and she hurried to the kitchen.

Bendin recovered from his spasm and looked at the Lightworth family, reunited at last.

"You may recall there was an earthquake," he said weakly.

"Lots of them," Jas replied.

"Yes, unfortunately for us," Bendin agreed with a tired smile. "That was part of a grand mal series of catastrophes, for lack of a better description. We had plans to stop what we—I—feared was coming. It did not go well."

"Do you mean what you and Andraste thought was coming?" Gen asked him.

That startled the old man, and he stared at her with a dawning horror.

"Tell me, child," he said quickly, "what has happened."

Gen looked at Jas and Mira, and they both nodded.

"Skaarden," said Gen.

It was a clap of thunder in the form of a name.

Bendin and Harris both cried, "No!" Bendin pushed his fists into his eyes.

"We failed," whispered Harris.

Gen felt adrenaline shoot through her body in spikes, and she stood up.

"No," she said. "No, you didn't. Nobody's failed. We're fighting him."

"Gen," said her father, "you have no idea—"

"Actually, I've met him," said Gen. "We all did, the Fireflies, I mean. So, we have a very good idea," and more tears stung her eyes. "He... he looks like *you*, Dad."

Harris looked at her with mouth agape, and then he turned to Bendin, who kept his eyes downcast.

"Tell me this isn't so," he asked Bendin. Bendin shook his head and sighed. "Why... why would he look like *me*?"

Bendin did not answer, instead saying, "If we are to save our land from that monster, you need to know what we're truly up against, Gen, Jas, and Mira."

"First," Reggie said in a voice laced with all the anguish of the past several days, "tell us where you were and why my husband couldn't be with us. We've been scared to death, and what with the attacks and the monsters, and now this—this Skaarden person? Just. Tell me. *Tell me!*"

Harris stroked her cheeks and kissed her. They held each other, touching foreheads for a long moment as they wept softly.

Bendin cleared his throat, and the room fell silent.

"I knew something had happened after Mira used Doc Bozzard's little age-defying magic trick for the Glowworm Ball," he began.

Mira closed her eyes and whispered, "Great."

Bendin continued, "It seems that trickery by Bozzard triggered a chain reaction, destabilizing multiple levels of redundancy we had worked hard to maintain for a long time."

"Centuries," murmured Gen, and Harris gazed at her in awe.

"Quite," Bendin said. He went on, "I knew only Bozzard could have done this. Since Bozzard had a hand in these events, I reached out to him for help. He didn't answer. So, I sent the invitation to you, Gen, as quickly as I could because I knew I would need to act away from the Inn, and it needed protection by someone I could trust. I also invited your father, separately and secretly, so that no one would know. I couldn't risk you knowing, Gen, Jas, and Reggie, just in case the worst scenario unfolded and Skaarden was awakened. That happened, but thankfully it appears he didn't know what we were up to. You see, I have a laboratory."

"In the Inn?" Gen asked loudly. "We didn't see a lab!"

"We checked a lot of rooms," Mira interjected.

"I'm glad you got the key, the pen, and the dosimeter," Bendin said, managing a smile at the three teens. "And trust me, Mira, you didn't see every room in the Hotel Lembrar." His eyes sparkled a bit then, and Gen and Mira looked at each other in surprise. "However, the laboratory is not in the Inn! It is in the Lantern."

Jas and Gen gasped.

"You've had a lab in the lighthouse this whole time?" Jas demanded.

"I have," Bendin answered. "Another level of redundancy, hoping no one would come looking for it. So, I invited your father to help me there, given his engineering skills and other attributes. The earthquakes, however, did not work in our favor, and we were trapped deep in the Lantern with no way out. The... system we were working on needed an important facet, and it was in the Inn; I had thought we might be able to come and go quietly, but I was injured in the quake and then worried that the light might be at risk, so I went back to the Inn to check on things. And to make sure you had what you needed. I made it back to the lab, and another quake wrecked our only way out."

"So, when you came back to the Inn, that's when you were bleeding?" Mira asked.

"Yes," said Bendin, coughing again. "I'm sorry to have worried you about either of us. It wasn't the best idea, going back injured, and then hearing the news about strange things crawling around out and about... something I had hoped would never happen, but we did anticipate it, long ago."

"What do you mean?" Gen asked.

Tam gave Bendin a special spiced tea, which he held under his nose to breathe in its steam.

"What I mean, dear Gen," Bendin answered, "is that, long ago, Andraste, Doc Bozzard, and I were part of a special group. We all worked together to protect the community of Glimmerbight in the event Skaarden and his team returned. We used our pooled technical knowledge to preserve our lives via both the Source in the Inn, in my case, natural mysticism for Andraste, and biotech prowess for Doc Bozzard.

"We helped each other out over centuries to stay alive and foster a new culture to survive after the Dawn of Dusk. Andraste knew that something had gone awry in the cryo chambers, and she had worried it would contaminate everyone, so she made dosimeters. Over time many of these were lost, but the last remaining one she kept and gave to your brother."

Jas brought forth the device and opened it. Bendin's mouth turned down.

"I see," he said, sighing, "that you've been exposed to one of those things."

"What does this mean for Jas?" Reggie asked as she and Harris looked worryingly at their tall son.

"I don't know what this secondary or tertiary contact will do to Jas, truthfully," Bendin answered. "Doc Bozzard would know better than anyone, and it would seem he's not around to tell us."

"Um," interrupted Jas, "he might be. I think... I think we saw him. I'm not sure, but... maybe. And he gassed us!"

Bendin jerked his head toward Jas and exclaimed, "What do you mean, he *gassed* you?"

Jas recounted the night they had gone to Doc's apothecary, and Bendin's face wrinkled into a peculiar configuration that grew increasingly red.

He's furious! thought Gen.

"What has he been doing?" Bendin asked, more to himself than to the group.

"I can't believe he would gas you!" cried Harris.

"I couldn't either," Mira said, her voice sad. "He gave me so much joy for the Ball!"

Tam said in a growl, "He'd better not cross my path again. I feel so betrayed by him. All of that dressed up as a favor to the family!"

"Ah," said Bendin. "Ah, yes, now I think I see it. Oh, how did we not foresee this? But how could we, then... he worked so hard to cultivate his image over the years. You all thought of him as this eccentric but kind doctor, yes?"

"Of course!" said Tam. "He was... well, I thought he was a friend."

"Oh, dear Tam," said Bendin sadly, "he used you. He used all of you, and me, and Andraste... all to set things in motion, I fear, for the very thing we had worked so hard to prevent: the coming of Skaarden. As for why? I can't imagine. All this time. An utter betrayal of everything we built. Of this beautiful town, of the Inn, of the Lantern... and now I wonder, what else did he set in motion? Oh, this wounds me. It wounds me deeply."

Gen looked at Bendin in alarm, for he seemed as though he might crumple up and die on the spot. Tam put her arm around him, urging him to drink his tea.

"So, it's not my fault after all," Mira breathed.

Gen jumped and glanced guiltily at Mira.

"I heard you," her cousin said. "You were dreaming," and Mira's eyes watered, "but I know you were telling me the truth about how you felt."

"I'm sorry," Gen gasped. "I'm so sorry."

Mira shook the tears from her eyes and said, "It doesn't matter. But there's something I do want to know. Uncle Harris, how did you and Bendin get out of the Lantern and get back to us? You could have been killed at any point!"

"Well, for that, Mira," said Bendin, "we can thank one Mr. Celestus, who has just returned from Umbradene!"

"Dad's home!" cried Mira. "Where is he?"

"Hopefully, showering at your house," Harris answered. Tam and Mira gathered their things and headed for the door.

"Be careful out there," Bendin cautioned. "The creatures you encountered underground are in various forms of metamorphosis, if my guess is correct."

"I think Doc is, too," Jas said grimly.

Bendin looked at the ceiling and groaned. "If so, we really are in greater danger than I thought."

The Bubble

Gen messaged the other Fireflies to see how they were doing and update them all about her father and Bendin. She exhaled with relief after speaking to Lyn, although his mother fussed in the background, and he had to go.

"Let me know when you need me," he whispered quickly to her holographic image, followed by, "Be right there, Mom!"

Even in her tired, emotionally overwhelmed state, she felt the urge to do more than sit around. She dressed for the night and fastened her firefly brooch below her throat. Her father passed by her room in the hallway, and he halted when he saw her adjust her cap over her indigo bob hairdo.

"Look at you!" he said from the doorway, smiling. He now wore a spare pair of spectacles, and she was glad he did, because it helped set him apart from Skaarden. His gentle demeanor did as well. Still, she felt traumatized by what she had seen and worried about what was to come.

"I'm gone for a little while, and I come back, and you've taken charge of the world," Harris teased.

Gen snorted. "Not really. I wouldn't want that job!"

Harris folded his arms and nodded. "Maybe you don't, but someone else does."

Gen put her hand over her brooch and then walked to her father to hug him.

"We were so worried about you, Dad," she said, and for a moment, her voice broke into a higher pitch as if she were a young girl again. "Why did you have to be in that lab? What was so important about it?"

Harris put his arm around Gen and smiled at her. "I'm the luckiest dad there is, with you and Jas working so hard and fighting monsters! It's because I'm your dad that I wanted to help Bendin, and I wish I could tell you everything we were working on, but we have to keep it secret for now. It's a... Well, I guess it's a last-ditch effort to get something to work in case we need it. And Gen, I really hope we don't."

Gen did not like the sound of that at all.

"Please don't go back there," she pleaded.

Harris put his hand on her cheek and said, "My sweet Gen, I can't promise that. We aren't finished. And I think our work is more important than ever. We're recovering from the ordeal, but we will have to go back, and soon, by the looks of things."

Gen held her father's hand against her cheek and closed her eyes.

"Please be careful," she said.

"I will, but promise me you will be as well," Harris replied. "Because I know you're going back out there, and I won't stop you. You have the tenacity of your mother."

Gen grinned. "And I have the stubbornness of my father."

"Touché," laughed Harris. "Oh! Sounds like your posse has arrived. I hear the housebots fussing and what sounds like some proper teenage swearing."

Gen laughed out loud. "That'll be Anisette and Phan, no doubt."

She was right, and after they burst in from the night air, redolent of jasmine, Anisette said, "Gen, I swear to Luna I'm gonna punt the small bot straight to the moon one of these nights."

"Ornery turd," agreed Phan. And then he saw Harris and Bendin and raised his arms up, then brought them down into a prayer pose. "Gents! Glad you're alive."

Harris chuckled and came forward to shake Phan's hand. Bendin stood haltingly and dipped his head at the boy.

"What have you got in store for us tonight, boss lady?" Anisette asked, lifting herself up and down on her toes.

"Wow, you're dressed for aggression!" Gen laughed, for Anisette bore earrings that mixed metallic lightning bolts and antique spark plugs, and around her neck, she had wrapped a spiked choker, as well as the long cord bearing the red gemstone conch shell from Andraste. She wore a violently bright yellow tank top, baggy black pants, and combat boots that she had rigged spikes on their toes.

Phan, in turn, wore a bright green T-shirt with large black letters that said, "EAT THIS!", gray cargo pants, and a holster around his waist; Gen could see the hilt of the dagger from Andraste peeking out of it. He seemed very relaxed and bopped to some music in his head, but that was a default mode for Phan. Gen loved him for it, too.

Nyota arrived next, after giving the bots a few choice words and a chiding tap from her staff. She walked in clad in silver and purple, her purple-tinged hair coiled high on her head, and she looked statuesque and confident. Her wounds had healed well but still shone, and she showed them defiantly through a sleeveless tunic. The red gem at the tip of her staff flashed from time to time, and it caught Bendin's eye.

"Ah," he said enthusiastically, "a fine choice by Andraste! I trust it helped you inside the Inn?"

Nyota bowed and said, "It did. I am glad you are well, Bendin. We found your library, by the way!"

Bendin's eyes shone from delight, and he clapped his hands together. "Brava! I hoped you would."

They all heard the shout, "Honestly!" that heralded Mira's arrival. She entered the house in what Gen could only describe as chic, asymmetrical athleisure via safari gear, down to a safari hat turned up on one side. She wore a small, black messenger bag slung across her body, and on her right wrist, a bracelet full of keys jangled. She put her left hand on her hip and rolled her eyes.

"Call off the bots, will you, Gen?" she said sarcastically. Then she jumped; Lyn walked in behind her.

"I find," he said, running his hand through his fiery hair, "that if you treat the bots nicely, they'll let you pass."

Gen rushed forward and hugged him fiercely. "They're set to let you in any time," she said into his shoulder, breathing in his sea-scent and feeling the comfort of his strong arms. "I'm so glad you're better."

"A little bump on the head couldn't keep me away," Lyn said, his aqua eyes holding her gaze just long enough that she shivered and looked away from him, blushing.

"Dhatura!" she exclaimed, and she watched as the elegant girl strode in, the sash across her body gleaming gold, inset with crescent moons embroidered in teal to match her pantsuit. Her copper peacock brooch sparkled on her sashed shoulder. She tossed back her thick, dark waves, cast her eyes about the room, and finally faced Bendin.

Suddenly her hands began to shake, and she held them tightly to still them.

"Hello," she said to him. "I'm Dhatura Lal."

Bendin regarded her with such a fascinating expression that Gen felt enthralled. It was as if the air itself had changed, and Bendin looked at the girl across a gulf impenetrably deep.

"Ah," said Bendin softly, "so you are."

Gen and Mira looked at each other fleetingly, and then Mira turned away from them.

Gen knew her cousin was scribbling in her notebook as fast as her deft fingers allowed.

Bendin strode forward to take the girl's trembling hands into his, and Gen saw Dhatura's eyes glistening. Bendin then looked at Gen and gestured for her to come forth.

"Dhatura," he said carefully, "I invited Gen here to take over the Inn and not you, not because I didn't think you could handle the job. Quite the opposite. And in many ways, it will take more than one person, for that was my failing: thinking I could go alone for so long. It's that... well, you're family, and while that makes you an heiress, it also means I must look out for you in other ways. You are the only family I have left, after all."

Dhatura nodded and wiped her eyes.

"Come, Dhatura, let us speak privately," Bendin said, and the two stepped outside.

As they did so, the shadow of a certain raven spiraled down above their heads, and up the lane walked Amber, wearing both black and white: her signature white fashion, of the highest couture, yet functional, in white leggings and jumper, with black riding boots, the black iridescent raven feather necklace, and her hair pushed partially back with a black headband.

Bendin greeted her, and his eyes opened wide with the thrill of watching Onyx land on Amber's shoulder. He grasped his hands together and smiled broadly.

"Ah! Well, this is rather perfect," he said. "Well met, Amber Glistenad! Your father Göran has been a great help to me over the years."

The blonde looked surprised. "Really? He's never mentioned you."

"As I said," Bendin said coyly, "he's been a great help."

Amber and Onyx walked into the Lightworth home, with the girl feeling quite unmoored for a moment. Onyx fluffed her hair a little, and she straightened.

"We're all here," Gen said, hugging Amber. "You okay?"

Amber blinked and said, "Yes. I just... it feels odd to learn things about your family you didn't expect."

Gen nodded vigorously. "Tell me about it!"

Dhatura reentered the house then, and Gen could not decipher the odd look upon the girl's face. *Is she upset?* She did not make eye contact with Gen. Bendin then followed, and nothing on his face revealed anything to Gen at all.

Grownups are good for hiding things, she thought.

Gen readied herself to address the Fireflies, which she still did not feel at ease doing, and frankly she would rather have just taken a nap, but she knew that there would be no naps in her near future if she didn't rally everyone to help stop Skaarden. And she still had no idea how they could. Then the bots' alarms went off.

"What now?" cried Reggie, exasperated. Then she looked sheepishly at the teens gathered in her house. "Not you, of course. It's just... it's been quite a week."

"No one can blame you for that, Mrs. L!" said Phan.

Bloop opened the door and waddled in, with a fresh *Biolumen Pen* pod on the top of its dome. It leaned over and the pod rolled out into the floor.

"Paper's here," said Bloop, and Gen could swear the bot spoke in a disgruntled voice. It waddled back toward the door to rejoin its companions in the yard.

"Bloop," said Gen testily, "can you dial it back on the security?"

The robot swiveled back around, its red eye flashing, and said balefully, "No." And off it went into the night again.

Bendin reached down for the *Biolumen* and the first page unfurled. He read aloud to the group, "SHIELD GOES INTO EFFECT AT MIDNIGHT," and then everyone's eyes darted to the clock in the dining room, its shining golden moon-dials and whirring silver gears ticking along, with a secondhand whirring, the hour hand nearly at twelve, and the minute hand inching closer. Bendin read on, " 'The Mayor of Glimmerbight announced a collaboration with the Lunadatrix Andraste to erect a sphere of shielding both above and below ground to contain the current threat. Authorities raced to determine the cause of the invasion'..." He stopped then, and the clock chimed.

"Outside," he said to them all, and they spilled out of the house to watch something extraordinary.

A shimmering, oil-slick-like film slid above their heads in the sky, and the earth trembled a moment, but not as strongly as in the recent earthquakes. Gen could still see the stars, but they were fuzzy with the shield. Her firefly brooch began blinking. She touched it, and the image of Andraste appeared before them all, in a shimmering, gold-tinged hologram.

She wore saffron and emerald garments, with many bangles swaying on her arms. Her hair curled and tangled in silver, gold, and copper masses, tamed only by the crescent moon crown that matched her extraordinary necklace.

"Bendin!" she said, and she smiled. Bendin walked forward to face her image, which was life-size. She was as tall as he, though both were bent from age; Bendin more so.

"My dear Andraste!" he replied. "It has been too long. And I know the night grows short. The shield is quite impressive." He gestured to the skies.

Andraste lowered her head for a moment, then looked up, "Nothing will stop Skaarden in the long run, I fear," she said. "But we can slow him down. I've erected the shield, with the mayor's blessing, to extend beyond the ventilation shafts to the bunkers. But I fear some of the... creatures may already have escaped. It's clear they're under his command now, given their escalation in the past twenty-four hours."

"We tried," Bendin murmured.

"We did, my friend," Andraste agreed. "But the man's greed knows no bounds. And he can break through my bubble if he accesses the Lantern's light."

"The Source?" asked Gen. "What exactly is it, and what can it do?"

Bendin and Andraste looked at each other, and he took a deep breath.

"I've been building the... Source, which is a much shorter name than the one I originally chose, ages ago... for, now, hundreds of years. I meant for it to provide unlimited energy and did not know how large I could make it, for it began quite small, you see. I grew it over time, adjusted it, and watched it become something remarkable. Something that could serve as both a power source and a conduit."

"A conduit for what?" Jas asked. "It's a frustrated system, isn't it?"

Bendin laughed. "Ah, yes, my young physicist. And it frustrated *me*! But I got it to work better than I could have imagined and crafted a way to use it for various tasks, one of which your father and I attempted to wrangle into something resembling functionality in the lighthouse. The configuration of the Lantern is quite unique."

"Did you build it?" Nyota asked.

"I did not," Bendin replied. "In fact, no one still alive knows who did, and its records are older than that of the Inn, and quite incomplete. It's almost as if whoever built it knew it might provide a greater purpose than simply guiding ships in at sea..."

He looked lost for a moment, his face swimming in the memories of an ancient shore.

A blaring horn echoed across the village just then, and they all jumped.

Andraste said, "That's a siren meaning there's been an attack. It's time for you to go to the Inn, fortify it, and wait. He's coming. Let us pray he's not already there."

"If he is," Bendin replied, "I've added one last layer of redundancy so he can't use that Source."

"I pray that it works, Bendin," Andraste said, her hands clasped against her chest.

"As do I," he said.

Bendin turned to Gen. "Do you have your pens?" he asked her.

Confused, Gen thought for a second, then she dashed back inside her bedroom. She found the special pens he had left for her in the Inn and put them in her pocket.

"Got 'em," she told him, emerging from the house.

Andraste addressed them, "Fireflies, the moment has come for you to shine. Remember your gifts. And I'm not talking about just those I gave you. Gen chose well. Fight for your home."

She vanished then, and a sense of doom spread upon them without her guiding golden light. Still, looking up at the sky, her work remained, giving Gen courage.

Bendin said to her, "Your father and I must return to finish our work at the Lantern."

Reggie let forth an exhalation of alarm, and Harris squeezed her hand and looked deeply into her eyes. "Guard our home your way," he said to her, "and I'll do it my way." She kissed him.

"What now?" called Dhatura.

Gen turned to them all, glancing at Bendin first, who nodded.

"We fight," she said.

In Too Deep

The procession to the Inn felt unnerving to Gen, with the strange sky from Andraste's shield causing a bit of bounce-back from the Amethyst Lantern's light as it still penetrated the thin layer. The siren, mercifully, had stopped by 1 AM, and that left them four hours before the light of dawn would impede upon the night that she loved so dearly and needed to survive. Amber let Onyx fly ahead of them to check for anything unusual. When he returned calmly, Gen relaxed a little. She and Jas hugged Harris on the hill overlooking the Inn. Harris and Bendin made their way down a separate path along the bluff, past the Inn, toward the white and purple-striped Lantern, and then beyond it out of sight.

She listened to the nonstop banter of Phan and Anisette absently, to distract her from her sense of dread.

"What are we going to find in there?" she muttered, and Jas answered, "Nothing fun, but it's bound to be interesting."

"Oh, you would think that," sniffed Gen.

Jas shrugged. "The Source is an engineering marvel. I'm in my element."

"I hope not too much that you get distracted," she said, biting her lip.

"I sort of wish that was all I was," Jas admitted. They gently nudged each other with their elbows in solidarity.

Approaching the Inn, Gen was relieved to see no monsters at the door, but everyone swiveled around to check behind them to ensure nothing was coming. It seemed unusually still, a windless night, the moon waning and obscured not only by the slight film of Andraste's shield but also by high clouds. Shadows were muted, and the stars were no more than smudges in the sky.

"Mira," Gen called softly, and her cousin made her way to the door and turned the lock.

"I hope there's no one inside," murmured Mira.

"You and me both," answered Gen.

The great rotunda of the dark inn welcomed them like a gaping mouth, and Gen felt that keen sensation that the Inn was not a structure but rather a creature. There pulsed its heart through the translucent floor: the white-purple light of the Source, which she now knew remotely powered the Lantern somehow. Nyota's staff gem glowed like a drop of blood, and Gen shuddered.

I hope nobody spills any *blood tonight.*

With the unwelcome mantle of leadership on her again, Gen spoke quietly to them all.

"Phan, Lyn, I want you to guard the elevator. Anisette, Amber, and Onyx, please keep an eye on the upper floors. Nyota and Dhatura, guard the door. Mira, Jas, come with me."

"And where are you going?" Lyn asked her.

"Below," she answered, evading his eyes.

"You need more people!" exclaimed Nyota.

"Not yet," said Gen, "I just want us three to look down there and see what we see. We'll head right back up at the first sign of trouble."

She felt a pang of guilt, for that was a lie. By the looks on everyone's faces, they all knew it, too.

"Yeah, good luck with *that*," Anisette said, drawing her mouth into a cringing, fake smile.

"Stations, please," said Gen then, and they all dispersed, with Phan and Lyn following her, Mira, and Jas to the elevator.

"Do *not* try to do this by yourself," Lyn cautioned her. "Promise me you won't, Gen."

Gen continued to avoid looking him in the eye.

"Gen, I—"

"No," said Gen suddenly. "Stop. I need you to guard this elevator. That's all I need from you right now."

Lyn sighed. "Fine," and he turned away from her to stand to the left of the door, while Phan stood to the right.

Gen swallowed and clenched her fists.

Why does Lyn have to be this way?

She, Jas, and Mira entered the great elevator and Jas worked the hidden buttons, looking through his infrared scopes to find them.

"You ready, cousins?" Mira asked them.

"Not really," admitted Gen.

"Same," Jas said, "but we're doing this, so."

"Yeah," said Mira, and the mood turned grim.

The scraping and disorienting movement of the elevator's long, corkscrew descent set them on edge. Gen felt queasy. Mira paced back and forth, and Jas fidgeted with his dosimeter, flipping it open and shutting it repeatedly until Gen marched over and closed her hand over the thing, glaring at her brother.

At last, the great elevator whined to a halt. The three cousins were pacing by that point, looking at each other and nodding in tandem. The door slid open, and they stepped out into a thick mist.

"Oh, I don't like this," Mira whispered. The three of them crowded together. The mist obscured the Source, making a bright, pulsating colloid so they could not see it at first. They walked toward it, though, and Gen could hear dripping sounds coming from somewhere in the immense chamber.

As Gen approached the great Source, she could hear something shuffling, and the cousins smashed into each other, back-to-back, Jas holding his knife. Footsteps rang through the fog-muffled vastness. A dark shape emerged from the mist. It was Styx.

"I'm glad you're back," he said, walking closer to her.

"Stay back," Jas warned.

Styx laughed. "That's not going to get you very far, bro. You've seen those things, haven't you?"

"Styx," said Gen urgently, "Skaarden's terrible," she whispered. "How can you follow him?"

He considered her and stepped forward, staring down at her, his large eyes filling her vision, and he took her hands in his.

"I don't know what else to do."

"I'll tell you what to do," she found herself saying vehemently. "Get away from him. Come with *us*. You need us to live. You don't need to fight us. Please!"

"Gen, if I do, it'll only threaten you more," Styx replied. "Skaarden knows what he wants. He's going to take tech he's made and whatever this mutation has become, and he's going to take your town. Then he's going to see what's outside this place and go out into the world."

She shook her head. "No. I'm sorry, but that's stupid. You know that, right? He already wants us all gone. Look at what he did in that chamber. You don't have anything to lose by coming with me, and only to gain. And either way, I'm fighting him. I don't know what I can do. But I'm going to find out, and I'm going to do whatever I can. This is my *home*. And you can't go back. So. It's your home now, too."

Styx took her face in his hands once again, and she placed her smaller, dirtier hands on his, and they stood there. Gen's heart galloped in her chest, and she could smell him, his sweat, his smolder, some essential scent she did not understand. But it was powerful. She knew that. He was out of time and out of his element, but he was also more fully confident than anyone she had ever known. More alive, more elemental. Just *more*. She leaned in...

An alarm blared, and she jerked, and Styx released her. They stared at each other and then up at the pulsating Source in the chamber.

"What is that?" she wondered, covering her ears.

"I'd say it's more," Styx said, his eyes half-lidded.

"More of what?" she asked.

"More of us, waking up. Gen, I didn't tell you, but—"

A waft of air met them, and they both froze. The fog dissipated. The air in the chamber smelled of a burning, preservative chemical that both tickled Gen's nose and made her throat contract.

"You don't need to tell her anything else," a low voice hissed.

The dim lights in the chamber went out, and in the absolute darkness, Gen swallowed, tasting salt from bile rising in her throat. Gen had never feared the darkness before. But now she did. She felt a hand reach for hers. She heard a scuffing sound of shoes from a long gait, and she could just pick up Styx breathing faster. They turned, and there stood Skaarden, his silhouette edged in red.

Regards

"Hello, moon children," Skaarden said in a low sing-song voice that made Gen's skin crawl. "Interesting world you've built for yourselves out there, I must say. Everything at night. Very charming. So very weak!"

"We're not weak," spat Mira. "You are. You buried yourself rather than face reality!"

He laughed, "Is that what that liar Bendin told you? Fake news. You're puppets, girl." He paced back and forth in front of them, observing the great Source stretching above and out of sight with bottomless, dark eyes glinting with greed and hunger.

"You held out on me, boy," he said to Styx.

Styx shrugged, belying the fear that Gen had seen in his eyes. "To be fair, I didn't know what I was looking at."

"Power," Skaarden stated. "Power that apparently sustained us for, what... five hundred some years? We can thank Bendin for that part, anyway. But he decided not to wake us. He decided to let nature and biotech take their course. He *experimented on us*."

"He did no such thing," gasped Gen.

Skaarden marched up to her, and Jas jumped in front of her, but Skaarden laughed at him.

"What good is that little toothpick going to do, boy?" he asked. He clapped his hands slowly: one, two, three claps.

Amorphous shapes clustered behind him in the shadow.

Gen's heart pounded in her ears.

"What good's a knife against *my* team?" Skaarden taunted.

Out from the shadows shot a long tendril, which looped around Jas's ankle and yanked, throwing him onto his back on the floor with an "Ungh!"

"Enough for now," commanded Skaarden, and the tendril sprang back into the darkness. Taller shapes walked up immediately behind the man, and they looked, from a distance, mostly human. But not completely.

Gen could see a few of them were indeed still people, but the others were in various states of metamorphosis, some of those bulging with too-large muscles, or bent too low or otherwise warped in some way, and still others were the black, quivering, tentacled creatures like those that had attacked the Fireflies near Moonbow Valley.

Skaarden towered over the three cousins, a formidable man in height alone, at least six-feet-five, taller than tall Jas. Gen and Mira helped Jas to sit up, and they stood to face the man and his strange group. The more humanoid members dressed in the faceted and tubed black outfits that he and Styx wore. Skaarden had black wrappings around his arms and chest as well and an insignia Gen could not quite make out.

"There was only one way out," Skaarden told them, "or so I thought. Styx here, for some reason, did not give us the clue for this," and he gestured up at the Source. "I wonder why you didn't, Styx?"

Styx stood erect, his chin up, and a vein in his neck bounced. Otherwise, his ice-pale eyes stared right back at Skaarden.

"We went to the closer exit to fresher air," he said simply, "since this way was locked."

"But you knew, didn't you," Skaarden growled. "You knew this was here."

Styx shrugged. "Does it matter? After all, there was no reason to keep the others from getting outside. Not when we had the open shafts to the outside to get through versus a locked door. You're here now, and you have this, whatever it is. I secured it earlier; there's no trouble here. Only two girls and a boy."

Gen realized then that she had led her brother and cousin into a trap. She looked at them, pained, but they were not looking at her. They were watching Skaarden's minions as they advanced slowly, bearing cords.

"I don't need you," Skaarden said, and for a moment, Styx flinched. Gen caught his eye while Skaarden looked at the Source again, his teeth gleaming in its light as it pulsed faster.

"I need Bendin," he said. "I know he's alive. I know he made this; I know him. I wonder who else he tricked into making this thing."

"Nobody," dared Jas. "He made it himself. He's that good."

"Good?" roared Skaarden, and he laughed maniacally, flinging the long, greasy black strands of hair over his shoulder. "There's nothing good about Bendin. He's pathetic, that Doctor Lal. Never could get the funding he needed, except from *me*. In exchange for finding a way to power us until things got better up top. Which it would appear they did."

"They didn't," Gen said, standing tall. Styx shot her an alarmed look and gave her one subtle shake of his head. But she felt searing rage. "Your people shut everything down and ran. You didn't face the consequences. You took your wealth, made bunkers, and hid in them. You didn't try to find a solution to catastrophe; you made more of it. Those who were left faced famine and war, and natural disaster. You just slept through it all. Out of greed."

"Then blame your precious Bendin for that, girl!" spat Skaarden. "Why didn't he use his apparent genius to help the world then, instead of sustaining his own life? There's your greed. Think of what this thing could have done: powered any machine needed to fix the world's problems. I'll use it the way it should be used. Return you cowards back to the light, instead of this unnatural cave-dwelling storybook you're living, like a bunch of fairy vampires."

Mira gasped, and Gen gritted her teeth.

"Glimmerbight?" he laughed again. "Really? This was a vast land. What did you do to it, you soft little worm creatures with your little twinkling lights?"

"It's called erosion, you bleak dumbass," Gen said quite loudly. "Guess you didn't think of that, did you?"

Skaarden stepped forward in two paces and seized Gen by the collar, and lifted her up, gasping, to face him as she flailed in the air. "Erosion doesn't carve away land in that time period, not even in five hundred years. Did Bendin engineer it? So that we'd be exposed and let nature take its course? Well, we're exposed for sure, but maybe not the way he planned."

"Nobody plans for every disaster," Mira shouted, "and because the climate shifted, the ocean currents did too. My geology teacher said—"

"Your geology teacher!" Skaarden cried, and Gen rattled from his shakes of laughter. He dropped her, and his fingers caught on her firefly brooch as he did. A drop of blood formed on his fingertips, and he licked it off.

The brooch began to flash.

"Not now," whispered Gen.

"All you are is a bunch of mutants," Jas said, scowling at the assemblage.

Skaarden looked over his shoulder.

"Do you hear that, team? This moon worm is calling *us* mutants." He leaned over Jas and spat into the boy's eyes. "I distilled us. Made us pure. Look at you. You're *dilute*."

A scraping sound echoed in the chamber, and Gen, Mira, and Jas looked over toward the exit to the elevator.

"Ah, another way out," Skaarden said, walking forward, and then a flash of something black struck his face, and he screamed. It was Onyx.

A great whirlwind of black feathers swirled all about them among the purple-white light of the Source, and raven upon raven flew forward, seemingly from nowhere. Onyx led the charge as dozens of ravens swooped, soared, and attacked Skaarden and his minions. Amber then strode forward out of the elevator, her necklace feathers glowing red around the edges, her hair wild, and she smiled in a haunting, mad fashion.

"You're not getting out this way," Amber said to Skaarden. "Andraste sends her regards."

And Onyx flew straight down and tore at the man's face with his powerful black beak, leaving a gash from the corner of Skaarden's right eye down to his jaw. Skaarden snatched at the bird, but four other ravens dove forward to peck at the man, and Onyx flew free.

The others in his team ran back into the chamber where they had come from, chased by ravens. The monsters, however, remained, and Skaarden yelled, "Get them!"

The creatures spilled forth, whipping, snapping, seizing, and the Fireflies ran back to the elevator, Onyx following Amber, but the other ravens did not. Mira turned the elevator's key, and Gen shouted, "Please shut, by Luna, please shut!"

Skaarden and the monsters ran toward the elevator too, but at that moment, a bright golden light shone forth from Gen's brooch: Andraste's image in hologram separated the teens from Skaarden.

"I suggest you surrender, Skaarden," she told the man.

Mira pulled on Gen to get her away from the door while Jas pounded on the panel for the doors to close.

"Hurry!" hissed Gen, pleading with a machine she had no control over, but also in a way to Andraste.

Skaarden skidded to a halt in front of Andraste's image.

"You," he snarled, wiping the blood from his face. "I should have known."

"Surrender," Andraste said coldly, "or it's going to get worse for you."

"Worse than being held prisoner down there for centuries?" Skaarden countered.

"You chose this," Andraste said. "Surrender."

The elevator door shut just then, and the connection with Andraste was broken, with the firefly brooch gone dim at Gen's neck. They could hear the hideous guffaws of Skaarden as the elevator rose slowly upward.

Entrapment

As Gen, Mira, and Jas gasped with relief inside the rising elevator, Amber sat with her back against the wall, cradling an agitated Onyx. Her necklace dimmed, and her hair settled, and her flushed face went pale.

"Thank you, Amber," Gen said to the girl, and her brother and cousin joined in.

"That. Was. *Amazing*!" cried Mira, tucking her notebook away after rough note scribbling.

Amber yawned, "You're welcome," and petted Onyx absently.

"How did you do it?" Jas wanted to know.

Amber half-opened her blue eyes and murmured, "I'm not really sure. Onyx pecked at my necklace; he was very upset, and I couldn't get him to settle. He kept saying 'monsters,' and after he pulled at my necklace more, I touched it, and it felt hot. I don't remember much after that, to be honest, just… wings, birds, shooting down from a hole in the ceiling of the Inn. I felt… strong. I followed Onyx to the elevator, and it opened, and all the birds flew in... and then I was down there with you."

"Crazy," murmured Mira in admiration.

Amber closed her eyes again, and Onyx tucked his head back, and they dozed until the elevator reached the top. It opened, and Lyn and Phan relaxed their aggressive stance, with Lyn groaning in relief.

"Thank Luna," he sighed, pulling Gen forth and hugging her. Phan and Jas helped Amber to her feet, and she staggered out, drooping.

"It took a lot out of her," Mira said, watching Amber. Then she fell quiet and locked the elevator chamber door behind them all. She looked at her keys and sighed. "But what a power to have."

Gen, overhearing her, said, "There's an old saying, that the most powerful people hold the keys to unlock anything. You don't need a flock of ravens, Mira."

"It's not just the ravens," said Mira, and then she straightened. "Never mind. We've got bigger things to think about."

"I know," said Gen with a sigh. "How do we protect the Source? What's Skaarden going to do with it?"

Nyota approached and held her staff, flickering at the end with its red gem, and said, "We'd better think of something soon. Your dad and Bendin are working on something in the Lantern, and my guess is, that's not going to work if Skaarden figures out how to use the Source first."

"Well, I'm ready to cut monsters," Phan said arrogantly, punching his right hand with his left fist. "Take me to them!"

"Um," Jas interjected, "it's not just monsters. There's people down there too."

"What people?" Anisette asked, fanning out her billowy pants with her hands in their pockets. "Let's kick them," and she kicked her spiked boots out.

"Big people," Mira answered.

"*And* monsters," Gen added. "And... some in-betweens. Like, different stages of mutations."

"Jas," said Dhatura suddenly, pointing a glittery fingernail, "your wrist."

Jas looked down at the dosimeter, strapped upon his wrist, and it hung open. He stared at it; its color had darkened. He pushed his lips together and closed the thing with a click.

Gen touched his arm.

"What does it mean?" she asked, fearing that she already knew, but did not want to think about it.

"One thing at a time," Jas said. "But... maybe I'm changing."

Gen felt sick. "Changing? Changing how?"

"I don't know. I don't... I don't feel quite the same," Jas replied. "It's too dark in here, can we lighten it up?" He fussed with his goggles and turned their dials until bright lights beamed from them, causing everyone he looked at to wince.

Mira took hold of Gen's arm and pulled her aside, "Oh God, Gen, he's mutating, isn't he?"

"We don't know for sure," Gen hissed. "Maybe he's just... tired, still recovering, or something."

"Gen," said Nyota gently, in her ear, "he doesn't look well. We should get him home."

Gen cast her eyes about and found Amber slumped against the wall, sleeping, Jas roaming the great rotunda with bright lights, and Phan and Anisette arguing and faux fighting.

Lyn nudged her and said, "I don't think we can do anything else tonight. The ravens chased those... people back where they came from. I'm hoping they left some marks."

"I'm hoping the birds are okay," said Gen.

"That too," agreed Lyn.

"But Onyx and some other ravens left Skaarden a nice little gift, at least," Gen said. "Now he'll have a scar, to match his name."

Lyn laughed. "Nice one, Gen."

"I guess your charmstone won't work on Jas at this point, will it?" she asked him soberly.

"I don't think so," sighed Lyn. "I don't know what to do for him, if he really is changing."

"I sure wish Doc Bozzard hadn't slinked off to the unknown," grumbled Mira, "or he could answer that question, I think."

"Hey," called Jas from across the room. "I can hear you all, just so you know. I'm not too far gone yet."

"Sorry," Gen called back.

"Can you come over here?" Jas asked them. "I want you to see something."

Everyone but dozing Amber walked across the room, with its glowing floor, and Gen was glad to see that at least for now, it still worked, whatever Skaarden might have planned for it. She looked at Jas, who shone his illuminated headgear upward on the curving arch of the great rotunda of the Inn, and the brilliant wedge of light fell on a large, stained old painting.

Gen gawked. The painting showed a group of adults, the background behind them lush and golden and coiling with floral vines, and the adults themselves were young and hale and beautiful. Three men and one woman stared out, smiling and laughing in the painting. The woman had wildly curled, golden-copper hair and golden hazel eyes, a noble nose, flawless skin, and an hourglass figure draped in emerald green. At her neck, a spiraling crescent moon necklace shone.

"Andraste!" Nyota cried in awe.

To her left, two men stood back-to-back with their arms crossed, one with curly, mahogany-colored hair, mustache and green glasses, the other with a shaved head and brown skin. To her right, a man stretched his arm behind her, and he was striking with chin-length, black hair, dark eyes, tanned skin, and bright white teeth, model-perfect. He looked exactly like Harris, without glasses and with slightly longer hair.

"Skaarden," Gen said.

"Then that must be..." Mira squinted upward. "That has to be Doc Bozzard with the glasses! Right? Which makes the man next to him..."

"Obviously Bendin," Dhatura said, gazing up with a smile.

"God, they were gorgeous," Anisette murmured.

"Andraste was..." Phan began, but he whistled instead.

"So, they all knew each other," Lyn added. "And apparently got along pretty well at one point. And maybe... maybe they were *here*? In the Golden Hour?"

"Not sure," Jas answered, "but I guess it fits. Or maybe it was just before the Golden Hour, because I think maybe Skaarden was frozen before that. Like he didn't know what was coming, maybe? It hadn't... the world hadn't ended yet, outside."

Gen tapped her finger on her chin while she looked at the painting.

"He wants that again," she said suddenly. "He can't let that image go, I'll bet. He must have thought it would be the same when they all woke up. That they'd all be together again."

"But Andraste didn't sound like she was still married to Skaarden," Nyota pointed out. "Something must've gone wrong."

"That might explain why Skaarden resents Bendin so much," Mira reasoned.

Gen paced. "Yeah, something went wrong there, for sure. But I still think maybe Skaarden believes he could have that again."

Nyota made a disgusted sound. "Who knows what a madman like that believes? I wouldn't waste my time trying to figure it out, Gen, when he probably just wants to kill us all."

"I mean, true," Gen agreed, "but don't we kind of need to understand where—or when—he's coming from, so we can try and stop what he plans to do?"

Phan said, "I'm more concerned that we beat monsters than trying to figure out how that ancient freak thinks."

Lyn held his hands out to Gen, who glared at him.

Amber woke then, and Onyx squawked, startling them all. "Search," he said in his strange raven voice, and he bolted up and out of the ceiling of the inn. Dhatura helped the girl stand.

"You okay, Amber?" Gen asked.

"Yes," answered Amber, smiling, yawning, and rubbing her eyes. "That took a lot out of me, but... I liked it! I felt so strong. Maybe that's how Andraste feels?"

"A little bit of magic goes a long way," Nyota told her with a grin.

Onyx hurtled back down quite suddenly and croaked, "Monsters! Monsters at the door! Monsters climbing!"

"Oh my God," Mira breathed.

Gen looked at the light, which still pulsed with its rapid lavender-white heartbeat. She looked up at the ceiling.

"By Luna," she cried. "We can't get out, but they can get in!"

She turned to Amber. "Amber, I hate to ask you this, but can we use Onyx to get a message out? Before it's too late?"

"Of course!" said Amber, and she held Onyx close for a long moment and kissed his beak. "Be safe, Onyx," she said to him.

"Onyx," Gen said to the raven, "go to the Lantern. Find Dad and Bendin. Tell them we're trapped!"

The bird launched skyward again and just made it through the hole when a ropelike, whipping black stalk sailed across it, missing the bird by inches. Screeching, Onyx flew higher. There came a great boom, and the teens covered their ears.

"Onyx!" cried Amber. Another boom.

"What is that?" shrieked Anisette. "Is it a cannon?"

"No," said Dhatura, deadly calm. "It's a gun. Onyx is being shot at!"

"Oh, Luna, no!" cried Amber.

Gen embraced her. "We don't know if he's been shot. He might have got away."

"We'd better hope they had a bad aim from stewing in their own juice for five hundred years," snarled Phan. "Cowards!"

"Bro," said Anisette, "if they've got ancient weapons like that, your knife is useless."

A slapping sound startled them, and they turned to see a black, sprawling shape land on the floor behind them.

Phan bared his teeth. "That thing doesn't have guns, though. Let's go!"

And he ran full tilt at the slithering, black creature, knife in hand, with Anisette and Lyn in pursuit and Nyota with her staff, and as the beast lashed out, another one fell from the hole above and skittered across the floor toward Amber and Dhatura. A loud ramming struck the Inn door just then as well, and Gen gasped.

"They're trying to get in any way they can," Jas said with a sigh. "We're surrounded, and no way out."

"Wait," Gen said, "we do have a way out. The elevator!"

"Won't they be down there too?" Mira asked.

"I don't think so," Gen said. "I think they're trying to get in here so Skaarden can get control of the Source. He won't be down there." She turned to see Phan slash the first creature with several quick thrusts of his dagger, and Anisette stomped and kicked it, while Nyota stabbed the other with her staff, its crystalline tip blinding red, and sizzling upon contact with the thing.

Gen looked up and could see another quivering form above, ready to drop, just as the first two were killed, but not without lashing at their attackers first. Her Fireflies could not survive much more of this.

"Anisette!" she yelled. "Make the call!"

"What?" cried Anisette, and then she looked down at her chest, at the conch shell hanging there. She laughed wildly, doubling over, "Hell yes!" and she blew on the conch.

Not a sound rang out, but Gen didn't wait for one.

"Get to the elevator!" she screamed, as a buckling, warping, banging sound rang upon the outside doors. She heard the shattering of old wood and glass high in the Inn's upper floors and knew that they had very little time.

And so, they ran; Gen ran so fast her legs burned, and she pulled and pushed her fellow Fireflies toward the elevator. They had enough time to hear a tremendous blow, and the doors of the Inn flew open, and in spilled Skaarden's goons, guns in tow. They ran in, fanning out, and Gen hesitated, but Lyn yelled, "Gen, hurry! The door is closing!"

A deafening crash made her look up, and she saw something incredible: the rotunda of the Inn collapsed, and through it emerged two immense, mechanical talons, and the largest owl she had ever seen. The pieces of the ceiling fell and both they and the weight of the tremendous owl crushed the invaders, with the bird's enormous yellow lamplike eyes driving the more animal-like mutants berserk and shrieking out of the Inn. Anisette bounded back out of the elevator to look at it, and screamed, "GigantOwl! Yes!" before Gen yanked her back in just as the doors began to close.

Rising and Falling

B ut it did not close. Something stuck in the door and stopped the elevator from going down. Gen wheeled around to see a curved piece of metal sticking through the gap as the elevator whined then began chiming. She could not understand what the object was at first, but then she saw eyes staring in at her through the gap: eyes as pale as ice.

"Styx!" she cried.

"I'm sorry," Styx said to her, and he pried the door open with the metal. She could see then that it was part of the smashed chandelier from the rotunda. "But I can't let you go back down there."

"Like hell you can't," Lyn snarled, lunging forward.

"Aren't you supposed to be going to bed soon?" Styx drawled, still holding the metal. "You could stay up, you know. You could be day living again instead of going against nature. It's not that you can't. It's that you won't. That every single thing you do is because you're safe and you want to stay that way. I never had that option. I'm awake now. But you're still asleep."

Lyn took hold of the end of the metal piece to shove it back out, but Styx was much stronger than he looked, and he thrust it back at Lyn with great speed, sending him flying onto his backside in the elevator.

"You need to get out of here," Styx told Gen urgently. "Shut the elevator off, Mira. You have the key, yes?" And he pointed to the keyring on Mira's wrist.

"We *were* getting out of here," Gen snapped.

"If you go down there," Styx told her, "you're going to find Skaarden waiting for you. It's a trap."

"And why would I trust you?" Gen asked him between the gap he had pried open, warping the doors.

"Because I know him," Styx answered. "I know his weaknesses. I opened up the other capsules; I know who you could trust going forward. Gen, I know you're trying to stop your world from changing, but you can't. He's determined. He's figured a way out. Even beyond the shield. It's too late."

"What do you mean?" she asked, and her friends crowded around to listen.

"That shield that Andraste... conjured?" said Styx. "It was too late to catch every mutant. Some got out of that ventilation shaft and kept going. I know because I went back and counted the capsules. Some had already been opened well before I was; too many to account for the ones you had killed, I would guess. So, they're out beyond the barrier. And also, there's drainage seeping out of the sea cliff below us, probably from those shafts. I think... I think sea life might be at risk now."

"What?" Gen gasped.

Styx fumbled with his free hand, straining with his right hand to keep the elevator open, and he brought something out of a pocket. They were green glasses.

"Those are Doc Bozzard's!" cried Mira.

"Let me see," insisted Jas, leaning forward. Then he fumed at Styx, "How do we know this isn't some new trick? How do we know you guys didn't kill Doc Bozzard and get his glasses?"

"You don't," admitted Styx. "I've got nothing to gain here and everything to lose. Skaarden finds out I helped you? I'm dead. That's okay. I may as well have been dead all this time. I've only felt alive since meeting you, Gen."

"Oh, come on," Lyn growled.

But Styx only had eyes for Gen as he said, "Don't go. Please. We can figure this out together. I know things about the past that you don't, that nobody else does, and we can save the world from what was let loose. I know it."

"Nice try, kid," a voice snarled, and out of Gen's range of vision, someone swung something and struck Styx in the back, and he fell to his knees. This person seized the wrought iron from the boy's hands, kicked him out of sight, and peeled back part of the doorway.

Jas showed his headlamp out and cried, "No!"

It was Doc Bozzard. Only it wasn't quite; not anymore. Half of the old man's face sprouted with black coils, and one of his arms quivered in an inhuman manner like a sleeved tentacle. Gone were his spectacles and his eyes... Gen and her friends pressed back inside the elevator in horror, for his eyes swam with strange, spiked swirls, dark black and green, and his grin revealed teeth missing and a black tongue.

"No, Doc," wailed Mira.

"Hello, little midnight dancer," Doc said in an oily voice. "You really opened Pandora's box, didn't you? Well, I did, anyway. Thank you for giving me the excuse. It was a long time coming."

The sound of gunfire broke out behind him, then a yell and the shots ended abruptly. Footsteps pounded the inn floor, and a voice yelled, "Doc!"

"Bendin!" cried Gen. "Be careful, he's not—"

There was a great crash and a burst of golden light, and Doc Bozzard turned so that half his body was bathed in gold. He hissed at what he saw and was distracted just long enough for Nyota to ram her staff into his belly. He bayed then like one of the monsters, his mouth stretching too far open to be human, and his tentacle arm whipped forward into the elevator toward the teens.

But Phan was ready and cut it off at what would have been Doc's elbow. The strange blood sprayed across his "EAT THIS!" shirt. Anisette kicked the amputated appendage with her spiked boots back out of the elevator. Doc fell backward, but the rod was still lodged in the damaged doorway. He rose from where he had stumbled, holding his bleeding tentacle-arm.

"Step aside," a voice boomed. It was not Bendin, however.

"Andraste!" yelled Nyota just as a flock of ravens engulfed Doc.

Onyx croaked loudly, and Amber let him fly out of the elevator gap to safety.

Andraste and Bendin then both appeared and with a wave of her hands, Andraste forced open the elevator doors and said, "Run, all of you! I've secured the room."

En masse, the Fireflies spilled out of the elevator. Lyn lingered a moment, standing over Styx, who was barely coherent from pain, and said, "Who's awake now? Guess you're the one that needed to sleep, after all." And he stepped over the boy in disgust.

"Where's Dad?" cried Gen, too worried to dwell on Lyn's behavior.

Bendin, struggling to pin Doc down, said in a strained voice, "Safe! Working," and he managed to wink at Gen. "Andraste, if you would…"

The woman nodded and held her hands out in front of her. Two bracelets flew from her arms, grew in size, and wrapped around Doc, binding his arm and tentacle to his body so that he could not attack them. Panting, Bendin stood and nodded to her, and she grinned.

"Look," Gen said, "Styx told us something important."

"Do you believe him?" Andraste asked her.

"By Luna, I do," Gen replied.

"Then tell us, child," Andraste offered, holding her hand out for Gen to take.

"First of all," Gen said, taking deep gulps of the night air from the exposed ceiling, "Skaarden is waiting down at the Source. He thought we'd go back down, and we were going to."

"Ah," said Bendin. "What else, Gen?"

"Styx said that someone had opened capsules long before he did and that some of those monsters must have got out some time ago. He found Doc's spectacles," and she pointed to the floor where they lay. "Then Doc attacked."

"She's raving," Doc muttered, spittle flying from his warped mouth. "You're not going to listen to these kids, are you, old friends?"

Bendin looked at him with contempt, an expression Gen had never seen before.

"How dare you call us *friends*," he said, biting the words out, "when you attack children. *Gas* them. Let loose your monsters upon the world, threaten everything we built over *centuries*?"

"And what did you do, old man?" Doc demanded. "You, dwelling away from the world, building your precious power source that could have helped others outside our land."

"You sound like *him*," Andraste said in a low voice. "I never pegged you for being Skaarden's lackey, but I should have expected it; you always wanted funding for your experiments, and he clearly gave it to you. And you've cosplayed as a doctor for people for generations."

"Let me guess," Bendin said, his lips trembling with barely contained rage, "the illicit magic trick you pulled with Mira's age disruption triggered your bitterness, and you let your genetic work run amok. Only it got hold of you, amplified your worst instincts, and now it's too late for you. You let them out of those shafts, didn't you?"

"So what?" spat Doc. "I was tired of waiting for you. That little pulse of 'magic' made the Lantern light activate those capsules. It was just the push the nanovirus needed. I didn't have to wait any longer. We would *survive* and flourish, not endure this fantasy night-living anymore. I've made us superior."

"You're not even human anymore!" cried Mira, gazing at Doc with revulsion in her face.

"I'm better than human, you ungrateful brat," Doc snapped.

Mira looked stunned and betrayed, and she shook her head and backed away from him. "Our family trusted you," she said, "and you not only failed us. You used us."

Mira turned away from Doc and walked toward her friends, and the huge cyborg owl presiding over the destruction in the rotunda.

"He's still down there," Gen reminded the three older adults. "What do we do?"

"We stop him from using the Source and taking control of this town, because he won't stop there," Andraste said. "He won't like that there isn't much of a world to go back to and exploit, but what he can control, he will. That's all he's ever cared about, really: control."

"Then why did you marry him?" Gen asked loudly but not unkindly. She truly did not understand.

Andraste cupped Gen's cheek with her wizened hand, and her hazel eyes shone brightly through the many wrinkles on her face. She said softly, "He was ambitious and hopeful, once, before greed got in the way, and success, and glamor. I did love him for a time until he grew warped, and wanted to take over the biggest corporations on earth. He even wanted the rest of the solar system in his grasp, too, before it all ended down here. But he couldn't love me back the way I loved him, and I had to let that go."

Gen was stunned by the words, their implication, and she mulled over "solar system" for a moment before her eyes fell upon Styx. Bendin reached down and checked on him. He groaned.

"So, he wasn't always bad," muttered Gen.

"Not always," agreed Andraste, "but now he is beyond reach, likely warped on a genetic level even, though not in the same way as poor Bozzard here."

Then she called, "Ruru!" and the immense owl replied, "Hoo?"

"Keep an eye on Bozzard," she said. "If he tries to get away, I'm sure you can find a way to convince him to stay still."

She grinned at that, and Gen smirked.

"Your friend will be okay," she added.

"Who, Styx?" Gen asked. "He's not my fri—"

"He may *need* friends," Andraste said gently. "He is out of his depth, to be sure, but he is also out of his time. There's hope still. Now let's honor the confessions he made to you, at great personal risk."

Gen knelt by Styx, who leaned back against the wall of the hallway, and she whispered into his ear, "Thank you."

She stood, and Bendin said to her, "Gen, you had better get back to your home since it's not too long until dawn. I know Reggie will be worried."

"When is Mom not worried?" Gen countered.

"Fair enough," said Bendin.

"We've got a problem," Andraste said suddenly.

"What?" asked Bendin, and then he followed her gaze.

The elevator door had shut, and they could hear distant scraping.

Bendin and Andraste, and Gen looked at each other.

"He's coming up!" gasped Gen.

Bendin put his face in his hands. "Andraste, make sure Ruru is ready."

"Oh, my friend," said Andraste, her voice mournful. "I am sorry."

"So am I, darling," said Bendin. "So am I."

Fractures

Bendin turned to Gen and said in an urgent tone, "Do you have the pen that I gave you?"

Gen fumbled with her pockets and pulled forth the pen he had left for her.

"Excellent," he said, smiling. "And the papers, behind the old desk, do you know where those are?"

"Yes," Gen replied, wondering where Bendin was going with this.

"I want you to run and grab some sheets of paper and one of the ink pots. Hurry!"

She did not hesitate and sprinted through the rotunda's wreckage. She was surprised to see her friends there.

"We, uh... we have prisoners," Jas said, looking sheepish, and indeed all the Fireflies had bound up the soldiers wounded by Ruru the owl's crash landing.

"Wow!" said Gen. "Good work. I'll be back."

"Do you need us, Gen?" Dhatura asked.

"I... I don't know, but be ready for anything, I guess. Skaarden's coming!"

Nyota slapped her staff into her hands like a long club. "Then we'll be waiting for him!" she said.

Ruru's lamp eyes illuminated the scene, showing some of the damaged frescoes and paintings fractured, but some remained.

I hope those can be restored, Gen thought fleetingly as she dashed to the Inn's check-in desk. She entered the side door, swept her hands through the mail slots, and pulled forth a sheaf of Bendin's paper and one of the iridescent ink pots. She sprinted back.

"He'll be here soon," Andraste warned, "so be quick, whatever it is you're thinking, Bendin."

Bendin nodded. "Ready your pen," he told Gen. She did, and he said, "Write this down: Initiate Lembrar Protocol Nepenthe: Forty-three point nine-nine by thirteen point nine two."

Gen scribbled in her atrocious handwriting.

"Nobody's going to be able to read this, you know," she muttered, shaking her head.

"Do you have it all?" he asked, noting the ink had gone invisible.

"Yes," Gen replied.

Bendin put his fingers to his lips. "Thank you." He said then, "I had this plan, and what a grand plan it was, let me tell you. Ah, hubris! My frustrated system, as your brother calls it, indeed is biphasic, and it's powered the Lantern, kept us alive," he dipped his head to Andraste, "powered our new technology, or magic... although that was something entirely new, and of your doing, Andraste... and it kept Skaarden and his team alive too. We just... didn't know, or at least I didn't, what a disrupted nanovirus would do to those who slept.

"Gen, I must tell you something. My pens have DNA tags activated by ink. Yours corresponds to DNA in your family, so when I wrote to your father, letters contained a special genetic marker, and they collapsed upon reading for those with the same markers in their genes. Skaarden will want to know how to power the Source. You're going to give him this paper."

"Wait, what do you mean?" Gen asked, just as the elevator made a final, scraping whine at their level. She whipped around, shoved the paper into her pocket, and stood face to face with her father's doppelgänger: Skaarden, and on either side of him, an array of creatures coiled and snapping and amorphous, ready to spring.

Skaarden stepped out of the elevator, imposing, raw, exuding power, his lank hair slicked back behind his ears, and said, "Go get 'em, boys."

And out the creatures snapped and slithered.

Andraste was ready: she threw her hands up before her, and a golden sphere formed around her, Bendin, and Gen, but the monsters slid and bounced and slithered all over it, and Gen curled up on the floor, hands over her head, terrified.

"Hello again, Skaarden," the Lunadatrix said, and Gen lifted her head up to watch the two of them.

Skaarden twisted his face into a strange expression, and Gen could not decide if it were disgust, anger, or something else, something she was not familiar with... *But maybe one day, I will be.*

"So, you chose old age and magic tricks," Skaarden sneered.

"I chose better than you," Andraste countered, "in more than one way." Her hazel eyes flashed with the fire of youth still and a layer of passion Gen had not seen before.

Skaarden arched his fingers toward the bubble, clawing at its surface before her face.

"Everything you've ever done has been a betrayal," he hissed. "I gave you everything. A roof over your head. All the money in the world. A clean slate. Power. And you threw it back in my face."

Andraste sniffed. "That was your doing," she said, her voice ringing like a sword on steel, "yours and yours alone. You made yourself the monster before you made these monsters. Call them off and face me like a man."

"Unshield yourself first and grow a spine," snarled Skaarden.

Gen felt the fire of the words between the two former lovers, and she cringed. Then the earth shook, and she heard cries in the rotunda as more chunks of the walls fell in.

"Ruru," Andraste called, her voice projecting deeply through the space, "lift as many of the children out as you can to safety."

Gen scrambled to her feet. "Fireflies!" she yelled, and for once she was glad of her loud, resonant voice, "get to the owl!"

"Gen!" cried Jas, and he rounded the corner and beheld the scene of the golden bubble, with Andraste, Bendin, and Gen within it, covered by the oily monsters, with Skaarden leering over them. The man turned to see Jas, and he smiled to himself.

"My recruit," he murmured, and Gen felt more shaken by that than by the earthquake. "Don't worry, girl," he said to her particularly, "it won't be today or tomorrow, but it will happen. You won't know him anymore, but he'll have orders from me. He's one of mine now. The girl with the staff and the twins, too."

"No!" gasped Gen.

"You'll never have them as recruits," Andraste spat back.

"Skaarden," said Bendin, "call off these... things of yours. After all, the real battle is between you and me."

Skaarden stared down at him, his brow drawn into a maniacal glare, and he said, "Give me this... Source of yours, and I'll let them all go. Back to their little moonbeam lives, every single one. Look at you," he spat, his eyes smoldering, holding them all in his sway, towering over them. "This is what humanity has come to while I slept? It is you who has slept. You couldn't adapt, so you went underground and into the night. Living in the dark like worms. Like animals, like cowards. You're an abomination, an obscenity. I can see we came back just in time. We'll set this right. You'll understand what true power means."

Gen could hold back no longer. "It's you who's the coward!" she yelled, her face nearly as purple in fury as the Lantern itself. All eyes turned to her in amazement. "You are the one who gave up. You ran away. You hid in a *bunker*. You're the coward, and you're lazy. You didn't want to fix anything; you didn't try to stop what ended the world the first time. You just waited like vultures to pick off the dead." Skaarden laughed openly at her, but she did not back down.

"Well, guess what!" and her hands were on her hips by now, "We were stronger than you. We *did* adapt. We made do, and we made life better. We made a beautiful new world. We never gave up and we never hid. There is nothing wrong with us: we love ourselves. This is who we are, and this is who we are going to be. You're stuck in the past. We are the present." And then she cried, "Jas, get on that owl and get out of here!"

"What about you?" he yelled back.

"I'll be fine," she assured him, and she hoped she was not lying to her brother.

"Go, Jas," said Andraste, and it was a command, not a request. He nodded and ran around to Ruru, as Andraste backed out at the entrance to the rotunda to oversee the giant owl's progress with the Fireflies. Everyone had climbed aboard, except for Dhatura, who was nowhere to be seen.

Nyota looked distraught at the sight of Andraste. "Lunadatrix!" she cried.

Andraste closed her eyes and said, "Ruru, tap upon the floor above the Source three times. Then fly away."

The owl made a resonant hiss, and rose and fell three times, as the teens held on tightly, and Ruru struck the translucent floor with the remnants of the chandelier scattering in all directions. A great fracture splintered that floor, and rays of white-purple light shone up between the shards, and the owl then thrust upward slowly and heavily into the sky and out of sight in the waning night.

"There's your precious Source," spat Andraste, as she and Gen and Bendin backed into the great, collapsed rotunda.

"Give it to me," bellowed Skaarden. "You've got my team crawling through every tunnel and you've trapped them all inside; but there are more outside, and you can't control them all without me. Give me the Source and I'll make sure they never hurt anyone."

Gen thought of what Styx had told her, and now she knew it to be true. Those creatures had ventured beyond Glimmerbight, she realized, and Luna knew where or what havoc they would bring. Bendin touched Andraste's shoulder.

"We have to do it, Andi," he said gently.

Andraste shook, her bangles tinkling together, and tears streamed down her face.

"We worked so hard," she whispered, staring out at Skaarden, but speaking chiefly to Bendin.

"I know," said Bendin.

Andraste exhaled. "I'll release Bendin, and he can show you how to manage the Source," she said, in a defeated tone.

"No!" cried Gen.

The bubble released, and the creatures dropped, but Skaarden raised his hands and said, "Hold," and they froze in place, quivering on the floor. He seized Bendin by the shoulders and marched him toward the Source light radiating from the broken floor.

"Show me how to control it," he ordered.

"I don't have the instructions with me," said Bendin. His eyes flickered to Gen.

"Bullshit," hissed Skaarden. "Tell me, or I unleash those things on all of you. I'll ask them to crush every bone in your bodies or make you one of them. Your choice."

"I don't have them," Bendin said again, and before Skaarden's rage-twisted mouth could open, he pointed to Gen, who froze in place. "She does."

Skaarden turned his dark eyes to Gen, and his face softened for a moment, enough that it terrified Gen, for he so resembled her father. She held her breath.

"Go on, then, girl, give them to me," he said in a syrupy voice. "I promise I won't hurt you."

"Promise me you'll leave my family and friends alone," Gen said in a shaking voice. "Forget about me: just promise me about them."

Skaarden shrugged. "Sure. Now, give them to me, before I change my mind," and he advanced on her, bending over her so that she smelled his chemical reek mixed with sweat. She dry-heaved.

"It's fine," Bendin encouraged her. "Go ahead."

Gen's shaking hands thrust into her pockets, and she felt around and brought out the paper she had written on earlier.

Skaarden laughed. "Paper instructions? Oh Bendin, you never changed. Old fashioned to the end."

He snatched them from Gen and opened them up.

"What the hell is this scrawl?" he muttered.

"The—the instructions," stammered Gen.

"I can't bloody read this!" he growled. "You read it!"

"I—I can't," Gen said, shaking, "It won't work for me."

He seized her and she cried out, so he pushed her onto the floor on her hands and knees and smoothed the papers out onto her back. Her cheeks went hot in rage and humiliation. "This is the worst handwriting I have ever seen. How did you devolve so much, Bendin?" The old man looked down at Gen in anguish. Skaarden then read aloud, "Initiate Lembrar Protocol Nepenthe: Forty-three point nine-nine by thirteen point nine two."

Nothing happened. The rotunda sat silent, with nothing but the whistling of the wind, and dark, with no light but the wedge of the Amethyst Lantern swinging overhead.

Skaarden shook the papers in Bendin's face. "What is this, a joke? This didn't work."

"Maybe you didn't say it right," suggested Bendin, his eyes glinting. "Say it again, maybe more slowly."

Skaarden held the papers out, and then they began to disintegrate. He gasped as they vanished into a little kernel, fell away from his fingers, and rolled away.

He stepped forward and grabbed Bendin around the neck, and the earth shook again.

"Andi," wheezed Bendin, "take Gen and run!"

"Bendin, no," cried Andraste.

"Do it, hurry!"

Andraste seized Gen's hands and pulled her away toward the wall. They watched as the fractures in the floor began to collapse, sending more cracks in all directions.

"Gen," gagged Bendin, "Write the future you want. Make it a good one, make it—make it last this time."

The floor began to collapse, and Bendin and Skaarden, who held his throat, and the monsters, who leaped upon Bendin's back and tore at his flesh with their tendrils, began to slide toward the center of the room, toward the light.

"Bendin!" screamed a voice, and out ran Dhatura, loosening her sash and running toward the two men. She threw the sash around Skaarden's legs. The copper peacock brooch, pinned onto the sash, struck a blow that forced him to yell, and the sash tripped him so that he lost his grip. The floor fell away in great chunks then, and she scrambled to hold onto the edge of it as brilliant purple-white light shot into the sky in an immense beam. Skaarden slid swiftly downward, and Bendin caught Dhatura's sash where its brooch snagged on one of the hanging shards of the floor. She and Gen dashed over to him, but Andraste stopped them with two of her golden bracelets, enlarged, and pulled them back from the edge.

Bendin gave one last look at Gen and Dhatura, and the floor fell away, and so did he and Skaarden into the brilliant, pulsing, violet-white light. "No!" the girls screamed.

Down the men fell out of sight, and another massive surge of energy burst upward, coupled with a beam in all directions from the Amethyst Lantern simultaneously. And then the Source withdrew down, deep into the bowels of the Inn, and there lay only a dark chasm.

Chasing Twilight

Gen and Dhatura held each other on the edge of the chasm, tears streaming down their faces, as Andraste murmured a series of chants that rose and fell as a keening for Bendin. Through her watery eyes, Gen could see that Andraste looked crumpled with repressed grief, older than she ever had, and frailer. Yet the older woman ended her lament and gestured to the girls to come to stand beside her.

"I am sorry," she said to them. "That did not go how I wanted it to go. I know Bendin must have felt there was no other way, but I... I am damaged by this. I will have to return to Moonbow Valley soon to rest. Making the shield around the city tired me enough, before this." She took each girl's hands in hers. "Thank you for your bravery, Gentian and Dhatura, and for your ingenuity. The Inn is truly yours now, though the state of it..."

And her voice trailed off as she gazed across the chasm at a collapsed painting, the one with her, Bendin, Skaarden, and Doc Bozzard. She darted her eyes to the prisoners and drew in her breath.

"He's escaped," she whispered.

Gen cast her eyes about, and groaned, "I knew we couldn't trust Styx."

"I meant Doc Bozzard," Andraste clarified. But then she and Gen looked at each other.

Dhatura said it for them: "They must have helped each other."

"But they can only get so far, yes?" Gen asked. "With your shield?"

"Over land, yes," Andraste said, but she gazed up at the Lantern, and the thin edge of softening of the horizon, signaling that dawn would arrive soon. The Lantern had returned to normal, and Gen took some comfort in that. But Andraste added, "We are quite close to the sea, though."

"Oh no," moaned Gen. "The drainage to the sea!"

"Possibly," Andraste said, and she lowered her head. Gen worried that the woman might collapse where she stood, so she and Dhatura helped her over to the little office desk and chair, and she gave a little laugh.

"Ah, I have not sat behind this desk in many moons," Andraste said with a sigh, and she looked out at the broken inn. She fell into a dreamlike state for a moment, her hazel eyes glazed over, and then she sighed. "A night to remember."

"The Hotel Lembrar," Gen murmured.

"Yes," Andraste replied, and then she stirred and sat erect. "You have a visitor, dear."

Gen looked up to see Harris running toward her, ungainly and wiry, his glasses crooked, and altogether quite unlike Skaarden except in his face. She felt a surge of relief and joy at the sight of him.

"Dad!" she cried, and they embraced, careful to stay around the edges of the walls, away from the chasm.

"Let's go home, Gen," said her father, and they began the march home.

Ruru had settled on the ridge line, and the rest of the Firefly gang came running down just before dawn began to break, to meet Gen, Dhatura, Harris, and Andraste. Harris hugged Jas and Mira, who had as usual been writing everything she had seen. Lyn caught Gen up in a huge hug and swung her around for a moment before setting her back down.

"Sorry," he said sheepishly. "I'm just so glad you're okay."

"I am too!" said Gen, in too loud a voice.

"Jas," Andraste called, and the boy looked at her in surprise. Her deep gold-hazel eyes looked concerned. "Are you still wearing that gem I gave you?"

Jas blinked, and then pulled from his shirt the tourmaline-hued crystal she had bestowed on him. "I never took it off."

Andraste closed her eyes and smiled. "Good. That'll help offset the... effects you were exposed to. But still keep an eye on your dosimeter."

Gen watched her brother. He took a breath and nodded. "Thank you, Lunadatrix."

Jas approached Dhatura, speaking to her in comforting tones. Before long, the two fell to talking about what had happened with the Source, in what Gen could only imagine was some sort of scientific flirting, but it felt right to her.

Harris helped Andraste up the path to the ridge and up onto the tremendous cyborg owl, which piped and hooted and clanged and clicked with its powerful beak. Gen watched in amazement as facets among the owl's back feathers unfolded, making multiple shielded seats.

"Anyone who wants to visit me in Moonbow Valley is welcome," Andraste announced. "Though mind your cloaking shields. Nyota and Amber, I'll have Ruru drop you off at your homes. But in the coming days, ask your parents if you can come on a school trip to the valley. After all, two Lunadatrices are better than one, and I had better start training you both." The girls gasped and looked at each other, exchanging excited smiles. Onyx flapped his wings in approval. "Harris, you'll put in a good recommendation for me?" And the old woman's eyes glinted mischievously despite her fatigue and sadness.

"Absolutely, Lunadatrix," Harris answered, leaning back to take a look at the magnificent Ruru. Amber, with Onyx on her shoulder, climbed aboard next. Nyota followed, settling in with her staff. The two girls looked at each other and grinned.

"Never thought I'd see the day, Amber," said Nyota.

"What do you mean?" Amber asked.

"You're going to be a witch!" Nyota answered, smiling broadly.

"Am I?" Amber asked, clutching her feather necklace and tidying her stained white outfit. "I don't know that Mom and Dad will approve."

"You're of age," said Nyota, nudging her with her elbow. "And you've obviously got the talent, or Onyx here would never have set foot on your shoulder!"

"A witch," murmured Amber, and Onyx rubbed his beak on her cheek.

"Witch!" he agreed, and Amber laughed.

Gen smiled up at them.

"Thank you for everything. See you soon?"

"Definitely," said Nyota.

Phan and Anisette saluted Ruru. "Goodbye, Gigan-tOwl!" called Anisette, waving furiously. The great bird pushed upward into the sky, its passengers enclosed in shields against the dawn, and Gen felt a sense of peace, watching the creature soar on its massive wings to the north.

Luna

Gen, Jas, Mira, Harris, the twins, Lyn, and Dhatura made a final mad dash to the Lightworth home and tumbled past the irate and overly sensitive housebots into the periwinkle house, spooking the cats to the far corners of the home. Reggie and Tam hugged everyone, and Tam again played nurse for various scrapes and bruises.

"What will you do about any remaining monsters?" Reggie asked Harris.

He raised his eyebrows and turned to look at the Fireflies assembled around the dining table, devouring plate after plate of food, so great was their hunger and exhaustion. "Ask them," he suggested. "They're the monster hunters!"

Phan grinned and threw his hand up to wave at Reggie before falling back upon his feast.

Gen said, "I think we'll wait until tomorrow. Let Andraste recover, see what the mayor wants to do, and hope for the best."

"I've not heard any updates from the *Biolumen* tonight," Reggie said, "which I find odd, because everyone saw that bright light shoot into the sky a couple of times!"

Dhatura flinched, and she looked across the table at Gen. Gen felt a bond with her now that she had not before. They would have to work together if they wanted what remained of the Inn to survive.

"Fight monsters, rebuild inns," Anisette said, "all in a night's work. Okay, maybe more than a night."

Gen blurted out, "Will you help us fix the Inn?"

"How could we not?" Mira asked. "Jas, you're not going outside! It's sunrise!"

Jas abruptly stood. "There's a paper," he said casually. "I'll get it."

He marched to the door and did not take a shield from the shield hanger.

"Jas, what are you doing?" his mother demanded, but he stepped outside before they had time to think.

Phan and Anisette looked at each other, stood, and sprinted after him. The light and heat that entered the home as they opened the door made everyone else cry out in pain and dread, so they shut the door.

"What are they doing?" cried Tam. "They'll be burned and sick in minutes!"

The three teens reentered after about five minutes, and their skin looked mostly normal, if a bit sunburned.

"How?" Harris and Reggie asked at the same time.

Jas pulled out a metal disk from his pocket and opened it. His dosimeter had darkened yet again.

"We're not the same anymore," he said. "I'm guessing Nyota isn't either."

Reggie and Harris clasped each other's hands and did not know what to say.

Mira trembled.

"It only got on my wrist a little while," she murmured.

"Then maybe you're okay," Anisette said. "Anyway, here's the paper," and she handed the pod to Mira, who quickly set about unfurling it.

The headlines read, "EARTHQUAKE DAMAGES THE INN AT THE AMETHYST LANTERN," but remarkably, the paper said nothing about the light. And nothing about Bendin, Doc Bozzard, Skaarden, or any of the monsters.

"I cannot believe this!" Mira cried, outraged. "Not a single thing about what's happened, not at all."

Gen laughed. "Mira, just start your own paper," she teased.

Mira, incensed over the lack of news, fished out her notebook.

"Maybe wait until you've had a full day's sleep," Tam said dryly, deftly removing the notebook from her daughter's hands and pointing down the hall to Gen's bedroom.

After a long sleep, Gen woke up sore and thirsty, and she scuffed along to the kitchen, where Sylvia and Smudge laced themselves between her legs, meowing, and she tripped over them and swore. Setting their separate food bowls on the floor, she opened the window to see the dusk. She leaned on the sill, tolerating the last remnants of the day's heat as the sky darkened and the stars winked out at her. She saw the purple arc of light from the Amethyst Lantern and pondered how it might still be working.

Almost in answer to her, her father walked in quietly to the dining room and sat down at the table, reading the cast-off leaf-pages of the *Biolumen* so scorned by his niece the day before.

"We should head up there later," Harris said casually, pretending not to take interest in anything other than the paper.

But Gen caught sight of something undulating down toward her... two somethings.

"Dad!" she cried. "Luna moths!" and she stood up straight. "Could it be...?"

Harris said nothing, and watched as two great, pale green moths descended, and hovered in front of Gen as she leaned out of the window. They carried something between them, and they dropped it into her reaching hands. Then off they flew, dancing softly in the deepening blues of the night, as deep as Gen's indigo hair.

She held an envelope in her trembling hands. On the front, in a looping script she could read "Gen."

"He's okay!" exclaimed Gen. "Oh, Dhatura will be so happy!"

She tore open the envelope and began to read, and her face fell.

Oh no.

"Dear Gen," the letter read, and she could almost hear Bendin's voice from his strange penmanship alone, "if this letter reaches you, it means that I have perished. Please do not be sad for me. My time in this world stretched longer than anyone else's, and a million of my hopes lived and died before you were ever born."

Gen wept openly, her shoulders shaking, her tears splashing down upon the iridescent ink.

"I know you didn't ask for this," the letter continued, "but I believed in you always. You have been determined, much like your father was in his youth, to discover and seek out. Yet you are like your mother, steadfast and pragmatic—perhaps not always, but when it's the most necessary. We need a little bit of imagination at least, but we also need to take a stand. Your cousin is a brave girl, but she is not a leader. She helped choose the team, but the Fireflies chose you to lead them. They sensed in you a leader, and now you are one. Make the Inn grand again, Gen. It was never meant to be as I left it, a shell of its former vibrant self. Write the future for you and your friends, and bring the Inn to life and light once more. Live and love, dear Gentian, and live up to your name, for your light is worth all the stars in the sky, and the moon besides. Your humble servant, Benjamin D. N. Lal."

Harris came over to hug his daughter as she held the letter close to her chest, and she sobbed as it began to melt away. It formed a little kernel, and the kernel fell outside the window of the house and burrowed into the earth out of sight.

Her father said, "Come with me to the Lantern, Gen."

She wiped her tears on the cuffs of her sleeves and sniffed, and followed Harris out the door. The housebots barked at them, and Gen managed to smile.

"Is that their new default?" she wondered.

"Maybe," Harris said with a shrug. "They just want to look out for us."

Gen followed her father along a different path, the coastal bluff path toward the Lantern, rather than toward the Inn. The wind whistled up through the tall trees, resilient against gales and from brutal sun, and yet still gentle somehow. She wondered how old they were, and how they had outlived other trees long ago; those that could not flourish in a changing climate or under a volatile sun. The moon was sheltered by a wreath of clouds as it rose, and the Lantern stood tall and proud, its thick stripes white and violet, gleaming against sky and bluff. The great light circled around and around.

She almost did not want to look at the Inn, for she knew that it was heavily damaged, and its lovely rotunda imploded. But she did look, and she was comforted by it despite the damage, for she realized it was hers now, hers and Dhatura's. And she began to daydream, just a little bit, of what Bendin had said in this letter. How could they restore the Inn? She remembered the flashing images he had shown her, Mira, and Jas, of what it once was.

Harris walked to the entrance at the base of the great lighthouse, and Gen looked out at a whitecapped sea from the bluff below.

"Ready for a climb?" he asked her. "The view is much better from the top, I guarantee it. But be careful. The stairs are quite steep, and some are broken. It's not only the Inn that needs repair. We need to retrofit this thing against any more seismic activity."

Inside the lighthouse, Harris switched on lights strung all along its spiral staircase, and they began to climb. By the time they reached the top, they were both quite winded and then they exited the stairwell onto the topmost platform, where the Lantern shone brilliantly from its glorious facets. Within a glasslike sheath, a huge crystal pulsed, though nowhere near as large as the Source in the Inn. The crystal both powered and gave light to the lighthouse lantern and was brilliant. At the base of the Lantern, a series of panels circuited the interior area of the topmost floor, and a railing protected the outside perimeter. Harris led her over to the opposite side so that she could look out and away from the dazzling light.

Sure enough, the view was astounding, and Gen could just make out the hint of a small island on the horizon, not visible from Glimmerbight. An ancient telescope stood propped up, aimed skyward, but Harris took it and looked through it, adjusting it and aiming it downward.

"I never knew there was an island out there," Gen remarked.

"Take a look at it," Harris offered her. "If you look north, you can see the lights of Umbradene and the Lucent Mountains. But I like looking out here once in a while. You never know what you'll see."

Gen took the telescope from her father and peered into it, squinting and adjusting the eyepiece. She looked out at the island, and it was nondescript and partly shrouded in fog. But something caught her eye in the water. She focused on it.

"There's a boat out there," she murmured.

"Really?" Harris asked. "That's unusual. Nobody really goes out there. It's a dead island, just volcanic rock."

Gen looked again, focusing more, and she could barely see a solo passenger steering the boat, and it was lean and had pale hair. Styx.

She straightened up, her cheeks aflame. Harris watched her, curious.

"Was there something else you wanted me to see?" she asked, trying to stay neutral while her nerves bounced.

"Just perspective," said her father warmly.

A tone began pinging behind them, and they both jumped.

Harris stepped quickly to the control panels at the base of the Lantern.

"It worked!" he gasped.

"What worked?" asked Gen.

Harris looked up at her, eyes shining. He took a deep breath.

"Bendin and I were working to restore an old feature of the lighthouse in case of an emergency. As emergencies started to unfold, we got back to work on it. And as you know, earthquakes trapped us for a time. But Gen, this is more than a lighthouse. It was a listening post and a beacon. Long ago. There are other... well, for lack of a better description... lanterns out there, or there were, before the Dawn of Dusk. We hoped someone had survived. So that surge of the Source that you saw coming from the lighthouse was a signal, a distress beacon. We were in distress, so what better time to test it? This tone means another lantern somewhere received our signal! It means... Gen, it means we aren't alone here. Others survived out in the world. It isn't just us!"

"Really?" Gen said, amazed, looking at the old flashing lights on the panels. "Where?"

"I'm not sure. I see two responders. So that's definitely two locations!"

Harris fidgeted with the controls and muttered, "I wonder—"

Gen found a switch and flipped it. Static erupted, startling them both.

A voice spoke: "Thank God, finally. We've tried, we've waited, and we finally got the signal."

"What signal?" Gen asked.

"This is Amethyst Lantern Base?" asked the voice.

"Uh... Yes?" Harris answered this time. "Who is this?"

"This is Commander Taunton."

"Um... where are you?" Harris asked.

"Tycho Base Alpha," said the voice in crackles.

"And where is that?" Gen asked, rather loudly.

"Tycho Crater. The last base on the moon."

Gen's indigo hair raised on her neck, and she stared into her father's comprehending eyes.

"By Luna," he gasped.

"By Luna is right," Gen answered. "We aren't alone!"

About the Author

J. Dianne Dotson, who also writes as Jendia Gammon, is a science fiction, fantasy, and horror author of THE INN AT THE AMETHYST LANTERN (Android Press), THE SHADOW GALAXY: A Collection of Short Stories and Poetry (Trepidation Publishing), and the four-book space opera series THE QUESTRISON SAGA® (Heliopause; Ephemeris; Accretion; and Luminiferous). Dianne is also a producer and small press publisher alongside her husband, Gareth L. Powell.

Dianne dreamed up other worlds and their characters as a child in the 1980s in East Tennessee. She formed her own neighborhood astronomy club before age 10, to educate her friends about the universe. In addition to writing stories, she drew and painted her characters, designed their outrageous space fashions, and created travel guides and glossaries for the worlds she invented.

Dianne's short fiction is featured in several anthologies and magazines. She holds a degree in Ecology and Evolutionary Biology and spent several years working in both ecological and clinical research. Dianne is also a science writer and an artist.

As a convention guest, Dianne provides insight into science fiction writing and characters (Nebula Awards Conference, Star Wars Celebration, San Diego Comic-Con, WonderCon, Cymera Festival, and BristolCon, among others), the science of science fiction films, and offers lectures on writing and world-building at conventions and universities.

Dianne is a member of the Science Fiction Writers Association, the Society of Children's Book Writers and Illustrators, the Horror Writers Association, the British Science Fiction Association, and the British Fantasy Society. She lives with her family in Los Angeles, California and is married to British science fiction author Gareth L. Powell.

Also By J. Dianne Dotson

The Shadow Galaxy: A Collection of Short Stories and Poetry

The Questrison Saga:
Heliopause
Ephemeris
Accretion
Luminiferous

also available from
Android Press
Science Fiction & Fantasy Punks
www.android-press.com

Bioluminescent
A Lunarpunk Anthology
edited by Justine Norton-Kertson

rivers
in
your
skin,
sirens
in
your
hair
poems
marisca pichette

WHEN WE HOLD
EACH OTHER UP
A SOLARPUNK NOVELLA
PHOEBE WAGNER

Star Scorched Fingertips
Melissa Ferguson

FIGHTING FOR
THE FUTURE
CYBERPUNK AND SOLARPUNK TALES
EDITED BY PHOEBE WAGNER

CAGED
OCEAN
DUB
Dare Segun Falowo
Glints & Stories

XAN VAN ROOYEN
SILVER
HELIX

MOTHERSOUND
THE SAUÚTIVERSE ANTHOLOGY
EDITED BY WOLE TALABI

STEEL TREE
SARENA ULIBARRI